Mortis Unbound

By Jessica Steiner

Dedication

For my wife, Miko. I couldn't do it without you.

Printed in Canada
First Printing, 2012
ISBN 978-0-9881516-1-1

Jessica Steiner
203 - 2760 Trethewey Street
Abbotsford, BC, V2T 3R1
Canada
http://jessicasteiner.dreamwidth.org/

Cover by Rebecca Potter.
http://www.rhpotter.com

This is the day, which down the void abysm
At the Earth-born's spell yawns for Heaven's despotism,
And Conquest is dragged captive through the deep:
Love, from its awful throne of patient power
In the wise heart, from the last giddy hour
Of dead endurance, from the slippery, steep,
And narrow verge of crag-like agony, springs
And folds over the world its healing wings.

—from *Prometheus Unbound*, by Percy Shelley

Chapter 1

Mortis heard the banging, felt the swaying, even in her dreams. It angered her, and she hammered futilely against the interior of her prison. The impacts of her own fists echoed in her ears, assaulted her senses, and did nothing. *Nothing.*

Sleep tried to drag her down again and she prepared to surrender. Nothing she did mattered, and she would never escape. It was better to live in dreams.

But then she heard shouting, a *"Be careful with that!"* and a jolt ran through the prison.

Then she sensed it: the tiniest of hairline fractures in the glass. It was too small to see, but for her, it was enough.

She burst from her imprisonment and rose into the air in a shower of glass, wings unfurling. There were humans all around her, men and women who wanted to put her back in the prison. She wouldn't let them. She wouldn't go back to that endless hell.

She spread her hands and the humans were falling, dying, their little lives snuffed out effortlessly. She felt nothing except the relief that they could not hurt her again.

Her feet touched the ground once more, when the last human lay dead on the floor. They lay all around her, like broken matchsticks and of just as little consequence. Glass sliced into her feet. Pain, strange and foreign and unpleasant, jolted through her body like tiny bolts of lightning.

She wanted to escape. Needed to hide, but she didn't know where to go. Where could she hide?

She stepped over one of the bodies.

The certainty she had felt was fading, subsumed by fear and memories of the endless sleep. She pressed her hands to her eyes, shuddering. Where could she go? Who was she running from? That didn't matter. What mattered was that she was running, and she was all alone in the world.

She straightened. She wasn't all alone. There was one person. He might be an enemy, but he was the only person in all the world whose face she could picture in her mind. Everything before that quickly became smothered in fog. If he was an enemy she would do...do something.

She would not go back to prison.

Death could find anyone. She stumbled out into the street, gavoxae tugging at her hair with their little hands, and savoxae wrapping their chill arms around her, toying with her skin.

She turned towards the place where she knew he could be found, and took flight.

Chapter 2

Liiran stepped into the elevator, leaned back against the wall and yawned, tugging his tie down a little further to let his neck breathe. He tried not to think about the fact that he had to be up early to go to work tomorrow morning. He had to be on the ball, get the information he'd uncovered in the desert written up and handed in fast so he could be ready when the next big story came in.

When no one ever died, there wasn't a lot of upward mobility. You relied on connections and luck to keep your place, as well as being better at your job than anyone else. It was something Liiran was good at, but there was always the potential to screw up, and screw up bad. If he lost focus, it could cost him his job.

Sometimes it meant going on crappy assignments, like writing feel-good stories about backwards, primitive tribes in the Sincovati Desert that no one really cared about. You smiled and did it, and sometimes you struck gold – as he had, this time.

Despite the exhaustion, the jetlag, and everything else, Liiran hadn't been able to resist treating himself at his favourite bar. The only thing that could have made it better would have been getting laid, but other than a quickie in the bathroom, that hadn't been in the cards tonight.

Too bad. But you won some and lost some. Maybe he'd used up all his luck surviving what happened back there and getting the story of the year at the same time.

Sal was going to do back flips.

Once inside his apartment, he got a beer, turned on the television and dropped onto the couch. Then he lit up a cigarette. He flipped restlessly through the channels, sipping on the bottle, tapping ash into the tray on the coffee table. It was a good brand, strong tobacco from the Norpal provinces, with just a hint of clove. He could already feel the last of the tension drain out of his body.

There was a quiet thud, from the door to his balcony.

Liiran's head jerked up with surprise. *Shit, a bird,* he thought, dropping the remote and setting down his bottle. He made a face as he crossed the room.

A corpse was really the last thing he wanted to deal with right now, or ever. Animals and plants could die, of course. Animal activists could never understand why the AND couldn't keep fuzzy pets and endangered species from succumbing to death. Liiran had stopped keeping pets after the third cat died on him – it was just too annoying getting attached and then watching them die after only a couple of decades, if you were lucky.

None of this actually passed through his mind as he walked to the window and reached for the drapes. What passed through his mind was 'Shit!' because just as he reached for the pull-tab, there was another bang, harder than the first.

No way another bird's that stupid! But what in Mortisor could it be? He was on the fifteenth floor. Not exactly prime cat burglar territory – and besides, cat burglars rarely knocked. So far as he knew.

He opened the drapes, looking into the darkness outside. The moons were both just tiny slivers tonight, but in the dim, silvery light, he could see a shape.

There was *definitely* a very *large* shape on his balcony. But he couldn't make out what it was. It almost looked like a bird perching on the railing, but no bird was that huge.

He stared at it for a moment, then realized that it had to be able to see *him* inside the well-lit apartment, far more clearly than he could see it.

He glanced around for some kind of weapon, but there was nothing appropriate within reach. He had a pair of ski poles in the bedroom closet, but they weren't really good at bashing things, and the tips weren't actually all that sharp.

As he followed that line of thought to its conclusion, he started to feel silly. What danger could he really be in? It was probably some homeless guy who'd moved in while he was away and objected to the sound of his television.

Boldly, he unlocked the door and stepped outside onto the balcony. "Hey, what do you think you're doing?"

The creature's wings flared, but no bird outside of fantasy books had a wingspan that wide. It flapped its wings and buffeted him with wind, and he stumbled back inside the apartment, more out of shock than from the force of it. And then it stepped down from the railing.

No, it hopped down. It had been *sitting* on the railing, not perching. And it wasn't a bird. It was a woman.

A woman with wings.

And Liiran recognized her.

"It's you," he said, staring stupefied at the woman he had last seen in a glass coffin in the desert. "What are you doing here?"

She stepped into the apartment, looking around with an expression of what looked like a mixture of wonder, fear, and confusion. Her skin was so pale it was almost blue, and her hair tumbled in waves down her back.

She was completely naked.

Her irises were so dark in colour, Liiran couldn't tell where they left off and her pupils began.

But it was her wings that his eyes kept being drawn to. He ran a hand through his hair. "Look," he said, "you can't just barge in here without saying anything. What do you want?"

She looked at him, and he felt as if he might drown in her eyes. "I'm sorry," she said. "I don't mean to be rude. I was looking for you, but there were so many people at the other place, I waited until you were alone."

She might as well have been speaking gibberish for all the sense she made.

"No really, who are you? What are you doing here?" Bluster seemed to help keep the terror at bay. "Why were you looking for me?"

"I don't know." Her eyes dropped towards the floor, which at least made it easier for him to breathe, released from their spell. "I'm sorry. It was dark and I was trapped, and then I got out and I knew that I needed a safe place."

"So you came to me? You don't even know me." *And what* are *you?* Liiran's mind supplied.

She shrugged. "I thought you might help me."

Liiran sighed. This was just going in circles. He folded his arms, and took a breath, inhaling a lungful of calming nicotine. It helped.

Keep it simple, stupid. "What's your name?" Later, he could revisit the more complicated stuff.

She was silent for a moment, her brow furrowing. "Mortis."

"Okay, that's a start. Now *what* are you, Mortis?" His fingers itched for a notepad, but he didn't want to lose momentum by going to look for one.

"I don't know how to answer that question," she said softly.

He paused for a moment, then hazarded, "I don't suppose you could be some kind of vox?" Liiran didn't know much about magic except what little he remembered from high school, but the larger voxae Liiran had seen had had wings, and were sort of human-shaped. But they were tiny. The biggest he'd ever heard of was no more than the length of his pinkie finger. Still, it really *was* the only explanation.

"I guess I must be," Mortis said, without any reassuring level of certainty. "I mean, I'm not like you." She spread her wings slightly, as if he needed a reminder that they were there, and then folded them securely against her back.

"Right." Liiran rubbed at the bridge of his nose. "Well, I'm Liiran Uwis. And I've got to say, Mortis, whatever's going on, coming to me was the wrong thing to do. I have to take you back to where you came from. They'll figure out what to do with you."

He was pretty sure the experts had taken her coffin to the Museum of Magical History. That was what he had been told, anyway. So that was a place to start. And maybe once he got her back there, they'd be able to give him more information. He obviously wasn't going to be able to get much more out of her directly.

Mortis shrugged, but said nothing, and he turned and marched to his phone. He dug in his pocket for the business card he'd been given, dialled, and it rang. And rang again. After a few rings the line clicked and the curator's voicemail message ran.

"Professor," Liiran said, keeping his voice neutral. "It's Liiran Uwis, the journalist. I imagine you're pretty busy, but I've got something it seems you've lost. Call me as soon as you get this message."

He hung up and glanced at his guest. She looked small and fragile, standing in his living room with her wings dragging on the floor.

He sighed. "You can stay until someone contacts me," he said. "That probably won't happen until tomorrow."

Relief was obvious in her face. "I thank you, Liiran," she said. "I really didn't mean to be a bother. I just...remembered your face, and I thought you seemed kind. I was afraid, and I didn't know where else to go."

"I'm a reporter, Mortis," Liiran said wryly. "I'm not kind." He shook his head. "Do you need anything to eat? Or are you hurt at all?" She had left a trail of smudges across his carpet that looked like dried blood.

She frowned and shook her head. "No, I don't think so. My feet were hurting when I left, but they don't anymore."

He grunted. "Take a seat. Let me... get you something to wear. Are you sure you don't want some food? Or a beer or something?" Did voxae eat? If so, then all the voxae in his lights, and heating unit, and air conditioner, not to mention his watch and a hundred other things, would all starve to death. It wasn't as if you had to feed *them*. Thinking about it again, he didn't think voxae needed to eat.

She sat down on the couch and he escaped into the bathroom.

He dropped his half-smoked cigarette into the toilet, then leaned on the counter.

For a moment he just leaned over the sink, staring at his own reflection and trying to tell his stomach that it didn't want to eject the half-bottle of beer he had just drunk, along with the other three he'd had earlier. There was a vox in his living room. A naked, beautiful, vox, with the most terrifying eyes he'd ever seen, and she apparently had amnesia.

This was *crazy*.

This story had just gotten a million times better.

He ran a hand over his face, then grinned at himself in the mirror. There was really only one course of action. He had already made a start at interviewing her. Tomorrow he would return her to the museum and get more answers out of the scientists, but not without taking a couple of pictures first. They weren't going to be nude photos, though, so he had to do something about that.

He pulled a bathrobe off of a hook on the door, then strode back out to the living room.

She was examining the bottom of her foot. He could see it was dirty, and there was blood, but as he watched she rubbed at the skin of her foot and the blood flaked away. There was nothing but smooth skin underneath. She had no calluses he could see.

"Do you think you could put this on?" he asked, eyeing her wings uncertainly.

Their fingers touched as she rose and took the bathrobe from him. Her skin was warm. Why would a vox seem so human? It was amazing. His heart sped up a little again every time he looked at her, and it wasn't just because she was easily the most gorgeous woman he had ever seen.

"Yes... yes, I think so." She frowned with thought for a moment, and suddenly her wings were gone.

If he'd still had that cigarette in his mouth, he'd probably have swallowed it. "What did you do?"

She worked her shoulders, craning her neck around as if to check that they really weren't there. "I'm not really sure. I just felt as if I could change if I wanted to. The wings are natural for me, but this is all right, too."

Abruptly, a disturbing thought occurred to him. "I wonder what kind of vox you are," he said. "Do you have the urge to...*do* anything?"

"Like what?"

She was still naked, and it was almost one in the morning. This wasn't really the ideal situation for an in depth discussion about magic, but now they were on the topic and he wanted to know. Curiosity had always been Liiran's downfall.

"How should I know?" he asked, spreading his hands helplessly. "I don't know what it's like to be a vox. Don't you have any urges? To... move things, or make things cold, or—" He looked at her cautiously. "Set things on fire?"

She shook her head, but there was something wary in her eyes. "No, nothing like that."

He sagged. Well, once he got her back to the experts, maybe he'd be able to shed some light on the situation. There was no way Liiran was abandoning this story now.

"Well, put that bathrobe on. I'm going to head to bed," he said. It was all far too confusing, and he was really too tired to deal with it right now. "If you do decide you want something to eat, you can take anything you find in the kitchen. Watch TV if you want. You'll have to sleep on the couch, but I'll bring you a blanket and it should be pretty comfortable."

She nodded. "Thank you, Liiran," she said softly, then wound the bathrobe around herself and belted it. Immediately it felt a little less stuffy in his apartment, though he regretted it, a little.

A few minutes later, she was stretched out on the couch, the blanket arranged over her, and she looked as comfortable as one could be. Though she was lying down, her eyes watched the television with a palpable fascination, as if she had never seen one before. He watched her for a moment, conflicted, then turned and headed to bed.

Though at first he wasn't sure he'd ever sleep again while she was in his apartment, Liiran fell asleep to the unceasing hum and chatter of the television.

Tomorrow was going to be a bigger day than he'd originally thought.

Chapter 3

The booms of the explosions and the clash of swords had been steady for an hour now. They were loud, even in Grand General Hason's tent, which was some distance from the thick of the fighting, but close enough that the battle messengers could get quickly back and forth, bringing detailed news of how things were progressing. Even in this modern age of voxihanto magic, runners and written communiqués were really the only reliable means of communication in this wilderness. Wires could too easily be cut, and soldiers couldn't carry telephones into the fray, dragging miles of cabling behind them.

Each time an explosion went off, the walls shook, but the atmosphere inside the tent was celebratory. Hason moved to the mouth of the tent, the boy on his chain following obediently behind him.

Beyond the open doorway, the desolate Monson mountains rose up sharply, craggy and forbidding. Every shadow contained a pool of ice and snow, and the upper reaches of the mountains were white and blue, glittering like diamonds in the sunlight.

Beyond the immediate crags were the valleys where the last enemies of the Laxam Empire scrabbled for a pathetic, primitive life in the desolate passes and caves. Hason couldn't imagine how they managed without going mad, let alone why they continued to put up a fight. They should welcome a chance to live and work in comfort, to pursue a proper life, rather than eking out an existence in this horrible place.

When the Laxam Empire finally conquered those rocks, it would usher in an age of peace that would last forever. And the resistance fighters who styled themselves the Monson Alliance would look back upon their stubbornness and wonder why.

All over the mountains, knots of soldiers crawled, clad in green and grey camouflage uniforms, each wearing the white rose emblem of Laxam. The resistance fighters were guerrillas, directing hails of rocks and crossbow bolts from shadowed hiding places, using their knowledge of the terrain against the more disciplined soldiers.

Even as Hason watched, he saw a boulder fall from a high crag, slamming into a knot of soldiers and scattering them widely. He wasn't concerned. It wasn't as if death was a possibility, and with the boy standing beside him, they couldn't lose.

"What do you think, Certos?" he asked, glancing at the vox. Certos was slender and small. In all the time Hason had known him, he had changed not at all. A collar, composed of chips of glass and etched with runes, adorned his neck. A gold chain ran from the collar, and Hason held the end of it.

He had held that end – figuratively, even if not always literally – for over two hundred years.

"Victory is assured, sir," Certos said softly. He raised a hand and pointed. "The soldiers will break through there, where that notch in the rocks gives them an easy route over the ridge. We will lose a few dozen, I think. No more. It will be difficult, since the fighters can attack from above, but they will get through with sufficient numbers."

Though death had been conquered by the medical Breakthrough over three hundred years before, war could still be devastating to a soldier. One could lose a limb, or be injured so badly that they could never recover. Hason had been told that one day medical science would advance to the point where even the most gravely injured could be revived. He paid it little thought.

There were no true sacrifices in war when everyone was effectively immortal.

"And after they capture that pass?"

"We must gather as many soldiers as possible, and begin a systematic takeover of the lands beyond. Intelligence reports show nothing but small hamlets and farms. All of their defences are focused upon that ridge, and keeping us from getting through it," Certos said, his tone not varying in the slightest. He seemed scarcely to care one way or another who won this battle, but Hason knew that wasn't the case. Certos would ensure they won.

"When those defences fail, all that's left is the mop-up," Certos went on. "They will throw everything they have at us, but it will not be enough. We have more resources, more fire-power. In a month—"

The boy suddenly stopped talking, his eyes seeming to turn inward to look at something only he could see. He remained silent for a full minute while Hason watched, perplexed.

"In a month?" The grand general prompted finally.

Certos seemed almost to shake himself. He looked up at Hason, a wide grin splitting his face. "She's out. It'll be over. Soon."

Hason felt a chill run down his spine. He had never seen Certos act this way before. The expression on his face was... mad. Inhumanly so.

"You mean the war?" he asked, his tone clipped.

The smile faded abruptly from Certos' face and he looked away, towards a phalanx of soldiers making their way up a narrow ridge to attack a vulnerable group of guerillas.

"In a month, or less, the war will be over. The Laxam Empire will control the world."

Is that all you meant? Then who is 'she'? Still seeking his equilibrium, Hason reached out and petted the boy's hair, then rested his hand on his shoulder. "You have done our country such service over the years," he said. "What will you do when there is no more war?"

Certos actually *twitched*, visibly, and Hason relaxed. The creature's emotional reactions, rare as they were, were fascinating. Certos didn't answer for a moment, and when he spoke his tone was measured. "Whatever Prime Minister Niveus would have me do."

"As do we all," Hason agreed, smiling. Apparently the odd fit had passed. Certos seemed normal again.

The sounds of distant shouting and the cracking of rock attracted Hason's attention. He looked up and saw a large boulder roll out from amongst the seemingly vulnerable guerilla fighters. The soldiers were utterly devastated from the trap, and the boulder then struck a large laser cannon below. It shifted, the rock of the cliff where it had been situated collapsing. Then a bomb went off underneath, obviously set by the enemy, and the cannon slid off the precipice.

"Voxae ma nema uto," Hason swore, his eyes fixed on the unfolding drama as the soldiers tried to save the cannon, or save themselves. The huge piece of machinery fell, and struck an outcropping. The voxmar inside ruptured and covox erupted in all directions, sending burning rubble up in a fountain, high into the air. Hason's eyes widened when he realized a burning ball was headed, through a freak, seemingly impossible series of chances, right towards them.

"Sir," Certos said, looking up disinterestedly and watching the ball arc through the air. "I think you will die now. Goodbye."

"You did this!" Hason hissed, and turned to flee. He didn't get more than two steps before the impact and explosion knocked him off of his feet. He saw burning wreckage flying all around him and Certos standing motionless over him, untouched by the chaos. Smiling.

Then he knew nothing more.

Chapter 4

The telephone chimed, a soft ringing that Calam Veliir reached out quickly to stop. It was past three in the morning, and the minister of laws had been deeply asleep.

He brought the receiver to his ear with a heavily tattooed hand. Almost every inch of his skin, which had already started out so dark that it was almost ebony, was infused with ink. When you had an interest in body art and over three hundred years to exercise it, you had a lot of time to be creative.

"Yes?" he grunted.

"Calam, it's Maenos." The head of the Ministry of Research and Development wasn't usually the sort of person that the head of the secret police got late night calls from, and Calam frowned. Maenos was an academic. Though they had known each other for centuries, Calam didn't think he had ever heard her sound afraid. She sounded downright terrified now.

"What's wrong?"

"I just got a call from a colleague of mine," she said. "He's third tier mage, the head of the Museum of Magical History. He was called in by some idiot lost in a sandstorm in the Sincovati Desert." She swallowed, then finished in a choked voice. "They unearthed a *huge* voxmar."

Calam was up and out of bed in an instant. His lover shifted and muttered, but went back to sleep as Calam strode out of the room, naked and not bothering to cover up. He closed the door to the bedroom and went into his study before responding. "Why was a tourist even in that area?" His voice was even, but just short of a snarl.

"How should I know?" Maenos' voice rose. "I'm not the one in charge of security!"

Calam ignored the implicit accusation. "Have you told Minister Itolan?"

"Yes, he told me to call you," Maenos replied. "He's on a plane, with the certovox. Some kind of accident, he said. The grand general is hurt."

More good news.

"What else do we know?"

"The voxmar is in the capital," she said. She seemed to be calming, thankfully. "My colleague has already transported it back for study. He called me because I'm Headmaster of the University, and thought I might want to take a look. He has no idea what he's got."

There were many universities in the Empire, but there was only one University – the University of Magical Studies, which was the only place in the world that trained magi.

Calam breathed out a sigh. Security had been breached, but it might still be contained. At least they knew where the bottle was. They would have to ensure the silence of anyone who had touched or seen it, but that was just a part of Calam's job.

"Give me the address. I'll deal with it tonight. Meet me there in one hour."

"What? Why?" Maenos asked.

"Magic and voxmar are your areas," Calam said. "Security is mine. I may be a mage, but I don't practice. I don't want to miss anything."

"Oh. All right."

That was all Calam waited for before hanging up and going to find some pants.

Fifteen minutes later he was dressed. Ten minutes after that, he finished the last of his phone calls, and left. He didn't say a word to his lover, who shifted restlessly with his pillow over his head as Calam spoke orders quietly into the phone and got dressed at the same time.

The drive across town to the museum took twenty minutes at this time of night, with only the odd late night taxi cruising along at low altitudes, propellers moving lazily as it trolled for pedestrians, of which there were few in this part of town. The commercial districts, bars, and night clubs would still be hopping, but this was a street of art galleries and museums, which were only open during daylight hours, and it was too early for even the most dedicated scholar to be at work.

When Calam arrived, a large black van was already there. It sat squat and gleaming under the streetlights, just outside the loading dock at the back of the modest-sized artificial sandstone edifice called the Laxam Museum of Magical History.

Twelve men piled out of the van as Calam got out of his car. They were dressed in black police uniforms, but their emblem was the crossed swords of the secret police. Though Calam was in charge of all aspects of the Empire's legal system, from the judges to the lawyers down to the regular police, these men were special. Strictly loyal and highly trained, they worked directly for the Circle of Magi, cleaning up messes like this one.

"Secure the area," Calam ordered. "I want all exits covered. Don't let anyone in or out." The men bowed their acknowledgement and scattered, going around both sides of the building and up onto the loading dock.

By the time they had strung the yellow caution tape, a cherry red coupe pulled up, cruising in at head height, then lowering to just a few inches above the pavement before coming to a stop. It was the latest model, and didn't even have wheels. Like all modern vehicles, voxmarae kept it aloft like an airship, to completely eliminate vibration that could easily break the fragile glass capsules.

A slender, willowy woman with skin the colour of light mocha unfolded herself from the car, which hovered motionless as she got out. Unlike Calam, who wore a police uniform, she wore the robes of a mage. They were a fashionable green and blue, cut to accommodate her figure. In fact, the outfit was more of a dress than a robe.

Calam approached her. "We were just about to go in."

Maenos nodded in a curt way, smoothing her fingers down her robes and squaring her shoulders. "Let's go, then."

Calam led her around to the loading dock. There was a white van hovering at the dock, and the large garage doors were standing wide open. The truck was still running. He peered into the front cab and switched off the key.

The fact that the van had still been running might have been disquieting, but Calam wasn't worried yet. Engines were nearly silent, since a car's motive power came from a voxmar full of vavoxae hooked up to wires. Hundreds of years ago, the cities had been filled with vehicles that ran on, of all things, fossil fuels. The air had been choked with pollution. Now, with magic replacing nearly all of the old technology, and no need for fuel to keep a car going, there was no reason to turn a vehicle off, except to keep it from being stolen. In fact, there were many reasons why the van might still be running without anyone attending it – the most obvious being that they might still be in the midst of unloading it, and would be driving it off shortly. But he still had a bad feeling.

They poked around the loading dock, but it was very clean, with no signs of any boxes or containers large enough to house the voxmar. They must have brought it inside.

"What are we looking for?" Maenos whispered.

"A large crate," Calam said shortly, in a normal tone of voice, and Maenos blushed.

"Of course."

Four officers joined them. "All exits secured, sir," the platoon leader said, saluting crisply. "No reports of anyone trying to leave the building, yet."

"Let's go inside. I want every person in the museum rounded up and brought to me for questioning. Alert me if you find any boxes large enough to house a human being, and I will investigate them personally and tell you if it needs to be removed," Calam said.

"Yes, sir," the officers acknowledged in unison and the one closest to the door grabbed the knob and twisted it.

It didn't take long to round everyone up, or to find what they were looking for. Through the door, they found a large room filled with a dozen unmoving bodies. The people didn't have a mark on them, but the rest of the room looked as if a bomb had gone off. Wood splinters and shards of glass covered the floor.

Maenos gasped with horror and Calam stopped short in the doorway, realizing immediately what had happened. The less informed officers were slower to comprehend and fanned out cautiously, weapons at the ready.

Calam bent and pressed his fingertips to the neck of one of the bodies. With a sigh, he straightened, his suspicions confirmed. "No pulse."

The effect was instantaneous. Calam stood still for a moment, listening to the shocked and horrified sounds of his men, who had not encountered or even heard of someone dying in over three hundred years. They were understandably distressed. Death just didn't *happen* anymore, not since Dr. Nexalum made her Breakthrough.

He let it go on only a few seconds before taking control. "Search the rest of the building," he snapped. "Find anyone left alive in here and bring them to me."

"But sir, what could this mean—"

18

"Go," Calam said. His voice was low and calm, and it had an immediate effect on the men who, almost as one, managed to steady themselves and filed out of the room.

Calam and Maenos exchanged glances. The woman mage's face was pinched. "This is... a complete disaster," she breathed. "The mortivox loose after all this time. There'll be a panic."

Knowing it was true, Calam didn't bother to respond. He bent over the dead men one by one, checking each one for signs of life and finding none. Glass and bits of wood crunched under his boots, and he was doubly glad that he didn't bother with the trappings of mage hood, such as long flowing robes.

Maenos examined one of the larger shards of glass, then tilted it up so Calam could see. The corner of a rune was etched into it. "The idiots definitely broke the voxmar," she murmured, and pulled out her cellphone to call Altus. The leader of the Circle needed to know that the situation was even worse than they'd feared.

Death had been unleashed upon the world once more.

Chapter 5

Liiran's alarm woke him too early. He stumbled out of bed in search of coffee, only to be surprised when he discovered the vox on the couch, still watching his television.

He'd had his share of people stay the night, of both genders, and not always only one at a time, but they generally stayed in his *bed*. In his caffeine-deprived state, he'd momentarily forgotten he wasn't alone.

"Good morning," Liiran said awkwardly as he padded on bare feet into the kitchen nook and started the coffee pot. Her hair was just as perfect as it had been the night before. How did she *do* that? He scratched his own tousled locks and thought about his shower.

"Very good," she agreed, and smiled, rising from the couch and letting the blanket fall away, revealing that she was still – barely – wearing the robe he'd given her the night before.

How in *Mortisor* was he going to get her back to the museum in broad daylight? She was barely wearing anything. Liiran didn't own a car, since it wasn't really necessary in the downtown core. The subway normally served his purposes.

Well, there really was no choice. She'd made it here somehow. He'd just take her back and wash his hands of the whole thing.

The covoxae in the glass bulb embedded in the side of the coffee maker danced and spun, boiling the water. He eyed the voxmar gloomily as the liquid started to drip into the pot. Were those motes of light tiny people, trapped in a prison of glass?

Forget about it. Am I going to start advocating to destroy all our technology and live like savages like the tribes in Sincovati do? It doesn't concern me. He shook the questions off firmly.

"If you're ready, I'll get you something else to wear, and we'll go," he said. "I'll see if I have some stuff in my closet that might fit you."

She smiled once again. "You're very kind, Liiran," she said. "Thank you."

"Don't worry about it," he told her, and headed into the bedroom with his coffee in his hand.

He found her a dress in the back of his closet – a cast-off from an old girlfriend. He wasn't even sure which one. It was a dark blue and had a flattering, if not terribly practical, flaring skirt. At least it was a bit more modest than the bathrobe. Not that Mortis really should be encouraged to hide her assets, in Liiran's opinion, but it was better that she not attract more notice than she could help. That wide-eyed look of wonder would probably attract enough attention as it was.

As he expected, travelling to the museum on the subway was surreal. Everything was new to Mortis, and she stared with equal fascination at the glimpses of the city visible between tunnels, and at the other travellers in the crush all around them. She asked questions about nearly everything, and Liiran finally placed her against a wall, with his own body between her and the rest of the passengers, their heads close together so she could whisper her delight without everyone around her looking at her as if she was crazy.

Of course, here he was even more aware of how attractive he found her, but he struggled to ignore it and concentrate on explaining the myriad of things she found fascinating. The last thing he needed to think about was *that*, since he'd likely never see her again after turning her over to the magi.

Why did that sound like a horrible thing to do?

Not. My. Problem, he told himself sharply as they stepped off the subway, allowing the stream of people to carry them along out of the station and onto the street. He grasped her hand to keep her close as they went. *I have a career I need to think about, and there are lots of nice human girls out there who don't have wings and aren't very, very strange.*

They both balked at the same moment, but for completely different reasons.

Liiran saw large yellow signs on the door, and barriers set up between the sidewalk and the front entrance reading, 'CLOSED FOR INVESTIGATION BY ORDER OF THE MINISTER OF LAWS'. Two black-uniformed guards stood by the door – they might have looked like rent-a-cops except they held themselves too perfectly erect, and Liiran wondered if they were secret police. He couldn't see from here whether they bore the emblem, and even if they didn't it wouldn't have necessarily meant anything.

Mortis, on the other hand, simply stopped dead when she saw the building. "No!" she said, starting to move backwards and away. "I didn't know you were taking me here. I won't go back there. I won't!"

Her voice carried and people turned to look. Liiran saw one of the guards glance in their direction and he quickly tugged Mortis away down the street. She was only too happy to follow.

"I won't go back there, Liiran. I won't let them put me in a prison again. I thought you were going to help me!"

"Hush," he hissed. "I'm sorry, I thought you understood. Keep your voice down, Mortis." They were out of view of the museum now, walking rapidly down the street and hopefully just part of the anonymous crush of people once again.

"I didn't understand," she said, tugging her hand out of his angrily.

"Look," he said, growing impatient. "What am I supposed to do with you? The people at the museum aren't the ones who put you in the prison, Mortis. They just wanted to learn about you."

"They put me in a box," she replied, folding her arms around herself as if she were cold. "They weren't going to let me out, either. It was an accident."

Liiran could believe that. He sighed. "Well, what do you want me to do, then? I don't know what you need."

"I need a safe place," she said softly. "And I need to remember what happened to me. If I remember, then I'm sure I'll know what I need."

That did make a little bit of sense. Liiran struggled with himself as they walked, but he just couldn't do it. "All right," he said finally, "you can stay with me – for *now* – but I don't want to get mixed up in anything illegal. I don't want anyone finding out you're not normal, all right? At the first hint that this is going to cause a problem for me, you're on your own. Got it? I never asked you to come to me, and something like this could ruin my life."

She looked at him with a mixture of relief and fear. "Yes, I understand."

Why did he feel like such a jerk?

He sighed. "Then let's get you back to my place so I can finally get to work. The last thing I need now is for people to start wondering what's going on with me and start asking questions."

Mortis looked at him, her lips pulled down at the corners. "Is it really wrong for you to keep me with you?"

He shook his head. "I don't know," he said. "All I know is that *someone* put you in that voxmar, and I doubt that they'll be happy when they find out you're not in there anymore. I don't know who they are, and I don't want them coming after me."

Chapter 6

Grand Minister Altus Itolan entered the prime minister's office, towing a large wooden crate on wheels. He left the box in the middle of the room and moved to Niveus' side, looking out over the city.

The prime minister's office occupied almost the entirety of the top floor of the Parliament building in Laxamora, the capital city of the Laxam Empire. The office boasted windows on three walls, through which the sunlight streamed at all hours of the day, from when the first rays peeked over and around the tall skyscrapers in the morning to when they sank below the horizon to the west, over the ocean, at dusk. Niveus liked the sunlight. Perhaps it had something to do with his nature. In this gold and white edifice, Prime Minister Niveus Exalan fit perfectly. His blond hair swept back artfully from a handsome face, fixed and poised. He always wore suits of white and cream. Standing at the window watching the sunset, bathed in the sunlight, he seemed to glow.

Sometimes, all this showmanship irritated the hell out of Altus. Usually, it was useful. Niveus wasn't human, but his subjects, who adored him, didn't need to know that.

Right now, jetlagged and having barely slept in almost twenty-four hours, it irritated him even more than the box he was towing around. It had been morning in Talgar when the accident happened, and now, having just landed in Laxamora, it was morning again. Given what Maenos had told him, the grand minister was facing another very long day.

"What's his condition?" Niveus asked. His blue eyes, the exact shade of his tie today, turned to regard Altus, but his head didn't move. There was a certain stillness to Niveus, and even after over three hundred years of knowing one another, it never ceased to strike Altus as creepy.

He was, of course, asking about Grand General Hason.

"The doctors say he was struck on the head during the accident, as well as being badly burned. There was a lot of bleeding and swelling inside the skull." He folded his hands, the long sleeves of his robe covering them. "Frankly, Niveus, even if he ever does wake up – which is in doubt – he will likely not be the man he was. There was certainly brain damage."

"Forever is a long time," Niveus clucked his tongue in remonstration. "Since he won't die, there will one day be a solution to the injury and he will wake up."

Altus rolled his eyes. "Technically, you are correct, of course. But that does not solve the immediate problem, unless you want to wait for that day before crushing the Monson Alliance," he said wryly.

Niveus was silent for a moment, then crooked a smile. "Of course not," he said, as if the suggestion had been a serious one. He had never quite gotten the hang of sarcasm, though with Altus by his side, few had ever noticed his deficiencies. "We'll have to find a replacement."

Altus kept his face neutral, nodding. "I've been giving this a great deal of thought all night. Obviously the replacement would have to be scrupulously loyal, but also open-minded. The post carries such complications. We may not be able to find the right person quickly – or at all. It took us months to vet Hason."

Niveus looked at him sharply. "Speaking of complications, what is Certos' status?" he asked.

Altus gestured towards the box. "The certovox is safe," he said, and now his lip curled with contempt. "There was nothing stopping it from simply walking away, but it just stood there in all the confusion. I took possession of it as soon as I arrived. It's fortunate I was in Talgarora."

"He's broken," Niveus said, turning to look out the window again. "Who wouldn't be after three hundred years of imprisonment and slavery?" His voice was calm, but Altus thought for a moment he detected a hint of melancholy. No, that had to be his imagination.

"Yes, Prime Minster," Altus said quietly, keeping his voice neutral. Certos wasn't a person. It wasn't 'slavery' to use a tool for its purpose. But Niveus was biased, though he certainly had never had compunctions about using said tool. The whole thing had been his idea, after all.

"That brings me back to my earlier point," Altus said. "I already have possession of the certovox. Why don't I act as grand general until the end of the campaign? It won't be much longer, and this way we can focus on more... immediate problems."

He was referring, of course, to the calamitous escape of the mortivox.

Niveus glanced at him sidelong. "You aren't a military strategist, Altus."

"What difference does that make?" Altus gestured at the box again. "That, right there, is my military strategy."

He waited, almost holding his breath. He had already been working towards the next phase of his plan, and this accident had presented an opportunity to him that he had never expected. But for him to take advantage of it, he had to have control over the certovox, otherwise the opportunity was wasted and the future was far less certain.

He had discussed his plan with the certovox all the way back, but it couldn't affect Niveus with its powers directly. No vox could. That was why Niveus had agreed to work with the human magi in the first place.

It frustrated him quite often that he couldn't just use magic to influence Niveus, and frequently he cursed the fact that he hadn't taken full control of the nivevox from the beginning, as they had done with the certovox. But Aevi Nexalum had been so against it, and without her none of it could have been possible.

*　　*　　*

324 Years Ago. Eight years P.B. (Pre-Breakthrough)

"Sir? Headmaster, are you busy?"

Altus looked up impatiently at the young woman standing in his doorway. Actually, that was a poor description of what she was doing. She had opened the door only about a quarter of the way, and was peeking through, so that one eye and half a thin mouth was visible.

It was late, the havox lamps hung about the room the only source of illumination. Altus wouldn't have still been at the University if it weren't that he'd gotten involved in some very interesting calculations, and he was frankly shocked that anyone else was still here at this time of night.

But no, he'd heard of this girl. Aevi Nexalum, he thought her name was. A graduate student, already on the cusp of being declared third tier, yet she was only twenty-four. He vaguely recalled her presenting a shocking thesis about voxmar runes a year before, which had revolutionized their understanding of magic. In fact, the very havox lamps in his office had been greatly improved due to the theories she had developed.

He supposed he could give her a minute of his time.

"Aevi, is it? Come in," he said, gesturing. "What do you need?"

Aevi slipped into the room and shut the door. She held a clipboard in front of her like a shield between him and her slender body. "I'm sorry for bothering you, Headmaster. But I... He wanted me to tell someone important, and you seemed like the most important person I could talk to right at the moment. And also, since it's so late, I figured no one else would be around— it's a bit of a secret." She said this all in a rush, tripping over her words, so that he could barely make sense of it.

He got to his feet and raised his hands to stop her. "What are you talking about? Who wanted you to tell me what?"

"Niveus," she breathed.

There was a moment of silence. "Who is that?" Altus prompted, his voice tightening with irritation.

Aevi visibly swallowed, then scurried forward and placed her clipboard down. It was covered in runes and calculations, like nothing he had ever seen. "I've been working on new runes," she said, her brown ponytail swinging forward as she pulled a piece of paper towards her from on top of a pad on his desk, and began to draw a circle. "You can't trap him. It would take so much power. At least eight or nine magi, and a very powerful collective will, very focused energy. But if he wants to come, it's not that hard to call him, you see." She looked up at him, wreathed in smiles. "I practically tripped over it by accident."

Altus couldn't follow what she was doing. The runes she drew inside the circle were completely unfamiliar to him, yet there was a pattern he couldn't quite grasp. "Aevi," he snapped. "Slow down and *speak*, girl! What are you talking about?"

"Oh," Aevi said, her thin fingers flying to her mouth. "I'm so sorry, Headmaster. I've learned that there are vox that are very complex, as complex and intelligent as you and I. One of them – I've named him Niveus, you know, for the nivevox, the genus nive, highest in the classification of order on the order/chaos dyad."

"What?"

"Please, let me show you," Aevi said, seemingly oblivious to his shock and disbelief. She completed the drawing and touched it, and light erupted from the paper.

Sparks coalesced just inside Altus' window, whirling and dancing and growing more coherent. Finally it formed into the shape of a man, nude, massive white feathered wings folded against his back. The man smiled at Aevi, then bowed to Altus.

"Headmaster Altus? I am Niveus. Aevi's told me all about you."

As Altus gaped, Niveus' smile widened. "I have a... I believe it's what humans would call a 'business proposal' for you."

*   *   *

Niveus wasn't looking at Altus. Instead he stared out the window as he considered Altus' proposal. Finally, he opened his mouth.

"No," he said, and Altus' fingers spasmed with frustration, hidden in his voluminous sleeves. "No, I think I need you working exclusively on the Mortis problem, not running the war campaign. That is a much higher priority. I'll select a replacement from the top generals. I'm sure one of them will be suitable."

"But Niveus," Altus protested, almost against his better judgement. "I can handle this."

"Don't you agree that Mortis is more important, Altus?" Niveus sounded genuinely puzzled.

"I... do. Of course."

"Then it's decided." Niveus made a gesture of his hand, dismissing the subject. "Thank you for the report. Is there anything further?"

Altus took a breath, steadying himself. All wasn't lost. He had the certovox until Niveus passed it on to someone else. He would just have to do what he could until then. He had already been making plans without it, so this was only a lucky bonus, not necessary to success.

"Nothing, yet. The resistance fighters seem content to let our army camp out on their doorstep, and I've ordered the fighting to cease until we have a new grand general. Your secretary has the detailed report on the day's victories and casualties," he said. "As for the mortivox, I plan to meet with Maenos when we're done here and get an update. I don't know any more than you do as of yet."

"Excellent," Niveus said, turning back to gaze out of the window again. "I'll let you know when I need you again."

Altus bowed and took a step back before turning. "Yes, Prime Minister."

Niveus nodded and made a gesture of dismissal, but Altus was already leaving and only saw it out of the corner of his eye. He didn't bother to acknowledge it before he left, pulling his precious box behind him. He had even more to do today than he initially thought.

Well, he could sleep later.

Chapter 7

The University, an edifice of black and grey stone punctuated by gleaming windows, was one of the taller skyscrapers in the downtown core of Laxamora. Not only was it full of thousands of busy students doing their post-secondary studies in first-tier magic, but it housed hundreds working on their second- and third-tier degrees.

There was no fourth tier. Or so most people believed. In fact, a select number of third tier magi had been elevated to a greater status. Nine of them, in fact, and these were the Circle of Magi, headed by Altus, and directly in control of the government of the world-girdling Laxam Empire.

Altus knocked perfunctorily and then opened the door to the Headmaster's office, pulling the box in after him. The room was filled with books, neatly set in rows on bookshelves, along with boxes of glass bottles and experimental devices.

Maenos wasn't working. She was sitting at her desk, fiddling with a glass bottle and a tiny etching torch, but as far as Altus could tell she was just doodling with it. She looked up as the door opened and set down the tools as she rose to her feet.

"Altus," she said, her eyes falling on the crate. "Is that...?"

Altus closed the door and turned the lock, then pressed a button just next to it. There were bottles full of sound voxae embedded inside the door which would create white noise when the button was pressed, making it impossible for anyone outside to hear what they were saying.

Maenos was his oldest friend, and they had been lovers, once. He moved around the desk, clasping arms with her and stepping close, then drawing her towards the window. They stood arm in arm, looking out on the world, which was growing heavy with grey clouds, though it had been sunny earlier. "Yes, it's the certovox." He grimaced. "I don't know how Hason dealt with it for so long, dragging it all over the place." The box annoyed him. Why did it have to be so primitive? It even had wheels, rather than far more efficient magical suspensors, and every bump and carpet snag irritated him anew in his sleep-deprived state. If he weren't going to be handing it off soon to someone else, he'd redesign the thing.

"I guess you can't take him out?" Maenos asked, casting a glance back at the box. Was that sympathy? Really?

"Don't be ridiculous." Altus said. "No one can be allowed to see it. What would people think?"

"Hason sometimes did," she pointed out, "in camp. So I understand."

"Hason isn't me," Altus growled. Why were they wasting time on this discussion? "And this isn't camp— there are magi everywhere who don't need to know there are vox like it out there." He changed the subject. "Have you started work on a new voxmar for the mortivox, yet?"

Her lips tightened, but she answered readily enough. "My best students are working on it on an emergency basis, and assure me it should be completed and ready for etching by tomorrow."

"I hope there aren't too many questions being asked."

"Don't worry about that," Maenos snapped. "I can handle my end of things."

Even after three hundred years, she could still be defensive, even with Altus. Especially with Altus. "I know you do. I never meant to imply otherwise." He shook his head and modulated his tone. "What about the etching? You'll be handling that yourself?"

Nodding, Maenos gestured towards a large painting of Aevi Nexalum on her wall. Altus knew that her personal safe was secreted behind the painting. "The designs are still in there from last time."

She shuddered visibly and went on softly. "Three hundred years, Altus. Every minute, people are going to be dying. And why now, right before it was almost over?"

There was no answer to that question, and Altus just shook his head. Outside, it was beginning to drizzle.

After a moment, he spoke. "Speaking of everything we wanted, there is something else I must discuss with you."

"Hmm?"

Altus chose his words carefully. "This is nothing new. It is a secret that I have been keeping for some time, but now I feel I cannot stand by any longer. I need your counsel, my friend."

Maenos hesitated, then shifted away, grasping Altus by the arms and turning him to face her solemnly. "What is it?"

Good, she was listening.

"It's Niveus," Altus said. He drew back, out of her grasp, and folded his hands together. "He's not human."

Maenos stared at him for a long moment while that stunning revelation sank in. "What are you talking about?" she asked finally, in a whisper.

"I have known for some time now," Altus admitted. "Niveus is the nivevox. He manoeuvred himself into becoming the prime minister because he wanted to bring order to human society. It turns out that that is the reason he initiated this war, and the reason he helped us to develop a way to trap death and eliminate it from the world."

"Voxae ma," Maenos covered her mouth with a hand. Wide green eyes looked at him over shapely fingers.

"I can't argue with the results. I believe in what we have done, but I cannot remain silent any longer. I have come to realize that the time has come for humanity to determine their own direction again."

She lowered her hand. "Damn right." She looked up at Altus, eyes narrowing now. "How long have you known about this?"

Altus had hoped that Maenos wouldn't ask him such a direct question. He hated to lie to his best friend, especially since she very well might figure it out eventually. "Mae..."

"Just answer me, Altus. You're a conniving bastard sometimes, and don't think I don't know it just because I happen to like you as well." Maenos' mood was worsening by the moment.

This wasn't going at all as well as Altus had hoped. "I've known all along, as you probably expect," he said stiffly.

Her eyes were now storm clouds, filled with lightning. "You knew all along?" she exclaimed. "And you were playing all of us like fools, then? Like you always do! But me, Altus? Even *me*? I should have known!"

Rubbing his forehead, where a headache was coming on, Altus kept his voice even, resisting the urge to look at the box containing the certovox. Why was this going so wrong? Why wasn't it working? "I thought you would have some difficulty understanding the necessity."

"Oh I understand!" Maenos snapped, her fists shaking. "I understand that you handed the entire human race over to a *creature*. A vox, which can't possibly have any kind of *real* understanding of the complexity of human behaviour and interaction. You handed all of our fates over to something that might not even be a *person*! Just a personification of pure order! Well Altus, humans aren't orderly. They are chaotic, and emotional, and they don't fit neatly into slots."

The pure rage buffeted Altus and he struggled not to answer in kind. "I'm aware of that," he said, his voice growing colder and more clipped with every exchange between them. "Don't think I've just let him run amuck and determine everything. Why do you think I formed the Circle? I am Niveus' advisor, and I have been the true power from the shadows all along. You and I *both* know that."

"I'm starting to wonder how much of what I know is true."

"I assure you," Altus said shortly, "that I have told you the truth about everything else of substance. You *are* my friend, Maenos."

"But you didn't bother until now tell us what we'd really done!" Maenos replied, turning towards the window. Rain drummed against the pane. "What do you want, Altus? Why did you tell me now – you have to want something from me."

Altus struggled for control. "I want to tell you that I need your support," he said. "In a coup."

Maenos cursed. "Typical," she muttered. "Get out of my office."

The grand minister's head jerked up. "But—"

"Get out."

"You don't want Niveus in power, do you? You can't mean that you don't support me in—"

"I'm not inclined to support you in anything right now," Maenos said. "I suppose you need me for some part of your cunning and devious plan, or you wouldn't have bothered to tell me at all."

"That's not true—"

"Then you don't need my support at all!"

Altus lost it. "I *meant* that I would have told you regardless of whether I needed you or not. It so happens that I need your help very much! For one thing, I need you to make a voxmar for Niveus."

She made a violent gesture. "Fine! Whatever! Now get out of my office, I said, you lying, conniving, deceptive snake, and go manipulate the people who actually need to be tricked into helping you. You *knew* I'd say yes before you walked in the door, so don't give me that."

There was nothing for it but to turn and walk out of the office.

Damn, Altus thought as he walked down the hall, dragging the stupid box. *That was one of our more spectacular arguments.*

He smashed the elevator call button, only then realizing that he was shaking with repressed anger. He took a deep breath to try to calm himself down, but it only half-worked.

Once he had pushed the box into his rented van, he wasted no time in opening it.

Certos blinked up at him from inside, the size and shape of the case such that it had to curl into a ball, knees against chest.

"What went wrong?" Altus demanded. "Why didn't you stop her from getting angry at me?"

It seemed to cringe away from him, as if afraid. "My... my powers don't work that way, sir. I can't affect individuals so precisely. The plan is working... she said she'd help. You just have to be nicer if you don't want them to be mad at you. Sir."

Despite the servile attitude, Altus had a strange feeling the creature was laughing at him.

Still, the words were reassuring. She *had* agreed to help. Sort of.

She'll come around, he told himself firmly as he latched the box and moved to the driver's seat to move on to his next appointment. *She always does. It'll be fine.*

Chapter 8

When Varil Ordoba, daughter-assassin of Talgar, had been a child too young to hold her first blade, she saw the queen for the first time in person. It was at a blade-marriage where the year's best were raised to the level of daughter-assassins. The ceremony was an important one. Only a handful of those who trained their entire lives until their first bleeding would be raised. The rest remained sisters and daughters and wives and raised the next generation of apprentice daughter-assassins.

Afterwards, she had gushed about the gilded throne, the fluted marbled columns lining the long, high-ceilinged hall with so few places for a blade to hide, the opulent tapestries depicting famous assassins of the past.

Her mother had told her that it wasn't the surroundings that made the queen, but the queen herself. And then she'd sent her to climb the walls a hundred times. Literally.

These days, she knew it was true, but also that the surroundings *had* helped.

This hall was a rough shelter of unmortared rocks and stunted tree trunks with the branches stripped off. There were no tapestries, and the queen's dress was faded and patched. The queen sat on a cut and polished stump instead of a throne. But she was still the queen.

Fifty years of living in a primitive village in the Monson Mountains, north of the kingdom she had ruled for the more than 250 years that preceded it, hadn't dimmed the way her eyes could pierce straight to your soul and pin you like a butterfly to the ground.

As she was doing right now to the poor Laxaman messenger who stood nervously before her.

From her position as honour guard just behind and to the right of the queen, Varil couldn't see her queen's eyes, but she could imagine them. And see their effect reflected in the man's eyes.

His fear only increased when his eyes flicked to Varil. Laxamans were notoriously afraid of the Great Mother – Death. Varil only hoped she'd get a chance to show him her steel teeth, though she knew she'd have to compete with the dozen other blades in the room that he *didn't* know were there.

The twenty male guards who lined the rough walls were pretty much for show.

"Give your message," The queen said. her voice was soft, but sonorous, and carried without effort. "Aloud."

The dusty man had obviously traveled hard and not easily to get here, and he looked exhausted. Despite that, and his obvious fear, he managed to straighten his back.

"I was told to deliver the message to the former Queen of Talgar, alone."

Varil heard a hiss, like a cat, from her left side, and glanced at Turil, the other member of the queen's honour guard. "*Former*," Turil muttered venomously.

The queen held up a hand, calling for quiet. "Here, in this room, you are surrounded by my people, either by birth or adopted as they were driven here by conquering armies. Here you speak only to me. Give your message."

His eyes darted around, then reluctantly he spoke. "Altus Itolan, grand minister of the Laxam Empire, sends his regards to the queen. He, uh, has a proposal you will find intriguing. A kingdom, for a single life. If you agree, send one of your famous assassins to him in Talgar Castle for instructions." The man swallowed. "He also sends word that your woman will have no trouble passing the blockade."

Varil didn't bother to hold back a guffaw at that. What game was that man playing?

"Altus Itolan sends his greetings, not Niveus Exalan," the queen said with heavy irony. "And he offers a rich bond as prize for the use of a hound."

"Your Majesty—"

"Go. I will consider your proposal."

The man was bustled from the room quickly, protests ignored. At a gesture, Varil, Turil, and the other daughters in the room moved forward to kneel before their queen.

The room was freezing, and Varil had to fight to control her shivering as she knelt motionless on the bare dirt floor. In only a few more weeks, all of the passes would be closed by ice for the long, hard winter. If any of them survived the army's onslaught that long, Varil wondered if any of those remaining would live through another winter.

None of them could *actually* die, of course, but starving made some do what they could to escape it eventually. Cliffs were a favourite, and knives a close second. The oblivion of an endless coma was still oblivion.

She waited, watching the queen's foot tapping on the floor as she thought.

Finally, she spoke. "Varil, Turil, and Navil, you will go. You are our best, and we cannot spare you, but cannot afford not to send you. Altus Itolan is likely plotting a coup. Niveus will go to the blade if he wishes, but we will not be merely his hounds."

Varil looked up and met her queen's eyes. Now they weren't sharp, but very, very tired. Even worse, she suddenly noticed that the lines in her face were even deeper with worry than they had been even a decade before.

"As you command, my Queen," Varil said, chilled even further by the sight. She heard her two sisters echo her words.

"Do what you can for us, daughters," the queen added in a whisper. "Anything you can. I trust you."

Varil closed her eyes and felt a tiny prick of tears at the corners. "Thank you, my Queen." They had no other hope.

They would have to grasp the poisoned knife in the dark, and hope it was the handle they held, not the blade.

Chapter 9

Calam was in his office this time when the phone rang. He'd been fielding and making calls for most of the day, in fact, and he'd expected to receive a call from this man sooner or later.

"Calam, it's Aros. I have some news for you." Aros was another member of the Circle, the minister of arts in fact, and they coordinated quite often, enforcing censorship of anything Niveus and Altus felt was on a 'need to know' basis.

"What have you got?"

"Nothing too important, but it could be a loose end."

Aros always took forever to get to the point. "Yes?" Calam prompted.

"The 'tourist' who discovered the voxmar wasn't a tourist at all. He is a journalist," Aros said, quite cheerfully. "Works for the Laxam Daily newspaper. He goes by the name of Liiran Uwis. Pretty sure he's still alive."

A loose end, indeed. All of the bodies had now been identified, and there was no reporter named Uwis among them.

Calam sat back, rubbing the bridge of his nose with finger and thumb. "Anything else?"

"That's all I've got." Aros said. "You gonna bring him in?"

"I'll take care of it," Calam said, and hung up the phone.

No sooner had he done that, but there was a knock on the door.

"Come." He was expecting one of his officers, and he rose to his feet quickly when he saw the grand minister.

Altus had black circles under his eyes and was towing a large wheeled wooden crate like a recalcitrant dog on a leash. Calam wondered how long Altus had been awake.

"Altus," he said. Despite the informal use of the Minister's first name, his tone was deferential.

The Circle of Magi were largely friends, or at least closely tied professionals. It was almost impossible to keep a clear boundary between people who had schemed and worked together so long, and whose fates were so inextricably entwined. Especially when they shared so many secrets.

But Calam tried, with this man especially.

The mage closed the door, engaging the lock and smiling as he approached. "Good afternoon, Calam. How are things going with our little problem?"

"It's not a little problem," Calam said, watching Altus carefully. What had rated the personal call? A status update could have been communicated over the phone.

"It will be contained. I've already met with Maenos, and she's working on a new voxmar," Altus said, lacing his fingers together. His hands were slender and deft, so pale against the black of his robes. They looked like white spiders under the bright overhead lights.

"We'll have to do a major summoning as well," Calam said, folding his arms across his chest. His muscles bunched and strained to do it. "What do you want from me?"

He wasn't a conversationalist at the best of times.

Altus hesitated. "Things have become complicated very suddenly. We're in need of a new grand general, and the war is on hold. Even if we find one quickly, we may hold off until the mortivox is recaptured, so as not to panic the soldiers."

Calam shrugged. "I figured."

"But we don't want to hold off too long, either," Altus went on, only a flicker of his eyes acknowledging that Calam had said anything. He moved to the side of Calam's desk, close to the tall man and leaned against it. "The Monson Alliance may see it as weakness if we wait too long after losing Grand General Hason. They may gain popular sympathy, or even make some kind of strike against us. More urgently, winter is coming, and soon we won't be able to reach them, let alone fight them. We'll have to wait until spring, when the snow thaws, and who knows what could happen between now and then?"

"I am not involved in the war effort, Altus," Calam said. "Why are you wasting my time with this?"

Now Altus' face flickered with annoyance, but smoothed quickly. "Calam, there is a secret that you must be aware of. The time has come for us to take care of another vox."

That wasn't at all where Calam thought Altus was going with this rambling, and he lowered his arms, resting his hands on the desk and giving Altus his full attention. "What vox?" He was already embroiled in a search for an *escaped* vox, couldn't this wait? Presumably, it had something to do with the war effort, but the war had been going well, until the – in his view relatively minor – setback of Hason's injury.

Altus fixed him with a firm gaze, but Calam detected a smug smile playing about his lips. "Niveus."

For the second time, Calam was surprised. No, surprise was far too mild a term. Calam felt dizzy, as if the world had been rocked on its foundations and he had been knocked off of his feet. Niveus, a man that he had followed faithfully for centuries, was nothing but a vox?

The man who had built Laxam into the great Empire it was. The leader of the country for which Calam worked with fanatical devotion every single day to protect from those *inside* it who would hope to bring it down, was himself a liar. Calam's true loyalty had always been to his country, but Niveus was the golden-haired prince, the charismatic leader. If Calam were to close his eyes and picture the face of his Empire, it would be Niveus' face he would see.

Yet despite that, he didn't question the truth of it. He was sure Altus wasn't lying to him. Not now.

As if giving Calam time to digest this shattering news, Altus straightened and turned away, walking to a board on Calam's wall, covered in pictures of fugitives and traitors who had yet to be captured. He touched a photograph of a woman, dressed in a gown and hair dripping with jewels. The queen of Talgar, who had fled when her Queendom was annexed fifty years earlier. She was still at large.

Calam waited with as much patience as he could muster for Altus to explain.

"Niveus is the nivevox," Altus said finally. "I learned this some time ago, but it has taken me until now to decide what to do. Clearly we cannot allow human history to be directed by anyone but humans."

"Clearly," Calam said shortly, frowning deeply. "How long have you known?"

Altus shrugged. "Some weeks," he said vaguely. "It's not really relevant. What is relevant is that Niveus is our prime minister, and he must be brought under our control. But doing so in the wrong manner would have political ramifications. Obviously our citizens must not know that we have entrusted the leadership of our world to a vox all of this time. It would cause chaos."

Calam nodded. He was irritated at Altus' delay in bringing him this news – and sure he was understating its length. But ultimately that was in the past. He knew, now, and Calam had to face what was. He didn't much care about politics, but he cared about chaos, and preventing it. "What do you need me to do?"

The slender man smiled, and Calam saw the triumph in it, but was far too distracted by his own inner turmoil to care. Altus would want to step into the vacuum that would be created, but that was not only expected, but logical and correct. He was the leader of the Circle, and Niveus' right-hand man. He was their *true* leader, it seemed – had been so all along.

"I know this is shocking. There is nothing I need you to do except to do your job while I put my plan into effect. For now all I need is your support." Altus looked up at him squarely. "I do have your support, do I not, Calam?"

Calam took a breath, then nodded. "Of course, Grand Minister Itolan," he said. "I could not support anyone else."

"Good," Altus said. "If I do need more, I will let you know. But for now, focus on your task – apprehend the mortivox. If you must speak to the nivevox, I am sure you will not have difficulty keeping your knowledge of his nature secret. I know how good you are at poker."

Calam was known for his ability to keep his face composed, and now was no exception. In fact, his face felt like wood, stiff and unyielding. "Don't worry."

"I'll leave you to it, then." Altus nodded, smiled once again and then left in a rustle of robes and the rattling of wheels as he took the case with him.

Calam waited until the door closed behind him, then finally sat down in his chair. He stared at nothing for a long time, then rose and moved to his board and looked at all of the photos. Face after face of people who wanted to bring down the empire, wanted to halt and reverse their march across the face of Aeria, wanted to kill Niveus, or his advisors.

And now was he one of them? Or was Niveus' face the one that should be stuck right in the middle of that collage of traitors, liars and enemies of the state?

Calam couldn't honestly say he knew.

Chapter 10

Liiran was just putting the finishing touches on the first draft of his story about finding Mortis in the desert when his email beeped with a message from his editor, Salmo Lina.

Lii, meet me in my office, soon as you can. Bring all your materials from the desert find.
—Sal

"Fucking Mortisor," Liiran muttered and grabbed the spools of film and his notes.

He didn't bother to argue. Two hundred years ago, he definitely would have. Even fifty years ago he would have moaned about it. But today he just dropped off the notes and the film and watched them go into a locked box Salmo kept in his office for the purpose. The contents probably went to the secret police, or were simply incinerated. Liiran didn't know, and didn't ask.

He muttered rote assurances that he would delete all the data from his computer and then went back to his office to do it. Sometimes he found things moved about in his office, and Liiran was pretty sure that his computer was checked regularly by someone – not Salmo or anyone else at the Laxam Daily News. There were people who did stuff like that professionally, Liiran was sure. People in the employ of the Ministry of Arts.

But they wouldn't find anything. Liiran was a good little journalist, and didn't print anything he wasn't supposed to. It was for the good of the Empire, after all.

He wiped the data, emptied his trash and scoured his desk for anything else that might pertain to the obviously now-off-limits matter, then decided to take the rest of the afternoon off. It was only an hour until quitting time, anyway, and he had nothing to do.

As he walked out of his office he came upon his boss coming up the hall, and paused expectantly. "Sal, was there something else you needed?"

Salmo shook his head. "No, I was just in Sunac's office and now on my way to grab a coffee." The break room was just down the hall. "You headed out?"

Liiran spread his hands. "Didn't seem like much point in sticking around."

The editor in chief of the newspaper hesitated, then patted Liiran on the shoulder. "I'll have an assignment for you tomorrow. There are a few things coming up the pipeline. You'll be cursing me for having too much for you to do, I promise."

Somehow, Liiran believed it. "See you tomorrow, then," he said and started down the hall.

"Lii?"

Liiran paused and glanced back at his editor, who was looking at him. Suddenly he felt a cold sweat spring up on his palms. Did he know there was something he hadn't mentioned?

Voxae ma, some people at the museum were probably injured or something. Maybe I should just come clean and let the police pick her up. I was all ready to send her back this morning.

What's wrong with me?

He opened his mouth, his heart thumping in his ears, but all that came out was a weak, "Yeah?"

"I'm sorry, Lii. I know you didn't even want that project, and now the work you did is wasted."

Lii swallowed bile and shook his head, shrugging. "It's just the business," he said. "Forget it, Sal. It wasn't your fault."

"Yeah," Salmo said. "It's just shitty, though. Better day tomorrow, am I right?" The editor smiled encouragingly and Liiran answered the smile with one of his own.

"Right."

"Good man," Salmo replied, then turned and glided down the hallway. How anyone as fat as that could move so easily, Liiran would never know. Half the time, he seemed to be dancing

Liiran turned and hurried off, cursing himself. *The longer I don't tell anyone, the more trouble I'll be in when it comes out,* he thought as he rode the elevator down to ground level. He leaned his head against the wall, feeling the cool of the metal soak into his skin. *Why didn't I just say it?*

He wondered that the whole way home.

*   *   *

286 Years Earlier. 30 A.B. (After Breakthrough)

Liiran adjusted his tie and smiled as he crossed the office and extended his hand across the desk. He'd made it through two interviews already, but this was really the man he had to impress – Salmo Lina, head editor of the Laxam Daily News.

"It's an honour, Mr. Lina," he said, shaking his hand firmly and taking a seat.

"Not at all, Mr. Uwis," Salmo said, a smile spreading across his broad face. "Can I call you Liiran? Good. I've read your credentials. Very impressive photography work you've done. I've seen your work before, actually. Didn't you do that spread in Economic Focus Magazine last month?"

"The month before," Liiran said, flushing slightly.

"Of course, the one about the Norpal vineyards. That must have been a fun assignment," Salmo laughed, and Liiran found his smile grow more genuine. He already liked this guy, and was thankful that – if he landed this job – he wouldn't be working for some insufferable douchebag.

"Yeah, it was great," Liiran agreed. "Nothing like a month drinking wine and enjoying the hot southern weather. But I'm looking to move on from pure photography, so I was really glad to learn about this position at Laxam Daily News," he went on, trying to steer the conversation towards the actual topic of the interview.

"Yes, of course," Salmo said, spreading his hands and sobering. "Quite a shame about Halis. They say she may never recover." Salmo cleared his throat and leaned forward. "So tell me, Liiran, why do you want to be a journalist? You've already got a promising career as a photographer. And may I say, quite a good eye. Why switch streams now?"

Liiran drew in a breath as his heart began to beat more rapidly. Of course he was nervous – this was really his big chance, and all he had to do was impress this big shot. So far he'd done well with his photography, but what he *really* wanted was so much more.

"Well, sir, the truth is I really enjoy being a photographer, but I feel like I'm not fulfilling my potential. As a journalist I'd have far more control over what I cover. I wouldn't just document what I see. I'd be able to really dig in, seek the truth, and bring it to the people." He smiled sheepishly. "This is really important to me. But I hope that's a point in my favour, Mr. Lina."

From the way Salmo was smiling, he had a feeling he'd just made a fool of himself.

But Salmo's expression was kind, as well as bemused. He chuckled softly. "It's refreshing to hear your passion, Liiran. Would you be surprised to hear that that was why I became a journalist, myself? Back in the dim and distant past." He laughed again and rose to his feet, coming around the desk towards Liiran with surprising agility.

He jumped to his feet. "Really?"

Salmo patted him on the shoulder in a fatherly manner. "Really. Within a couple of decades, you'll understand that things are a lot more complicated than that. You'll be older and wiser, and understand – like I now understand – that truth isn't always what people need. But I hope you don't completely lose that enthusiasm. It's a shame when a journalist gets too jaded."

Then Salmo stuck out a hand. "Congratulations, Mr. Uwis."

Liiran hesitated, eyes widening, then he grabbed Salmo's hand and shook it, heart in his throat. "I won't get jaded, sir," he said, his smile spreading from ear to ear. "And you won't regret it."

*　　　*　　　*

Liiran unlocked the door to his apartment and entered. He toed out of his shoes and, realizing that he couldn't see Mortis, called out. "I'm home!"

Silence met his call.

That was strange. Liiran searched his apartment, poking into every room. He leaned way out over the balcony, even searching the skies, but there was no sign of his house guest amongst the high-altitude passenger vehicles buzzing between the sky scrapers.

While he was in his bedroom, he got down onto his hands and knees and pulled a pile of boxes of books and sports equipment out of his

46

closet. He felt around the carpet until he located a loose corner, pulled it back, and lifted a board out of the way.

Beneath the board next to one of his water pipes was a large file box, which he lifted out and opened. Inside was his biggest – and really only – secret. The box was filled with reams of paper, piles of photographs, and spools of film. Hundreds of years of unanswered questions, censored articles, forgotten news stories.

Over the years, dozens of stories Liiran had personally worked on had been censored by the government, and the data destroyed. Hundreds more that he hadn't worked on, but had been aware of, had suffered the same treatment.

Liiran couldn't let it go.

So when he could, he had made copies of articles before deleting them, rescued film from the trash, developed extras of photographs before destroying negatives. He had smuggled each item out and put it in this beat up old cardboard box.

Sometimes he'd gone decades without doing it, but eventually, like an addict, he would fall off the wagon and risk everything yet again. He would see something that didn't add up, and he would save it.

He shoved the copy he'd made of his notes and the film right to the bottom. The contents were all mixed together and disorganized, and a couple of rolls of film fell out, but he shoved them back in and closed the box again.

Once he'd rearranged his closet again to hide his felony, he stood and stared at the pile of boxes for a few minutes. Even now, he didn't know why he kept things like that. He knew if anyone ever found it, he wouldn't just be fired. He'd be imprisoned for life – which meant forever and ever, for eternity. It wasn't worth it.

Yet even though he often lay awake at night fantasizing about setting fire to the box and being rid of it forever, he never did.

But none of this would help him find Mortis. He walked back out to the main room and fished a cigarette out of the package on his coffee table. Standing in the middle of the living room and smoking it, he considered the situation.

I guess she remembered something. She could have at least left a note.

He frowned. *Forget it. I'm better off, anyway.* And then, *hopefully she won't mention my name to anyone.*

Suddenly he had a strong, very strong, desire not to be alone – and not to be sober. Without further hesitation, he headed for the door. Maybe a few drinks and a pretty girl, or boy, would make him feel less as if he'd just done something stupid and lost an irreplaceable opportunity, both at the same time.

A blond, maybe, or a redhead. Definitely not black hair, tonight.

*   *   *

Sincovati Desert. Two days earlier.

The wind whipped Liiran's light brown hair into his eyes as he looked back nervously at the clouds behind them. What had been barely a smudge on the horizon when this jeep had picked him up from the airport was now a boiling mass of dark clouds that stretched from horizon to horizon and blotted out the setting sun. The sand storm sparkled malevolently with the concentration of voxae it contained.

Liiran fingered the camera around his neck and grabbed for the rail as the jeep went over a ridge too fast and landed on its wheels with a crash. He winced, but by some miracle the engine kept running. He could no longer see the road and wondered if they were even still on it, or if it were just covered with the shifting sand that stung his eyes and rasped his exposed skin.

He glanced at his companions. The big guy driving he hadn't caught the name of, but hunkered down in the rear with him was Shaala, the tribal chief Liiran was supposed to interview. In the front passenger seat was Vitaale, their tribe's best hunter, or spiritual guide, or something like that. Liiran hadn't learned much before this headlong race with the wind began.

Voxae ma, did he want a cigarette.

"Does this happen a lot?" Liiran shouted over the wind and squeal of metal on metal as the old hulk struggled to keep up with the demands of the vavoxae in the engine.

The chief looked up at him and Liiran realized from his clasped hands that he had been praying. "Not often, Mr. Uwis. Not so early in the season. But the storms have been worsening in recent years."

Normally, Liiran would have smelled a story, but right now he just didn't care. "How far to Shulash Village?" His tongue tasted like sandpaper.

"Hours yet," he said bleakly.

"With no shelter, we are all doomed," the wise man said from the front. The driver was clearly too busy to add his opinion to the general gloom.

Liiran cursed and hunched down a little, peering out at their surroundings. Curtains of blowing sand obscured his vision like rain. But a dark, squarish shape in the distance caught his eye and he pointed. "There! What about there?"

The driver risked a look, then exclaimed something in a language Liiran didn't understand, and the jeep jerked a bit.

The other two exchanged a glance and the chief nodded. "Go, Maalak. We have no choice."

With another screech of tortured metal, the jeep made a turn. Liiran caught a glimpse of a razor wire fence, down and half-buried in the sand. *Where are we? This doesn't look like something a tribe would build.*

They pulled up in front of the building and rolled the last few feet to the door when, with a great grinding noise and a shudder, the engine finally died. Liiran suspected it was the sand that was the culprit, not a broken voxmar, though he wondered if this vehicle even *had* a voxmar. He had heard the tribes thought magic was blasphemy and refused to use magic or trap voxae for any purpose.

It was like refusing to use flush toilets because you like water too much, to Liiran's mind, but right now he was prepared to be grateful. He doubted a voxmar-driven vehicle would have survived even half of that wild ride.

The foursome leaped from the jeep and raced to the heavy steel door. Between Liiran, the hunter, and the driver heaving on it, the lock snapped, and they crowded into a hallway lit by harsh, white havox bulbs.

The place was so clean, silent, and bright after the dark chaos of the storm that it was a shock. The three Shulash villagers huddled by the door, while Liiran took a few steps inside. There was only one other door, straight ahead. What was this place?

"Where are we?" he murmured. The smooth white walls threw his words back at him.

The tribesmen just shook their heads. "Laxam soldiers kept us away from here for many years," the driver said breathlessly. "No one comes here now."

Liiran resisted the urge to tell them that they were Laxam, too. Not only was it irrelevant right now, but he doubted they would agree, no matter what the maps said.

He pulled his camera out of his duffle bag, checking that none of the sand had worked its way inside or gotten on the lens, then let it hang on the strap around his neck. It was a familiar comforting weight there. He started for the door at the end of the hall.

Despite its cleanliness, there was an air of disuse about the place. It was dry and stale, like a tomb that hadn't been opened in centuries.

He had no idea what he would find, but his heart was pumping and his brain itched with curiosity. So long as they were trapped here until the storm subsided and he could get enough cellphone signal to call for help, he might as well get some pictures and take some notes.

He pushed the door open. Unlike in the hallway, the lights were off in the room beyond, but the light from the hall spilled inside and illuminated the small space, if dimly. He raised his camera expectantly.

Then he lowered it again, forgetting it completely as he gasped at the sight in front of him.

The light from the hall reflected off of a huge glass coffin, refracting and splitting into a hundred cold white sparkles as it hit the runes etched into the glass. Each rune was the size of Liiran's palm.

It looked like a voxmar, but Liiran had never seen one so huge.

And even stranger, there was a woman inside.

She seemed to be sleeping. Her long lashes rested on her cheeks, which were pale and almost as blue as a corpse under the harsh artificial light. Long, dark hair fanned out around her head, shifting as she dreamed. She was nude, and so far as he could see her body was perfect, completely devoid of scars or blemishes.

But, even more amazing, Liiran then saw that something else lay beneath her. Large, black feathered wings.

"Voxae as nema uto," he breathed involuntarily. The oath echoed loudly in the silent room.

Liiran stepped closer. His camera still hung forgotten around his neck.

"Who are you?" Liiran whispered, bending over to try to get a good look at her face. *Shouldn't I try to get her out of there?* he wondered. She was beautiful. And she was *alive*. Surely she couldn't be human, but in three centuries of journalism he'd never heard of anything like this.

Liiran abruptly realized he had rested his palm directly on the glass as he bent over. He jerked away and saw his sweaty hand had left a palm print on the formerly pristine glass. Flushing, he used a corner of his shirt to wipe it away. *Real professional there, Lii,* he thought ruefully, taking a quick glance around the room, but it was empty except for the huge voxmar.

Something moved in the corner of his eye, and he started. For one moment, he thought the woman had opened her eyes and looked at him. But when he looked again, she was just sleeping. Her full lips parted slightly in breath, and then closed again, as if she sighed.

Maybe I should take some pictures and then just... wait, he thought reluctantly, taking a few steps away and raising his camera again. *Salmo is going to tap dance when he sees these.*

But I wonder what the University is doing, locking this... thing away in the middle of a wasteland no one sane would go to?

*   *   *

Liiran shook off the memory and smiled at the blonde girl sitting on the bar stool next to him, her leg brushing against his as she smiled uncertainly up at him.

"Am I keeping your attention, sugar?" she asked wryly.

"Sorry," Liiran said, giving her thigh a little rub and picking up his glass to drain the last of the amber liquid inside.

It was his third, and the liquor was just starting to hit, but from the way the girl swayed on her seat, she had had a few more. And from the way she was drinking he suspected it wasn't anything out of the ordinary for her. He stubbed out the last of his cigarette and turned the full force of his smile on her. "I was just thinking I wanted to get out of here. My place is two blocks away, if you want to come."

She giggled and leaned close to speak into his ear. "It's cold for a walk. You're gonna have to warm me up when we get there."

"That's the idea," he returned, and gave her a kiss. Chapstick and something sour underneath. Drugs? It didn't matter.

A flicker of movement in the direction of the bathrooms attracted his attention. He glanced up and spotted Mortis. As their eyes met, she gave him a frantic wave, then disappeared into the hall.

What the hell is she doing here? he thought, his heart giving a lurch of foreboding. *Did she follow me? Where did she come from?*

Liiran swallowed, then smiled at the girl as he slid from his stool. "Just a minute, honey. The beer is calling. But I'll be right back, and then we'll go."

"Don't keep me waiting," she sang out gaily as he made for the bathroom. He glanced back and saw her ordering another drink as a beefy man rose from a table in the corner, his eyes on her. Well, that was one catch he'd probably lost, but there were plenty of fish in the urban cesspool.

It was no big loss.

As he stepped into the hall, someone grabbed his hand. He turned and looked right into the eerie black eyes of Mortis, who quickly put her finger to her lips and then dragged him to the end of the hall and outside to the rear of the building with surprising strength.

"Mortis! What—"

"Liiran, I'm glad you're okay," she said. "Did they see you? I tried to watch, but I was afraid to get too close."

The alley was deserted and smelled of sour beer and garbage. Liiran shook the vox off, taking his hand back. "What are you talking about? I thought you had left for good."

Her eyes were wide, but when she spoke, it was quietly, as if afraid of being overheard. "Liiran, earlier while you were gone some people came to your house."

"People?" Liiran's heart suddenly began to pound. "What people?"

"I don't know," she said with a shake of her head. "They wore uniforms like the man outside the museum this morning. I left right away. I don't think they saw me."

52

"You don't *think*?" For a moment, Liiran was blindingly angry. Because she had forced herself on him, because she had shown up and begged to be allowed to stay, and because he, Liiran had allowed her to stay, he could lose everything. He could be arrested!

People who were arrested by the secret police simply disappeared.

Her eyebrows rose. "If they had seen me, they would have arrested you, wouldn't they?"

Liiran drew a breath and let it out. Something about her tone calmed him down from his panic. "You're right," he said. "But... damnit, I have to know why they went there."

He turned and strode towards the side of the building.

"Liiran, wait!" He ignored her. She'd already made enough trouble for him.

There was a black sedan parked in the lot out front. Was it a police car? He turned in the opposite direction and hurried towards his apartment, trying to stay in the shadows.

Had they bugged his apartment? The visitors must not have found his secret file box, at least. But why had they gone there? Because he'd found Mortis in the desert? There could be some other reason, some previous association of his who had come under suspicion or a story he had worked on before, but he doubted it.

He was so absorbed in his thoughts and worries that he was halfway up the block before he realized that she was still following him. She was like mist, soundless and swift, following behind him.

"Look," he said, rounding on her. "What are you doing?"

"I'm coming with you," she said defiantly.

A headache flared in his temples. "Fine, but you're not coming up until I tell you. If they came because of you, they might be monitoring the apartment." He frowned. "But I don't think so. They didn't find you, so they *probably* don't have a reason to hang around. I just need to check."

"Okay, Liiran," she said in a more subdued tone. "I won't come inside until you're sure it's safe."

That was, at least, an acceptable compromise. Liiran nodded and continued up the street with his beautiful, dark shadow.

I'm probably overreacting, he thought as he let himself into the building and left her standing on the sidewalk. *They were probably just doing some kind of routine check, like they do with my office. For all I know, they do it every damn week.*

He entered his apartment again and stood for a moment, looking around. He didn't even know what he was looking for, but suddenly his apartment felt cold and alien. Hostile. Filled with traps and dangers.

There was nothing out of place. At least, nothing he could see now. How had he not noticed anything earlier, when he got home from work? Shouldn't *something* have twigged him? Surely a pack of strangers couldn't come to your own house and riffle through your things without leaving some sign of it?

Liiran moved through the apartment, this time looking for something, *anything* that seemed odd. Had the coffeemaker been there yesterday, or was it only moved because he had made coffee that morning? What about that magazine on the table?

Carefully, he unhooked the telephone from the wall and turned it over. There was a very small glass bottle attached to the underside, filled with little whirling sparks.

Had it always been there? He touched it and it came away, revealing a bit of a white sticky substance that had held it in place.

Fuck. That's not right. Monitoring my calls?

Swallowing hard, Liiran pressed it back into place and hung the phone back up on the wall. He didn't even know how long it had been there, but he couldn't take a chance. If it had been there for a long time, that meant they would have heard his call to the museum. If it had been placed there only yesterday, then something else had aroused suspicion.

He headed back downstairs and met Mortis on the sidewalk outside. She looked relieved to see him. He scarcely looked at her, his eyes darting back and forth. The street seemed filled with people wearing black.

"Okay, they are watching me, and they probably know about you."

She clenched her hands together so hard he saw her knuckles go white. "What are we going to do?"

Liiran drew a breath and let it out, then started walking down the street. She followed him. "There's only one thing I can do now," he said. "I'm sorry, Mortis, but I have to turn you in."

"What?" She sounded stunned, hurt.

He didn't care. He *didn't*. "If I don't turn you in, then they'll figure I just let you escape. I'll still be branded a traitor, and I'll still be arrested. Do you know what they do to traitors?"

He saw her hair move out of the corner of his eye as she shook her head.

"Neither do I," he said grimly. "All I know is that no one ever sees them again."

He expected her to turn and run, and he didn't think there was much he would be able to do about it if she did. What he didn't expect was to hear her soft voice. "Okay," she said. "I'll come with you so you can turn me in. Maybe I can escape again. I'm sorry I got you into this, Liiran."

"So am I."

Chapter 11

As Garelon Unitar strode into the prime minister's office, he kept his hands at his side and his chin up. Though anyone watching him would have only seen a decorated general, blue eyes icy and totally in control, inside he was sweating.

He'd never been summoned here for something like this in all the centuries he'd been a soldier. Generally he attended war planning meetings, and that had only been since he'd achieved sufficient rank to be part of the planning. Not that Grand General Hason had done much consultation. He'd always had the plan, and issued orders with a certainty that Garelon had always admired.

But yesterday Hason had been injured in a freak accident, and by all accounts might never recover. Then only an hour ago, Garelon had suddenly been summoned to a secret, personal meeting with the prime minister himself.

The timing only meant one thing – he was on the short list to replace Hason. But why was it being done like this? A secret meeting with the prime minister, just to conduct a job interview? And with such little warning. Surely a job like this would take months to fill, and with the passes due to close in the Monson Mountains, there seemed to be no need to hurry. The whole thing seemed fishy.

Well, he would find out in a moment.

Niveus was sitting at his desk, and Altus stood to one side. Waiting. Garelon stopped just inside the door and saluted crisply. "Prime Minister." Then he inclined his head to Altus. "Grand Minister."

Garelon had met both of them before, though he didn't know them personally. The grand minister was a mage of some repute, apparently, though Garelon knew little about how magi ranked themselves. He wore long black robes that obscured his figure, but he wasn't merely some weedy academic. There was strength in his thin-fingered hands, and an erectness to his bearing that some would probably find intimidating. His hawk-like eyes watched Garelon enter and gazed at him piercingly.

Niveus smiled and rose to his feet, gesturing Garelon forward. "At ease, General. How are you today?"

The friendly, casual response caught Garelon off-guard and he hesitated before stepping towards the desk. "Fine, sir," he said, darting a look at Altus, who smiled tightly and gave him no hint of what was going on. Garelon had the sense he was upset about something. What, was anyone's guess.

In response to a gesture, Garelon took a seat opposite the prime minister, and Niveus sat down.

In his experience, Niveus didn't mince words, and he didn't disappoint this time. "My sources tell me that you are a very intelligent man, loyal to the Empire. As I recall, you distinguished yourself at the Battle of Carhal."

There was a thick file on Niveus' desk. It was, in fact, the only object on the desk. It had Garelon's name on it. Garelon glanced at it, then met Niveus' gaze.

"Yes, sir. I have done my best to serve the Empire in whatever way I could."

Niveus' blue gaze was penetrating, and seemed to look into his very soul. "Running an empire is a complex matter, especially in wartime," he said, his casual tone at odds with the look in his eyes. "Sometimes one must make decisions that are not clear, which test the conscience."

Where was this going? Garelon searched for a response. "I'm sure we all have done things we're not proud of, which became necessary for the greater good." He felt off-balance. If this was a job interview, it wasn't one he felt completely prepared for.

Was this a job interview?

"Yes, indeed, the greater good." Niveus smiled. "The Empire has been embroiled in war for the better part of three centuries, but it is close to an end. Though circumstances may change, we must ensure that we do not falter now."

"Oh, yes sir," Garelon said. He felt as if he were on surer footing with this topic. "The Empire has brought peace to warring nations all across the world. I was there. Once we've completed the campaign, I expect I'll be out of a job and have to find something new to do." He chuckled. It sounded a bit forced to his ears, but his words were sincere. Niveus smiled as if he'd said the right thing, then bent his head and opened the file in front of him, flipping through it without seeming to read anything.

"You had a tragedy in your past, as I recall," the prime minister said. "You once had a wife, and a son?"

Garelon felt those words like a physical blow. They were completely out of left field, so unexpected that they left him gasping, and he had to struggle to answer without losing his composure. "Yes sir," he said. "There was a plane crash eighty years ago. My son is in a coma. My wife... left after that."

Niveus' eyes speared him again. "Marriage is rare these days. People tend to shun commitments of that type, feeling that nothing lasts forever."

"I love my wife," Garelon said stiffly. "The accident was just too much for our relationship." He licked his lips and waited, suppressing a rush of anger. Was he failing the test now? What did any of this have to do with *anything*?

"And not only did you marry, but you applied and received permission for a child," Niveus went on maddeningly. "Also a rare event. Once again, few wish to be tied down with such a commitment, and of course we cannot permit the human race to multiply out of control. But as a decorated general, you were well-positioned to receive the license."

"Yes, sir."

There was a moment of silence, as Niveus plainly waited to see if he would say anything further, but Garelon simply stared ahead, his gaze fixed on a point just to the left of Niveus' ear.

Finally Niveus shut the file. "You are a steadfast man, Garelon," he said. "When you make a commitment to something, you do not waver, no matter the pain it might cause you. You are brilliant, loyal, and have centuries of military experience. You are the perfect candidate for the position of grand general, which is what I wish to offer you."

Garelon's jaw dropped open and he jerked his gaze back to meet Niveus' smiling eyes. He had... passed?

"Yes, sir," he said, a little too quickly. "It's an honour, sir. I will bring victory to the Empire—"

Altus cleared his throat. "There is one small matter. Before you accept, you must fully understand the post you have been given."

Garelon looked at the grand minister. What was there to know? The grand general issued the orders, determined the overall strategy. He was the tactician, and the one who directed the war from the highest post.

Garelon had worked closely with the grand general for a very long time, and knew the purpose of his job almost as well as he knew his own. What more was there?

"What do I need to know, then?"

Altus inclined his head, then took a step to one side, revealing the presence of a third person Garelon had utterly missed.

There was a boy sitting on a couch against the wall, who was so small that Altus' figure had completely hidden him. He was dressed simply in a wide-necked tunic-style shirt and pants. A strange sort of necklace glittered around his neck.

No, it was a collar, made of what looked like irregular plates of glass, and a gold chain hung from it, which Altus held in one hand. The boy wore no shoes.

"Stand," Altus commanded.

The boy got to his feet. He looked as if he might float away in a strong gust of wind.

"What in Mortisor is this?" Garelon demanded, losing his cool for a moment. Then he recalled where he was. "Sirs," he added belatedly.

Altus snorted softly and made a gesture. Certos stepped towards Garelon until the length of the chain forced him to a stop, though he didn't strain against it, standing placidly in the middle of the room.

"This is Certos," the prime minister said. "He is the vox of war."

Garelon's head turned with such quickness that he felt a muscle clench in his neck. "A *vox*?"

"That's correct," Niveus said. "This is not well-known. Some voxae are especially powerful and sophisticated, compared to the basic, simple ones you're familiar with. They grow so large and intelligent that they can blend in with human society if they try. Certos is one of these voxae. There are others."

Garelon sat still, trying to comprehend this. He had never contemplated anything of the sort. "I don't understand this, sir," he managed. "What are you trying to tell me?"

Niveus rose to his feet and turned, walking to the window with his hands clasped behind his back. "I will be frank. Certos is the secret to our success. Just as we harness tovoxae to make clocks tick, and vavoxae to make cars move, we have harnessed the certovox to make war go the way that we want." He glanced at him over his shoulder. "Obviously it is more complex than that. We lose soldiers, we lose battles, but with Certos in our corner we cannot lose the war."

Garelon realized he was on his feet, and didn't remember how he'd gotten there. "But sir, this is incredible. How is this possible? It... it's..." He turned and stared at Certos, his emotions swirling.

"Incredible, yes," Altus said quietly.

It was unfair. It was *wrong*. Garelon swallowed hard.

Niveus turned towards him once more. "Perhaps you think there's something wrong with this. But why? He is nothing more than a weapon, General. We have thousands of weapons, far more powerful than anything our enemies can muster. Certos is only a human-shaped one."

Garelon turned towards the prime minister again. "You're saying he only *looks* like a person?"

The prime minister's face was inscrutable. "That is the way to think about it, yes."

Garelon let out a breath. The shock had been great, but he clawed inwardly for a core of calm as the world rearranged itself around him. "What do you wish of me, sir?"

Niveus smiled. "If you choose to accept this promotion, your job is to work with Certos. Use him. He will provide you with tactical information, and you will interpret it, translate it into orders to transmit to your troops. He will be your constant companion from now until the conclusion of the war."

Garelon bowed. He still needed time to absorb all this, but the time for that wasn't in the offices of the two most powerful men in the world. He would accept his orders, and figure out how he felt about it later. That was how the military worked, and he had been a military man for so long he scarcely recalled a time when he wasn't.

"Thank you for this opportunity, sir," he said. "May I ask one final question?"

"Of course."

"What is the meaning of the collar and leash?" Garelon asked, careful to keep his tone neutral.

It was Altus who answered. "You know of voxmarae, of course," the mage said. "Vox bottles are very effective ways to contain voxae and direct their energies. But voxae as complex as the certovox can be contained in another way, which preserves their versatility while ensuring they obey. That is the purpose of the collar. It keeps it tractable." The mage held up the chain. "This signifies the person who it is bound to. If you accept it, you need not hold it at all times, but it can serve to punctuate the point that it is to obey you, and remain with you. It is your responsibility to ensure that the certovox doesn't escape your control."

"Yes, sir," Garelon said. Voxae were notorious, after all. The tiniest crack in the voxmar and they'd escape, and you'd need a new bottle. Surely Certos would be the same way, though he certainly didn't seem anxious to run away.

Niveus was watching him with penetrating eyes once again. "Do you accept this promotion, Garelon Unitar?"

Garelon glanced at Certos one last time. Could he do this?

What sort of question was that? It was the height of arrogance to turn down such an incredible opportunity to serve his country, whatever the reason. Certos had been helping them win the war he had been fighting for centuries. Who was Garelon to judge the method now?

He squared his shoulders and faced Niveus. "Of course, sir. I am honoured by your consideration, and your trust."

Altus stepped forward now, tugging Certos lightly until they both stood next to Garelon's chair. Then Altus poured the fine link chain into Garelon's palm. Without a word, Altus retreated to stand by Niveus' elbow. For a moment, he glowered at both Garelon and the boy as if he wasn't sure who he was angrier at, but then his expression smoothed into placidity once more. Again, Garelon wondered what he was so upset about, but it wasn't his place to ask.

"If have any questions, ask me," Altus added. "I am your direct commanding officer now, as you know, and I am the foremost expert on this subject."

Niveus smiled. "There isn't exactly an owner's manual for a certovox, and no protocols for this eventuality, so we'll just have to deal with issues as they arise."

He had a million questions, but they were all a jumble in his head. He bowed numbly. "Thank you, sir."

"Get to know Certos, obtain his counsel," Niveus said. "You will fly to Talgar tomorrow, and then we'll crush the last resistance, and this interminable war will be over. You are dismissed."

Garelon was more than ready to get out of here and sort out his thoughts. He bowed again and turned away. Certos followed him like a silent ghost.

Before he went more than a few steps, Altus spoke suddenly. "General, the certovox's existence is a national secret. You can use that crate to transport it in public."

Garelon's eyes followed the direction Altus pointed, and he stared at the wheeled crate sitting incongruously by the door. After some consideration – and effort to keep his face in check, he turned to look at his superiors again. Now, it was Niveus who looked disquieted, while Altus was smiling.

"Very good, sirs," Garelon said stiffly, and nodded to Certos. "Go ahead. Do you need assistance?"

There was no hint of dismay – or any other emotion – on Certos' face. "No, sir."

A few moments later, the boy was boxed up tight and Garelon wheeled him out, the leash emerging from a hole in the lid and looped around his wrist.

He felt faintly ill.

Chapter 12

As Liiran entered the police station, Mortis was still right behind him, looking around at the activity with as much amazement as she had on the subway. Police officers buzzed all around them, as well as other people not in uniform. Even as he addressed the man at the front desk, a woman was taken past them, heavily chained and reeking of alcohol.

On some level, he was shocked that she was still there, and despite his reasons for being here, he wished she'd just fly off instead of obediently allowing this to happen.

He ignored the activity as best he could. His palms were sweating and his heart was beating too hard. "I need to speak to someone, but I'm not certain what the protocol is. I have information about a matter that is being investigated by the secret police."

The secretary looked doubtful, but he put a hand to the phone. "Just a moment, sir. May I take your name?" he asked.

Liiran hesitated. "No," he said. "If necessary, I'll give it to your superior," he added when the secretary's lips thinned.

Giving his name was probably going to be necessary to exonerate him, but he wasn't about to start throwing it around willy-nilly.

The secretary spoke into the phone, and a few moments later, a uniformed man with the bars of a section chief emerged from an office and came to meet them. His eyes were grey and serious, but his lips smiled and he shook Liiran and Mortis' hands warmly before ushering them into the office and closing the door.

The man sat at his desk and leaned forward. "I'm Section Chief Phiiro," he said. "What can I do for you two?"

At least it was a chief, not some lower functionary. "I'm not sure there's anything you can do for me," Liiran said. "I have information that may be of interest to the secret police."

The chief's smile didn't falter, but his eyes narrowed. "If you'll just tell me what it's concerning, then I can pass the information on to the correct department. Of course the different police sections cooperate closely and pass information back and forth."

That was, Liiran was pretty sure, bullshit. The journalist straightened in his seat. "Why don't you just call your contact within the secret police and I'll speak to *him* about the matter."

Not that he really cared about the internal politics of law enforcement. He just didn't want to get caught in a turf war. Maybe Phiiro was trying to block him, or take the credit for gathering the information himself, but either way, Liiran didn't want any part of it.

Now the smile grew chilly. "I'm sorry, sir, but that's not how this works. I'm not going to bother them with every person who comes in off the street claiming to have information the secret police needs. How do you even know the secret police cares about your information?"

To Liiran's surprise, Mortis answered before he had the chance to open his mouth. "Because we saw them, and this is the kind of thing they would deal with. We want to speak with Calam Veliir."

"How the... how do you know that name?" Phiiro's face had gone as pale as a sheet.

Mortis flushed. "I don't know."

Liiran had heard that name before, too. He was mentioned in several things Liiran wasn't supposed to have in the box in his closet. He swallowed and returned his gaze to Phiiro. "Call him," he said with more authority than he felt.

Phiiro stared from one to the other, looking as if he'd just realized he'd let a pair of poisonous snakes into his office instead of people.

"I can't just call him. Not just like that," he sputtered. "Are you crazy? He's got better things to do than talk to a couple of random kooks who say they have information for him. He's got people for that—"

"Kooks who can ask for him by name?" Liiran said.

Inwardly, Liiran thanked Mortis fervently for the name-drop. It was just the sort of thing that a journalist might do to get in somewhere he wasn't supposed to be, but Liiran wasn't sure he would have dared to drop *that* name himself.

Phiiro went silent, and his pale cheeks slowly suffused with heat. Looking almost as if his hand was operating against his will, he reached out and picked up his phone receiver and pressed a single button.

He didn't get put straight through to Calam, but Liiran and Mortis sat patiently as the chief worked his way through the bureaucracy. There weren't as many layers as Liiran might have expected, and then he saw Phiiro's entire manner change.

"This is Section Chief Unara Phiiro of Section 12," he said. "I'm very, very sorry for disturbing you, sir, but there are two people here in my office who are insisting that they need to speak to you directly."

There was a pause. "No, sir, I don't know who they are. A man and a woman. They wouldn't give their names to my receptionist. They just walked in a few minutes ago."

Another pause. Liiran was trying not to fidget.

"Yes, sir." The receiver was held out towards Liiran. Phiiro's eyes were haunted and his eyebrows drawn sharply together. "He wants to talk to you."

Liiran took the phone. "Hello?"

A deep voice answered him. "With whom am I speaking?"

Though the speaker didn't identify himself, from Phiiro's manner Liiran didn't question who it was. He was speaking to the head of the Ministry of Laws, a man who was not actually officially supposed to exist. Sure, there were people in the government who ran the judiciary, the police, and the secret police, but Minister Calam Veliir was an official myth.

Liiran tried to swallow, but his throat was dry. "My name is Liiran Uwis."

"Ah."

The note of quiet recognition in the man's voice made Liiran's blood run cold. So he *was* being watched by the secret police. And not just by the organization, but the man at the top of the heap actually knew his *name*.

Suddenly all his doubts about whether he should have come here faded like mist.

It was also obvious what he should say.

"I have a woman here with me," he said. "I think you might be looking for her. She's agreed, I mean... I've come to turn her in." That was less graceful than Liiran might have wanted.

There was a short silence on the other end of the line. "Very well," Calam said. "Pass the phone back to the section chief, please."

And that was that. Liiran stared for a moment, then passed it back. Calam Veliir, or whoever that really was, was a man of few words, obviously.

"Chief Phiiro here." Pause, then, "Uh, yes sir. Thank you, sir."

Phiiro hung up the phone and then pressed the intercom. "Send some officers in here, please."

Liiran tensed a little and glanced at Mortis for the first time since speaking to the minister of laws. She was sitting bolt upright in her seat, staring straight ahead, her cheeks very pale.

The door opened and three police officers entered. The chief glanced up at them and nodded. "Arrest them both."

In an instant, both Liiran and Mortis were on their feet. Liiran felt one of the officers grab him by the arm, rough because he was trying to pull away. "What the fuck is this?"

"Why would you arrest him? It's *me* you want," Mortis exclaimed. An officer was trying to grab her arm, but she somehow seemed to avoid it without any apparent difficulty.

Phiiro spread his hands helplessly. "I'm sorry, those are my orders. I'm sure it's just to get things straightened out. He probably just wants to ask you a couple of questions."

"If he wanted to ask questions, he had a chance," Liiran growled, but it was futile and he knew it. He was in a police station, and what was he going to do, fight his way out? That wasn't exactly possible.

He sagged, but Mortis was not so easily cowed. "No," she snapped, her black eyes flashing with angry fire. "We came here – I *agreed* to come here – because Liiran was in danger because of me. You are *not* arresting him. He's not a traitor!"

The chief stood up hastily. "Look, miss. No one's saying anyone's a traitor."

Mortis wasn't listening. Her voice rose with anger, taking on an edge of hysteria. "Leave him alone. You can't imprison him, too."

"Mortis." Liiran tried to reach towards her, but an officer was holding his arms behind his back while another one fumbled with handcuffs. "Mortis, calm down!"

The third officer reached for her arm again. "Look, just calm down, lady—"

66

The instant the officer touched her, the man's eyes rolled up in the back of his head and he dropped like a stone.

"You won't take him."

Liiran felt something pass through him – a pulse like a single heartbeat. The other three people in the room keeled over soundlessly, crashing to the floor like sacks of grain, or broken dolls. Somehow, whatever it was, it had left him alone.

"Mortis, stop!" Now freed, Liiran leaped forward, but hesitated before he could touch her, afraid he would suffer the same fate as the first officer. She looked at him, startled, and he saw that her eyes were so black that they were like holes in her face.

He felt himself being drawn into them, the eyes filling his vision. Then she blinked, and the pull vanished, her eyes returning to normal. "What did I do?" she asked, the anger replaced by confusion.

He had no idea. "Come on," he said, taking her hand and tugging her towards the door.

The moment Liiran stepped out of the office he stopped short and stared. All around them people lay, unmoving. They were slumped in chairs, lying over desks, collapsed on the floor. The secretary sprawled over his desk, phone receiver dangling from still fingers.

"What have you done?" he asked, scarcely realizing he had spoken.

"I... don't know."

He turned and looked hard at her, but her expression was as confused as ever as she gazed around the room. Though in some part of his shocked mind, he recognized an utter lack of anything resembling the horror he was feeling.

Did she even understand that there was something bad about what she'd done?

Liiran wanted to run, but he released her hand and bent to touch the neck of a woman who was lying face down on the floor near his feet.

No pulse.

Numb, Liiran straightened. "We've got to get out of here. Now," he said, and started towards the door. Mortis followed him, silent.

Chapter 13

The idea that the certovox, being a vox of war, might actually attack him had crossed Garelon's mind, but when he wheeled the crate into his house and opened it up, Certos merely stepped out and stood there, staring with an expression of blank disinterest.

"Make yourself at home," Garelon said to the blank-faced vox, somewhat helplessly. "But don't try to leave the house." Certos nodded and slowly wandered deeper into the house, glancing around without any hint of curiosity.

"Yes, sir," Certos said, looking at a vase of artificial flowers. He sounded as if he didn't care about anything. Didn't feel anything.

It was unnerving.

Garelon cleared his throat. Perhaps a kinder tack was better. Certos had to be unhappy that the previous grand general had been hurt, surely. Hason was a good man, and they would have been close companions for many years. Surely they had been friends.

"Well, let me show you around your new home," he said. "You will be staying in my son's room. This way."

He moved down the hall to the stairs, narrating a brief tour as he walked, pointing out the various rooms as they passed them. Though he tried to be upbeat and welcoming, Certos followed him without comment or questions. It was hard to tell if he was even listening.

Upstairs, he steeled himself and opened the door to his son's bedroom. The hinges creaked from disuse, though Garelon did dust and clean up in here about once a month when he was home, so it was pretty much free of dust or dirt.

"This will be your room," Garelon said, his voice tightening though he tried to stop it. "I'll box up all of Orphas' things and put them in the closet." He glanced at Certos, who was examining a chess set on a small table in the corner, with the pieces still arranged mid-game. He still wasn't paying any attention to his words so far as he could see.

Garelon raised his voice slightly. "Wait here, Certos. I'll just go get a box. Please don't touch anything, I... I'll put them away to be safe so nothing gets broken."

He waited expectantly.

Finally, Certos glanced at him. "Okay." He straightened up and stood in place, his hands clasped together.

Now Garelon felt like a heel. Did he think he wanted him to just stand there and not touch *anything*? "You... you can take a seat on the bed, or the chair at the desk," he said. "Just wait for me. I'll be right back."

He turned on his heel and left, his face prickling with heat from a mixture of anger and frustration. He couldn't tell if Certos was acting this way because he was a vox and voxae just were different, or because he was being deliberately difficult and uncooperative.

Except that was the worst thing – he was the last thing from uncooperative. The more Garelon interacted with him, the more he saw it was almost too easy to think of him as simply a tool, a weapon to be used to win the war.

He was back in a few minutes with a couple of old boxes, and found Certos sitting on the bed as close to the chess set as possible, leaning way over so he could examine the pieces. Orphas had been an excellent chess player, and Garelon was amateur at best. He hadn't beaten his son at chess since the boy was seven.

Garelon tried to be pleased that the vox was interested in *something*, but he felt a surge of fatherly protectiveness over his son's most precious belongings. Did the creature have to be *so* interested in Orphas' favourite chess set? A game couldn't possibly mean anything to Certos.

Garelon tried to ignore it, moving to Orphas' desk and beginning to clear it of personal items. The silence was thick and oppressive, and he finally searched for some way to relieve it.

"Do you have any questions?" he asked, sorting through the detritus in Orphas' desk drawer.

"What are they for?" Certos asked, startling Garelon. He honestly had been expecting a simple 'no'. He looked up to confirm that Certos was pointing at one of the chess pieces, his finger hovering over it an inch away but not touching.

Garelon swallowed. "They're not 'for' anything, Certos. My son liked – likes – to play chess, and they are pieces for playing the game."

Warming up to the subject, he picked up the piece Certos had pointed to. "This is a knight. It can only move diagonally across the chess board. All the pieces move in different ways to capture the king."

"Oh," Certos said, and looked away. He sounded *disappointed*, and Garelon felt a flash of anger.

"Well? Is something wrong with that?" he demanded, clenching his fist around the figure. The edges of it cut into his palm.

Certos' head whipped around and he looked up at Garelon with wide eyes. "No, sir. Nothing's wrong, I guess."

Abruptly, Garelon wanted this chore over with. He started throwing things into the box quickly, though he was careful not to break or damage anything. "I suppose you think it's a stupid, pointless exercise. Do you even understand games or creativity?" *Why did I have to be saddled with this creepy, irritating kid?*

"Yes, sir, I... I mean, no sir—"

"Well of course you don't," Garelon said, closing the first box and shoving it deep into the back of the closet, then swept the chess pieces into their case, packing the board away. "How could you? I don't know why I bothered. The prime minister was right to tell me not to worry about you, that you were just a tool."

He ran out of words and heard Certos say very softly, "As you say, sir."

That made him look up, finally. Certos was in the corner, on the bed, his legs drawn up to his chest. His expression was still so blank, though. Try as he might, Garelon couldn't see any emotion in that narrow face.

Acting on a hunch, he stood up and strode quickly towards Certos. As he'd half-expected, he saw the boy flinch.

That broke the anger, and he stepped back, horrified at himself. *It's just this room. Just the memories,* he thought to himself. *I'm not a cruel person. What was I doing, yelling at him?*

He sat down on the edge of the bed and dropped his head into his hands. "I'm sorry," he said.

There was no reply from Certos, only a rustling as he shifted.

Garelon drew a breath and forced himself to look at the boy. "*Do* you understand games?"

Certos' face was turned towards the wall. "Yes, sir," he said softly. And then, rather earnestly. "I don't think they're stupid."

"No, I'm the one who's stupid," Garelon said wryly. Certos looked up at him then and, to Garelon's astonishment, laughed. It was a quiet, dry chuckle, but it did qualify, if only barely.

There was a moment of silence. "Did you like Hason?" Garelon asked.

Certos shrugged faintly. "He was all right. He wasn't really anything to me."

"Why not? Why wasn't he anything?"

The vox was silent for a moment. Garelon wondered if he was being so careful of his words because he was afraid of saying the wrong thing, or if that was just the way he was. Finally, he spoke. "He thought of me as a weapon. Like a talking book that could tell him what he needed to know, and then he could put me on the shelf until he needed me the next time. He didn't hurt me, or do anything nasty, if that's what you're asking. He just was there."

Garelon nodded. "You're not really a talking book, are you?"

Certos shrugged. "It was all right being that way," he said. "I'm not like you. I don't need food, or sleep or people to talk to. You could lock me in a closet and ignore me for a year and I'd come out the same as I was."

"Would you really be the same?" Garelon frowned.

Again, those thin shoulders rose and fell. "Essentially."

This was stamping all over territory that Garelon didn't want to think about. If Certos was a person, then he was a slave, not a weapon. And then what would Garelon do?

No. He would serve his country, either way. This wasn't the first thing he'd had to wrestle with his conscience over, after all. Regardless of how he felt about it, his duty was clear.

But he didn't have to be nasty about it, like Certos had said. And he wouldn't be.

"Well, I'm not going to lock you in a closet," he said. He offered Certos a smile, which the boy didn't return, then got to his feet. "And maybe you'll like me better than Hason."

"I'm sure I will, sir," Certos said, and Garelon knew it was a lie. But who could blame him?

He forced himself to look at the boy and not be disappointed at the response. "Why don't you pack up the rest of the things yourself?

Anything you'd like to keep, you can leave out and arrange however you like. All I ask is that you treat the things in this house with respect. But this is your room, now," he said. "If you want anything, just tell me and I'll get it for you."

Certos' response was so quiet Garelon almost missed it. "A chess game?"

Garelon started in surprise. "But you've never played before, right?"

The vox frowned. "No, but I like it."

That sounded strange to Garelon, but after all, Certos was strange. He hesitated, then picked up the case with the chest board in it. It was a little battered, and well-loved, but made of sturdy leather and wood. He held it out to Certos. "You can have this."

That startled Certos visibly, and he looked up. "Really?"

Garelon nodded and set the case down next to Certos on the bed. To his slight surprise, Certos reached out and touched the shiny leather cover with what looked like reverence, a tiny smile curving his lips.

Garelon knew immediately he had made the right choice. "Really. This is yours, Certos. There's an instruction booklet inside to teach you the rules. And if they replace me, you can take it with you. I think Orphas would want you to have it."

Certos stared at him with open-mouthed amazement. "Um, thank you," he said after a moment.

"You're welcome. I'll leave you to it, then." Garelon found himself grinning, and couldn't remember the last time he had worn that particular expression. He turned, and headed out of the room, closing the door behind him.

There, he thought as he headed for his bedroom to change into civvies. *Maybe it won't be so bad, after all.*

Chapter 14

Thankfully, whatever it was Mortis did seemed confined to the police station. Outside on the street, people passed them without any hint they knew something had just gone horribly, horribly wrong. Liiran struggled not to quicken his steps – or act suspicious in any way – as he left the station, but he knew it was futile. He'd given his real name to the secret police, and cameras in the station would have shown everything.

Even if he hadn't already been doomed, he sure was now.

He didn't say a word to Mortis, completely absorbed in his own thoughts and worries as he rode the subway back towards his building. In fact, he was so lost in it all that when Mortis finally spoke, as they walked up towards the building he lived in, he was startled nearly out of his skin.

"Why did we come back here, Liiran?" she asked, in an urgent tone. "We already know that they're watching you."

Liiran knew it was stupid. And yet.

And yet.

"There are some things I really need to get," he said quietly, walking with purpose towards the front door.

He fumbled for his cigarette pack, then shoved it in his pocket again unopened as a new, disturbing sight distracted him. There was a car parked just outside the front door, the running lights lit. It was a dark-coloured van, not a police car. Liiran tried to ignore it. If he started seeing every car as being a possible surveillance vehicle or undercover police vehicle, he was going to go crazy.

"I really don't think this is a good idea," Mortis said as he entered the lobby.

"Then you stay out here," he said sharply. He realized in that moment that he was not only completely spooked, but he was *blindingly* angry. Mostly at Mortis.

But he really didn't have time to think about that. He needed to focus on what he was doing, and then figure out what he was going to do next. Otherwise he was going to panic.

He was no hero, damnit! He was just a newspaper reporter. He was supposed to *cover* the news, not create it.

He wasn't cut out for this shit.

Liiran entered the elevator and watched the numbers count their way upwards. Each one seemed to take at least twice as long as he remembered it taking. When the doors opened he hesitated and leaned out, looking up and down the hall. His own apartment was on the end, and there was no sign of anyone nearby so, breathing a sigh of relief, he strode briskly down the hall to his door.

There was no reason to believe that anyone would be waiting for him here. The disaster at the police station had happened so fast, he doubted that anyone had had a chance to get word out that something was wrong.

His mind shied away from thinking about what had happened there, as well.

The apartment was silent and so far as Liiran could tell, nothing had been disturbed. He moved quickly to his bedroom, and dragged a duffle bag out of his closet. He began stuffing clothes into it, moving almost mechanically, grabbing things that seemed important almost at random.

He paused, looking around for anything he might need, saw nothing, then hurried into the bathroom to keep packing.

What am I doing? he thought a moment later. He stood in the middle of the bathroom, toothbrush in one hand and razor in the other. He whispered out loud. "What in *Mortisor* am I doing?"

He walked back out to the bedroom and tossed the toiletries into the bag, then stared at them. With a violent motion, he shoved the bag and dumped it onto the floor. Toiletries and small necessaries scattered over the carpet.

"Where the fuck am I going to go?" he demanded of the empty room. "I'm packing?" With a flash of anger, he turned and kicked his closet door. It closed with a bang, and a shock ran up his foot, which started to ache.

"What am I doing?!" he shouted, then collapsed to sit on the edge of his bed, his head in his hands.

"Liiran?" It was Mortis, calling from his living room. "Liiran, come quick, there are people on their way up!"

The words galvanized him into action. He grabbed the duffle bag, threw everything he could see that had fallen out of it into it again and zipped it closed. In a moment, three hundred things he might probably need ran through his mind, but there was no time.

He darted back out into the living room. The patio door was open, and Mortis was standing on the balcony, her wings visible and spread wide. Her eyes were wide as well, and she waved to him. "Come on!"

Someone banged on the door hard. "Open up, police!" came a muffled, gruff voice.

"Fuck," Liiran swore, and raced towards her. But before he reached her, he stopped. He was so high up. "I'm trapped. You go!" he said, flapping his hand. "I'll give myself up. There's no point, anyway."

"Don't be silly." She grabbed his hand, yanking him through the patio doorway onto the balcony.

He heard a loud cracking sound and a bang. Glancing back, he saw that the police officers had forced the door and a half dozen black-clad people spilled into his apartment. "There they are!" one of them shouted, and Liiran heard clacking sounds as they cocked their crossbows.

Then Mortis wrapped her arms around him and there was a rushing of air as her wings flapped. His feet parted ways with the ground and suddenly they were airborne and flying away from his balcony into the sky.

Liiran resisted the urge to scream, or drop the duffle bag and clutch madly at Mortis' arms. He didn't look back, but as no bolts zipped past them, he figured they must have surprised the Mortisor out of the police officers, and were already out of range before they had a chance to react.

They winged past several buildings, and Liiran started shivering in the cold wind. Mortis' arms were warm around him, as was her softness, pressed against his back. But it wasn't enough to shield him from it as they moved higher.

"Where are we going?" he asked. Beneath them, Laxamora was spread out like a child's game, though they weren't above the level of the highest buildings, which rose like silver spires into the sky. He could see the white parliament building, brightened even during the day with floodlights so it seemed to glow. It stood right on the edge of the cliff that the city was built on. Cars and trucks mostly flew closer to the ground, no more than five stories up, but the biggest vehicles drifted lazily between the highest buildings, or even higher, propellers whirling to push them through the sky.

The Grasha river, a large tributary that came down from the mountains to the north and east, ran right through the city like a blue wedding ribbon and terminated at the cliff, where it cascaded down hundreds of feet into the Unaecon Ocean, a wide strip of sea between the two main continents of Aeria. In the distance, he could see boats out in the water, pleasure cruisers and tours as well as commercial ships, like tiny scale models built right out of the box.

Then they banked and were heading back into the city again. "I have no idea where to go," Mortis said. "I don't know the city, Liiran. I'm just flying. Where should we go?"

He closed his eyes for a moment, trying to distance himself from the distracting and terrifying sights long enough to think. The anger and fear that had caused his small melt-down in the apartment was still quite close to the surface, but he knew it wasn't productive. He had to think. Where could they go, where at least he would be safe long enough to figure something out?

A hotel was a bad idea. He'd have to give a credit card to reserve the room, and chances were his credit was flagged. He didn't have nearly enough cash in his wallet to pay for a hotel room, and accessing his bank account would only help them find him, even if Calam hadn't yet frozen his accounts, which he probably had.

Finally he opened his eyes and gave Mortis an address. "It's on the south side of the city," he said. "I'll direct you when we get closer. But we should be careful not to be seen flying around. Maybe we should land and take the subway. It'll help throw them off our trail."

"Okay." She ducked between two buildings and slowed and he made the mistake of looking down. The walls of the buildings were very close, and the ground was rushing up far quicker than he had expected; he nearly swallowed his own tongue.

"Mortis, slow down!"

"Hush!" she said, sounding more irritated than concerned, much to his dismay. "Be quiet, Liiran. I know what I'm doing."

Her wings flapped a few times, and Liiran felt his body shift abruptly in her arms. His duffle bag swung in his hand and banged him hard in the knee, and then his feet touched the ground as lightly and neatly as you could ask for. She had landed in a narrow alley, thankfully out of sight of traffic.

She released him and stepped back a pace. By the time he turned towards her, her wings were gone and she was gazing at him with what looked to him to be an inappropriately smug expression.

"I told you it was a bad idea to go back to the apartment."

Liiran glared at her. "Look, the last thing I need from you is an 'I told you so' when it's your fault I'm in this mess in the first place."

He watched her face turn contrite, and he turned his back towards her, starting off down the street. "Just come on," he snapped, feeling pettily triumphant at the look on her face. He swung the duffle bag onto his shoulder and walked on.

The trip was long, especially since neither of them said anything. It was the middle of the day, right around lunchtime, so the subway was full of people taking a break from work, but it wasn't packed. Liiran and Mortis managed to get seats easily, but by some kind of silent agreement they sat on opposite sides of the train, not looking at one another.

They had to change trains, and then take a bus. By the time they reached the right neighbourhood, a lot of Liiran's anger had cooled. After everything that had happened, and the long silence, he didn't quite know how to start up the conversation again, so the silence reigned until they had reached their destination.

The house was small, and identical to all the other houses on the row. It had been a nice neighbourhood at one time, but it looked as though maintenance had been falling down on the job for some time. Even as they approached a shingle came loose, skittered and fell off the roof into the grass.

Liiran winced at the sight. It had to be xhovox – chaos vox that caused wear and tear over time. Since they were in their natural environment, they were invisible, but their presence was obvious from the advanced wear on the roof. He'd never seen an infestation that bad before. Most hardware stores sold little vacuum-like appliances that could suck up xhovox, and then there was a service that collected the bottles and released them into the desert where they wouldn't bother anyone. Except, presumably, the people who lived there, but no one seemed to care about that.

He strode up to the door, which had once been painted green, but the xhovox had faded the color. Liiran rang the doorbell and a slender man with sandy-blond hair and a narrow blade of a nose soon answered. The man looked startled for a moment, then grinned.

"Hey, Lii, you're lucky you caught me. I had a squash game tonight, but my knee's acting up, so I had to cancel." The man spotted Mortis behind him, and quickly moved out of the way, gesturing them to enter. "Who's your friend – and what's up? You couldn't call?"

"I'm sorry for showing up like this, Tanen," Liiran said. "This is Mortis, a... friend of mine. I was wondering if we could crash here tonight. There's a bit of a problem, and... it's complicated. Do you mind?"

Tanen and Liiran had been friends since university. After graduation, Tanen had worked in the business for a while, but had branched off into freelance photography, not liking reporting work and the rat race of working in the media industry. Over the centuries, Liiran's friend had moved even further out of the field, and now was a full-time painter, a pursuit that didn't pay well but which he apparently found rewarding.

Tanen's house was filled with an unimaginably huge assortment of crap. Liiran picked his way past an easel with a sheet over it, and a few boxes of what were probably art supplies, searching for a place where he could park himself.

"Vox turds, Liiran, do you need to ask? How long have we been friends again?" Tanen rolled his eyes and ushered them both inside the house. "You can stay as long as you like."

There was a shower of objects, most of them paper and the rest probably pens and brushes, and then Tanen presented them both with a reasonably clear couch. Their host himself dropped down into a nearby chair, after clearing it of a pile of sketchbooks.

"So," he said, leaning forward. "What's going on, Lii?"

Liiran sat down on the sofa, and Mortis sat beside him. She looked at him, and he turned away, focussing his attention on Tanen. "Don't ask. You don't want to know, Tan. I really mean that."

The other man's hazel eyes flickered with disappointment. If there was one thing that Tanen and Liiran shared, it was an insatiable curiosity. It was what had drawn them both to journalism, though only one of them had stayed.

"Are you serious?" Tanen asked. "Whatever it is, Lii, I know you wouldn't do anything *that* bad. And you know you can trust me."

78

"It's not that, Tan," Liiran said. "I don't want to draw you into something that doesn't concern you. We'll just stay the night, and then we'll be on our way. Maybe I'll be able to tell you when it's all over." He doubted that.

Tanen locked eyes with him, and Liiran could see him practically willing him to change his mind, as if pure *want* would actually cause him to capitulate. Liiran stood firm, hyperaware of the presence of the dangerous woman behind him, and just praying that she wasn't going to cause any more trouble tonight.

Finally Tanen sat back, and grinned as if it didn't matter to him at all. "Well then, why don't we see what's on television, hmm?" He grabbed the remote control, and switched it on. There was an ice skating competition on, and the music filled the room. Liiran deliberately turned and focused his attention on the screen, determined to shut everything else out for a while.

He'd decide what he was going to do in the morning.

They whiled the afternoon away that way. Liiran allowed himself to be hypnotized by the television, trying to figure out how to get himself out of a multiple murder charge. Tanen left him mostly alone. Eventually the living room was filled with the scent of oil paints as Tanen absorbed himself in another painting.

Mortis rose and excused herself. Absorbed by equal parts his own worries and some ridiculous movie, Liiran barely registered her leaving, until a few minutes later when Tanen dropped down beside him and handed him a cold glass.

Liiran tasted it, and discovered that it was a screwdriver. He sighed and settled back, feeling Tanen's arm slide across his shoulders.

"You sleeping with her?" Tanen asked softly.

Liiran jerked and looked around, but Mortis wasn't in sight. He glanced at Tanen, who was looking at the television, but Liiran suspected that he wasn't really paying attention to it. "No," he said, "it's not like that."

The hours of thinking hadn't really eased any of his worries, but he did feel a little less antisocial. His lips no longer felt numb, and he smiled weakly at Tanen, feeling a strong urge to simply spill every detail even though he knew it would only endanger his friend. At least if he told him, he wouldn't have to work it all out alone.

"Surprising, for you," Tanen teased him. His hand rested on Liiran's shoulder and squeezed. Sighing, Liiran shifted closer, until his own shoulder bumped against Tanen's ribcage.

There was silence for a few moments. "You're being a hero for this girl, aren't you? I thought you'd beaten that out of yourself in that soul-sucking job you have."

"I'm not being a hero," Liiran said sharply, glancing at him. "She came to me by chance, and now I'm in shit up to my eyeballs. That's all."

Tanen smiled. "I think that's the definition."

Liiran shook his head and averted his gaze.

They watched in silence for another few minutes, before Tanen gave him another squeeze. "You want to sleep in my bed tonight, or hers? You know I've only got the one extra room."

Liiran didn't even have to think. "Yours."

It wasn't a relationship. It was a friendship. Liiran and Tanen hadn't even seen each other in years. They kept up over email and phone. But when you knew someone for over three hundred years and committed relationships had fallen out of fashion, friends with benefits arrangements had become common.

Tanen grinned and nodded, giving him a squeeze and then rising. "I'll just make sure there are fresh linens for your friend," he said. "Come on in when you're ready."

"Where is she?" Liiran asked, looking up as Tanen started away.

"I think she went upstairs," Tanen said, waving vaguely as he disappeared into the den. There was a guest bed in there, probably buried under canvases, if Liiran knew Tanen at all.

Frowning, Liiran trotted up the narrow steps to the top floor, which was a loft bedroom. It was actually relatively neat up here, with the blank canvases in piles and the bed rumpled but clear of debris. The operative word was 'relatively'.

And it was quickly obvious that Mortis wasn't in here, either.

Liiran's frown deepened and, operating on a suspicion, he stepped over to the window, which was open a crack. He pushed it the rest of the way open, craned his neck upwards and saw a shape on the sloping rooftop, hunched over and curled up tight.

There was a small ledge on the windowsill. Liiran placed his foot on that, and squeezed out the window, clinging precariously to the eaves trough. "Mortis?"

She looked up and turned her head towards him. Her hair stirred as a chill wind picked at her clothes, and her feathers rustled. Her wings were wrapped around her like a cloak.

Seeing him, she unbent a little, the wings flaring out and then settling against her back. "Oh, I'm sorry," she said. "Were you looking for me?" She rose to her feet and walked across the roof towards him. It was sharply raked, but she walked as if gravity had no pull on her.

He supposed maybe it didn't.

"I guess I was," he said. He hesitated, and she offered him her hand.

For a second, all he could see was the young man at the police station earlier that day. The man had touched her, and fallen over dead. But he gritted his teeth, grasped her hand, and let her pull him up onto the roof. He sat down immediately, and she lowered herself to sit next to him. "Tanen's just arranging your bed, but I guess while I've got you here, we need to talk."

She nodded silently, looking at him with eyes like liquid pools of ebony, open and uncertain.

Liiran sighed, rummaged for a cigarette, and lit up. He inhaled, and waited for the rush of nicotine to fortify him before he spoke. "What exactly happened back there, Mortis?"

She hesitated. "I'd say that I don't know, but I suppose I have some general idea," she admitted. "I don't know why it happened, or exactly what. The main thing is that I panicked. The same thing happened when I first came out of the prison, only then I was angry, too." She spread her hands, which were blue-veined and pale, with slender, shapely fingers. Those fingers had held his weight as if it were nothing.

"And what happened?" he prompted. "Even if you don't have a word for it, what can you tell me?"

She was silent for a moment, but this time he sensed she was choosing her words. "Something inside me came out. It touched those men and women, and that was when they fell."

"They were dead," Liiran said bluntly. "That shouldn't even be possible. There was a medicine that was invented, three hundred years ago. Everyone got an injection, and now no one can die. But you killed people tonight."

She stared at him. "An injection?"

He nodded. "I guess that was after you were sealed away?"

Shrugging, she spread her hands. "I can't remember," she said. "If I ever did know about it, I'd forgotten. But if I'm a vox, it's not very surprising that I wouldn't know much about what humans do, right?"

"I guess not."

He turned away from her, cogitating for a moment as he smoked. "Mortis, you shouldn't have killed those people. You can't do it again."

"They were going to arrest you," she said, and he turned to stare at her.

"That's not the point," he exclaimed. "You killed I don't know *how* many people, and for what? To stop me from getting arrested?"

"I didn't really mean to do it. I just panicked. I don't..." Her eyes dropped away. "I was afraid. Frankly, I would do anything not to be put in that prison, but I tried, because I knew that you were in trouble because of me, and I didn't want that. When I realized that it was all for nothing, and they were going to arrest you anyway, after everything you said, I just had to stop them."

"Maybe so," Liiran said. He felt mollified, somewhat. He couldn't imagine what it might have been like for her in that glass prison for long, and it was natural she wouldn't want to be placed in that position again. Perhaps it was unfair of *him* to expect it of her.

"But it's still drastic," he said firmly. "Drastic isn't anything close to being a strong enough word. It's damned wrong. I don't want you to do that again. I won't have any more deaths on my conscience, you got it?"

He glanced at her, and saw no guilt on her face, only hesitant confusion. "Well, I'll do my best," she said. "I can't promise that I won't panic ever again, but I promise I'll try not to."

"You really have no idea what I'm getting at, do you," Liiran said flatly.

She frowned. "What do you mean?"

"You don't know why I have a problem with what happened."

Mortis hesitated. "Well, I understand that you don't want people to die."

"*Do* you?" he asked sharply. At her blank expression, he sighed. "You don't really see why killing is wrong." He shifted and took her hands. They were cool, and his own hands were even more chilled. He held them tightly, struggling to find a way to explain it to her.

"Let me explain it this way," he said. "I'm as afraid of dying as you are of going into that prison again." Her eyes widened faintly and she nodded with evident understanding. Liiran squeezed her hands, encouraged. "But that's not all. So is everyone else you killed today. And everyone else in the world. That might not matter to you, but it matters to me. Is that good enough for you?"

She sat for a moment, then nodded slowly. "I don't really understand why. Death is just the end of life. It's natural."

He winced. "Maybe so," he said. "But every one of us is afraid of it. Because we don't want to lose our life, lose our friends and the things we've done. We don't want to just disappear. That's natural, too."

Mortis sighed softly and freed a hand, brushing a lock of hair back from her forehead. "I guess it's wrong to force someone to do something they don't want to do. I don't really get how something so natural can be a bad thing, or why you would be afraid of it, though. I mean, are you afraid of the wind?"

"Death isn't like the wind," Liiran said, letting go of her and stubbing out his cigarette on a shingle. "Not to us."

She looked at him, her lips curving in a smile. "I don't understand, but that doesn't mean you're wrong," she said. "And I'm very sorry for what I did today, Liiran, if it caused you so much distress."

He shook his head. "Just try not to do it again. Can you do that?"

She nodded. "Yes, I think so. I know what triggers my fear, now, and I'll have better control over it." She stood up, brushing her hands down her skirt and straightening the fabric. He noticed that her feet were bare, and her toes gripped the shingles. "I'm glad that's settled."

"Me too," Liiran said, and realized with amazement that he was. "I'm not really sure what we're going to do tomorrow, but for now let's get some sleep and then discuss it in the morning."

"Sure," she said, and turned a smile towards him. She picked her way easily down the roof and then dropped down to the windowsill. "Come on," she said, holding out a hand. "I'll help you down so you don't fall."

Grateful for that much, Liiran worked his way down to her and let her help him down. He noticed that her wings had disappeared again as he stepped back into the room.

Tanen came up the stairs as Liiran's feet touched the carpet. "Oh, here you guys are," he said cheerfully. "Mortis, your bed is down the stairs and on the right." Liiran saw the searching look in his eyes that he knew meant he was making sure that the arrangement was still the plan.

Liiran smiled and nodded, and Mortis moved towards the top of the steps, a smile on her face as well. "Thank you, Tanen," she said. "I do apologize for all the trouble."

Tanen bowed to her, his long hair falling around his face as he did so. It was a bit of an overly dramatic bow, and Liiran found himself rolling his eyes inwardly. "Not at all, my dear," he said. "It's no trouble at all."

When Mortis had gone downstairs, and Tanen and Liiran were alone together again, Liiran moved towards the bed, shedding clothes casually. He knew Tanen wouldn't mind that. Tanen was suddenly behind him, his arms going around Liiran and crossing over his stomach.

"Were you guys on the *roof?*" Tanen asked, his chin resting on Liiran's shoulder.

Liiran rolled his eyes and turned his head, kissing the other man. "Didn't I tell you not to ask?"

Tanen laughed and pulled him down onto the bed.

*   *   *

316 Years Earlier, 0 A.B.

"Hey, Lii, have you seen this?"

A torn flyer was shoved under Liiran's nose, between his eyes and the essay he was in the midst of writing for his Journalism 101 class. It came accompanied with the strong smell of turpentine and oil paints. Though his roommate was in the same classes he was, Tanen was also doing a minor in Fine Arts and instead of working on their essay, he had been working on a project for another class.

Liiran blinked a few times until the page came into focus, then plucked it out of Tanen's fingers. "Voxae ma, really? The clinic's opening tomorrow? For *everyone*?"

He turned his chair around while Tanen flopped down onto his bed on the other side of the dorm room, and bent to remove his shoes.

"Yeah," Tanen said, with an odd lack of enthusiasm. "I never thought it would happen so fast. I mean, they just started reporting about the – what's it called?"

"The Aevi Nexalum Drug," Liiran said, his heart thumping a little faster in his chest. "That's what they're calling it in the papers. Apparently some doctor by that name laid the groundwork, but she died in that big airship crash a couple of months ago, and they had to complete it from her notes. But they named it after her."

Tanen looked up pensively. "You've really been following this, haven't you?"

"We really should be following current events, Tan," Liiran said sternly. "How in Mortisor do you expect to make it as a journalist if you don't read the fucking newspaper?"

Tanen shrugged and grinned crookedly, like he always did. Then he sobered. "Do you think you'll go?"

Liiran stared at him. "Of *course* I'm going. It's *immortality*."

"What about kids?" Tanen asked, cocking his head. "You know, this could really fuck up the environment. Can you imagine if no one really died? And all the kids growing up and not dying. We'd outgrow the world in ten years."

"There are only something like fifty million people in the whole world, Tan," Liiran argued. "It'd take a lot longer than that. Besides, I heard the drug comes with a chemical sterilization. If you want kids later, you'll have to apply for them. If you're one of the people who's gotten the drug, that is."

Tanen nodded and flopped over onto his back, putting his hands behind his back. "Yeah." He grinned. "It'd be pretty cool, right? Being immortal. Not getting any older, just being young and hot forever."

Liiran grinned, relieved. He couldn't understand why Tanen seemed uncomfortable with it, but he wouldn't want to lose his best friend over this. How terrible would it be to be immortal and for his friends to get old and die? They were lucky that the drug was being manufactured and distributed for free. That new prime minister, Niveus, was really doing some amazing things.

He bet the other countries were just looking at Laxam in envy, right about now. No wonder there were rumours of war brewing on the borders.

"Right? So we're going tomorrow?" he urged, waving the flyer at Tanen.

Tanen glanced over at him, and nodded. "Let's do it."

*   *   *

Afterwards, Liiran lay in the circle of Tanen's arms, his head resting against the other man's chest and his hand on his stomach. "You're not eating enough," Liiran said, walking his fingers upwards and counting the ribs.

"You know I've always been a skinny twink," Tanen replied carelessly, batting his hand away. "That tickles."

Liiran rested his hand on Tanen's hip instead. "Hm. Art doesn't pay shit."

"That's only because every asshole in the world thinks they can do it, just because they've had three hundred years to pick up a hobby," Tanen said. "Someone's got to make money at it."

"That someone doesn't have to be you."

"Just because you hate your job doesn't mean everyone else should follow your example."

"I don't hate my job."

There was a long silence.

"I don't know what to do," Liiran said softly. "Tan, I'm so fucking screwed."

"What, again?" Tanen's voice was light and joking.

Liiran cuffed him on the hip. "Shut up. This isn't funny." Something about his face must have shown how *not* funny it was, because Tanen immediately sobered.

"What's going on, Lii? Seriously."

Liiran swallowed. He knew he shouldn't say anything. He *knew* it, but he needed to talk to Tanen about it, or he felt as if he might explode. "Somehow I've been saddled with a vox who needs my help, because

86

she's got amnesia, and now the secret police is after both of us. Today, they tried to have us both arrested, and she killed everyone in the police station. They've been bugging my house, and they tried to come after me again, and we had to run."

Once he got started, he couldn't stop, but he quickly ran out of words and fell silent.

"Voxae ma," Tanen swore, "are you serious?"

Liiran felt a flash of irritation. "Do you really think I'd tell you something like that if I weren't serious?"

"Okay, okay," Tanen said, rubbing Liiran's arm quickly to try to calm him down. "I didn't mean it like that. I'm sorry. It's just..." He lifted a hand and ran it through his hair. "It's hard to take in just like that."

"I know," Liiran said. "Sorry."

Tanen was silent for a moment. "So Mortis is a vox? Really? I didn't think they came that big, and... pretty."

"Neither did I," Liiran said. "She was in a voxmar, which was in some kind of building I stumbled on by accident. It broke when they brought it back here, I guess." Briefly, he explained in a bit more detail. It was more helpful than he had expected to unload this, but there wasn't actually as much to tell as he might have thought. Soon they lapsed into silence again.

"I don't know what you should do, either," Tanen said finally. "But hell, Lii, you can stay here until you figure out what you want to do."

"Don't be idiotic," Liiran said, closing his eyes. "If they find us here, you'll be arrested, too."

Tanen shrugged. "Maybe they won't find you here."

Liiran just shook his head, but didn't argue. Tanen stroked his arm, and it was soothing, but not soothing enough.

Chapter 15

Patient 1167-287-24576 read the plate above the small steel door, one of hundreds in this block, and thousands in this building alone. The doors lined the hall in endless rows, each with their identification plate.

No names, just numbers.

Aevi Nexalum adjusted her surgical mask and then inserted her key and opened the door. It swung to the side, and the plastic pod beyond slid out on rails into the sterile hallway where she stood.

The woman inside the pod lay still and unmoving, except for the slight rise and fall of her chest and the steady beat of her pulse in her throat. Tubes and wires ran from her body to an array of machines, feeding her a proper balance of nutrition and delivering electrical stimulation to keep her body from atrophying and wasting way, simultaneously monitoring her vital signs.

She looked healthy, almost as if she was sleeping, except for a deep crease that ran from her eyebrow into her hairline.

"Has there been any improvement with the therapy?" Aevi asked, bending to examine the EKG printout. There was a single straight line running down the centre of the paper with a few small wiggles here and there. She sighed.

"Nothing statistically significant, Dr. Nellexe, but there is an upwards trend. Perhaps if we increase the dosage?" asked her assistant.

Since death had been eradicated, brain damage was one of the few real medical problems of consequence remaining. Many things could be repaired *eventually* through the normal healing processes of the body, though of course it was always a tragedy when someone was crippled. But a paralyzed person could still interact with the world on some level, while oxygen starvation would leave a person brain dead, even though their bodies still breathed and functioned.

There were dozens of buildings like this around the world. Storage units for the almost-dead. And doctors like Aevi worked tirelessly to try to find solutions that might one day allow them to awaken and rejoin society. Eternity was a long time. One day a solution would be found, she hoped. Occasionally a person recovered, from incurable illnesses or cancers, as their bodies finally overcame something that would have killed them before the Breakthrough.

In this case, a new drug had been developed that was supposed to promote brain blood flow and replace brain cells, generally considered impossible a few short centuries ago. For someone like Patient 1167-287-24576, who had suffered a contusion and lapsed into a coma, it could get her out of this facility one day.

Assuming it worked.

She completed her examination and prescribed a higher dosage of the drug, then emerged from the storage block and removed her surgical mask and sterile gloves.

There was a man waiting for her. Altus Itolan sat in a chair, reading a newspaper.

"A-Altus," she stammered, surprised. "I wasn't expecting you."

He folded the paper and set it aside. "Any breakthroughs, Eve?" he asked as they turned to walk together down the hallway towards her office.

He had used her assumed name. For three hundred years she had been Eve Nellexe. It was a choice that hadn't been hers, but she was glad of it. The world knew Aevi Nexalum as the surgeon who had conquered Death, and been one of its last victims. If she were still 'alive', she would be a celebrity, and unable to continue her work.

Of course, she hadn't done it alone, either, but that was how mythology worked. The Empire needed heroes, and she was one of them.

It often surprised her when she looked at her own face on the back of coins that no one ever recognized her. Even after the plastic surgery and radically changing her hair colour and style, she could still see herself in the mirror. Usually. Sometimes it felt to her like a stranger was staring out of the mirror, even now.

She shrugged. "Nothing today, but we keep researching."

Altus shook his head. "I can't imagine how you stand it, working in this depressing place. Your brilliance is wasted here." Though his tone was mild, Aevi felt like the words were a reprimand.

"I continue my work, Altus," she said apologetically. "I like to keep my hand in the truly worthwhile things. Saving lives." She was both a scientist and a mage, but few knew about the latter.

She swallowed, immediately regretting her brashness. Altus had always petrified her, especially when she had just been a student, and he had taken a personal interest in her discoveries. Even now, she found him frightening, even if only out of habit.

"Have I been derelict in my duties in some way?" she asked. "Is that why you came here, because of some complaint?"

"No, no," Altus said, his tone kindly. "Come, let us talk about it in your office."

"Of course, sir," she said, and fell silent until they had passed through the door. He locked it, she saw, and engaged the anti-eavesdropping device. She swallowed again, and took her seat at her desk. "How can I help you?"

Altus didn't sit, but moved to inspect a portrait of Aevi on the wall. It wasn't there because of vanity – in fact, she hated the portrait with a passion – but because if a medical facility administrator had failed to have a depiction of the greatest doctor of all time on the wall somewhere it would have seemed odd.

He stared up at the picture. "I have two reasons for coming here, Aevi," he said without looking at her. "Firstly, I require your assistance with something very important."

She folded her hands. "What do you need?"

Now he fixed her with that icy stare of his. "I have decided that it's time to collar Niveus."

She simply stared at him for a moment, shocked. "What? Why?"

Altus moved towards her, and rested a hand on her shoulder. Her skin crawled. "I have always been able to trust you with our society's deepest secrets, Aevi," Altus murmured. "You are the only one who has shared with me the secret of Niveus' true nature, all this time. Back then, you begged me to trust you, and leave him free. Now I'm asking you to trust *me*. The time has come."

He squeezed her shoulder, then released her and walked around to the other side of the desk, to face her. "Can I count on you to work with Maenos and develop the runes necessary to contain and control him, just as you did with the mortivox and certovox before?"

Her throat was too dry to speak, but she managed to croak. "But... but why?"

Altus' eyes narrowed. "I know that you have a... fondness for him, Aevi, but you and I *both* know that humans are different from vox."

She dropped her gaze. "Yes, naturally we are different."

"And do you not agree that humans should control their *own* destinies? We needed Niveus to get this far, but we cannot be ruled by a vox forever! Vox are necessarily limited in their viewpoints, not like humans. Sooner or later, Niveus' leadership will lead us down a path that isn't good for us as a race, and we must not allow that to happen." His passion caused his voice to rise, and she felt her shoulders tightening in response.

It left a bad taste in her mouth, but she also knew he was right. Niveus had been a tool, though she didn't like to think of him that way. Perhaps...

Perhaps Altus was right.

Niveus had done well with Altus' guidance, but if Altus was taking this step, that meant that they were starting to move down that path. A vox of order only understood and wanted order, and she had long wondered if Niveus could really understand what humans needed beyond his limited worldview.

She bobbed her head in acceptance and whispered, "Of course." She swallowed and managed to add, a bit more briskly, "Of course, I'll do whatever is necessary."

He smiled and leaned across the desk, patting her clasped hands. "Good," he said. "I knew I could count on you."

He straightened up. "You don't have much time, I'm afraid. We will want to move as soon as the next phase of the war begins. Can you have it ready by the day after tomorrow?"

That soon? Aevi hesitated. "It should be closely related to the runes we've already developed," she said. "I'm sure between Maenos and I, we will be able to come up with something—"

She was interrupted by a frantic banging at her office door. Emergencies were rare here. Had the new dosage of the drug caused an allergic reaction? Aevi started to her feet and started to call out, then remembered that Altus had locked the door.

As she rounded her desk, Altus moved out of her way and all but faded into the background.

One of her assistants was standing outside the door, her eyes wide with shock and panic. "Doctor, Doctor, it's not possible," the woman gasped. She was winded, as if she had been running.

"What is it?" Aevi demanded. The timid woman she had shown Altus simply flowed away in the face of an emergency, and her voice was hard as a rock. "Calm down and explain."

The woman seemed steadied by her manner and she swallowed visibly, putting a hand out to the doorframe. "I'm sorry, it's just that—" Her eyes darted quickly from side to side. "Doctor Nellexe, remember that man who came in yesterday, the car accident victim? Cranial trauma with facial lacerations?"

Utterly confused as to what could possibly be so urgent about a man who might never wake up from his coma, Aevi nodded. "Yes, I recall," she said.

The woman's words were delivered in a hushed whisper so soft that Aevi nearly didn't catch it. "Doctor, he... he *died*."

For the second time in as many minutes, Aevi couldn't believe what she was hearing. "That's impossible."

"I'm sorry, Doctor," she said. "But we checked the equipment three times, and even took his pulse manually. There's no brain activity, no heartbeat, no breathing. He's... just *gone*."

How is that possible? It's just not possible! Now it was Aevi's turn to lean on the doorjamb for support, but she only did so for a second before straightening. "Take me," she said, starting forward.

The sound of a throat clearing reminded her that the grand minister was still in her office. She turned towards him. "Altus, I'm sorry, we'll need to chat later—" she began.

"Eve, I apologize, I know you have something very important to deal with," Altus said, and by his unruffled expression she saw that he already knew. "I will be only a few moments more, if you would please close the door."

Going cold with horror, Aevi shot an apologetic look at the assistant and then shut the door in her face.

"Altus, please. What is going on?" she whispered.

His expression was grave. "I should have told you first. I'm sorry, Aevi, but I didn't think it would begin so soon." He shook his head. "Death has escaped her prison."

Aevi stared at him for a few long moments, her ears filled with the rapid tattoo of her heart.

"Voxae ma," she whispered. "Save us all." One death was bad, very bad. But what would happen to their carefully built society when the deaths multiplied beyond their ability to keep it quiet?

It would fall like a house of cards.

She left her office at a run, all but dragging her assistant behind her.

Chapter 16

A loud banging at the door sent Liiran from a relatively peaceful sleep into a state of panic like a spring uncoiling. He sat up before he'd even opened his eyes, his heart pounding and the metallic taste of adrenaline in his mouth. From the pale sunlight slanting in through Tanen's bedroom window, it was just after dawn.

Tanen had always been a poor waker. He groaned and pulled his pillow over his face, groping for Liiran. His hand spidered over Liiran's bare hip, tickling. Liiran smacked at it.

"Tan!" he snapped, searching for his pants. "Someone's here."

"Who cares?" Tanen muttered. "If it's important, they can wait. Come back—" A crashing sound and the pounding of multiple feet downstairs had Tanen also sitting up, blinking the sleep from his eyes. "What the fuck was that?"

"Shit, shit, shit," Liiran said, pulling his shirt over his head. His duffle bag was open, and he started shoving things back into it. Thankfully he hadn't unpacked much.

Mortis emerged from the stairwell as if she'd been shot from a cannon, feet barely touching the floor. Her eyes were wide with worry. "Liiran, it's—"

"Police!" came a gruff shout from downstairs. "Everyone come down with your hands up and you won't be hurt. The house is completely surrounded."

Tanen was out of bed as well now, still looking befuddled, but searching for clothes now.

"How did they find us so fast?" Mortis asked. Despite the fact that it was dawn, her hair was smooth and unruffled, though her dress was in slight disarray.

"I have no idea," Liiran said. The three of them gathered together in a tight knot in the centre of the room and listened to the stairs creaking. The officers were coming up.

Liiran turned to Mortis. "Can you carry both of us, if we can get out of the building?"

"Mortisor's fiery pits, Lii," Tanen said, shaking his head. "How're we even gonna get out of here?"

"The window," Liiran said, pointing. "Let's get onto the roof, then we can fly away like before."

"I don't know if I can carry both of you," Mortis said.

Liiran rounded on her. "You're damn strong, Mortis. You can do it!"

"It's not about strength! Should I hold you one under each arm? I'll drop you!"

"We'll figure it out!"

"I could..." Mortis began. Her eyes were beginning to glow, the black deepening, and her wings suddenly spreading wide. Tanen stumbled away from her, swearing.

She hadn't finished her sentence, but there was no doubt of what she was suggesting. Liiran grabbed her by the shoulders and gave her a desperate shake, ignoring his mental image of the officer yesterday.

"Oh no. You are absolutely not going to kill anyone," Liiran shouted.

"Guys!" Tanen's shout pulled Liiran out of the argument and he looked. The first officer was almost at the top of the steps. He was dressed in black, his body armoured and his face covered. He carried a large crossbow of some kind. It was a thoroughly terrifying sight.

All three backed towards the window.

"There's no time," Liiran said. His heart was pounding with terror as the officer looked from side to side, panning the bow along with his eyes as if searching for others who might be hiding in the corners.

Then Tanen took a step forward, raising his hands to shoulder height. "You guys go," he hissed. "I'll be okay."

"What? No, are you crazy?" Liiran grabbed Tanen's shoulder, but his friend shook him off. Mortis had already started for the window, and the officer shouted for her to stop.

"I haven't done anything wrong, I don't know anything," Tanen snapped to Liiran in an undertone. Then he walked towards the officer. His position blocked the officer's line of fire. "I surrender," he said. "What's this all about? How dare you come into my home like this? I'm a law abiding citizen, you know—"

Taking a deep breath, Liiran dove for the window. *Damnit, damnit, this was a bad idea. How could I have done this to him?*

Ignoring the shouts from behind him, his shoulder blades itching with the anticipation of a bolt burrowing into his back at any moment, Liiran clambered through the window, dragging the duffle bag after him.

Before he'd even had a chance to climb onto the roof, Mortis grabbed him under his arms and launched into the air. He cried out, his feet dangling and his body hanging far more precariously than before, almost dropping the duffle bag.

There was a sound, like a low twang, and Mortis suddenly banked. A crossbow bolt grazed Liiran's right leg, drawing a line of fire across his skin. She flapped her wings strongly and they continued to rise, the buildings rushing by underneath them, as they left the police officers far behind.

Then Liiran heard a rhythmic throbbing sound. The sleek black ship with its angled propellers blurring slid out from behind a tall building and angled towards them at shocking speed. This was no passenger liner or pleasure cruiser. This was a military vehicle.

"Fly, Mortis! Fast!" Liiran screamed, and Mortis dove, banking and dodging as crossbow bolts rained down on them from above.

Mortis flew desperately, weaving between the buildings, but the high rises were far enough apart in this part of the city that the beetle-like airship kept them in sight. The flying crossbow bolts stopped – either the angle was too difficult for the sharp shooters, or they were afraid of causing innocent casualties in such a populated area.

Either way, Liiran was sure it was just a matter of time before they found their shot. He didn't know if Mortis could be taken down by a crossbow, but the ache in his leg was a constant reminder that *he* was vulnerable.

The airship might not be able to gain on them in this environment, but sooner or later reinforcements would get there, or they'd run out of city to hide in.

"Liiran!" Mortis cried, rounding a building and skimming the leaves of a rooftop garden so close that Liiran had to draw his legs up or lose his shoes. His body was aching from how tightly she held him around his waist. "Where can I go? Where is safe?"

"We have to lose that airship!" he said. "Can't you go faster?"

"I'll hurt you," Mortis wailed. "You can't take my maximum speed."

He was pretty sure she was right. Even at her current speed, he could feel the strain on his body from the wind.

"Then find somewhere it can't follow," he said.

"I'll try," she said, and circled around the building to head deeper into the downtown core.

The police had anticipated them.

As they headed west, the airship hot on their heels, a second one suddenly rose up from the top of a low building and headed straight for them. The front windows looked like the eyes of an insectoid monster, starting at them, and the harpoon turrets swivelled to bear right on Liiran.

A speaker crackled to life. "Attention fugitives. Surrender by order of the police and your sentence will be fair. Continue to flee and we will have no choice but to put you down!"

Mortis turned too fast and accelerated. Liiran cried out as the G-force slammed into him. The airship turned to cut them off, and Liiran could see that she simply couldn't move fast enough while carrying him to get out of the way.

He opened his mouth to tell her to surrender, fighting to get the words out.

Then a black shape shot from between two buildings. It went straight past them, and Liiran caught a glimpse of skeletal bat wings and a pale face like a skull, then the creature flew directly at the airship.

Huge wings draped over the windshield, and the pilot clearly panicked. The airship dove to the side and the creature disengaged. The machine plummeted, the pilot struggling to regain control.

"Hide!" Liiran heard the vox – it was clearly another vox – yell as it blurred past. "Wait for me!"

Then he was heading for the other airship. Mortis dove again, and Liiran clutched at her arm, gasping. "Find an alley," he shouted to her past the wind in his ears.

Who is that? he wondered dizzily. He couldn't hear the grinding noise as the first airship's blades cut into the side of a building, but he felt the shudder as it crashed into a rooftop and all the vavoxae escaped explosively.

By that time, Mortis wasn't too far up, and it didn't take much longer before Liiran's feet touched the sidewalk again, sending a jolt of pain up his leg that settled into a dull throb. She let go, then landed beside him.

They gazed at each other for a moment, in silence. Liiran knew, somewhere inside him, he was filled with seething rage and fear. But there was so much of it he was overwhelmed and couldn't feel anything at all. He was completely numb, as if he'd been doused in ice water.

Without a word, he turned and ducked into a nearby alleyway, out of sight of passersby.

"Liiran," Mortis said, following him into the shadows. She folded her wings and they vanished once more. "Maybe I should just give myself up."

Liiran gaped for a moment, then closed his mouth. He gazed at her, at the fear in her eyes, mixed with genuine guilt and worry.

He turned the idea over in his head, tasted it, savoured it.

"Maybe if I turn myself in now, they'll let you and your friend go. I'll tell them I made you help me, or something. I'll tell them *something*," she went on earnestly. "You shouldn't have to pay for this. It's my problem, and I got you into this terrible mess."

Somehow, even though Liiran had agreed with her only yesterday, and only minutes before had been ready to give up himself, it was different hearing her say it. Hearing her offer to give up her freedom in exchange for his and Tanen's, his anger at her died. All this time he had blamed her, but it was the police and the government who had *really* created this horrible situation.

He shook his head and reached for her. The action was completed before either of them quite realized Liiran was going to do it, judging by Mortis' hiss of surprise. Liiran gathered her to him in a tight hug.

She smelled of incense, smoke, and cinnamon, his mind noted in a distant way. Her arms went around him after an awkward hesitation, squeezing with equal strength despite her obvious uncertainty.

"Liiran?" she whispered after a while.

He cleared his throat in embarrassment, straightening as he realized he'd just been standing there for almost a full minute, embracing her and shaking lightly with reaction. "Sorry."

She frowned at him, her arms still held in a half-embrace, as if she wasn't sure if she should let go or not. He somehow found a smile as he released her.

"You don't have to turn yourself in," he said. "We should concentrate on getting your memory back, and on finding out why you were imprisoned in the first place. Everything else, we can evaluate when we have more information."

Her mouth went slack, and Liiran couldn't blame her. His new resolve was probably giving her whiplash at this point. But now his thoughts were clear, as they hadn't been since this whole thing started.

"But what about the police?" she asked. "What about Tanen? I'm sure they arrested him."

Liiran was sure of that, too. But he shook his head, clenching his fists. "Tanen knew he was going to get arrested for helping us. And you giving yourself up won't help either of us. They want to silence us, or they wouldn't have tried to arrest me at the police station. If there ever were a point when turning you in would have saved me, we're long past it now."

Mortis nodded regretfully. "I suppose you're right."

"There you are."

Liiran stiffened at the unfamiliar voice, and they both turned. A man was in the alley with them.

He was very slender, with a long, sallow face, and eyes set deeply in his sockets. He was wearing a simple t-shirt and jeans, both ragged and worn.

"Who are you?" Liiran certainly had never seen this man before, and Mortis didn't look as if she recognized him, either. But even as he asked the question, he recalled the face of the vox that had rescued them. He had caught only a glimpse, and the wings were gone now, but it had to be the same person.

"My name is Phames," he said, lifting a hand to his cheek to scratch with ragged fingernails. Though he answered Liiran's question, he stared fixedly at Mortis. "So you've finally managed to get out, have you, Mortis?"

Mortis' jaw dropped. "You... you know who I am?" she demanded. "You really know who I am?"

"Shit," Phames said with feeling. "I thought something was wrong. Look, we've got to get under cover, now. You've caused a stir, and they'll find you if we don't keep moving."

He turned away and took a step towards the mouth of the alley before glancing over his shoulder at them. "You coming? I've risked a lot by revealing myself, you know."

Mortis glanced from Phames to Liiran and back. "Of course we'll come. You know a safe place we can stay?"

Phames turned back. "We?" he echoed. For the first time, he looked at Liiran, staring hard. His eyes were a light sandy colour, a few shades lighter than hazel. It was very unusual, and Liiran couldn't help staring back at him, caught by those strangely coloured eyes, the same shade as the desert sand around Mortis' tomb.

"Yes, 'we.' Liiran and I are together," Mortis said. She glanced at Liiran. "I'm not leaving you behind for a moment. Not after everything you've gone through for me." Addressing Phames again, she folded her arms. "Where do you intend to take me? How do I even know I can trust you?"

Phames' head swung to look at her, and he stared for a moment in obvious shock. Then his mouth shut with an audible click. "Fine," he said in a sullen, sulky voice, "he can come." He sighed and tilted his head up, looking at the thin slice of sky visible overhead. "But we're walking from here. I won't risk flying with the magi watching the skies for us. Especially with a human slowing us down."

Liiran grimaced. The mention of walking had caused his leg to start throbbing, reminding him of the injury. "Just a minute."

He bent, dropping the duffle bag and thanking the voxae of luck that it had survived two wild rides through the air. He sorted through it until he found the first aid kit he had packed and retrieved a roll of gauze.

His pants had a tear through them at mid-calf and were soaked with blood. The gash from the crossbow bolt that had grazed him was only bleeding sluggishly, but if they were going to be walking from here, he was sure it would open again.

He wrapped his wound as quickly as he could with gauze. He was very aware of the thrum of airships circling, and couldn't tell if they were getting closer or not.

Phames had his arms folded and he was fidgeting, tapping his foot on the ground. It wasn't very loud – Liiran now saw that he was barefoot – but it made him vibrate just at the edge of Liiran's vision in a very irritating way. "Do you *mind?*" Liiran asked him. "I'll be ready in a second."

"Humans are so useless," Phames sneered in reply.

"Excuse me," Mortis said. "Liiran's the reason why I haven't been recaptured yet, so be nice."

"Oh really?" Phames asked sarcastically. "Are you sure he isn't the reason why you have almost been recaptured several times already?"

"What are you talking about?" Mortis' eyes flashed with anger. Liiran struggled to finish a little faster, but didn't want to do a sloppy job and wind up leaving a trail of blood all the way to wherever they were going. Finally he tied off the gauze, while Phames stalked to his side, grabbed the duffle bag, and rummaged inside it.

"Hey!" Liiran exclaimed.

Phames' hand emerged with a small object, and he turned it over, displaying Liiran's electronic organizer. "Look at this," he said, glaring at Liiran.

He opened the cover that hid the voxmar and displayed a tiny glass bottle, the size of his ragged pinkie fingernail.

"That's my organizer," Liiran said, reaching for it, but Phames pulled it out of his reach.

"Don't be stupid," Phames said, prying the voxmar out. Liiran saw a second bottle still nestled inside the guts of the device, about twice as large. "This is the one that makes your stupid thing work. This one." He held up the small one, then dropped it deliberately on the ground and crushed it under his bare heel, "was a bug."

Liiran felt his jaw drop, then quickly got to his feet, tugging the cuff of his pants down to cover the bandage. "How do you know that?"

"When you've been evading the Circle of Magi for three hundred years, you learn their dirty tricks," Phames said, rummaging inside the duffle bag again. This time, Liiran didn't object.

Within a minute, Phames had found a second bug inside his camera, and had searched through everything Liiran had brought with him. Liiran felt a little ill, and it wasn't the loss of blood on the flight that was giving him nausea.

"That's how they knew," he moaned. "That's why they found us at Tanen's house."

Mortis put a hand on his shoulder. "You didn't know. It's not your fault." Phames watched them impatiently, the duffle bag slung over his shoulder. He gazed at Mortis especially, scowling.

"I should have realized. I knew my home phone was bugged. I should have checked."

"Stop moaning and carrying on," Phames snapped, and stomped towards the street. "And *if* it's not too much trouble, can we get out of here before they come to arrest us all?"

Swallowing, Liiran followed him, Mortis at his side.

Chapter 17

They took buses, subways, and even a taxi, and over the course of two hours Liiran and his two vox companions criss-crossed half the city before they finally reached their destination. By that point Liiran's wound had mostly stopped hurting, which would have been a mercy if it weren't for the fierce pain in his feet from all the damn walking.

They finally reached a run-down part of the city, several of the shops along the street boarded up and the others barred tightly. Even in the great city of Laxamora there was crime, after all, though it was combated ruthlessly.

The last bus stop was two blocks away, and then they passed down a blind alley before they reached a small wooden door recessed into the brick wall of a building. There was no sign, nothing that indicated that it was anything but the side door of the apartment building above it.

Phames looked around with obvious nervousness, but there was no one nearby but a cat rooting around in a stray bag of garbage that filled the narrow, dark space with a sickly sweet smell. Finally he produced a key and pulled the door open to reveal a staircase heading downwards.

"Go in, hurry," he hissed.

Mortis hesitated, then stepped in boldly and Liiran followed. The stairs were steep and narrow, and the railing was rickety, held on by about half as many screws as there should be.

Phames stepped in after him and pulled the door shut. The lights were abruptly extinguished and the click of the lock was overly loud in the suddenly dark space. "Shit," he said, stopping where he was. Liiran didn't want to try to grope his way down in the dark, with a bad leg and a shaky rail. "Isn't there a light in here?"

"Oh, for..." Phames flicked on the light switch, which Liiran hadn't noticed. Above them hung a bare, cobwebby bulb. Mortis was almost at the bottom of the stairs, silhouetted by a second light below them. "I forgot that humans can't see for shit."

Liiran resumed his limping descent. He was really getting sick of this attitude from Phames, which had not let up an inch over their journey.

"Well I'm sorry that we're not as perfect as you are," he muttered under his breath.

"You should be sorry," Phames sneered

"Phames. Liiran," Mortis called, "both of you shut up."

"Why did it take so damned long to get here, anyway?" Liiran asked, ignoring Mortis' half-hearted attempt to stop them from bickering. "We could have easily gotten here in two transfers, as far as I could see."

"Sure," Phames said sarcastically, "and then if someone had been following us, we wouldn't have known until it was too late."

That shut Liiran up for a moment, and he worked his way down to the bottom before speaking again. "Was anyone following us?"

"No, but that doesn't mean it was stupid to make sure."

Liiran wanted to strangle him.

The space at the bottom of the staircase might be called an apartment, but it barely qualified for the name. There was only one room, and it was populated by a sagging couch, a few other rickety pieces of furniture, and a massive television.

Liiran gaped at the latter, stunned by its incongruous presence in this hovel. There wasn't even a bed, or a kitchen. Hell, there wasn't a bathroom. As he looked around, he saw that there was also a desk, tucked up next to the staircase, with a laptop sitting on top of it. A thick internet cable snaked across the floor and disappeared into a hole in the far wall.

"What is this place?" Liiran asked.

Phames ambled across the room, switched on the television and perched on a chair. He actually *perched*, drawing his feet up and crossing them in front of him on the seat of the chair. The TV was showing four different news stations at once, the sound so low that it was only a vague buzz to Liiran's hearing.

Phames pointed at the couch. It looked extremely lumpy and uncomfortable. Liiran sat down gratefully anyway, suppressing a groan.

"This is my home for the moment," Phames said. "I move around a lot. Actually, I just came back to Laxamora a few months ago. I had to leave again a few decades back to avoid the magi."

Mortis eyed Liiran with obvious concern in her eyes, but he waved it away. He was sore, that's all.

Apparently reassured, she then turned to Phames. "I think you'd better start from the beginning."

Phames met her eyes and nodded. "Yes, I think so," he said. His pale eyes darted to Liiran for a moment, then fixed on Mortis and stayed there. "But before I start, am I right in understanding that you don't remember who you are, or anything?"

Mortis nodded, folding her hands together tightly. "I don't remember a thing before I broke out of my prison," she said. "A few impressions of being trapped for a very long time, but nothing from before that. I know I'm a vox, and... some things have happened to me, but I don't really know anything at all."

Phames nodded. His fingers picked restlessly at the threadbare fabric at one knee. "You're the vox of death," he said without sugar-coating it in the slightest.

Liiran's jaw dropped, and he blurted out before he could stop it. "There's a vox of *death*?"

The other vox looked at him coolly. "Why do you think you haven't died in three centuries?" he asked. "She's been trapped all this time, by the Circle of Magi."

"But..." Liiran looked at Mortis, his heart beginning to pound. "It was a medical advancement," he said weakly, not sure he even believed his own words. He turned back to Phames. "They gave everyone an injection."

"Did they give everyone *outside* the Empire – or as it was then, the Laxam Republic – an injection?" Phames asked. "None of them are dead, either."

Liiran shifted uncomfortably. "I know that all the more civilized nations that we had treaties with at the time benefited from the advancement," he said, aware that he was practically parroting the press releases coming out of Parliament at the time. "And I always figured that the terrorists stole what they needed."

Phames made a rude noise. "Well, that's a big pack of lies," he said, as if Liiran was stupid for not having known all along.

Annoyed, Liiran looked away, struggling not to rise to the bait. This time, at least, he suspected his irritation didn't really have anything to do with Phames. Mortis' cool hand rested on his knee, and he rested his hand over hers in return, grateful for her presence.

"Tell me," Mortis said, "what has really happened?"

There was a moment of silence, then Phames sighed. "Like I said, you're the mortivox. I'm the vox of decay – a related type," he said. "They wanted to capture me around the time they got you, probably so they could solve death and hunger at the same time, but I managed to evade them. I've been on the run ever since."

Liiran could only shake his head, struggling to fit what he was hearing into what he knew about the world.

It was easy to understand things like covox, or savox. Gather a bunch of covoxae in one place and things got hot, and the exact opposite thing happened with savoxae. In most places you got a mix, of course.

But how did the mortivox work? Were there a billion tiny voxae like Mortis? Did she individually have to go around and kill people?

The morbid tenor of his thoughts sent a shudder through Liiran's body.

"None of this makes sense," he murmured, though he remembered the blast that had erupted from Mortis, and how all the people in the police station had collapsed and not gotten up again.

"What about it doesn't make sense?" Phames asked with an edge in his voice. "Maybe you could enlighten me, human."

Liiran drew in a breath, gritting his teeth. "First of all, why don't you explain why I'm not dead, then? If Mortis is the mortivox, why hasn't she killed me yet?"

Phames' face folded into a glare. "That's what *I* want to know."

"Is... there a reason that he should be dead?" Mortis asked.

"Of course!" Phames said, making a violent gesture. "He's three hundred years old. Shouldn't he be dead by now?"

Liiran *really* didn't like that idea. "Now see here!" he snapped. "If you look at it that way, then shouldn't everyone in the whole world be dropping dead right about now? There aren't that many people having babies these days, even if they can get licenses to do it."

"Licenses to procreate," Phames sneered, shaking his head as if at a private joke. "Humans are so unnatural." He fixed Liiran with a glare. "Maybe they should all be dropping dead. Ask me if I care?"

Liiran felt his face growing hot with rage. "I don't get why you're being such a jerk about this. I don't blame you for not liking the people who tried to hurt you, but why do you hate all humans like this? I've never done anything to you!"

Phames snorted and folded his arms. "I don't need to justify myself to a monkey."

Mortis shot to her feet and physically planted herself between them, blocking Liiran's view of the phamevox. "That's it!" she snapped, her hands on her hips. She was facing Phames, so Liiran couldn't see her expression, but he could hear the anger in her voice. "Phames, I'm not going to tell you again. Liiran helped me, and he deserves your respect." She whirled around, her skirt flaring. "And Liiran, give Phames a break. He's obviously been through a lot."

"Fine with me," Liiran said, though he couldn't keep a certain sulky tone of resentment out of his voice.

Phames started it.

The vox just snorted. "Fine," he growled, "but I still don't see why you don't kill him."

Mortis sat. "Well I—" She stopped, and frowned. "I think it's that he's not sick," she said stubbornly. "I can't just go around killing everyone, even if I am the mortivox. That's not right."

Phames leaned back in his chair. "I suppose you're right," he said. "Humans rarely drop dead for no reason. Not that it stopped you before."

"Those times were accidents," Mortis said tightly.

Her hand crept back into Liiran's, and he squeezed reassuringly. If he were in her position...

...No, he had absolutely no idea how he would be feeling in her position. How did you take being told that you were the mortivox?

It did explain the way she had reacted to him telling her not to kill anyone else, though. He bit his lip and tried not to think about that. He couldn't very well sanction killing, especially after their society had functioned for so long with no death at all.

Mortis spoke up again. "Phames, you never told me why you came back to Laxamora now. Did you know something?"

Phames shook his head. "No, I've been travelling for a while, but I do come back here every so often, when the heat is low," he said. "I run a small newspaper, trying to fight back in a way."

Liiran barked a laugh at that. "A newspaper? The phamevox runs a *newspaper*?"

Phames met his gaze steadily. "It's called *The Truth*. I do everything I can to tell the humans that what they've been reading about in the other media is a lie, that everything they know is a lie."

Wait, what? Liiran's mouth worked for a few moments. "Hang on," he said in a voice that shook with shock and disbelief. "You... *You* are Phamile Sandar?"

Phames smiled for the first time since Liiran had met him. "You've heard of me," he said with deep satisfaction.

Chapter 18

Liiran lay on Phames' lumpy couch, a spring digging into his side. With nothing else to distract him, he couldn't help reflecting on how close he had come today, for the first time in his life, to winding up in jail.

He imagined that the beds in jail might be more comfortable than this couch.

Worse, he might have actually *died*.

He could hear the clicking of the keys as Phames did something on the computer. The voxae were still talking in low voices, and had been for hours. Liiran had listened for a while, but had eventually given up the ghost and turned in. He had drifted in and out of wakefulness and eventually found that the voxae had lapsed into a mode of speech he couldn't understand. Their voices were soft and musical, and the best analogy Liiran could come up with for how they sounded was like the wind rustling dry leaves. Another language?

He stirred and shifted, unable to suppress a grunt as he turned over. The discussion stopped abruptly, and then Mortis whispered again and Liiran could understand it.

"We're disturbing him."

The response from Phames was still in that strange language, but he didn't sound sympathetic.

"He's our friend and it's my fault he's here, that's why I care," Mortis said. "How many times do I have to say it? And speak human, he can hear."

"He shouldn't be listening," Phames said, grudgingly switching to something Liiran could understand. "Besides, it's late. He'll be asleep again in a second."

"It's almost dawn," Mortis said, "let's go up to the roof to talk before it becomes too light to fly without someone seeing us."

Phames grunted and Liiran heard rustling as he stood. "Fine. It's stuffy in here, anyway. I'd like to stretch my wings."

Liiran felt a gentle hand land on his shoulder and opened his eyes to see Mortis smiling down at him. "We'll be back later, Liiran," she said softly. "You rest and sleep."

He nodded and closed his eyes, listened as the two left.

Then he opened his eyes again and sat up. A plan had been forming nebulously in his mind since yesterday and now he had probably his last opportunity to put it into motion.

He got up and slipped his feet into his shoes, climbed the rickety staircase, and poked his head out of the door into the alley. A sickly sweet scent of rotting garbage assaulted him, but he ignored it, scanning the sky. It seemed clear.

There was a pay phone a block away, which he'd noted on their way here. He walked to it unhurriedly, resisting the urge to look around or hide his face from passers-by. No one had followed them to Phames' safehouse. There was no reason to believe anyone would recognize him. Not that there were a lot of people on the street, anyway. It was nearly deserted, in fact. This wasn't exactly a happening spot.

When he reached the telephone booth, he pulled the door closed behind him, dropped a coin into the slot, and dialled a number from memory.

It rang, over and over, but finally someone answered clumsily and then a sleepy, rumbling voice spoke over the line. "What?"

"Sal, it's Lii," Liiran said quickly. "I'm sorry for calling you at home."

"Voxae ma, Lii," Salmo growled. "What the fuck is going on with you? First you vanish without a trace, don't call in to work, *nothing*. Then the police are calling me every hour demanding to know where you are, and going through your office files, tearing the place apart. Now you call me out of the blue in the middle of the night? What kind of trouble are you in?"

After having his home bugged and tracking devices inserted in his belongings, Liiran had been pretty much expecting to hear this. "I'm really sorry," he said. "I haven't done anything wrong, Sal, I swear. But I've gotten mixed up in something, that's for sure."

"You gonna tell me what it is? I don't want to have to fire you, Lii."

"You don't want to fire me. Why do you think I called you?" Liiran said. "I have a scoop for you, and I want you to meet me."

"Voxae nema uto ma, Lii," Sal groaned. "Are you fucking kidding me? Is this some kind of joke? I haven't seen anything big coming down the pipeline at all, and now you're telling me that you've got something yourself?"

"This isn't going to come down the pipeline," Liiran said forcefully. "Do you want it or not, Sal? Are you a journalist or a fucking parrot?"

Despite his complaints, Liiran could tell from the tenor of the silence that ensued after that comment that Salmo was listening, and very intrigued.

"Meet me at Savaer Park in an hour," Liiran said, his mouth dry with terror.

"Fuck, Lii... you're going to drag me out of bed at this ungodly hour?"

He had him, Liiran could tell. "Take it or leave it, Sal. You won't regret it," he said.

There was a heavy sigh. "I'll be there, but only for you, Lii."

"Good," Lii said, and, just in case, "come alone, Sal."

*   *   *

Liiran fingered his cell phone in his pocket as he crossed the park and sat down on the bench. The sky was a pale blue and the sun was only just touching the buildings in the distance as it rose. A courageous pair of joggers trotted past on the concrete path and nodded to Liiran as they sweated by in their spandex.

The air coming off the river was cold and Liiran pulled his coat around himself, sticking his hands in his pockets and letting out a breath that misted around his face. His leg jiggled nervously, but then it started to throb, and he forced himself to stop. He felt exposed out in the open like this, but at least he couldn't fail to see the police if they showed up. The only trouble was, where would he run to?

He couldn't help feeling that he was doing something wrong, but he pushed that out of his mind. There was no other way, and Mortis and Phames would just have to understand.

If it had just been Mortis he would have brought her along, but he knew Phames wouldn't allow this. Of course he wouldn't. The vox was the creator of the only independent journalistic source on the planet, the only one that wasn't subject to the censorship of the government. Others had tried to accomplish the same thing, but Phames was the only one who had never been caught, and now Liiran knew why.

He must see people like Liiran as merely catering to the status quo that Phames hated for good reason. He had to see Liiran's paper, his coworkers – and especially his bosses – as the enemy. He certainly saw humans in general as the enemy.

"There you are, Lii!" Salmo walked towards him, breath steaming in the cool air. Though he had had to carry his bulk halfway across the park, his face was flushed more with irritation than exertion. He looked rumpled, as if he hadn't slept in days.

Liiran could sympathize.

"I can't believe you called me out of the blue and dragged me out to this place," Salmo grumbled in a quieter tone as he came to stand next to the bench where Liiran was sitting.

The tone wasn't a surprise. He had expected to catch flak from making his boss come out here at the time normal, committed journalists were expected to go to work. Of course, Liiran hadn't been at work in two days. Busy, busy.

"I'm sorry, Sal," Liiran said. "Thank you for coming, and I'm sorry that the police have been giving you a hard time."

"So what?" Salmo snapped, not at all mollified. "What's the story, Lii? What are you up to?"

"Are you really listening?" Liiran asked. "Because, like I said when I called you, I have a huge one for you. Bigger than anything since the Breakthrough."

"That's shit," Salmo retorted, but Liiran could see he was leaning a bit closer, like a dog scenting a fox. Yet despite that underlying interest, his eyes darted quickly from side to side, and Liiran got to his feet warily. He had expected grumbling, but something was off here.

"Sal, why don't you sit down? It's been a crazy few days. I've got a lot to tell you." *Plus you're creeping me out.*

"Lii, listen to me," Salmo said abruptly. He wasn't looking at him, instead staring at a pair of men in dark clothing, walking up the trail in their general direction. They were bundled up against the early winter chill, and Liiran tried not to let them distract him, even as his mental alarms started pinging.

Liiran tried to catch his friend's gaze. *We've known each other for three centuries. No way he would turn me over to the police. No way!* "I'm listening."

Salmo jerked his head to face Liiran, but his eyes skittered over him as if he were made of ice. "You know we're friends, right? I tell you this as a friend, Lii – just give yourself up. All this shit, it isn't like you. You're a straight-up guy – and practical. I've always admired that about you. A good investigator's got to be curious, but practical, too, I always say."

"Sal," Liiran said, every bell in his head now ringing at once, "what——"

But Salmo wasn't listening. "But this, I mean, voxae ma... they're saying there are cops de— in storage because of whatever you're mixed up in—"

Liiran snapped. "They're dead, actually. Really dead. But Sal, that wasn't my fault, and if you'd just shut up and listen to me you'd understand—"

"No!"

The word was said with such force and conviction that it cut off Liiran's attempt at an explanation like a door had been slammed in his face. When Salmo continued a moment later, his tone was hushed and apologetic.

"No, whatever this is, I'm not going to be a part of it. I've got my own career to consider, and I... I just can't let you drag me into this, too. Three hundred years to build a career and you flush it down the toilet for one story? Well, that's fine for you, Lii, but not me."

"Then why the fuck did you even come?" But then Liiran felt a hand land on his arm and jerk it roughly behind his back. He looked around into the face of one of the men he'd seen walking by, and began to struggle. All he could see were a cold set of blue eyes over a ski mask. Liiran began to struggle, but the man just twisted his arm tighter, the blinding pain stealing Liiran's breath with its intensity.

"Liiran Uwis, you are under arrest," the man holding him said in a gruff tone.

Black-clad men, all with covered faces were converging upon him now, seemingly from every direction. Liiran looked up at Salmo, glaring.

Salmo backed away as if Liiran were contagious, his hands raised and his face creased with apology. "I'm sorry, Lii."

"Fuck your sorry, Sal!" Liiran heard himself shouting as if from far away. A cold circlet of metal closed around his wrist, and then the other. He tried again to jerk away from the policeman, but another one grabbed him and the next thing he knew he was on the ground with both on top of him. He yelled as he tried to push them off.

"Thank you for your assistance, sir. I have no doubt that the prime minister will be personally in contact with you." Liiran dimly heard one of the police officer saying to Salmo, but his boss was shaking his head and waving his hands.

"Look, look, it's fine," Salmo said. "I was just doing my civic duty. Now there's no need for any further investigation, right? You've got your man so you can leave us to do our jobs. All this has been hell on my employee productivity."

"I just do what I'm told, sir."

Liiran's attention was taken from this extremely infuriating conversation as someone dragged him to his feet ungently, his shoulders screaming with pain. He tried to get his feet under him, to take some of the pressure off, but the police officers barely let his feet touch the ground. He could see now that a large black van had been driven right into the park and hidden behind a stand of trees, and the secret police officers were dragging him straight for it.

"I haven't done anything wrong!" he exclaimed, his heart in his throat. He was going to disappear, just like Tanen. He was going to be put in that van, and it was going to drive away, and no one would ever see him again.

He struggled, but the handcuffs made it all but impossible to break the grip of the two police officers. One of them snapped at Liiran to stop struggling or he'd get his arm broken, but it didn't make much of an impression on Liiran's panic.

Then the most welcome rushing sound of wings made Liiran look up. Mortis and Phames arrowed down towards them out of the low clouds, their wings back like a pair of stooping birds of prey.

"Get him, Phames. I'll take care of these," Mortis called, and her wings suddenly flared out, and she stopped in mid air as if she had unfurled a parachute, only without a single wobble, her momentum

114

cancelled out with perfect grace. She hovered, impossibly, twenty feet above them, and spread her hands wide above her head.

Liiran couldn't see her eyes from here, but he knew exactly what they would look like – like drowning, infinite pools of black.

The police officers scattered, but Liiran knew it didn't matter how far they ran.

You couldn't outrun death.

Phames ploughed into Liiran from behind, grabbing him under the armpits and literally ripping him from the grasp of the officers.

The pull sent another ripple of pain through Liiran's shoulders and he convulsed as his arms were forced up and the cuffs cut deeply into his wrists. He screamed and Phames adjusted his grip to take the pressure off, beating his wings to bring them higher.

Liiran took a deep breath, then another. His ears were ringing with his own scream, but there was something he had to do, something very important.

Mortis' hands were still rising, as if in slow motion. Energy seemed to crackle around her.

"Mortis!" Liiran cried. "Don't kill them!"

She hesitated, he *saw* her hesitate, and then he felt something punch him in the chest so hard it knocked all the wind out of him. Phames dipped in surprise, his wings flaring and beating wildly, and Liiran heard Mortis call his name, saw her dive towards him.

Liiran looked down and saw a spreading stain on his shirt, red blood, right over his heart, and caught a glimpse of a figure with a long-barreled rifle, lying prone on top of the police van.

Gunshot? Who bothers with guns anymore?

Then with that thought, everything went black.

Chapter 19

Mortis snatched Liiran from Phames' grasp on the wing and clutched him close to her chest. She flew so fast the buildings blurred to her vision, leaving the sounds of crossbow fire far behind. She could feel hot blood soaking into her dress, spreading warm and thick across her skin. Liiran was completely limp, a dead weight in her grasp.

But he wasn't dead. His heart continued to pump strongly, though much of the blood it pumped flowed out of the gunshot wound in his chest. Mortis could feel his vitality, feel his life hanging on.

From everything Phames had told her, she knew that it would hang on like that until she cut that thread.

In a twinkling she had reached the safe house. She hadn't realized how much power was crackling around her until the door opened without her touching it, something like lightning flashing out from her fingertips. The door slammed against the wall with a bang, and she hurried down the steps, pulling her wings in tight against her back.

The couch sagged under their weight as she sat and pulled Liiran onto it with her. She felt a strange sort of thrumming through her body as she turned him over, looking down into his face. It was so pale, and his face was slack.

Phames arrived while she was still staring in mixed fascination and terror down into Liiran's face.

"What the hell?" he growled, striding across the room towards her. "Why did you bring it here, Mortis? Are you insane!" His own wings mantled with a rattling sound.

Mortis heard him, but didn't look up. "He's not an it! We... we can't risk taking him to a hospital," she moaned. "Liiran... Liiran, wake up!" She shook his shoulder helplessly, but he only flopped. His hand dropped down and his knuckles rapped on the floor with a sharp sound. He didn't so much as stir.

His heart beat on and on.

"He's still *alive*?"

Phames' shout finally penetrated her attention and Mortis looked up into his sallow face. "What?" she asked, holding Liiran a little more tightly against her chest. She couldn't focus on Phames, and lowered her head to press it against Liiran's forehead, closing her eyes.

"How can he still be alive? He's got to have hardly any blood left in his body," Phames said, gesturing towards Liiran with a bony finger. "What are you doing, Mortis? End him!"

"No!" Mortis held on tighter. Her mind was swirling, and she couldn't think straight. All she knew was that the last thing she wanted to do was reach out and touch that thin thread of life holding Liiran together. And yet it was also the thing she wanted to do most in the world.

"End him, Mortis," Phames ordered. "We're just wasting time. He's as good as dead anyway. He's just a hunk of meat. Do you know how many mindless vegetables are lying in storage, because even though they didn't have any blood in their brains they didn't die? Humans can't survive this!"

"No! No!" Mortis wailed. He was dead, even though she hadn't acted? A droplet of water hit Liiran on the cheek and ran off. Water, not blood.

She frowned and touched the droplet. Her hands, soaked in Liiran's blood, left a smear of red in its place.

Phames had stopped railing at her, his tone going quiet. "What are you doing?"

The phamevox knelt on the floor and reached up towards Mortis, touching her on the cheek. His fingers came away wet. His pale eyes widened with shock.

"I..." Mortis touched her own cheek, felt the water there. "I'm crying."

"Why?"

She shook her head, closing her eyes. That squeezed out a couple more tears. "I don't want him to go," she whispered. She gathered Liiran against her chest and breathed in his scent, felt the thread of life pulse and weaken in response to her touch. "Humans cry at times like this. Why shouldn't I?"

"Mortis..." Phames said warningly. "He's too badly damaged. We need to let him go and focus on Certos and Niveus."

Phames had told her all about them, but she couldn't care less right now. All her attention was absorbed by that pulse of life, that heartbeat in Liiran's body, and how very, very weak it was becoming.

All because of her. If she hadn't escaped from her prison, he wouldn't have been hurt, not once, not twice. He wouldn't be bleeding out of a hole in his chest. He wouldn't *have* a hole in his chest. And he wouldn't be dying – he would *never* die, if it weren't for her.

Liiran was afraid of dying. As afraid as she was of being imprisoned again. How could she be the one to do such a thing to him, when he had risked everything to protect her from *her* worst fear?

She couldn't.

Hatred rose up inside her, a pure revulsion at what she was. Drawing in a deep breath, she took that rejection, and she *pushed* it towards Liiran.

Light filled the room and Phames recoiled. "What are you doing? Mortis, no! Stop!"

Chapter 20

It was hot in the manufacturing plant, a cloying, rippling heat that stripped the moisture from your skin faster than you could sweat. A huge oven dominated one entire wall, the element glowing so hot that it was difficult for Altus to see it through the haze of covoxae and havoxae whirling around it. Though humans normally couldn't see them outside of voxmar, when they were so energized they became discernible, at least to the magically trained human eye.

A swarm of magi, most likely all first- and second-level, worked at shaping the huge voxmar. Using hollow rods and metal plates on long sticks, they shaped the molten glass into the proper shape. The voxmar had to be a single, unbroken piece of glass, without any cracks or flaws, or the vox would easily be able to escape from it.

Altus spotted Aevi hurrying towards him, clipboard in hand and her hair escaping from its bun in little wisps that drooped and stuck to her face.

"Sir, the voxmar's initial construction is almost done. It should be complete by the end of the day, and ready to cool," she said, her eyebrows pulling together worriedly.

It would have to cool completely and evenly, which was the tricky part. If there was a flaw in the glass, or it didn't cool properly, it would cause a bubble or crack, and the whole thing would have to be remade from scratch.

"Where's Maenos?" he asked, nodding curtly to let her know that he had heard her. She hesitated, then turned and pointed towards a door, and Altus brushed past her.

In the office, it was slightly less cloying – but only slightly. Maenos had several coolers going, the rotating fan blowing the chill generated by dozens of savox out into the room. The voxmar themselves were embedded in a screen, which was coated in a powder of frost even in the warmest room.

Maenos was wearing a thin sleeveless top and shorts instead of a robe, and still she looked uncomfortable in the heat. Her face looked flushed even through the dusky tone of her skin.

Especially when she looked up and saw Altus. It didn't look as if she'd cooled down much at all since their argument.

"What do you want?" Maenos asked, then bent and shuffled papers on the desk, not looking at him.

Altus spread his hands. "I'm just looking for a status report."

"Aevi didn't give you one already? She's like a cute little puppy dog the way she hangs on your approval."

He sighed inwardly. "I want to know from you."

Maenos rose and stood in front of one of the coolers, the air from the fan lifting a few strands of her dark hair. Altus was beginning to drip himself, but resisted the urge to take off any layers. It was late fall outside, and he wouldn't be here long.

"One voxmar is ready to be etched. The second you saw out there. It should be cooled and ready by tomorrow. We had two losses already, so we're just crossing our fingers that this one will work. The workers had to take a crash course in advanced glass blowing and sculpting, but they're getting better. I think it'll be fine."

"What about the new runes I asked you and Aevi to develop?" Altus asked, trying not to let an edge of impatience enter his voice. The more he pushed, the more she would push back, and things were tenuous as it was.

"For Niveus?" Maenos glanced over her shoulder at Altus, her expression closed and difficult to read.

"Of course."

Most would believe the second voxmar was a backup. Half the Circle didn't know the truth because Altus didn't want to give them a chance to decide where their loyalties lay – if Niveus caught wind of the impending betrayal he'd make the whole thing so much more difficult.

Maenos shrugged. "He's pretty close to the polar opposite of Mortis on the voxihanto spectrum," she said. "Though there isn't technically an opposite to death, she's in the same family as the chaos xhovox and he's the vox of order. A few reversals and some redesigns were all that was needed. Developing the runes in the first place was the tough part, and Aevi did that three hundred years ago. The science has only developed in complexity since then."

The technical jargon was comforting to hear. Maenos was beginning to relax. "Sounds as though you've done everything I could ask for," Altus said.

She turned around, faced Altus directly for the first time. "The ritual," she said, folding her arms, "that's the sticky part. Three magi isn't enough power to summon a vox of that size across a room, let alone from another continent."

"I have faith in you," Altus said, moving closer and perching on a corner of her desk. "We'll have four of the Circle there. If we gather a few dozen weather magi, we'll have the necessary power for the ritual. I also have a plan to make the initial summoning unnecessary."

Her face lined with skepticism, but she nodded reluctantly. "Well, you know what you're doing. What does Niveus think we're working on?"

"Battle strategy, and a bit of mayhem for our side," Altus said with a thin-lipped smile. "He thinks I just want to use the weather magi to raise some fog to help crush the Monson Alliance once and for all."

"You'll be doing that as well, won't you?"

"Certainly. It'll be a help. The rebels have already gotten bold and more aggressive since we lost General Hason. They bombed a weapons factory just outside Talgarora yesterday. Everyone's wondering how they got through the blockade, but there are probably still sympathizers in the city itself, anyway."

Maenos nodded, her lips pursing sympathetically, but she made no comment. There was a short pause before she spoke. "Aevi assures me that she's almost got the entire ritual drafted. I'll be going over it tomorrow morning, and I'll send it to you to work out the kinks."

"That's cutting it close. The certovox and his new handler are on their way tomorrow to the front," Altus said. "Niveus is giving me a hard time about the mortivox still being at large, but we're about to hit our window of opportunity for dealing with Niveus, and it sounds as if you're telling me we probably won't have Mortis dealt with until afterwards. Two rituals in two days is going to be a nightmare."

"Not as much of a nightmare as conducting a battle where people can actually *die*," Maenos said.

Altus waved a hand. "That's Certos' and the grand general's problem, not mine. I'll inform them of the stakes before the battle and they'll just have to work it into their strategy. The distraction it causes the troops will only make our job easier. By the end of the day, Niveus will be caged and we can be free to deal with Mortis. We can pick up the pieces afterwards."

Maenos huffed in reply. "Sounds as if you're playing with covoxae to me."

"What else is there to play with after three hundred years?" Altus replied, almost under his breath.

Chapter 21

Liiran opened his eyes. He felt exhausted from his bones out to his fingertips, but he came awake all at once, and his eyes popped open.

"Oh voxae ma, it worked." Mortis' tear-stained face hovered over his. She looked far more upset than he had ever seen her, and as his memory of the near arrest and the sight of the bloodstain spreading across his chest returned, he looked around. He expected to see monitors and a hospital bed, but it was just Phames' crappy safe house.

And Phames was pacing back and forth across the room, his featherless wings flaring each time he turned, making a clattering sound like dry branches in a storm. He looked angry, but Liiran couldn't bring himself to care why.

"What happened?" He'd been shot in the chest, he was sure of it. So how had he survived?

His shirt was soaked red with blood, he noticed now, and so was the front of Mortis' dress. It looked to him like gallons and gallons, though it couldn't have been that bad.

"I saved you," Mortis said, her head coming up and her eyes narrowing. "Because I didn't want you to go."

Phames muttered something unintelligible and kept pacing.

Liiran reached up and touched his chest, felt the place where he'd been sure he was shot.

There was a hole in his shirt. But underneath, his skin was smooth and unbroken, though sore as if bruised deep inside. "Voxae as nema uto," he murmured fervently. "How is this possible? You healed me? I... I thought you were the vox of death. You can do that?"

"That's what I'd like to know," Phames said, rounding on them both and glaring like Mortis had done something horrible.

Of course he would be angry. He was probably pissed off that Mortis had saved a human, leaving this albatross around his neck, instead of acting like a proper vox that didn't interact with humans and hated them as much as Phames did.

Mortis shook her head. "I don't exactly know. I just did the opposite of what I wanted to do."

Liiran stared up at her, jaw slack. "Thank you, Mortis," he said, not knowing what else to say. He reached up towards her, but his arm felt as if it weighed a thousand pounds, and it fell back before his bloody fingers touched her pale, wet cheek.

He sensed that something truly momentous was going on, and that he was only scratching the surface of understanding it.

"Thank you," he said again, feeling as if the words were completely inadequate.

"You're welcome," she said. He could see something shaken and confused in her eyes as well, and he wondered if she had any better understanding than he did of what had just happened here.

Then the spell broke as she eased her arms out from under him and stood up, shaking out her wings and staring at Phames as if daring him to say anything. "Now that Liiran is all right," she said briskly, "we need to consider our situation." She turned towards Liiran. "Why did you go to that place? If we hadn't seen you leave, you could have disappeared forever."

Liiran tried to push himself up, but he could barely manage to sit up enough to rest his head against the pillows at the arm of the couch. He was so unimaginably weak, yet he didn't feel as if he was going to die. He just felt as if he wanted to sleep for a week. Or a year.

But he did have to explain himself, and he felt his face growing hot. Amazing that he had enough blood left in his body for a blush, but he managed it.

"I was trying to help us," he said, hearing his voice take a defensive tone despite his best efforts. "I figured that if my editor heard the truth about what's happening – and about how the government lied to us all these years about why no one can die – that it would take the heat off of us. They'd be so busy running around to contain the story that they wouldn't have time for us."

He was warming to his justification, and his voice grew more confident as he explained, though Mortis' frown didn't let up. Her black eyes bored into him like lasers, and it made his thoughts get jumbled on the way from his brain to his mouth. "Not only that, but there probably wouldn't be any reason for them to arrest me anymore, because arresting me wouldn't suppress the information. It'd be too late. Don't you see?" His voice grew a tiny bit desperate on the last few words.

124

Used to being a confident speaker, and persuasive, Liiran pulled his gaze away from Mortis, trying to reorder his thoughts. He felt as if he was trying to push his thoughts through molasses.

"I see," Mortis said. "It makes sense, Liiran. But why did you sneak out if it was such a good idea?"

Liiran hesitated guiltily, and that was more than enough time for Phames to pounce. "Because he knew it was a shitty idea, and because he was really selling us out to save his own skin."

"That's not true," Liiran said hotly, and it took him a second to realize that Mortis had echoed him at almost the same moment.

Phames glared at them both, his wings flaring out and reaching almost to the low ceiling of the room. This was an accomplishment, given his stooped posture. "Isn't it? Then explain it, reporter man. What were you going to tell that asshole that he doesn't already know?"

"You think he already knows about this?" Liiran asked, waving a hand towards Mortis.

"Of course he does," Phames snapped. "People are dying all over the city. You think no one knew what they really did when they trapped Mortis in the first place? You think that no one's ever tried to inform the media of all the lies? Salmo Lina has been in his position for a very long time. He *knows* what kinds of stories Niveus doesn't want shared."

The sick feeling in Liiran's stomach confirmed Phames' words.

"He doesn't know it all. He can't," he said, the words sounding hollow even to his own ears. "All that happened because the police were putting pressure on him, and he thought I was involved in something very illegal. If he'd known what was really going on..."

Phames made a rude sound and turned his back on them. "All that is true," he said, "but he also knows. I bet you anything. And you *knew* it when you left."

"No, I didn't!" But hadn't he been worried? Hadn't the thought at least crossed his mind? "He's been my friend for centuries. I thought he would honour that, at least." He struggled to sit up again, but fell back against the cushions. "I didn't know he would sell me out."

"That's what humans do," Phames said bitterly. "Sell each other out for gain, or to protect their own skins." He glanced back at Liiran. "Maybe you weren't thinking of doing that to us, but I think somewhere deep inside you were hoping it would go down just the way it did, and that at least all of this responsibility would be taken out of your hands. You could be arrested, then admit what's going on, sing like a little bird, and buy your freedom with information and cooperation."

Liiran's entire body had gone cold, and it wasn't from the blood loss. "No," he whispered through numb lips. "I didn't mean that at all." He hadn't... Right?

"How dare you say that?" Mortis said, her own wings mantling with anger as she rounded on the other vox.

Phames didn't even look at her, keeping his eyes on Liiran. They snapped with icy anger. "Oh no? Your eyes tell the lie, reporter man."

Liiran opened his mouth to respond, but Mortis had had enough.

"Phames," said Mortis, her voice so frigid savoxae all but dripped from her lips. "I'm grateful to you for all the information you've given me, and for your desire to help. I know that you have worked tirelessly for centuries to try to find a way to rescue me, and that you blame humans for all our woes. But I am finished with your attitude. Liiran made a mistake, but he didn't deliberately set out to hurt us, and he's suffered punishment enough. What you're saying is not helpful to anyone. Apologize to Liiran, or I fear we may be done with you."

For the first time since Liiran woke up, Phames looked directly at Mortis. His eyes darkened with such disgust and revulsion that Liiran's jaw dropped once again. "That's fine," he said, "because I was done with *both* of you when you perverted your entire existence to keep him alive. Death vox do not heal people. It's not natural, and it's *wrong*. I don't even know what you are now, but it's not a *vox*."

He turned and picked up the laptop computer from his desk, tucking it under his arm. "Enjoy your lives together," he said. "I'm sure they will be short. I'm going to finally find a way to release Certos from his bondage, and end this entire sordid thing before it's too late. It's clear I won't get any help from the two of you after all."

And with that, he headed up the stairs. The door banged shut, and Mortis and Liiran were left alone.

There was a short silence as Mortis and Liiran stared in the direction Phames had gone, and then Mortis turned to look at Liiran, dismay written all over her face.

"What was that all about?" Liiran asked, though he was pretty sure he knew.

126

Mortis wrung her hands for a moment, but shook her head and seemed to square her shoulders. "I don't care what he thinks." She crossed the room and helped him to sit up, then deposited herself onto the couch and slung her arms loosely around him for support. Despite her words, he felt tension in her body as he rested against her shoulder.

"He thinks... What, you're too human?" Liiran asked. Mortis was too human? She hadn't even been awake for a week, and her knowledge of human things had been shockingly poor when he first met her. Had she really changed so much in the time they'd known one another?

Had saving his life been so wrong?

She nodded. "He said as much to me last night, several times," she said. "He was trying to convince me to leave you behind while we deal with some things together, but I didn't want to. He insisted that you would only hold us back, get in the way."

Liiran was starting to get heartily sick of Phames' opinion of him, and of humans in general, but a small, niggling part of him admitted that – just this once – Phames might have been right. At least, he was certainly going to hold Mortis back now.

He didn't want to admit it, though. Nor did he want to suggest that Mortis go after Phames. As far as he was concerned, they were well rid of him.

"Get in the way of what?" he asked. Already both of the voxae had mentioned something that needed to be done, and he was starting to become truly curious about what it might be. Even if it no longer mattered. The constant mention of the prime minister was especially intriguing.

Mortis leaned back, sighing, and tightened her arms around him. It would have been lovely, if it weren't for the fact that he was so exhausted he could barely move, and the fact that her dress was stiff with blood.

"Phames said that when I was trapped in the voxmar, another vox was, as well. The vox of war, named Certos. And apparently they found a way to control him, so they let him out, and he's winning all their wars for them. He calls it slavery," she explained, speaking the last word as if she wasn't entirely certain what it meant.

Liiran's eyes widened. "That can work?" Voxae ma... That would certainly explain how Laxam had gone from a small – albeit

127

technologically and magically rich – country to a world-girdling Empire in a few short centuries, with scarcely any lost battles.

Maybe *no* lost battles. Liiran hadn't exactly monitored every single move in the endless war. Now that he thought about it, he wasn't sure there were more than a handful of setbacks, and none of them had been serious.

He had heard rumours of a 'secret weapon', but none had ever been revealed publicly. And now he knew why – the secret weapon was behind the scenes, a special vox that Liiran had never suspected existed. And now some of the things he'd collected over the years and didn't understand, which he'd locked away in his hidden box, were starting to fit together into a very frightening puzzle.

"I don't know," Mortis said. "But Phames seemed quite certain."

Liiran shook his head. "I was just surprised. It certainly explains a lot. It makes sense."

Mortis was silent for a moment, then tightened her arms. "I told Phames I would help him, of course," she said. "I can't stand to think of another vox in the same position as I was, only worse, because he is awake. But Phames thinks there's something wrong with me, now, and I can't take you there."

"Look," Liiran said, the reminder of Phames sending a fresh pulse of anger through him. "I don't understand what Phames' problem is, but there's nothing wrong with you other than this amnesia you have, and that's not your fault. Obviously you still have your abilities, too, so there's nothing for him to complain about."

"Perhaps," she said, sounding unconvinced.

For a moment, Liiran sat in silence. They were discussing releasing the vox of war from Laxam control. Putting aside how impossible such a task seemed right now, when he literally couldn't sit up without help, was this really something he should do?

When Mortis was released from her prison, people started dying - or so Phames had said. When this Certos was released, what would happen?

Then again, the world hadn't exactly been a paradise of peace and tranquility over the last three centuries. Sure, things had been good in the central parts of the Empire, but the Laxam Empire had swept across the face of Aeria, conquering every other country in the world.

They had been *using* Certos. Maybe if he and Mortis freed Certos nothing would change, except that Laxam's enemies would actually have a fighting chance.

Fighting chance. Pun intended. He made an effort and shifted enough to be able to look up at Mortis. She certainly wanted to do it. The worry and pain in her eyes was palpable. He'd just have to work out how he felt about this, later, when he knew more. "Listen to me," he said. "Whatever happens, we'll get this Certos guy out, and we'll deal with this mess."

It's the only chance I have to maybe get my life back, anyway, he thought, but the thought didn't have as much force as it once might have. The memory of her black eyes shining with all-too-human tears had more of a pull than he would have expected.

"I can't put you in danger again, Liiran."

Liiran started in surprise at the force of the words. Maybe she was getting a bit too human, at that. "Why do you say that?"

"I don't know!" She threw up her hands in frustration. "I feel strange at the thought of losing you, but I don't know why."

Liiran hesitated, then chose his words carefully. "Because you care about what happens to me."

"Yes." Her arms were around him again. Tight enough to make ribs creak. "I do care what happens to you. You are important to me. You have protected me, and I... I didn't want you to go away." She fell silent, then added, "Maybe Phames is right, and there is something terribly wrong with me."

Liiran mustered up the most stern look he could. "Phames is full of shit," he said. "If you have grown as a person, while he stayed the same, so you have the ability to feel something new – how can that be wrong?"

Mortis smiled faintly. "You're trying to make me feel better. But I like what you're saying, anyway."

Liiran smiled in return. "Good. Because I meant every word."

Chapter 22

It wasn't a bad place, as prison cells went. No rats or other vermin. In fact, Tanen suspected that the place was cleaner than his own house.

It was even a little bit homey. There was a sink and a toilet and a bed, and a cupboard with a second set of prison clothes in it. Self-contained.

But that made it worse, somehow. There was a certain finality to the way the door closed behind him – the heavy, steel door with the slot for a meal tray and a tiny window in it – that said there was no particular reason that the door would ever need to be opened again.

And it hadn't, since then.

He didn't know how long it had been – more than an hour, less than a day. He was pretty sure.

He'd had time to affectionately curse Liiran for choosing to come to his place to hide, then *angrily* curse him for the same thing. He had a feeling that getting really, really scared was just over the horizon. It danced there, like a black flag on a windy day, just visible, but if he was careful he could avoid looking at it. He knew it was there, though, and soon it would reach him.

After that, he didn't know. Stark raving insanity, maybe.

His thoughts were interrupted by footsteps outside his door, and a metallic rattling. He looked up from his perch on the bed hopefully, wondering if it was time for the anticipated food tray he imagined had to be coming. That would do something to relieve the boredom, at least, and he hadn't eaten since the night before.

To his surprise, the door opened instead. A dark-skinned man wearing a plain black outfit cut like a military uniform entered, carrying a folding metal chair. The door closed behind him with a bang.

The newcomer calmly unfolded his chair and placed it opposite Tanen, with his back to the door.

"I'm guessing you're not my new cellmate," Tanen said, shocked to discover that his voice sounded pretty steady. So far, so good.

The man shook his head. "No."

"Nice tattoo job."

A slight widening of the eyes was his reward. "Thank you. I am Calam Veliir, minister of laws and head of the secret police, amongst my other duties."

"I figured it was something like that," Tanen said, his heart giving a lurch in his chest. Secret police, not that it should be a shock. "I can't say I'm enjoying your hospitality so far."

"Perhaps that means you would like to be released from here as soon as possible."

Released? Tanen tried to push down the hope inside. "Is that a possibility?" he asked cautiously.

Calam straightened slightly in his chair. It squeaked under his muscular weight. "As of this moment, you have not been charged with a crime. Yet," he said. "You were caught harbouring two fugitives, but I would understand if you weren't aware of their status. If you were to cooperate with us, and satisfy us of your desire to remain a fully contributing and law abiding member of society, there would be no need to keep you imprisoned." Calam took a breath, arching an eyebrow. "We do not hand out life sentences lightly, Mr. Siitar. There simply isn't the room."

"Liiran's been my friend since school," Tanen said. "I never saw the girl before, though."

"I'm well aware of that."

"What is it you want from me, exactly?" Tanen asked, stalling.

Calam shrugged his shoulders. "Tell me everything Mr. Uwis told you about his companion, and his plans. Tell me who else he might have contacted, and the likely places he may have run to. If necessary, we may require you to participate in his capture in a small way."

Tanen felt the blood draining from his face, especially at the last thing. "What do you mean, 'participate in his capture'?"

"If your information isn't sufficient, we may need you to contact Mr. Uwis and persuade him to meet with you, or to turn himself in."

Tanen could see the bait hanging in front of him, not that Veliir had bothered to sugar coat it. He had to respect the man for that, at least – if you betray your friend you'll get out of here. There was no attempt to pretty it up.

Yep, he had to respect that. You couldn't decorate a turd and make it into something else. This guy didn't try.

Tanen gritted his teeth. Well, time to discover what he was really made of. He had two choices, and either one he made he would regret it for the rest of his life. Eternity. Either he would be a coward, or a prisoner. He knew which choice to make, easily.

"Liiran is my friend, Minister Veliir," he said, straightening his back and trying to inject as much conviction into his tone as he could muster. "I've known him for three centuries, and he has never been the kind of guy to do something illegal, especially for his own gain. Whatever he's doing, there's a good reason, and I'm afraid that I just can't become a traitor for you, sorry. If you want someone to trick him, it won't be his best friend."

It won't be the one who loves him, the womanizing, idealistic idiot, he added silently.

Lii, you had better be worth this.

Calam leaned forward in his chair and Tanen tensed, but a moment later the policeman stood and folded up his chair.

"Very well. When you change your mind, knock on the door. I will station a guard to contact me when you're ready."

Shit, Tanen thought, watching Calam head for the door. It wasn't just a one-time choice. He was going to have to make it over and over. How long could he hold out?

How long before it became moot, anyway?

Could he really be sure that there was any point in this sacrifice?

He struggled to keep his tone and posture casual as he called after Calam. "Hey, thanks, but that won't be necessary. Anyway, do you think I could have a book or something? It's boring as hell in here, no offense."

The door opened at his knock and Calam shot an unreadable look over his shoulder at Tanen.

"No."

And the door closed behind him with an echoing boom.

Chapter 23

An unmarked black van took Garelon and Certos to the airport at dawn, where an airship sat on the tarmac. This was the Cloudtoucher, the prime minister's personal airship. There were four upturned propellers, each one rising out of a voxmar as tall as a man, surrounding a long, sleek body studded with windows. The huge voxmarae glowed with a cool white light as the propellers started to turn.

Garelon was in his dress uniform, which jangled with medals, and had brought a medium-sized wheeled suitcase that contained his laptop and the few personal items that he would need while away from home. Though this was far from the first time he had travelled to war, he felt at loose ends at the moment, not knowing quite what to expect or what was expected of him. Despite requests, he had yet to receive any tactical information he could use to plan the next sortie against the Monson Alliance.

The boy had brought only one thing with him – his chess set. He had carried it with him as he climbed obediently into his crate for the journey to the airport.

The driver was in the uniform of the secret police, and hadn't said a word the whole way. Now she saluted Garelon, unloaded Certos' crate, closed the van doors and got back into the car, soaring away without ceremony.

The tarmac was now completely deserted. Not a single person – not even press – had been permitted to see them off.

After a few moments' hesitation, Garelon hauled the crate up the ramp and was greeted by a flight attendant. The interior was luxurious, with large couches lining the walls instead of narrow seats, and coffee tables next to them. He knew from press releases that the ship had several large rooms, and even bedrooms. It was said that all of Aeria could be operated from here for a year without the Cloudtoucher ever needing to land.

Garelon tried not to gawk. He'd never been on the ship before, and the pictures he'd seen didn't do it justice.

Niveus and Altus were sitting on one of the couches, and Niveus rose to his feet when Garelon entered. He had a glass of some amber liquid in his hand. "Garelon, welcome," he said with a charming smile. "You can let him out, now." He gestured offhandedly to the crate.

Relieved, Garelon saluted the prime minister, then Altus, and bent to do just that with a, "Thank you, sirs."

When the lid opened, Certos climbed out silently, clutching the chess set to his narrow chest. He stood beside the crate, head down, and didn't took at either Niveus or Altus.

Garelon seated himself on a sofa, and tugged on Certos' chain lightly until the boy curled up next to him like a pale, long-limbed cat.

He was intensely aware that Niveus was watching them with close attention.

But then Niveus' eyes flicked to Certos, narrowed, then he addressed the vox. "Certos, what is that you have there? Plans?"

Certos stared distractedly into the middle distance, somewhere between two of the windows on the port side, nowhere near any of the humans or anything interesting. "It is a chess set."

"A chess set?" Altus asked in a suspicious tone. "What for?"

Garelon felt he had to come to his charge's rescue, and he spoke up hastily. "I gave it to him," he said. "I thought since he's involved in battle strategy that it might be... er, useful."

It was lame, and Altus' suspicious expression turned towards Garelon. "There is no need for such sentimentality, Garelon. The certovox is not a person. Perhaps it would help you to think of it as a computer, merely providing you with data."

Garelon stiffened. Altus' attitude really grated on him, even more than it had before he had started getting to know Certos. "It is not sentimentality, sir. I am well aware of what he is. He expressed interest in a chess set I had at my home and I gave it to him. It does not appear to have affected his functionality."

"Altus, let's not be rude," Niveus said mildly. "Garelon, would you like a drink? I believe we're preparing for take-off." He signalled to one of the attendants.

As the steward poured, Garelon heard a soft whine rise to the level of his hearing. How Niveus had heard it before he did, he didn't know. He had to have excellent hearing, or maybe he had seen some other signal.

Garelon tried to sit at attention and concentrate on his superiors, ignoring the vox beside him. He felt as if he were being tested, and he had a feeling that the flight was going to be very long if he had to be under Altus' scrutiny the whole time.

The flight attendant placed the drink in Garelon's hand and the airship took off so easily and smoothly that he scarcely felt the push of gravity as they rose. Niveus chatted amiably about the weather and the economy, and Garelon found himself being drawn into discussion almost without meaning to. Soon the three of them were involved in an animated debate about economic policy and Certos was all but forgotten.

Until about an hour into the flight, when Niveus drained his drink and rose. "I think it's about time."

Garelon got quickly to his feet. "Time?"

Altus moved to follow Niveus. "He means, let's retire to the boardroom. We must discuss the battles to come," he translated wryly.

"But I haven't even seen any data yet," Garelon protested, following the other two men into the next room. A small boardroom table dominated it, with eight chairs surrounding it. They took seats clustered around one end of the table, but Garelon was still objecting. "I haven't received any paperwork. I don't know our strength, our position, nothing. What is it that you expect me to say?"

Niveus leaned back in his chair and smirked at Garelon, then flicked a hand at Certos. "What do you think we have him for?"

Certos set his chessboard on the table and opened it up. He ignored them all completely, setting out the chess pieces.

"What are you doing?" Altus demanded.

Garelon wanted to know the same thing, but he was still staring at Niveus, trying to decide if he truly believed what the prime minister was saying. "What are you trying to say?"

Niveus shook his head and gestured towards Certos again. "Just watch. Certos, tell us about the next battle."

Certos picked up a white pawn and advanced it, then grasped the black one opposite it and moved it forward a single space. "We must use the cannons as shields and distractions," he said. "It will be vitally important to hide our people from the enemy, and protect them as far as possible from the line of fire. Designate individuals who can be trusted, to sweep the front lines and remove anyone who is badly injured or dead before the rank and file can learn that they are in real danger." He moved a second white pawn up right next to the first.

"What do you mean, dead?" Garelon said sharply, the word hitting him with a feeling like an electric shock.

Niveus and Altus exchanged silent glances, and the shock deepened to concern.

"There's a chance that the Aevi Nexalum Drug may be wearing off in certain cases," Altus said, to the accompaniment of a solemn nod from Niveus. "We're reviewing the situation, but there's a chance some of these cases could be on the front lines, and there's no way to know. Certos is probably trying to avoid a panic."

Garelon shuddered at the thought, and glanced at Certos, who sat very still, fingers hovering over the board, as if waiting for permission to continue. The general looked at Altus. "Is it wise to continue this if it's possible there could be real casualties?"

"Isolated cases," Altus said dismissively. "If Certos advises that we move forward, then there's no need to wait. The matter will be resolved soon enough."

Garelon hesitated, then looked at Certos. "Continue, then."

The boy shifted a rook and looked at Altus. "There are new conditions available."

Altus raised an eyebrow, then leaned forward, looking only mildly surprised by this. "I have asked Maenos to gather weather magi and bring them to the front. She suggested that they might be able to sway the weather in our favour."

"Use them to make fog," Certos said. Garelon watched him sacrifice a white pawn, then use a white knight to begin decimating the black forces, a line of several white pawns holding strong. His voice was completely detached, as if he didn't know they were there. "If they can, make it rain in the mountains. The water will run down and foul their supply lines, making it more difficult for them to move their own equipment as well." The black queen had to keep retreating against the onslaught or risk being taken.

"What else?" Niveus prompted. He was leaning back in his chair, his hands steepled, watching Certos closely.

Once Certos had begun speaking in earnest, it took no more than five minutes before Garelon realized he was completely unprepared for this

136

very strange war meeting, and had started taking notes furiously. Though Certos spoke in generalities, Garelon had a feeling this was all he really needed. When he reached the front, he would have the resources Certos had estimated he would require. He added additional notes in the margins whenever he had time – required equipment and troops for each stage, that kind of thing.

Once they arrived, he knew he would have to question Certos further. Would he be able to give him more information, right down to individual troop movements?

As Garelon listened, he became certain that he could do that.

Certos spoke for almost half an hour, moving chess pieces one by one, pausing only long enough to be prompted occasionally by either Altus or Niveus. Somehow, as Garelon watched, it seemed as if he were playing out the battle with the chessmen. It seemed impossible that he could do such a thing, but in the end, all but a few of the black pieces were gone, and the king was checkmated.

So this is why we keep winning, he thought, watching Certos use a fragile finger to knock the black king over on its side. *They don't stand a chance.*

Chapter 24

Phames walked.

He had never wanted so much to throw off his human form, cast off these ridiculous, restrictive coverings humans called clothing, spread his wings and fly. But he hadn't survived being hunted by the Circle of Magi for so long by taking foolish risks, and he'd already taken enough of them today for the sake of that idiotic human and his equally idiotic friend.

So he walked. And fumed.

If vox could be said to have friends, Mortis and Certos had been his best. The greatest of the chaotic xho genus of voxae, they had stood together against Niveus' efforts to impose artificial order on a naturally chaotic world for millions of years. Ever since they had evolved enough complexity to understand the stakes, in response to a world that had also grown complex enough to need them, the three of them had been together, along with the others.

Then Niveus had taken this step, a measure so unnatural, so unthinkable, that no sane vox would ever consider it. He had gone beyond his own natural powers and had allied himself with humans, to impose order upon the world in a scale never before heard of, and – Phames was sure – thereby increase his own personal power.

Mortis, Certos and Phames had been completely unprepared.

Three hundred years was a blink of an eye in the lifetime of a vox, who had been created when the universe first exploded into existence and the laws of physics were made. But it was long enough still to despair.

For one moment, Phames had felt some hope. Death had returned to the world. The natural order of things would return, and he would finally have some help to overcome Niveus' perversions.

Phames couldn't fight, really. His abilities worked on plants, and supply lines and storehouses, and could do little more than make humans uncomfortable. He had done his best to frustrate supply lines for the army and ruin morale, but against Certos' tactical might he could do no more than slow down the Laxam Empire's inexorable march across the face of Aeria. He couldn't stop it.

But Mortis could kill with a thought. With her at his side again, they could free Certos, kill the humans that had imprisoned them, set the world right.

For a moment, he had hoped, and now all his hopes were dashed. This human had somehow poisoned her. Probably, her amnesia had made her vulnerable to it – she hadn't known what she was, hadn't recognized Phames at all. And the amnesia was a side effect of the imprisonment, Phames was sure, though he had no idea how to correct it.

Now it no longer mattered.

It was almost laughable. A mortivox who didn't kill. A mortivox who healed, even. What was the world coming to?

He barely noticed his surroundings as he walked, slouching past other pedestrians who barely gave him a second glance as they hurried along their busy lives. Even after being effectively immortal for three centuries, humans were still busy.

Well, even if Mortis didn't want to kill, many of them were still dying. Their lives were going to get a lot busier.

Then, even as he worked his way fiercely through that morbid thought, a voice intruded on his consciousness.

"A Parliament spokesperson issued this statement today on the Monson War: 'The void left by the grave, accidental injury of Grand General Hason has left us all shaken and saddened. Our condolences go out to all those who knew and cared for him. However, the day of victory and the end of this terrible conflict has only been set back. Our enemies cannot succeed.'"

Phames paused and looked up. He stood beside a large bank of televisions in the front window of a store. The same bland-looking woman on the same news channel stared out from a dozen pictures. She smiled vapidly as she continued to read the prepared statement.

"'The guerrillas who continue to plague the mountains and attack our good citizens in the West will be pleased at this announcement that Grand General Hason's successor Grand General Garelon has now been brought up to speed, and is to travel to the front tomorrow. Let his vigilance and confidence assure our people that the final conflict is upon us, and this war will be ended within the month.'"

Phames stared at the screen, his mind whirling as he thought through the possibilities, as the woman moved on to the next news story.

If Garelon was heading to the front tomorrow, maybe that meant Certos was going to be there as well. He might need to be in the vicinity if he wanted to control the tide of the battle with precision.

And if they were gearing up to crush the poor remnants of the Monson Alliance, the last few people left on Aeria who hadn't yet come under Niveus' sway, he didn't have much time. It seemed to him that when Certos had completed his function, he would be placed in a voxmar and hidden like Mortis had been.

Perhaps so deeply that Phames would never, ever find him. At least now he had some idea of where he was going to be. And in the confusion of a battle, something could go wrong.

Something had already gone wrong once – Hason had been injured and taken out of the game, without Phames doing a thing.

Another accident could occur. And if Phames engineered *that* one, perhaps he could break whatever spell they had on Certos during all the confusion.

But he couldn't do this on his own. He couldn't kill. And to try to use his physical prowess to do something spectacular was a laughable idea. He was slender, weak, and frail for something that couldn't actually get injured or die. That was why he'd never tried to interfere like this before.

He felt his stomach turn over, but he about-faced and began walking back towards the safe house.

He needed Mortis. He would have to swallow his pride and ask her again for help. This was bigger than they were.

And somehow, he would have to get through to her, and convince her to be who she was, to embrace it.

Otherwise, this phase of the war against Niveus was over before it began.

Chapter 25

While Liiran had brought a change of clothes, Mortis' dress was soaked in his blood, too. Phames had a lot of junk hidden away in closets, however, and with a bit of effort, Mortis found a shirt and a pair of jogging pants that strained across her hips, but fit.

Food for Liiran was another project, and Mortis went out to use some of their dwindling supply of cash to find something for him to eat. As he waited, trying to convince himself that his strength was starting to return, he wondered what they were going to do when that money ran out.

The fact was, it seemed hopeless. They knew they wanted to go rescue this friend of Mortis', but they didn't know where to begin. Liiran was badly injured, and Mortis still didn't have her memories. They had already gotten one friend of Liiran's arrested, and another one had betrayed them to save his own skin.

Considering everything Liiran had gone through to this point, he couldn't even blame him.

The first time they accessed Liiran's bank account, they would only be sending up a flag with the words 'here I am' on it for the police to see. He was sure of that.

And even if they did rescue Certos, what then? Niveus was still in charge, and he and his Ministers had control over all of Aeria. Would they go to the Monson Alliance and hope that with Certos' help they could fight back against Laxam?

It seemed more than difficult – it was ludicrous. Even with Certos, the Laxam army was gigantic, and the Monson Alliance was just a big name for a bunch of starving refugees living in caves.

But Liiran was getting tired of running away, too. For one thing, it hadn't gotten him anywhere so far, except nearly dead.

He reached into his pocket and pulled out his package of cigarettes, then looked at it as if seeing it for the first time. Mortis was the vox of death, and she was no longer sealed away. He was no longer immortal.

Suddenly the thought of putting one of these cancer sticks in his mouth and lighting up turned his stomach. Had he already given himself a terminal disease with these things? He'd been smoking for centuries.

He slowly dropped it on the floor.

He didn't want to die, but at the same time, he didn't want to just put his head down and go along with things. He *wanted* to fight back and get his damned life back, and stop all these lies.

Conviction wasn't enough, though. No matter how much he thought, he couldn't think of a way to get what he wanted.

Still, maybe he'd quit smoking.

The door opened at the top of the stairs and he opened his eyes. "That you, Mortis?" he called. There was one good thing in all this, at least, and that was Mortis. At least he wasn't alone.

"No, it's me." Phames drew into view as he slouched down the stairs, his eyes narrowed as he looked at Liiran.

Immediately Liiran struggled to sit up. "I thought you were done with us."

Phames' lip curled. "Too bad I was wrong." He put his laptop down on the desk and threw himself into the chair next to it. "Where's Mortis?"

"She's out."

"Out doing what?"

This was becoming a pissing contest, and Liiran didn't care. He was angry at pretty much everything in the world, and could barely sit up without help, let alone do something to affect his own fate. Phames was an easy target.

"None of your business. What did you come back here for?" Liiran demanded.

"It's *my* house," Phames said. "Did you think I was giving it to you for you to hide in?"

"I'm not hiding!"

Phames sneered. "Right, sure. Did you send her to try to save your skin again? I'll bet that you can't wait for the next chance to use her to save yourself."

"Fuck you!"

If Liiran could have he probably would have launched himself from the couch at the other man, foolish and pointless as it might have been. But then a soft voice called out. "Phames?"

They turned to see Mortis standing at the bottom of the stairs, eyebrows drawn together warily. Liiran hadn't heard her come in, he'd been so focused on the argument, and he could see from Phames' expression that he hadn't noticed either – and he seemed as chagrined as Liiran to be caught squabbling like children.

She held a small bag of take-out food and the scent of it made Liiran's stomach cramp. There was an awkward silence while Mortis looked at both of them, then she crossed the room and handed Liiran his food.

He tried to be dignified about it, but his hands seemed to move on their own. The bag was opened and he was wolfing down the food before anyone could speak.

"Why have you come back, Phames?" she asked. Even in a T-shirt and jogging pants, her figure was lovely, and Liiran had an excellent view of said figure, since she placed herself directly between him and the other vox protectively.

Phames eyed her reluctantly, then sat up a little straighter. "I found out that Certos is possibly being moved to the front tomorrow." His tone was urgent, but a little resentful, and Liiran wondered how much he had struggled before deciding to come back. "I need your help to go after him, Mortis. I... I can't do it by myself."

"Why not?" Mortis asked, with surprising harshness. "You seemed content to do this alone two hours ago when you stormed out of here, calling us a variety of terrible names."

"I... I can't kill. My powers—"

"Maybe you need to unbend a little," Mortis interrupted him. "You can wither plants, but can't harm a human? Ridiculous."

She planted herself on the couch next to Liiran and folded her arms across her chest.

Liiran was halfway through a box of spiced rice rolled in seaweed. Despite it all, he was inclined to just forgive Phames and move on, if only because it meant that they were moving forward and doing *something*. But he kept his mouth shut – or at least full of food – for now. He didn't mind if Phames got a few metaphorical bruises before they agreed to help.

There was a long silence. Phames wasn't looking at either of them. He was toying with a pen between his fingers, and watching the movement as if it contained the truths of the universe. "I can't," he said finally. "I just can't. And even if I could, I wouldn't be anywhere near as good at it as you are, Mortis."

He drew in a breath and looked up. "Please help me. Or if you won't help me, then help Certos. He's – I mean, he *was* – your friend, too."

Mortis eyed Phames with lips thinned and hands curled against her thighs. "Apologize to Liiran and myself for the things you said."

Phames looked away. "No," he said quietly.

Silence again, and Liiran finally decided to intervene. He swallowed a mouthful and put a hand on Mortis' arm. "You have your opinions, and some of them might be valid," he said to Phames. "The rest are shit, but we aren't going to agree on that."

Phames looked up, startled, when Liiran started to speak, but now his eyes narrowed. Liiran went on before he had time to retort.

"We need to do something, and Mortis and I already agreed that we wanted to go after Certos. Whatever we think of each other, we will just get ourselves caught, or... whatever, doing it by ourselves. We'll probably have the same result doing it together, but this is the best we've got. We won't get anywhere just sitting around here."

"Finally ready to stop running away?" Phames sneered. "Well, it's about time."

"You're right about that," Liiran said, his voice going a little colder. "I think it's about time for all of us to stop running, even you, Phames."

Mortis glanced at Liiran. "You're sure?" she asked, and he nodded.

"We'll probably never get along," Liiran said. "And I don't know what I have to offer, either. But I say we take this opportunity, since it's the best one we've got."

"I think you'll just drag us down," Phames said. "Especially injured like you are. But...you might be useful for something," he finished grudgingly.

Mortis sighed and raised her hands. "Fine, you both hate each other. But we're going. Together."

"And hopefully we aren't just walking to our doom," Liiran said wryly.

Phames snorted. "Not walking," he said. "You can't even stand, and it's too far anyway. We're going to have to fly." He turned away and opened up his laptop, smirking. "Prepare yourself for some discomfort, human."

Chapter 26

In the mountains, the sun sets early and rises late. At this time of night, the sun wasn't even a distant hope over the jagged snow-covered peaks.

The sheer sides of a volcanic bowl protected the bulk of the Monson Alliance. On one side of the ridge, the craters and caves protected those few freedom fighters who still scratched out an existence outside the formidable Laxam Empire. On the other, the land sloped down to the former Talgar capital, nestled in the valley below.

Between lay a physical barricade of Laxam soldiers and metal fencing, backed up by weapons of war.

The only way through was a single checkpoint in a natural cleft in the stone, watched by towers bristling with crossbows and lit by floodlights filled with so many havoxae they left afterimages if you looked directly at them.

It was this checkpoint that the three women approached. Their bodies, cloaked in a grey fabric, would be nearly invisible against either stone or concrete, but showed up starkly in the light of the floodlights. However, their red hair and faces were cowled and left in shadow.

A soldier met them at the gate, blocking their path in an almost diffident manner, his hand hovering by his belt knife.

"The Minister is expecting you," he said, his voice shaking and his eyes averted. "He said he's prepared rooms at a hotel—"

"That won't be necessary," said one of the women. "Tell him I'll see him tonight."

"But... Uh, yes, ma'am."

The three women exchanged worried glances as they continued on their journey, stepping back out of the light and losing themselves in the darkness.

Chapter 27

The highest tower of the Talgar Castle was windowed on three sides and afforded a spectacular view of the former capital city of Talgar, conquered only five decades before. It was a walled city of concentric rings, abutting up against the base of the volcano in whose cone the Monson rebels hid. The secondary cone to the south was small and filled with water, looking like nothing more than a circular lake, but the surface bubbled and mist filled the air above it.

Niveus stood at a window, gazing out. It was a lovely night, crisp and clean, the buildings just barely kissed by the sun's light. The nivevox felt the touch of havoxae against his skin as the last rays of sunlight reached him. The flutter of their gossamer wings was audible, a hushed whisper in his ears that never ceased. They told him stories no human could hear.

But they weren't telling him what he wanted to know. He had stood at the window of his office in Laxam for hours, days, whenever he hadn't had anything forcing him to his desk, straining his sight for a glimpse of black feathered wings. But of course he hadn't seen any.

And now he was even further away. There was absolutely no chance of seeing Mortis, but still he looked. Perhaps because the act of sitting at his desk felt confining, trapped, too human.

He glanced at the man standing beside him. Altus didn't look happy, and Niveus was vaguely pleased by that. If the world Niveus had worked so hard to create teetered on the balance, the least that he could expect was that the humans he'd done it for should be worried, too.

"Tell me what you're doing to recapture her."

Altus' face darkened. "We're doing everything we can, sir. Dragging me in here at all hours is not going to get her captured any faster. I've been halfway around the world and back in three days. I'm jetlagged and I have duties to attend to."

So it was going to be one of those conversations. Altus had been Niveus' most trusted advisor for centuries, but he might need to be replaced. Perhaps Calam would be better – he was a steady fellow, solid and dependable. But he lacked Altus' imagination, which was such a good resource for the nivevox. Altus simply needed to be reined in.

"I wonder. Do you want to sleep?"

"Unlike you, humans sleep," Altus replied sourly.

"A shame," Niveus countered, "since you also die."

That shut Altus up, as Niveus had known it would.

They were alone in the room. Niveus stretched and released his wings. They spread and relaxed and he let out a sigh. Altus had taken a step back.

Niveus sometimes got the impression that the mage was disturbed by the sight of his true form, though he couldn't understand why. He had never asked, either.

"So, tell me again what you're doing to solve this problem," Niveus murmured, his words now accompanied by the rustle of white feathers.

"We have every police force in Laxamora looking for them," Altus said in a more subdued tone.

Obedient now – good.

"We're leaning on his employer, watching his friends and his home. If he comes up for air again, we'll have him for sure."

"So far, that strategy hasn't worked well. All we have is an ignorant artist in prison. The journalist got away right from under the noses of the police. Twice. Whose screw-up was that?"

"I think they were helped by an ally. They were being pursued, but the airships were interfered with. We were following the tracker, but we think they were tipped off before we could catch up to them," Altus said, his hands folded together so hard his knuckles were white. "The second time, I don't know. We might have killed him, but his body hasn't been found so we're assuming he's still alive."

"Helped by whom?" Niveus said. "What ally?"

Altus shook his head. "No idea. It appears to be another vox, from the descriptions given by the survivors. And the trackers we had placed in his gear were destroyed. All of them."

Niveus' wings flared outward in irritation. It had to be Phames. Why had he surfaced after all this time? Long ago, Niveus concluded he was of no consequence, but here he was, interfering. Sometimes Niveus wished he could just go, just fly and leave these constant, annoying, messy disasters behind. Who could have predicted things would be like this? It had all seemed so straightforward in the beginning.

But he had responsibilities, and this was *his* world now. He couldn't turn his back and let it all fall to chaos.

"We're doing our best. They can't hide forever," Altus said stiffly. "The reporter will access his bank account sooner or later. *Something* will come up. If he puts so much as a toe out, we'll have him."

"Are you trying to convince me or yourself?"

Altus didn't answer.

The sun was well out of sight now. Covoxae and havoxae buzzed through the air, slowly disbursing.

"What about on the magical front?" Niveus asked.

"Maenos will arrive with the new voxmar tomorrow. When Aevi arrived this afternoon she reported that all was well with it. It's unfortunate that the war is causing these logistical issues, but it may be for the best."

"How are we going to get Mortis in the voxmar once it's here, Altus?" Niveus asked. "It was easy last time, because she wasn't expecting it, but we won't be able to lure her to a trapping circle this time."

The silence was deafening.

Finally, Altus spoke. "In light of the urgency, and the fact that the Circle are not all able to come together upon short notice without being noticed, we've been working on a summoning ritual powerful enough to work with only a few magi. Normally, the four that are here in Talgarora wouldn't be enough, even with the weather magi providing a boost, but..." He hesitated again.

What was he waffling about now? He turned to the human, searching his expression. It was always so hard to understand what humans were thinking – their minds were so disordered and clouded with emotion.

"What else?"

Altus hesitated a moment longer before replying, words obviously chosen carefully. "We may need your participation to add a boost of power."

Niveus studied him, then smiled. "Of course. Anything to conclude this matter promptly. You will tell me when all is ready and my input is required?"

Altus' eyes flickered. He was relieved, Niveus suspected, and trying not to show it. "Excellent. If we can summon her right to us, we won't need to bother with that damned reporter anymore."

"Of course we will," Niveus said, his lips pulling into a crooked smile. "He knows too much, does he not?"

Now Altus smiled, chuckling softly from the shared joke. For the first time in this conversation, Niveus sensed that the man was being genuine. "But without Mortis, he'll probably think his ordeal is over. He'll come out of his hole, and we'll get him off the table before he can tell anyone what he knows. Two birds with one stone."

"Efficient and reasonably devious. Let's hope the ritual works."

Altus bowed to him and left him alone at last, and Niveus returned to his contemplation of the symphony going on in the sky.

"Now I wonder, Altus," Niveus murmured to the empty room. "How much of an idiot do you think I am?"

Involving him in a difficult ritual was plausible. That was the problem – even though it had never happened before. Was he being betrayed, *now*, after all this time? Or was Altus telling the truth?

Only time would tell. But if Altus did plan to pull something, remove Niveus the way they had removed Mortis, or collar him like Certos, he'd find that Niveus was not as ill-prepared or naïve as Altus might think.

Chapter 28

The grand general's tent was in the centre of the well-established tent city south of the ridge that separated the Laxam Empire and the Monson Alliance. Garelon had been here before, of course. He had commanded a division under Grand General Hason at the battle that had felled him. So he was familiar with the surroundings as he floated over the rough road in a military jeep. There were several things that were different, though.

The honour guard of armed soldiers on motorcycles, hovering ahead and behind, was new. As was the awareness of Certos' presence, locked in a box behind him.

The energy at the base camp seemed heightened as well, compared to the last time Garelon had been here. The news of Hason's injury had been hard on the troops, and Garelon felt the scrutiny of hundreds of eyes as he got out of the jeep and walked to his tent to stow his gear. He knew that he was being weighed and measured, but was confident. This wasn't his first battle, and now that he understood Certos' capabilities, he had every confidence that things would go smoothly.

The news that Niveus was nearby had also somehow preceded his arrival, and it caused a buzz through the camp. Though Garelon was insulated from the gossip to a certain extent, he heard the rumour being whispered several times as he moved through the camp, inspecting equipment, speaking with soldiers that he recognized, and generally connecting with the troops. Of course, there were thousands, so there was no saluting them all, but he spent an exhausting evening meeting with everyone who ranked captain and up.

When the meetings were finally over, it was midnight local time, which meant that Garelon had been awake for almost 36 hours. He dismissed the last of the Division Captains, trusting them to carry out their own duties without further intervention from him.

He got up and poked his head out of the tent. There were two sentries standing at attention outside of his door, but they were the only ones he saw awake at the moment except for a pair patrolling the area. He nodded to the sentries. "I'm going to bed. Don't disturb me until oh-seven, unless it's an emergency."

"Good night, sir," one of them said, and they both saluted. Garelon nodded again and withdrew into the tent.

His gaze landed on Certos' box. It had been sitting there like an accusation all day, but now, finally, he was alone.

He watched the boy crawl out with his chess set clutched close to his chest, then sighed with distinct irritation and ducked behind the screen separating his bed from the rest of the tent to get ready for bed. "I need to sleep, so do what you like. Just stay out of sight if anyone comes in."

"Yes, sir." He heard a soft rustle as Certos moved about. "Are you upset about something?" the vox asked a moment later.

For a moment Garelon didn't know how to answer, though he did recognize the question as an odd one. Certainly Certos wouldn't have asked him that when they first met.

He answered honestly. "Yes. I'm angry at the way you've been treated. But that's a familiar subject by now, as you know. It was all I could not to snap Altus' head off, but I think I'd have lost my job."

"No," Certos said. "You'd have been killed, probably."

"They couldn't kill—" Garelon started to object, then frowned. It was a disturbing turn of phrase, but not important. "Well, regardless of what you want to call it," he allowed. "But I expect they'd imprison me forever, since I know about you."

"Maybe."

Garelon crawled into bed and laid on his back, staring up at the ceiling. He heard a soft clicking and presumed Certos was, predictably, playing chess.

"I just want you to know that I don't treat you that way in front of them because I agree with them. You're not a computer, or a tool, or anything like that. I don't believe that."

"I know," Certos said. "I wouldn't care even if you did, though."

Garelon doubted that seriously, but there was little point in trying to force Certos to admit otherwise. "I see," was all he said. "Nevertheless."

With the click of chess pieces a soothing background accompaniment, Garelon closed his eyes.

He was so exhausted that it seemed he'd merely blinked and was awake again. Only the fact that the time on the clock by his bedside had advanced told him that he'd actually slept at all. It was now past three in the morning, and he felt groggy rather than rested – not surprising considering he'd slept for less than three hours.

What had awakened him? There were no chess sounds, now. In fact, he couldn't hear a thing, but maybe Certos had made a noise and it had awakened him? Whatever it was, it was gone now. Garelon lay in the bed with his eyes closed, willing himself back to sleep.

Then he heard a soft rustle at the foot of his bed and opened his eyes wide. Was that Certos?

He turned his head minutely, back and forth. The room was very dark, but there was a little bit of light from the glittering voxmarae hanging from the ceiling, and the digital clock next to his head. Far too late he saw a shape lunge towards him, the golden covox light glittering on the blade of a long, wickedly curved knife.

Certos appeared out of nowhere before Garelon could so much as free an arm from the covers to ward off the blade. The vox launched himself over Garelon as if on the wing, straight at the assailant. Garelon felt something gossamer light and very cold brush against his face as Certos threw himself across him.

Garelon didn't see what happened to the knife in the confusion that ensued, but he did see Certos strike the dark attacker, who stumbled back against the fabric wall of the tent. The attacker shoved Certos hard and Certos, light and frail as a feather, sprawled onto the floor.

By now Garelon was on his feet, and the attacker fled for the door.

"Stop!" Garelon shouted uselessly, racing after them, but Certos overtook him and burst from the tent a moment before Garelon did, hot on the heels of the assassin. It was dark outside as well, but not as dark as the interior of the tent thanks to the lamps hung on every tent. Garelon saw a figure in a heavy grey cloak, the hood pulled up, and as the cloak flapped he saw that the assassin was wearing a Laxam military uniform.

Garelon's two sentries were on the ground, their throats slit. They lay still, blood pooling around them. It was probably the fall of their bodies, or a small sound they had made during the attack that had awakened Garelon, he realized now.

He realized something else.

Certos had wings. They looked as if they were made of metal, each feather taking the shape of a glittering blade ending in a wicked point. He spread them and flapped, rising up into the air. His eyes flashed with a red light like blood.

"You will not escape!" Certos snapped, and thrust his hands out forward.

Garelon felt some kind of concussion strike him and pass him, leaving him untouched.

But whatever Certos had done had an effect on the camp. People burst from tents, stumbling in their haste. The assassin put on a desperate burst of speed, but more people emerged and converged on it from all sides. The mob closed on the figure with an angry roar and it disappeared from view, pulled under by reaching hands.

A white light flared from the collar around Certos' neck and the boy screamed. His wings folded up and he dropped like a stone. Garelon lunged forward, but wasn't quite close enough to catch him before he hit the ground.

"Voxae ma," Garelon said, pulling Certos up and seeing that his eyes were open and still burning with a red, angry light. "What did you do?"

Certos blinked languidly, and his eyes went back to normal. "Rage." His voice was like a seductive purr, alight with satisfaction and pure malice.

The assassin was screaming. Fists rose and fell in the mob, and the soldiers gave their own cries of anger. Rage, indeed.

Desperate, Garelon shook Certos hard. "Stop it! Stop it now!"

Certos only turned his head away, and Garelon thrust the boy away from him, getting to his feet and sprinting towards the crowd. "Stop this," he shouted, his voice tearing at his throat. His normally booming voice seemed swallowed by the night air, scarcely loud enough to combat the pure emotion of the mob.

Aware that he might be risking his own safety, he started grabbing people, dragging them bodily away. "I order you to stop," he said over and over. "Stop! Get away from them."

The people he pulled away shook their heads in confusion, and slowly the mob began to break apart, the soldiers looking around and blinking as if waking up from an incredibly vivid dream. Garelon forced himself to the middle of the crowd, but it was far, far too late. The broken form of the assassin was barely recognizable as human, and

Garelon couldn't even tell for certain if it had been a man or a woman, after all.

He swore again and turned around. "You, and you, take that to the hospital tent," he said, pointing to two soldiers at random and then down at the assassin. Not that the doctors would be able to do anything, but at the very least the damage could be assessed and the body could be put in storage.

He pointed to four more soldiers standing in a confused and frightened knot. "And you, take care of these soldiers. Hurry!" He indicated the sentries. He doubted they would fare any better than the assassin, but maybe with a blood transfusion, they could recover. Who knows?

Abruptly, he recalled that there was even a chance that these people could die, and he faltered for a moment, staring hard at the sentries. He couldn't see them breathing, but it was hard to say. Either way, he had to get all three bodies to medical attention, and even now the soldiers were hurrying to obey his orders.

He shook himself and pointed to two others. "You two, send word to Captains Phovon and Rasel that there has been a serious security breach and I want all patrols doubled. Anyone found in the camp who cannot be accounted for should be held for interrogation."

He glared around at the rest of the would-be mob. "All the rest of you, back to your bunks," he said. "Immediately."

He stamped back towards Certos, who still lay on the ground. His wings were draped over his body like crumpled fabric. "Come," he snapped at the boy and walked past him without slowing. He heard Certos rise and follow docilely.

*　　　*　　　*

Garelon pushed the tent flap aside and stalked inside, then threw himself into a seat. No sooner was he sitting, but he reached and hunted through a cupboard. He grabbed a bottle and splashed water into a cup, unable to find anything stronger. The water was room temperature, but the cup rimmed with frost as the savoxmar embedded into the base activated from the addition of a liquid. He drank.

Certos stood just inside, stock still, his wings folded against his back. His eyes were averted in that unfocused, vague way that Garelon was well acquainted with by now. He expected to be punished.

Garelon honestly wasn't certain that he *wasn't* going to be. He couldn't remember ever being so angry or horrified before.

But even as the thought occurred to him, he realized he was fooling himself – he didn't want to give Certos more of a reason to loathe humanity, if he could possibly avoid it. He closed his eyes and rubbed his thumb and forefinger over them, then ran his hand up over his forehead and through his hair. Adrenaline still thrummed through his body.

Hopefully he could deal with this more constructively than Hason would have.

When he felt ready, he opened his eyes and pointed to a chair. "Sit."

Certos sat. His wings made a soft musical sound as he moved, the feathers chiming together like bells. But as he sat down, they vanished and the sound ceased abruptly.

Garelon eyed him for a few long moments, then drew in a deliberate breath and let it out. "Certos," he said in a gentler tone, though there was still an edge to it. Then he paused, staring.

He hadn't noticed it before, but there was a line of drying blood on Certos' arm from an ugly gash in his shoulder. Immediately Garelon jumped up and crossed to him.

Certos flinched and shied away, but Garelon bent to examine him. "What happened?"

The boy looked at his own shoulder, then shrugged it. "The knife," he said. "I pulled it out, already."

"Let me see," Garelon demanded, taking his arm. Certos went rigid, but Garelon scarcely noticed. He pressed his fingers to the wound, trying to apply pressure, stop the bleeding. But the blood just flaked away under his fingertips, revealing smooth, unbroken skin underneath.

He brushed the last of the drying blood away, stunned.

Certos looked at him expressionlessly.

"I see," Garelon said. He released Certos and moved back to his chair, falling heavily back into it. Too many shocks in too short a time, and he was still trying to digest the fact that he had nearly been assassinated.

"Explain to me what happened tonight, please," he said, turning towards the boy. "I need you to try to help me understand what you did."

"I sensed the human as she killed the sentries," he said. Certos stared down at his knees, at least, rather than into space. Garelon considered that to be an improvement, though he wasn't really sure if it was one or not. "Then she entered the tent and I knew she hated you, and was going to kill you. Your death by assassination would throw our army into confusion, necessitate your replacement with someone else, likely in haste, perhaps someone less capable. It would reduce morale. It would buy them time."

Garelon was shocked to hear the cold, tactical analysis spilling from Certos' mouth as if it were relevant, especially accompanied by those words - 'killed', 'death'...

"Go on," he prompted, struggling to control his own emotions.

"I stopped her from hurting you." Certos looked up and his eyes flashed with that red light again, narrowed with anger. "I didn't want them to try again, so I used my abilities to inspire anger and cause the nearby soldiers to attack. I had to be hasty, so it was merely a mob. It would do the job, though. The story will spread. Other assassins will be reluctant to try again."

He lifted his chin. "I will do it again, no matter how many times they try, no matter if you punish me. No matter if the collar pains me."

Garelon's throat was dry at this pronouncement. He struggled for a safe question to ask while he thought about the rest. "Why did the collar hurt you?" he asked finally.

"I'm not permitted to use my powers without being ordered," Certos said with a defiant shrug. "If I try hard *enough*, I can." He smiled suddenly, and it was a terrifying expression. "I learned that tonight."

Garelon considered for a moment the ramifications of that piece of new information. The collar didn't normally allow Certos to use his abilities except as ordered, because Certos' abilities were dangerous if unchecked. That was obvious from what he had done tonight. What could Certos do to his captors if he knew he could use his abilities at will, so long as he was willing to bear the pain?

The thought of Laxam torn apart by mob violence flashed through his mind, and he shuddered.

156

He had never thought there might be a type of vox that could manipulate his emotions, but how else would Certos operate? Perhaps he wasn't just concerned with tactics that governed war, but the emotions that drove it.

It made his blood run even colder.

He shook his head and tried to push the reactions away. Certos was still watching him with defiance, but uncertainty was starting to creep into his expression the longer Garelon remained silent.

"Certos, why did you attack the assassin?" Garelon said, trying to figure out how to ask the question he really wanted answered.

"Because I didn't want them to try a—" Certos began, but stopped as Garelon held up a hand.

"No, I mean, why didn't you want the assassin to try again? If I were killed, it would give you an opportunity to escape."

Certos froze. The light was dim, but Garelon could swear that his cheeks were growing paler. "The collar doesn't permit me to escape. I can't fly for long. I can't use my powers without permission. There's no point."

Garelon eyed Certos. To call him a tactical genius was a brash understatement. And Garelon knew for a fact that even before tonight, he had been using his powers in a limited fashion without being directly ordered to – he could play chess. Certos had to have known, even subconsciously.

"If you went with the Monson assassin," he said, hoping he wasn't making a terrible mistake, "you could have tricked them into removing your collar. Or if they were not easily tricked, you probably could have worked out some deal with them that would protect you. They don't know what you are exactly, nor what the collar does. At worst, you would be no worse off than you are now – in slavery, but at least working against those who hurt you so badly."

Certos stared at him, his face as pale and colourless as ice. "Is that what you wanted me to do?" he asked, a strange note of hope in his voice. "Will you come with me?"

The questions, asked so innocently, floored Garelon. "No," he said, his voice slightly strangled as he spoke through a closed throat. "No, Certos, that isn't what I wanted."

"Oh," Certos responded, dropping his eyes once more.

Garelon struggled for a moment. "What I'm trying to ask you," he said, growing desperate, "is why it matters to you what I want, when you have to have come up with that idea on your own? You *did* think of it, didn't you?"

Certos stared firmly at the floor. "Yes."

Of course he had. If Garelon had thought of it, Certos had to have thought of ten alternative plans that were even more likely to succeed. "Then why?" Garelon demanded.

The words were pulled with visible reluctance from the boy's throat. "I didn't want you to die," he said. "You're the nicest human I've ever met. I want to be with you forever."

Garelon sat back in his chair. In all honesty, the words were not totally unexpected, but they were still incredible to hear. And they made him a little angry, to be honest.

"You shouldn't have done it," he said, and Certos' head snapped up, his eyes wide with astonishment.

"What?" Certos blurted. "But I—"

"No," Garelon said, pointing a finger at him. "Why haven't you escaped, Certos?"

The boy shrank back into his chair and shook his head.

Garelon got to his feet and began to pace. "Why didn't you take the opportunity when Hason was injured? He treated you abominably, and you had never met me at that point! Why did you just stand there and wait when you could have left? Don't tell me you had no tactical alternative."

"I... I..." Certos swallowed and shook his head again. "I couldn't."

Garelon rounded on him. "Why not?" he demanded, his voice raised almost to a shout.

Certos just sat in the chair, trembling visibly, his inhuman eyes staring out of a face that was utterly white. "I don't know."

The sight broke Garelon's anger and he sagged. He wasn't actually angry at Certos, anyway. He wasn't even sure who he *was* angry at. He just couldn't accept the possibilities that were presenting themselves to his mind.

Either Certos was planning some spectacularly horrible vengeance against them all that required him to remain ostensibly under their control for a while longer, or he was so completely broken down and beaten that even if Garelon took off his collar and set him free, he wouldn't go.

Both alternatives were so awful that his mind shied away from them.

"I'm sorry," he said, all the emotion running out of him like vox from a cracked voxmar. "I'm not angry at you. I shouldn't have yelled at you. I shouldn't... I just shouldn't have."

Certos remained still for a moment, then slowly lifted his gaze to meet Garelon's. "You're not mad at me any longer?"

"No," Garelon said. His heart warmed, despite its heavy burden of guilt. "Thank you for protecting me, Certos."

"You thank me even though you think it was wrong." There was confusion in his voice, and a bit of wonder.

"Humans are strange to you, I'm sure," Garelon said. "As strange as you are to us."

"Mmm," Certos agreed with a nod.

At that moment, a voice called from just outside the tent. "Grand General, sir! Prime Minister Niveus requests your presence!"

Chapter 29

"Doctor? Doctor? Another one's come in, Doctor Nellexe. Where should we... where should we put... it?"

The distress in the nurse's voice pulled Aevi part way out of the report in her hand. It was the fourth time she had read it. At least the fourth— she had lost count. Ever since she'd opened the special sealed black envelope that classified reports always came in, she found her eyes going back to it every time she had a spare moment. She found herself reaching for it, letting her eyes scoot over its lines and phrases, certain words burning themselves ever more deeply into her brain with every pass.

"Long-term patients..."

"...condition worsening..."

"...last count 50% have succumbed to true death..."

"...appears that the victims, by and large, succumb without additional pain..."

"...injections of the Aevi Nexalum Drug have no measurable effect..."

"...application of an IV with blood and sucrose solution seems to improve prognosis and in some rare cases may have prevented death..."

"...no improvement in those subjected to either AND or IV treatment..."

"...appears at present to be no explanation..."

Ripping her eyes away from the stark lines on the page, she looked up. She was a military nurse, in uniform with an erect bearing, but her face as white as paper.

Aevi realized that her own hands were shaking, the paper rustling in her hands.

"Another...?" she murmured uncomprehendingly.

"Yes, Doctor," the nurse said. "There was a... a problem. Some kind of fight in the camp. The injured and... and..." She seemed to steel herself. "Th-the *dead* are coming in now. The first one's just arrived."

"All right, I'm coming," Aevi heard herself saying, as if on automatic.

This is my fault.

160

She moved towards the flap of her tent, walking on autopilot to the hospital tent with the nurse hot on her heels.

This is all my fault.

The area outside the huge tent was chaos, with stretchers being carried in all directions and people shouting orders, the moans of the injured rising up over it all. But worse were the stretchers whose occupants lay still.

How many of these were merely unconscious, and how many dead?

No one seemed to know how to tell, and Aevi saw one corpse carried past under heavy guard despite the fact that it was obviously nothing but a lump of bloody meat. His carriers were hurrying past, shouting urgently for a doctor as if it would make a difference.

If I hadn't lied to everyone, they wouldn't be suffering now.

She entered the tent and looked around, struggling to make some kind of order out of the chaos all around her. Rows and rows of beds stretched ahead of her, each one looking identical from this vantage point. Each one an island of pain.

Someone plucked the report from her hand and pressed a coat on her. She put it on with mechanical fingers.

If I hadn't lied, it wouldn't all be coming to an end.

"Doctor, over here— we're just getting him prepped for emergency surgery," someone shouted almost in her ear.

She blinked and turned to follow, pulling latex gloves onto her hands. Someone tied her hair back out of her face, and she pulled a mask over her mouth and nose, looking down at a mess of blood covering a bare torso.

If I hadn't done this, I wouldn't be here, now.

"What happened to her?" she heard an authoritative voice ask as if from a very long distance away. She realized vaguely that it sounded like her own.

"Took a knife to the chest in the confusion, Doctor," a trembling voice advised her. She turned and looked into the pale face of a soldier, her clothes and face covered with blood. It was impossible to tell if she was hurt, but since she was standing up, she wasn't as bad as the woman on the table. "Is she going to be okay? Is she going to—"

"Get her out of here, so we can work," Aevi ordered, and a nurse grabbed the soldier's elbow and led her away.

I should be dead.

The scalpel cut through flesh, opening skin and muscle already sliced open by metal. She hadn't just been stabbed once, but twenty, thirty times, in a frenzy. The wounds were small, but so numerous, clustered all over her torso. Blood filled the wounds, and she suctioned it away, then began to suture damaged organs.

The heart was inches from her fingers, pulsing slowly. Blood leaked from it from a gash, bright red under the lights. Aevi tried not to let herself be hypnotized by its regular motion, which was weakening seemingly with every beat.

I should be dead.

Monitors screamed as the heart stopped. Aevi felt like screaming along with it.

"Get the paddles! Get them now!" The needle flicked in and out as fast as she could, closing the holes, and the heart lay still and dead. The brain monitor was flat-lining as well, emitting a shrill whistle even louder than the heart monitor.

A nurse was massaging her heart, trying to get it to beat again, but it lay like so much meat. "We don't have paddles, Doctor," he exclaimed, his voice high with confusion and panic. "What are they for?"

That should be me.

Suddenly the soldier seemed to sparkle. Though no one else could see it, Aevi's magically trained eyes watched in fascination as the voxae that held her body together began to swirl away in a riot of colourful sparkles.

It would take hours before they were all gone, but it was far too late to save her. Death had taken her.

I SHOULD BE DEAD!

Aevi sank to the floor, the scalpel and needle slipping from her bloody hands as she pressed them to her face and started to scream. She screamed and screamed, certain that she would never stop.

Chapter 30

Altus opened his window shutters and looked out into the night. To his eyes, Talgarora was still and silent, deserted at the current hour. The grand minister set a small lantern on the sill and moved back to his desk.

He only had to wait five minutes before there was a soft rustling at the window. Turning his head just slightly, he watched the woman climb through the window and straighten up, pulling back a hood to reveal her face.

Her cloak blended with the night and the desolate surroundings to the north of the city as well as it blended with the stones of the castle itself. Her long red hair was bound up tight in a bun that was intended to be more utilitarian than attractive. Her bone structure was slender, but there was nothing fragile in her bearing.

Certainly not a hint of fragility in her eyes, either.

"Glad you could come," he said, rising to his feet. "And you are...?"

"Varil. Spare me, Altus," she said, leaning back against the windowsill. Every movement she made spoke of her excellent shape and training. The female assassins of Talgar were legendary.

But he was determined not to be dissuaded. "Did you have any trouble getting through the blockade?"

Her lips curved upwards in a smirk. "No, you did very well," she said. "I'm sure all the money changed hands in the right places. We got through without any difficulties."

That reminded him. "'We'," he echoed, his brows pulling down. "Yes, the report said that there were three of you."

She sniffed. "You don't think I would take on a job as complex and dangerous as this without backup, do you? There are enough of us to ensure things go smoothly." She paused, and smiled. "By the way, the queen sends her regards, and wanted me to tell you that if either you or that overgrown snake Niveus is sleeping in her bed, that I'm to leave a poisoned knife in it for the next time you lie down."

What an irritating woman. Altus forced his face to remain bland. "I'll keep that in mind." His eyes narrowed, then. "Considering the opportunity I am handing you on a platter, I should think that you would not be so rude to me."

She let out a laugh, a bray of mirth that would have been startling if she hadn't kept it quiet so it wouldn't carry. She all but doubled over from it, folding her arms across her stomach. Altus had to clench his fists to stop himself from doing something stupid like approaching to slap the smirk off her slender face.

"What's so damned funny?"

The laughter stopped so abruptly that he wondered if it had been affected just to annoy him. She wiped her eyes, though, then shook her head. "Itolan, do you think we're friends now, because you've decided to let us be the ones to remove the only thing between you and being king of the whole damned world?"

That was precisely what he'd hoped she would think, but of course that was too much to expect. She wasn't an idiot, after all. He smiled silkily. "Of course not, Varil. But we are partners for the moment, at least. And as you said, I am giving you this opportunity. I did not need to do that."

"Oh, I'm well aware of that," she said, her blue eyes penetrating his. He affected a bland, friendly expression again. "I can think of a few reasons why you might have come to my sisters for this instead of knifing him yourself. I think you're just too cowardly to dirty your own hands."

"On the contrary," he said, spreading his hands and turning them over, palm up, "I have no illusions about my hands. But you do have to admit that yours are far better suited for handling knives."

She snorted again, but looked slightly mollified. "Be that as it may," she said, in a mockery of his own tone.

Altus shook his head. "I am well aware of what you think of me, and quite frankly, I can't say that it's undeserved," he said. "But this is really nothing more than it seems. You help me with this, and the war will come to an end. It is Niveus who is determined to conquer every square foot of this planet."

She shook her head. "Uh huh."

Irritated that she was so skeptical, he went on. "After Niveus is dead, we will withdraw from Talgar, and honour the old treaty of 247. You can move out of the mountains, and we will live in peace."

164

"With you as undisputed ruler of ninety-nine percent of the world, instead of a hundred percent," she said sarcastically. "*How* will you restrain yourself? And what about all the other people you conquered? What about all the rest of the treaties your people made? The Wanderers, the Yoltar, the Desert nomads on both continents."

Altus shook his head. "Most of those other people have been Laxamans for hundreds of years now," he said, and eyed her sternly. "I have sympathy for your position, but I suggest that you take my very generous offer and be done with it, Varil. Unless you are having second thoughts."

She looked away. "Don't be ridiculous."

"Good," he said, enjoying a glow of satisfaction. "I should think that you'd be grateful for the chance simply to get out of those mountains and live a normal life once again."

She folded her arms and said nothing, her lips thinned.

He couldn't resist a smirk. "The battle will begin tomorrow afternoon," he said. "There will be fog. Use that to cover your movements."

Her head jerked up and she glared at him. "There's no fog in any forecast I've seen."

His smile widened, and he didn't care that it wasn't a particularly attractive expression. "I have ways of arranging things to my liking."

Her eyes narrowed. "Fine. Is there anything else?"

"No," he said mildly, pleased to have won an unconditional victory. He watched as she bowed with a distinct lack of deference, and turned away.

Just as the woman swung herself out the window and vanished, Altus heard a rapid tattoo of knocking at the door. He hesitated a moment and glanced out the window to make sure she was well out of sight, seeing a dark shape vanish around a tower far to his right.

Only then did he cross to the door and pull it open. "What is it?" he demanded, seeing a woman in Laxam military uniform standing in the hallway, her chest heaving as she struggled for breath.

"Sir," she said, bowing deeply. "I've just come from the base. Grand General Garelon was attacked in his tent. Two sentries and an unknown number of other soldiers are injured, and the assassin as well, sir. The grand general is unharmed."

Altus narrowly stopped himself from whirling and glaring in the direction the treacherous woman from Monson had gone. Instead, he swore and slammed the side of his fist against the doorjamb. "Come in and report."

No wonder she had looked so smug. You couldn't trust an assassin. She had taken advantage of the opportunity to go after Garelon. Probably the only reason she hadn't tried to hurt Altus himself tonight was because he was going to give her the chance to go after the big prize – Niveus.

Not an unconditional victory after all. She had gotten him, and Garelon had almost paid for it.

Well, no matter. She'd get what was coming to her, but not until after she'd helped him with his own problem.

Chapter 31

Phames hadn't been kidding about discomfort. The trip across the ocean and then over the Eastern continent to Talgarora was pure hell.

The voxae didn't tire, especially while flying, which seemed to be their natural element. Their wings beat quickly and strongly, and they soared through the air effortlessly, unaffected by buffeting winds, harsh cold, or thin atmosphere. But Liiran was blood-deprived, weak, and all too human, and was affected significantly by all three.

All he could do was hold on, shiver, and hope it wouldn't kill him. Dying once had been bad enough. He didn't think he could cope with a second time.

Thankfully, the interminable voyage only *felt* as if it took forever.

They finally landed a few miles from Talgarora. It was well past midnight and the city glittered with lights, a rough semi circle around a large, dark stone castle, built into a high cliff-face. Jagged mountains rose up behind the castle, but they were only the foothills to the even higher mountains to the north, where Liiran knew the war was raging. He recognized it, even from the air, having been here before.

It took Liiran some time to get his feet under him, but soon they set off towards the city on foot. Despite the harrowing flight, his strength was returning in leaps and bounds, but he still had to stop and rest frequently.

Eventually, they found and stole a car from a nearby farm. After that, the going was much easier, all three of them riding as the old junker jolted up the street, Phames' hand on the steering-wheel directing the vavoxae that turned the propellers.

Mortis was unusually tired and leaned on Liiran in the back seat, watching the buildings of the outer city pass by in silence. Talgarora's city was ancient, and stone buildings crowded the narrow streets. The population had benefited from Laxamoran rule. The air buzzed with modern vehicles, and the pedestrians looked no different from those one might see in Laxamora itself. Yet the history of the city created a different backdrop, and they passed more than one frieze-covered building or marvellous statue that took Liiran's breath away.

But Mortis seemed disinterested, even when Liiran pointed some of these out, and Liiran wondered if she was nervous. His own stomach had a tendency to do flip-flops every time he tried to turn his mind towards the question of getting Certos away from a vox and an unknown number of soldiers and magi, but all he could do was hope that a plan would present itself when they got there.

There were guards at the gates of the inner city.

Talgarora had sprawled out of its confines long ago as the population expanded and modernized. To get to the centre of the city, one had to pass through one of the gates.

Phames stopped the car as they came in sight of the gate, and they watched a car get pulled over and inspected closely. The guards opened the trunk and searched the interior while the driver shouted at them angrily. Quickly, Phames turned down a side street and parked, and they all got out of the car.

"Have you ever been here before?" Liiran asked Phames, wracking his own brain. The last time he was here on a story there hadn't been any guards, had there? He was pretty sure there wasn't.

"Sure, lots of times," Phames said. "I've spent most of the last three centuries outside of Laxam as much as possible. They haven't had guards there for a couple of decades, not since right after they were originally annexed."

They ditched the car – without ownership papers, they couldn't possibly get through the checkpoint with it – and returned to the corner. They stood outside a shop, just out of sight of the guard station, and pretended to be inspecting merchandise in the dimly lit window of a store. Though it was out of sight, they could hear the guards issuing orders to the motorists who tried to enter the inner city. They weren't letting anyone through without a thorough inspection.

"What does it mean?" Mortis asked anxiously.

"Are they looking for us?" Liiran mused.

Phames snorted, but looked thoughtful. "They can't think we're here. How could they know?"

"They must know you can fly," Liiran said. "They might not think I'm here, but all I've done is slow us down." Phames glared at him, and he felt a flush of anger. "I *mean* that we only got here later than they might have expected, if they thought we were going to follow them here."

Mortis shook her head. "If they are looking for us, and don't think we're with you, Liiran, then why would they post guards at all?"

The two men looked at her in confusion and she held her hands up. "Think about it. Phames and I shouldn't have any difficulty passing a couple of guards. We can just fly straight over, invisible."

"Then they're looking for me," Liiran said, "or maybe it has nothing to do with us at all."

"Either is plausible," Phames said, folding his thin arms, "but we have to assume they're looking for us, for now. I'll need to try to contact some people from outside and find a new way into the city. For now, let's take a room in the outer city."

They nodded in agreement, though Liiran touched his wallet, worried to use his credit cards.

No sooner had they started walking, however, but a feminine voice hailed them. "Phamile, is that you? I thought you said you wouldn't be caught dead in this sewer, now that it's fallen to Laxam."

Liiran turned around in shock, his heart thumping hard, and saw a woman standing on the sidewalk, one hand on her hip. She was dressed plainly in grey and black, in a surprisingly utilitarian outfit that left little of her petite curves to the imagination. *Who the hell is she?* he thought in sudden panic. *How does she know Phames?*

Phames' eyes lit up, though, and he took two rapid steps towards her. "Varil. I could ask you the same question."

"Have I got a story for you," she said in a distinct purr. "But first, who are your friends?" She glanced straight at Liiran. "You look dead on your feet."

He felt himself redden. "I'm fine," he lied, shocked at her phrasing.

Phames shook his head. "That's a story, too. They're safe, though. How about an exchange of information?"

She grinned. "Sounds like a deal. This way." Without hesitation, she turned around and strode off down the street, fast enough that Liiran had to push his exhausted body to keep up.

She led them through alleys and streets, taking a twisting, switchback route that made Liiran wonder if she was trying to avoid being followed. It reminded him of their trip to Phames' safehouse, only shorter.

Even still, by the time they finally reached their destination, Liiran's vision was starting to grey at the edges and he was so tired he was afraid his legs were going to fold up under him and pitch him to the ground on every step. He was doing well for having died earlier that day, but he had pushed his body way too hard, it seemed.

Varil paused at a small wooden door set into a featureless stone wall in an alley way. She knocked twice, and the door was opened a moment later. Another woman in a set of clothes similar to Varil's looked them over with suspicious grey eyes. But after the two women exchanged silent glances, she stepped aside to let them all in.

She was more heavy-set than Varil, but she moved with the same grace, like a dancer or a gymnast, and had the same long red hair.

They entered a small, dimly lit room with a distinct smell of must. It may have been meant as a storage room, but clearly wasn't being used for that purpose now. The floor was dirt over stone, or maybe just covered in years of tracked mud from the streets outside. There was a small cot in the corner, and four mismatched chairs set in a rough circle, and that was the end of the furnishings.

"This is an old safehouse from the time of the war. And this is my blade sister, Turil." Varil said. She turned to the woman. "Turil, you may have met Phamile Sandar before, but I didn't catch the names of the others?" She raised an eyebrow at them.

"I'm Liiran," he said, dragging himself over to one of the chairs and sitting down gratefully.

Mortis hovered over him, a hand on his shoulder, but her eyes were on the two women. "And I am Mortis. Who are you?"

Phames perched himself unceremoniously on one of the chairs. "They're assassins from Talgar," he said. "Varil and Turil. Old friends of mine, since we've both been fighting against Laxam expansion for centuries."

Liiran felt his heart almost stop. Talgar assassins. They were all women – actually, Talgar was traditionally a female dominated society. Women occupied most levels of government, most professional occupations in Talgar, while Laxam had always been more equal between the sexes. According to Talgar tradition, women were faster, more vicious, and therefore more suited to powerful careers and law enforcement.

And the assassins were feared around the world. It was said that they could get in anywhere, slit your throat, and be gone before you knew you were dead.

Liiran had never met an assassin before, and the idea that he was now trapped in an extremely tiny and claustrophobic room with two of them, all but crippled, didn't sit well with him. The fact that they were friends with Phames didn't make him any more comfortable with the idea, either.

"Assassins?" Mortis echoed. Liiran would have expected her to sound mystified – there were so many human concepts that she didn't remember. But instead she sounded interested.

In retrospect, that made sense.

Varil draped herself in one of the remaining chairs. She leaned back, her leg flung over the rickety arm and her foot in the air. Her outfit made her all but blend into the wall behind her, except for the violently red hair, which was common in Talgar.

"So cough it up, Phamile," Varil said, her eyes serious despite the smirk curving her lips. Turil couldn't be any more different, taking the remaining chair and sitting ram-rod straight, eyeing them all with a steely gaze. She hadn't yet made a sound, and her expression was still harsh.

Phames drew his feet up onto the seat, perching like a bird with his arms wrapped around his knees. "Hmph," he sniffed. "We're here to throw a wrench into the works. Specifically, we're here to steal something vital to the Laxam war effort."

Varil's eyebrows rose. "A little hands-on for you, isn't it?"

Phames glowered at her, obviously caught off-guard. "I'm altering my tactics. And what are *you* doing here?"

Turil finally spoke up. "Why should we tell you?"

Phames shrugged, his sandy eyes darting only momentarily towards Turil. "We're allies. Maybe we can help."

Turil snorted. Her voice was a bit high and raspy, the voice of a woman older than she looked. Of course, no one aged past middle-age. "We know you, Phamile, but we don't know them."

"Mortis is a very old friend, and Liiran... is all right. He's an enemy of our enemies," Phames said with a trace of irritation. "They can be trusted."

Varil snickered and reached up, pulling a few pins out of her hair, which promptly spiralled out of the tight bun. It fell almost to the floor, a long red sheet. "It's all right, Turil. As far as I'm concerned, Phamile's friends are our friends." She straightened up slightly, but her tone didn't lose any of its carelessness as she added. "We're here to kill Prime Minister Niveus Exalan."

Liiran couldn't stop a soft gasp from escaping his lips. The two voxae exchanged a startled look. He felt Varil looking at him sharply, and struggled to school his expression again.

If Niveus was a vox, how could they kill him? Liiran restrained a strong urge to voice this thought. He couldn't be sure whether Varil knew about Phames' true nature, and suspected strongly that she thought he was human. He doubted Phames would want him to spill the beans on the existence of human-sized voxae.

As if to confirm his thoughts, Phames shot him a cold and angry look, as if ordering him not to say anything.

"Sounds difficult, even for you," was all Phames said. "Why haven't you tried that before?"

"You think we haven't?" Varil shot back. "His security is the tightest in the world. He's got guards around him all day and night."

"Then what's different now?" Liiran asked. It all seemed like too much of a coincidence, to him. Why would these assassins be here at the same time they were? Unless Niveus was especially vulnerable, and yet Liiran couldn't imagine the prime minister sticking his neck out.

Varil snorted faintly, her foot bobbing in the air as she rolled her eyes. "Because the one who hired us to do it is Altus Itolan."

That produced an immediate response. Liiran sat up, despite his exhaustion, and Phames nearly came right out of his chair. "Are you crazy? It's a trap!" Phames exclaimed. "The two of them have been friends for centuries."

"Of course it's a trap," Varil said with a dismissive wave of her hand. "But the queen believes that Itolan is trying to grab power. The timing's good for it, right at the end of the war. He can sew things up

172

nice and neat for himself and take all the credit. And honestly... the offer's a bit too good to refuse."

Phames snorted. "Of course he'd make it too good to refuse. But he's a liar. He's broken every promise he ever made, Varil."

"I know, but he *did* promise to withdraw from Talgar. Besides, we've done a few things to make sure he has no opportunity to change his mind. If my knife is at his throat, he'll give in."

"And conquer you again next week," Phames said darkly.

Varil spread her hands. "Not if he's dead, too," she said, with a wicked smile. Then she sobered. "We have no choice, Phamile. We really don't."

Phames just shook his head and fell silent. Liiran was still trying to come to grips with the fact that they were talking about killing the prime minister. And the grand minister, apparently.

Even discussing the concept was usually so taboo that Liiran couldn't remember the last time he'd heard the word 'kill' out loud.

"But how are you going to... to kill him, if," Liiran began. Phames was glaring at him. "If he can't die," Liiran finished in an innocent tone. He felt Mortis' hand squeeze his shoulder, and saw Phames relax.

Well, he wasn't an idiot. Honestly, what did they take him for?

Varil shrugged. "Well, I've heard some rumours that the injection's starting to wear off," she said. "Not really confirmed, or anything, but I've heard stories of people actually dying recently. But that's not really the point. We've always referred to it that way. I guess you city folk aren't used to it, but the methods we use..." She drew her finger across her own throat. "You're as good as dead in seconds. No chance of recovery, so why not call it by the same thing?"

Liiran felt his stomach squirm with nausea at the blasé way in which she discussed this. "Oh," he said faintly.

"So Phamile," Varil said, turning back to the vox perched tensely on the chair. "You won't tell us what you're here for, but at least tell me what you need from us? No way you came here just for a chat."

Phames didn't hesitate. "We need a way inside the city without being seen by the guards. Can you help us get in to do some investigation, and then out again?"

Varil looked them over skeptically. "All three of you?"

"Eventually, yes," Mortis said, speaking up for the first time in a firm tone of voice. "Though I think it won't hurt to allow Liiran to rest for a day or two while Phamile and I reconnoitre."

Varil's eyes rested on Phames, and he nodded. "Yes, that's right."

She shrugged, then. "No sweat," she said. "I can manage something. Right now?"

"No," Mortis said at the same moment that Phames said, "Yes, tonight."

They looked at each other, and Mortis surrendered. "Yes, very well, we shouldn't waste time. So long as we can find a place for Liiran to rest beforehand."

"He can stay here," Varil said. "I have to go over the wall anyway, and you two can come with me. Turil can stay here and keep an eye on your friend."

She jumped up from her seat, suddenly animated. Liiran got the impression that, for an assassin, she was highly energetic. On the other hand, he didn't know what was normal for assassins. But Turil wasn't nearly so fidgety. She barely moved, in fact. Like a watchful gargoyle.

"You take the cot, Liiran," Varil said, gesturing to the bed. "And I'll just get ready to go. Leave in five?" She was already binding her hair back up in a bun once more, pinning it in place.

"Thanks," Liiran said and got to his feet, moving towards the cot without a moment's hesitation. He didn't care if the mattress was infested with fleas, he was going to sleep, in a real bed.

"Mortis and I are ready to go immediately," Phames said.

Varil shot Mortis a skeptical look, but Mortis drew herself up. "I can keep up with you, I assure you," she said.

"You want a change of clothes?" Varil shot back, her lips twisting wryly. "Those jogging pants don't exactly show off your curves, honey."

Mortis glanced down at herself, looking perplexed, and Liiran let out a soft laugh as he sat down to pull off his shoes. "Get changed, Mortis. It'll help you blend in a bit better if you're wearing clothes that fit you."

"Oh, very well."

Liiran lay down. The last thing he saw right before he closed his eyes was Mortis pulling her shirt off over her head without an instant of modesty. He would have liked to watch a bit more closely, but his eyes seemed to close of their own accord and he knew nothing more for quite a while.

Chapter 32

As Garelon entered Niveus' office, Certos glued to his side, the prime minister was standing at a window with his back to him. At their entrance, he turned and walked towards them with a serious expression.

The room had a set of two chairs arranged around a decorative wall hanging, and a desk and chair that looked to have been placed there recently. It didn't match the rest of the decor. Three walls were all windows, providing a panoramic view of the city.

"Garelon, I'm glad to see you. Are you quite unhurt?" Niveus asked, gesturing to Garelon to sit. Despite his congenial tone, for the first time since Garelon had met him, Niveus didn't greet him with a smile.

Garelon sat down in the indicated chair. Certos curled up on the rug near his feet, his knees drawn up to his chest.

"I'm fine, sir," he said politely as Niveus took the seat opposite him. "The assassin grievously injured two soldiers on duty outside my tent and entered, but Certos took a blow intended for me. When the assassin fled, it was set on by several other soldiers, and unfortunately... well, there was little left that was recognizable, I'm afraid."

Not knowing how much Niveus already knew, Garelon gave a report that was essentially true, though the last part was slightly edited, of course. If he could avoid mentioning that Certos had used his powers without permission, causing the assassin to be torn apart by an angry mob, he would.

He was just glad that Altus wasn't here.

Niveus gazed at him unblinkingly as Garelon spoke. "It's wonderful that you weren't injured," he said finally, his face smoothing into a smile.

But the smile vanished as soon as it appeared, making Garelon a little dizzy at the shifts. It reminded him of Certos' mood swings.

Niveus steepled his fingers together in front of him. "You say he took the blow intended for you?" His eyes darted down to the boy on the floor and then back up.

Garelon nodded, his mouth dry. "Yes. He got in the way of the knife. But he's all right. It healed almost immediately."

"Of course it did." His eyes were growing more penetrating by the moment. "But why would he do such a thing for you?"

Garelon swallowed hard, trying to moisten his throat. Did Niveus have the same thought as he had had? Did he think Certos was plotting something?

"Honestly, I don't know for certain, sir," he said. He felt Certos lean against his leg and tried to ignore him. "I questioned the boy afterwards, but he couldn't give me a satisfactory answer."

"What answer did he give?" Niveus asked in a mild tone that Garelon didn't trust for a moment. What the hell was going through that man's mind? His eyes were completely unreadable.

"He said... that he didn't want me to get hurt."

Niveus' eyebrows rose. "Indeed?"

Garelon struggled to remain impassive, trying to give the impression of mild confusion. "Well, that's what he said, sir. Yes."

There was a short silence, and then Niveus glanced down at Certos. "Is that the reason, Certos?"

Certos picked at a rough spot on the rug and didn't answer for an uncomfortably long period of time. "Yes, Niveus," he said finally.

"Why?"

Niveus' voice had sharpened, and Garelon felt Certos cringe against him. "Sir, may I ask what concerns you about this behaviour in him? Perhaps I can give you better answers if I understand—"

"I want to know what he's up to," Niveus replied, looking up at Garelon again. "He did nothing to prevent it when Hason was injured. I don't know if he arranged it or not."

Certos made a wordless noise of protest, his head coming up for an instant and then bowing again as he squeezed himself so tightly against Garelon that the feeling was starting to go in his leg. "I... I didn't do anything to him. I was good. I was very good."

Niveus pursed his lips. "So you say."

"I was good," Certos said. "I did what I was told."

"Prime Minister," Garelon said through clenched teeth. "I don't believe he would lie. He seems quite... quite obedient to me. Perhaps he didn't try to protect Hason because he simply couldn't."

Niveus glared at him, and Garelon found himself glaring right back. This was insubordination, and he knew it, but he couldn't stand seeing

Certos so frightened. He bent down slightly and squeezed Certos' shoulder, trying to reassure him, but didn't take his eyes off of Niveus.

"You're soft on him," Niveus said. "I knew you would be the moment you laid eyes on him. But I thought that it wouldn't matter."

Garelon struggled with every fibre of his being to keep his voice even. "Sir, if you please. I see no reason why he should be treated with cruelty. If my attitude is incorrect, I hope you will enlighten me."

"Cruelty?" Niveus echoed, sculpted eyebrows drawing together.

He got to his feet suddenly and paced away from Garelon, his hands clasped behind his back. As Garelon looked up, he thought he saw something flash past the window, nearly invisible against the dark sky. He blinked and looked again, but whatever it was had gone, and he returned his gaze to the prime minister as Niveus turned back towards him.

"I see no need for cruelty," he said, the frown deepening. "Who said anything about that?"

"No one, sir," Garelon said, very quietly. "Except that you told me that I'm 'soft' on him, and perhaps I don't understand your meaning."

Niveus turned and eyed him. "I just want to know what you're doing differently from Hason."

"You'd have to ask him, sir," Garelon said. "Since I never saw how Grand General Hason treated Certos. But if I may be so bold, I would imagine that Grand General Hason treated Certos as if he had no sense of self."

He remembered Altus telling him that Certos was a tool, that he wasn't a person, and was doubly glad that the grand minister wasn't here now. But he watched Niveus closely, wondering if he had just made a terrible mistake by admitting this. Would Niveus take his promotion away, give Certos to someone else?

His fingers tightened slightly on Certos' shoulder. He couldn't stand that. Knowing that Certos would be handed over to another person who would treat him like nothing more than a talking piece of furniture?

Niveus sighed and ran a hand through his hair. "I know that's how Altus feels he should be treated. To keep him in line."

"With the greatest of respect, sir," Garelon said. "I may not have his expertise, but I have to disagree with Grand Minister Itolan. I have had no complaints about Certos' performance, and the fact that he did what he did tonight argues in my favour, in my humble opinion."

Niveus sighed and moved to the window again, staring out in silence for a few moments. "My concern is that this change in behaviour is not because of anything you've done, Garelon. Forgive me, but it's difficult for me to believe it."

"Niveus."

The whisper came from somewhere around Garelon's right knee, but it obviously carried all the way across the room to Niveus, because the prime minister turned.

Certos gazed up at Niveus, face pale, but set. He was all but shaking, but determined. "Don't take him away. Please."

Niveus gazed at Certos. "Tell me why. What do you want him for, Certos?"

"Nothing!" Certos exclaimed. "I don't want... he's not part of a plan. Please believe me."

"You know that I can't believe that until you give me a satisfactory answer. We both know what you are."

Garelon snapped before he could control himself. He was so sick and tired of this poor child being treated like a dangerous bomb. "What is he, sir?"

"He is the very *embodiment* of tactics and strategy," Niveus said. And then, his expression flickering with distaste, he added, "Worse, he can manipulate human emotions, such as rage. As he demonstrated tonight."

The image of that angry mob flashed across Garelon's face and he was shamed into silence. Niveus was right about that, of course. Hadn't Garelon had the same thoughts? The same suspicions?

Certos wrapped his arms around Garelon's legs and buried his face against them. His voice was muffled. "I won't let you take him. I'll make this whole city burn!"

"Certos!" Garelon said, shocked.

But Niveus didn't look surprised. "I won't allow that, Certos," he said, amazingly calm. "But there's no need for such histrionics. I haven't said that I'll reassign him. Just tell me now, why do you care so much whether he's the one?"

There was a long silence. Certos shook, clinging tighter to Garelon. But eventually, as if the words were being dragged out of him, he spoke. "Because he's nice to me. Because he doesn't hurt me. He... he gave me that chess set, and he treats me like his son."

Garelon choked at this last part, feeling his own cheeks flush. "I wouldn't say that's precisely true," he said stiffly, feeling the blue eyes of the prime minister boring into him, though Niveus had a strange smile playing about his lips as well. "I gave him my son's old room, that's all."

Niveus turned again, looking out at the stars. "Very well. It seems to me that if Certos really does have a... fondness for you, that it can only be an advantage to us in the long run. It would have been most unfortunate if you'd been hurt tonight, Garelon."

"Er, yes sir," Garelon said.

"I feel satisfied that nothing untoward is going on with Certos," Niveus went on as if he hadn't spoken. "Though I expect you to inform me immediately of any other strange behaviour, particularly anything that seems to speak to an unusual amount of initiative."

Garelon thought about Certos discovering that he had the ability to use his powers without being ordered to, and how he had done so even though he knew it would be painful. Niveus knew some of it, clearly, but did he know it all? "Yes, sir. Of course, I'll inform you immediately."

Niveus turned to face them and smiled. "As for the reasons for Certos' change of heart, I think we shall just keep quiet about that with Altus, don't you think?"

Garelon had to fight not to smile. "Quite so, sir."

"One last thing." Niveus' expression, so lately smiling, suddenly grew grave. "I believe it's time you learned of another development, which has unfortunate implications for the battle tomorrow."

Once again, Garelon felt almost dizzy at Niveus' changes in demeanor. He straightened attentively, glad to put aside the question of Certos' behaviour. "Another development, sir?"

Niveus crossed the room and sat once more. "When Certos was captured, there was another vox we captured at the same time. Her name is Mortis, and she is the vox of death. I'm sure you can appreciate that it was no drug that prevented everyone's death all of these centuries. It was she."

Garelon felt his mouth go dry. After learning that there was a vox of war, it wasn't difficult to believe in a vox of death. But why was Niveus explaining this to him now? "I understand."

"I don't think you do, just yet." Niveus sat back in his chair. "Mortis escaped her imprisonment, a couple of days ago. Tomorrow, in the battle, people will die, for real. Not just a few, but many."

"Voxae ma." The words were out before Garelon could choke them back.

"I knew it. I felt her," Certos murmured, and Garelon looked down into a face shining with pleasure. He didn't want to know what Certos was thinking, and quickly met Niveus' gaze again.

"Yes," Niveus said. "I think you understand now. The Mortis issue should be dealt with soon, but it's important that there not be a panic." He waved a hand. "If there aren't any questions, Garelon, you are dismissed."

Garelon couldn't believe that Niveus had just dropped this bomb on him so casually, but at the same time, he didn't want to have to sit here in front of the prime minister while he processed the implications of what he'd just learned. He got to his feet, just glad that the interview was over. "Thank you, sir," he said, and headed for the door.

"Garelon," Niveus added, just as he reached the door. Garelon froze, heart beating too fast.

"Yes, sir?"

"Take a room in the castle. I think it would be safest for all if you were close."

Garelon went cold. Safest for all, not just for him. Niveus definitely wasn't certain of Certos, whatever he claimed. Or was he afraid of another assassin with a knife that was truly deadly?

He turned and gave a bow. "I think you're quite right, sir."

And he left.

Chapter 33

Mortis flew around the castle, pausing every few moments and carefully peeking into each window to catch a glimpse of their occupants. Up and down she flew, around towers and along walls, searching.

She saw kitchens and bedrooms and sitting rooms, but very few people considering the number of rooms – the castle seemed all but deserted. Those people she did saw were asleep in darkened rooms, but she had little difficulty seeing them even in the darkness.

She realized after a while that she could taste their breath, hear their heartbeat, feel something *alive*. But she was careful not to reach out towards any of those little pulsing, shivering, *living* creatures for fear that the flame would snuff out if she got too close.

None of them was Certos.

She knew there were many people within the castle that she didn't see. The network of hallways was enormous, and there were likely dozens or hundreds of rooms in the interior, or underground. She could feel them as well, flickering, a hundred candles inside a large stone box.

She suspected that Certos would feel different, but she wasn't sure what he would feel like. Phames was different, after all. She knew enough now to understand why.

Dawn was beginning to approach. The covoxae were becoming agitated as the sun approached the horizon and the city began to warm. She came to rest on a slanted roof, watching Phames spiral around a tower she'd already checked, his skeletal bat wings beating the air furiously as he flew.

She spread her own wings, intending to go meet him and ask for suggestions. Maybe there was some way they could get inside the castle without being seen.

But just at that moment, she saw a light come on in the very highest room in the tallest tower. There hadn't been anyone there the last time she had looked, and instead of flying towards Phames, she headed upwards towards the tower. She could feel something up there, now, though she wasn't sure how to interpret the sensation.

That room looked out over most of the city. She approached cautiously, taking her time and trying to find an angle of approach that would keep her hidden if someone looked out the massive windows.

It took several minutes, but finally she hovered just below the level of a window, her wings beating slowly to keep herself aloft, and peeked just over the windowsill.

She saw two men, sitting in chairs, speaking to one another with heated emotions.

One was human, one... not.

She stared at the man in white. Was this Certos?

Then she heard him speak.

"Is that the reason, Certos?"

A soft voice answered his ringing tones, so soft that Mortis almost didn't hear. "Yes, Niveus."

"Why?"

As the two men in the chairs argued, Mortis shifted upwards, placing her hands on the windowsill and struggling to catch a glimpse of the third one. So the white man was Niveus, and the other one, the human... Who was he? From the deferential words he spoke, he was obviously an underling of Niveus'.

She thought back to what Phames had told her about Niveus and Certos. Was this man one of the Circle of Magi, who controlled Certos and made him do their bidding? Or was he General Garelon?

She finally caught a glimpse of Certos. He was so very small, clinging to the legs of the human man and shaking with obvious fear.

Mortis felt a flash of anger. Look at what he'd been reduced to!

The men were still arguing, and suddenly Niveus jumped to his feet and moved away from her, towards one of the other windows.

She'd seen enough anyway, and quickly flapped her wings, diving away and heading towards Phames, who was a black shape against the lightening sky.

"I found him," she hissed in their special language as she came within earshot. "He's in that tower room up there."

Phames whipped around, his wings flaring. "You found him?" He started towards the lit room, but then stopped dead in the air. "Niveus is in there."

"You can tell that?"

"Of course." Phames looked at her, eyes wide. "If you went anywhere near him, he would have sensed you, too. You shouldn't have gone there."

For a moment, she paused. "Well, I didn't know that. Anyway, Niveus didn't even look in my direction. I don't think he noticed me—"

"That's impossible."

She gritted her teeth in frustration. "*But* the important thing is, I found Certos. We know he's here in the castle, and I know what he feels like. All we need to do now is figure out how to get to him."

Phames hesitated, calming. "Who else was in the room other than Niveus and Certos?"

"Just one other human."

"The human doesn't matter," Phames said. "You can just kill him. And Niveus isn't much trouble on his own. We can go get him right now."

Not this again. "I can't just kill the human, he's not sick," Mortis argued.

"He's *old*—"

"Are you going to tell me what I can or can't do? What's right or wrong when it comes to my own sphere?"

Phames fell silent for a moment, glaring at her. "No," he bit out finally. "But anyway, even if we don't kill him, the human is no threat."

"I know," Mortis said, turning her back to Phames and looking up at the tower room, "but I don't think going in there with Niveus there is a good idea. For all we know, it's a trap. It was so convenient that he used that room, where it was so easy to see him. Maybe I'm wrong, and he did sense me. What if we get to Certos, and we can't get him away? We don't know anything about how they're holding him hostage, either."

Phames considered this. "You're right," he said. "We can't risk losing everything right now, just when we might be so close. We should plan this properly."

"At least we know where he is," Mortis said. "We need some time, perhaps to talk to him alone. A diversion would be helpful."

"Yes, a diversion," Phames smiled. "Like Niveus getting attacked by assassins."

Mortis glanced at him thoughtfully. "You mean Varil?" By mutual, silent agreement, the two voxae started heading back towards the safehouse.

"Exactly," Phames said. "Security will have to be lax that day, if Itolan wants her to get in to attack Niveus. She's not stupid. She won't go in at all if she's just going to get herself caught. Which means we can probably use the same opportunity to get in and get at Certos. The attempt will throw the castle into confusion, giving us more time to talk to Certos and try to find out how to break whatever spell they've put on him."

"The attempt – or her arrest," Mortis said. "You're not going to tell her this can't succeed, are you." It wasn't really a question.

"No, I'm not," Phames said shortly.

"But she's your friend."

Phames' eyes shot towards her, narrowed. "I don't have any *human* friends. She's just a source for my newspaper. And I've helped her a few times to try to make Niveus' life more difficult."

Mortis wasn't surprised to hear him say this, though she wondered if it were really true. Phames really did seem to hate humans, though. It was possible.

"What is Certos like?" she asked, changing tack to what she hoped was a safer subject.

Phames shrugged. "He has wings with feathers like knives, and he is tall and strong, very angry, but very intelligent."

Mortis thought about that shaking child she'd seen. It didn't sound anything like that description, and yet Niveus had called him Certos.

"Do you think being captured like he has been would change him?" she asked. "Really change him?"

"Change him how?" Phames asked, glancing at her sidelong.

"I don't know," she said, reluctant to speak about what she'd seen. Somehow, it would make it more horrifying. And she wasn't sure if Phames would even believe her. "Change him mentally. Like the way I've lost my memories."

"Well," Phames said, frowning, "probably. Maybe that's how they're controlling him. If he can't remember who he is, then it'd be easy to get him to do what they want him to do." He glanced at her again, significantly, but she pretended not to have seen. Did he think that she was acting strangely because Liiran had told her something? Some kind of lie? Did he think that Liiran was somehow controlling her?

Preposterous. Liiran wouldn't have the first clue how to control or change her.

"Maybe," she said "That would make a lot of sense."

But she wasn't so sure. Nothing really explained how frightened and helpless he'd seemed, not at all what she'd expected to see in a vox of war. And not at all what Phames had described either.

She only hoped that if it were a spell of some kind, they would be able to break it.

Chapter 34

Certos sat in the darkness beside his master, gazing at the human's face as he slept. The night seemed to stretch on without limit, but he had no urge to do anything.

The castle was cold and a little drafty, but this didn't bother the vox, either. A room had been found for them at the castle, but Certos knew it was only a matter of time before they found themselves on the battlefield once more. Stone walls gave humans an illusion of security, but this was war, and enemies were everywhere.

Certos hadn't mentioned that, from a tactical perspective, it was far easier to get at Garelon through a window in a sparsely inhabited stone castle in an open city compared to penetrating a city of thin-walled tents filled entirely with the equivalent of armed guards.

Foolishly, no one had asked him for his input. But more importantly, it didn't matter, since Certos himself was still here to guard Garelon.

But then there was movement at the window, and Certos looked up. He saw a soft light, human-shaped, white wings spread wide. Niveus beckoned him from outside and Certos swallowed hard, sitting up obediently and inching carefully off the bed. The magic didn't compel him to obey, but habit was strong, and there were other kinds of penalties for disobeying Niveus.

Garelon didn't stir, even as the vox of war spread his own metallic wings and they chimed softly.

He stepped towards the window, opened it an inch, then slid through the tiny space, and found himself outside, the chain trailing down.

Niveus caught the end of it, and Certos' eyes narrowed.

"Come," Niveus murmured in their common language, and the voxae flew together, up and up, finally landing on the roof of the tallest tower. Niveus folded his great feathered wings against his back, brilliant against the starry night sky.

It hadn't been long since they'd last seen each other, during the interview in the room just below. Certos crouched low, his eyes averted, wondering what the nivevox wanted to see him alone for. In all the years since he'd been captured by the Circle of Magi, they hadn't been alone together very many times. To him, Niveus seemed almost like a human most of the time, talking to them, working with them, always busy and distracted like them.

Maybe he'd become violent and unpredictable like them, too. Maybe he was angry at Certos, and wanted to punish him for something, but knew Garelon wouldn't want to do it.

"Certos," Niveus said. His voice didn't sound angry, at least. He took two steps towards him and crouched down, trying to catch his eye. Certos cringed and tried to keep still. Better not to look, better not to seem to care at all.

"Certos, I just wanted to talk to you, without your general here. It's all right," Niveus said. His voice was silky smooth. Certos knew that tone well. It was the tone Niveus used when he was trying to persuade someone to do something they didn't want to do.

Well, he didn't want to talk to Niveus, so that was logical.

"Yes, sir," Certos whispered, staring at an old bit of shingle, at a couple of tiny xhovox determinedly wearing away at the edges.

Niveus wound the chain loosely through his fingers, though it was pointless. Niveus couldn't control Certos using the human magic, the way Garelon now could. Each human who had touched the leash – Hason, then Altus, and now Garelon – gained that power, breaking his connection to the previous one.

Still, whether Niveus held it or Garelon held it, Certos wouldn't try to escape. Though it looked slender, it had a very real hold on him, and was a part of the collar that kept him tame.

Mostly tame.

"I'm not going to punish you, Certos," Niveus said. "I just want you to tell me honestly what happened tonight."

Certos sighed and began a dull recitation of everything he had heard and seen, right up to and including his retaliation. He would have liked for Niveus not to know that he could resist the collar a little, but it was obviously too late for that, if Niveus had gotten reports about the mob. From what Niveus had said to Garelon, it was clear he knew.

Niveus listened in silence, utterly still down to the fingers of the hand which held the chain. A light breeze ruffled their hair, clothes and wings, but that was all, until Certos finally finished his narrative. He didn't mention the argument he and Garelon had had afterwards, either. That was private.

"So Garelon has won your loyalty, has he?" Niveus asked. "How is that possible?"

Certos pursed his lips. "I told you, he's nice to me."

"Why should that matter to you?"

At this, Certos felt anger flare inside him. His head jerked up and he glared up at Niveus with sudden heat, his wings flaring and clattering. "You don't *know*," he said. "You sit there in your office, friends with humans, doing whatever you please. You don't know *anything* about what you've done."

"What I've done?" Niveus murmured. He seemed almost pleased by Certos' reaction, but Certos was too angry to wonder why, and too angry to be afraid.

"Yes. Capturing Mortis and I. You don't know what... what it's like. Is this what you wanted?"

Niveus was just staring at him, looking bemused. "I'm about to win, Certos," he said. His voice was soft, though lacking that silky tone it had before. "Surely you know about winning."

Certos twitched as if struck, and looked down again, the anger draining out of him. Even he could make tactical errors, at least in areas where he was weak. Interpersonal skills – human interaction – were hard for him.

"Yes," he said in a more subdued tone. He had lost, of course. That was what Niveus had just reminded him. He had lost badly, and had kept on losing for three hundred years, until it was hard to remember what it felt like to win.

Niveus gazed at him for several minutes, the time long past what would have been awkward for a human, but for them, it was a blink. "I never wanted to create this out of you, though," he said, in a tone that sounded – even to Certos – apologetic.

Certos didn't know what to say, so he said nothing, staring down at the shingles as if Niveus hadn't spoken.

After a while, Niveus stirred again. "Did Hason hurt you so badly?"

"Hason..." Certos murmured. "Hason's human. He gets angry if I misbehave. He wishes for me to be obedient, and silent and unobtrusive when he doesn't need me. I did what I was instructed."

"You hate him, don't you?"

"Yes." The single word drifted on the wind, calm and almost unemotional.

"He died," Niveus said. "Many of those in long-term care have died – perhaps most of them – since Mortis escaped."

Certos smiled with true pleasure. "Good."

"But Garelon's different? Truly different? And you'll obey him even still?"

"Yes, Niveus," Certos said. Obeying Garelon was as easy as scattering. He *wanted* to make him smile with approval. "That's right."

Niveus sighed and straightened up. "Very well," he said. "I believe you. Come now, I'll take you back to him."

Certos didn't question why Niveus had believed him now, why he was willing to accept this. He merely straightened and followed in response to the tug at his throat, back towards the only man who had ever treated him decently.

Chapter 35

Garelon was awake and pacing the room when Certos finally returned. A flash of light outside the window caught his attention, but he had no time to react before Certos was through and landing lightly on the floor, his wings chiming like bells as he folded them against his back.

His shock at Certos' return was genuine. When he had awakened to find the boy gone, he had been certain that despite his words, Certos had found a way to escape.

And he couldn't honestly claim that the way his heart had started hammering was out of fear for his job. After all, if their weapon had disappeared, escaped out from under his very nose, the least he could expect to get would be a reprimand, but that thought didn't occur to him until he saw Certos' bare feet touch the ground.

No, he'd been afraid to have *lost* Certos. He didn't like to admit it aloud, but what ran through his mind was that he had vanished from his life, like Orphas had.

The way his heart leaped again when he saw Certos once more, only made it harder for him to deny it.

"Where did you go?" He tried to sound stern and then wondered if that was entirely too fatherly.

Voxae ma, that conversation with Niveus had messed with his head.

Certos cringed back, but Garelon caught his hand and tugged him forward into a tight hug.

He expected the feathers of Certos' wings to be dangerous, to be hard, with sharp edges. But as he wrapped his arms around they felt as soft as real feathers, though they chimed together as he disturbed them.

Certos remained tense for a few seconds, but slowly relaxed and put his arms around Garelon in return.

"I thought you'd left," Garelon whispered. "Where did you go?"

"I... I didn't mean to," Certos said in a very soft, tremulous voice. "Niveus ordered me to come to him."

Garelon frowned. How had Niveus done that without waking him? He couldn't have been *that* tired. The prime minister couldn't have come into his room to give that order. Could he somehow command Certos remotely?

It bothered him that anyone could give orders to Certos without his knowledge. "He wanted to question you further, without me there as a buffer, didn't he." He released the boy, drawing back enough to look into his face.

Certos nodded, and Garelon grimaced. "Are you all right?"

The very question felt like treason, but he couldn't help himself. Though Niveus had made his protestations that he had no desire to be cruel to Certos, he had been the one to enslave him in the first place. And Altus was always around, complaining if Garelon showed Certos the slightest bit of courtesy. Either of them could have added to Certos' mistreatment, added to the reasons why Certos flinched away from Garelon as if he were going to be struck.

"N-no, sir. He just asked me more questions, and I... I told him what I told him before, that I protected you because I want to stay with you. He asked me about Grand General Hason, and how he treated me, and asked me how you treat me."

This startled Garelon for a moment. "He wanted to know if I treat you well?"

"Yes, he wanted to understand why I want to be with you, but I hate Hason."

Garelon nodded, not questioning the word 'hate'. He was getting to hate Hason a bit, himself, and he had always liked the man when he encountered him professionally. He had seemed friendly enough, though with a professional demeanor that he had always admired, and was widely known as a brilliant tactician. But clearly he hadn't treated Certos very well, and most of those tactics – if not all – were clearly to Certos' credit, not Hason's.

"He also said that Hason is dead," Certos whispered. "He and many others in long-term care have died. I guess he thought I would like to know."

The simple, almost innocent words struck Garelon like a sledgehammer. He thought for a moment that his heart had stopped, the pain in his chest was so acute. "Died?" he choked. "How...how many others?"

Certos shifted, looking up at him with what looked like concern. "He said maybe most of them."

Garelon straightened up abruptly and turned towards the door, not caring that he was wearing nightclothes, not conscious of his bare feet.

There was just one word that drove him at a run towards the door. *Orphas.*

"Sir?" Certos was right behind him, and caught his hand. "Sir, what's wrong?"

"My... my son," Garelon said, stopping in his tracks as if caught by a chain. How could the boy be so strong? He fought to free himself, but Certos clung to him stubbornly. "Did he say if my son..." He couldn't get the words out, and rounded at Certos. "Did he say what happened to my son?"

Certos' eyes were wide and he shook his head quickly. "No. He... he didn't say."

"I have to go," Garelon said, running his free hand through his hair twice and then trying again to tug his hand from Certos' grasp. What could he do? If Orphas was dead now, he had been as good as dead long ago. But he felt as if he needed to run to his rescue. "I need to ask him. I just need to know."

"He's not there," Certos said. "He's not in the tower where we saw him before."

The words snapped Garelon slightly out of his fugue. "Where is he, then?"

Certos pointed mutely towards the window. "Outside. He hasn't returned to the castle."

Garelon gaped at him. "How do you know that?"

"I can sense his location, sort of," Certos said earnestly. "But it'll be faster for me to find him for you. You can stay here and I'll ask him about your son."

And Certos spread his wings, moving quickly towards the window.

"Wait!" Garelon exclaimed, as his mouth caught up finally with his floundering brain.

Certos stopped as if his feet were glued to the ground and turned, his eyes wide in a white face.

Garelon stared at Certos. Could he let him go? He was showing so much initiative.

But there was only one answer. When it came down to it, he didn't care if Certos betrayed them, compared to his concern over his son. He nodded slowly, then, in case Certos needed a more explicit order after being ordered to stop moving, he opened his mouth.

"Yes. Go." He swallowed. "Please, Certos."

That was apparently enough, because Certos spread his wings and arrowed for the window, barely beating them at all before slipping back out again.

The agony Garelon went through was worse than it had been on the day of the accident. He paced the tiny room, measuring it with his strides, his hands clenched tightly behind his back as he waited for news. It reminded him of pacing for hours during the surgery, only to learn that it had been too late, that his son had suffered brain damage and needed to go into long-term care, but that he would awaken as soon as a cure was found for his condition... He had wanted to cry. He had wanted to punch the apologetic doctor in the face. He hadn't been the same since that day, and he knew it.

The only thing that kept him from breaking down now was the fact that Certos came back within minutes. Ten minutes, which felt like an eternity, and Certos slipped back through the window.

"What did he say?" Garelon asked before Certos' feet had even touched the ground. He clenched his hands together so hard they hurt with the effort not to grab Certos and shake him until the answer fell out.

"He's dead," Certos said, the words so painfully blunt, but his eyes wide with fear and uncertainty.

"Oh..." Garelon whispered, no swear word or invocation strong enough for the stab of horrible pain that went through him at those two simple words.

He felt pain in his knees and realized he'd dropped down to the stone floor. Tears slipped down his cheeks and he covered his face with his hands. He'd cried just once since his son had been hurt, but no one had been there to see it, then.

A few moments later, he felt small hands on him, slender arms going around his shoulders. He shuddered and wrapped his arms tightly around the boy, burying his face against that bony shoulder. The floodgates opened and he shuddered as the sobs burst forth.

Pain such as he'd never felt choked him, but then slowly, very slowly, began to ease.

Certos held him as he mourned his son, mourned the death two hundred years before, mourned the time he had squandered, hanging onto him in vain.

Chapter 36

Niveus glided down, down a long flight of stairs. As he walked, the light slowly grew dimmer. The lamps that hung at intervals along the stone walls were spaced more and more widely as he descended, but he didn't need light to see. He imagined it had been designed this way to terrify prisoners as they were dragged down these steps, and he regretted that it had been necessary to place anyone down here, particularly someone he had known for so long and who had been of such assistance to him.

When he reached the bottom, he strode up the hall, which was lined on both sides with heavy, steel-banded doors. Each one had a small window at eye level, but he passed them without pausing.

The silence was broken only by the muffled sound of sobbing behind one of the doors.

There were no guards – they were unnecessary. Aevi was here for her own protection, not because she had committed some crime. He had decided it was for the best, this way. Assassins had already attacked Garelon, and it was clear to Niveus that there was a security problem. Altus had summoned Calam to assist, but he wouldn't arrive until the following day. Altus and Maenos had been unable to shed any light on the situation.

Also, while madness wasn't something that the nivevox could fully understand, it had occurred to him that if he placed Aevi in a high tower to protect her, that she might just jump.

A character had done that in a book he'd read once. One of many human things he had experienced over the last few centuries.

Better not to risk it. Better to keep her safe in this dark and soothingly silent place.

He reached the door and knocked, hearing the sobbing hitch and pause.

"Aevi, it's me."

"Niveus?" Her voice was tremulous, nearly inaudible.

He drew a key from his pocket and turned it in the lock, then pulled the door open. A lamp had been hung high on the wall of the small room, driving back the darkness that would have otherwise been almost total. There was a small cot in one corner. Someone – probably Maenos – had thoughtfully provided a sizeable pile of books. But they sat stacked against a wall, untouched as far as Niveus could tell.

Aevi sat on her cot, her tearstained face turned towards Niveus as he entered the room. Her eyes looked hollow, sunken in her face, and far too large for it. Her hair was unbrushed and wild.

Niveus sat down on the edge of the cot. His fingers twitched and then he gave in to the impulse that seized him, and reached out towards her. He smoothed his fingers through her unkempt hair and withdrew them, leaving it smooth and shining in the lamplight.

Her eyes closed with a look of rapture on her face, as if he had caressed her. "N-Niveus, I'm sorry," she whispered.

He shook his head, folding his hands in his lap. Poised and unconsciously perfect, he was like a marble statue next to the trembling human with tears still rolling down her face. "Aevi, what happened? What's put you in this state?"

She drew a breath like a shaking sob, and lowered her face into her hands. "P-please... please, don't. I can't..."

"Can't what?" he murmured, his voice carefully sympathetic. "I'm not angry at you, Aevi. There's nothing to be afraid of."

"Yes, there *is*!" she cried, suddenly loud. Her hands clenched into fists, fingernails dragging over her cheeks and leaving angry red lines in their wake. "Yes! Everything is going to end! And it was all my fault!"

"Your fault?" His hands shot out and grabbed hers, prying at her clenched fists. "Aevi. Aevi, calm down."

She sobbed and screamed and fought him for several seconds. But the vox held her hands tightly, holding her still. "It's my fault! We'll all die, and we should all have been dead a long time ago!"

"Are you scared of Mortis?" Niveus shouted over her ravings. "Is that what you're afraid of?"

"No! Yes!"

She made no sense. He wanted to run, to fling himself from the room and flee in the face of this chaotic emotion. But he was the vox of order. He could *impose* it.

He took a breath and *pushed*.

Aevi's screams cut off with a choking sound, her tight, tense and shaking body slumping against the wall and her head lolling to one side. Her eyes stared glassily up at him and for a horrible moment he thought he had killed her.

Then she drew a soft breath and let it out, her eyes sliding shut.

"Aevi," he whispered. His hands still held hers, but they were no longer clenched fists, slack in his grip. He folded her hands together and held them gently in both of his. "Tell me."

"Altus. He made me help him, make the voxmar."

"Yes, yes," Niveus said. "So there's no need to fear, Aevi. We'll capture Mortis again."

"No." She shook her head fractionally. Another tear slipped out from under her eyelid and tracked down her cheek. "We should never have done it. It's wrong."

"Not at all," Niveus said, a touch of severity in his tone. "Aevi, you are brilliant. None of the great things we've done could have been possible if you hadn't made the advancements you did."

"I always loved you," Aevi whispered, and Niveus' blood suddenly ran cold. Love? What nonsense was this? "I thought you were so beautiful. I thought with you, everyone would be safe and happy."

"That's what I want. Have you forgotten, Aevi?"

"No," she said again, shaking her head. Her voice was still eerily calm, forced into it unnaturally by the influence of the vox, but he could feel her turbulent emotions still bubbling under the surface, a maelstrom of conflict he wasn't strong enough to eradicate completely. He had tried, in the past, but such changes were too fundamental. What was left would be no longer human.

He leaned closer to her, squeezing her hands in his own. "Then why are you so upset? What's wrong with you?"

"I always loved you," she said again. "But now I know you're bad, you're wrong for us. Everything you've done is wrong. And I helped you do it."

He straightened, a pulse of foreign emotion running through him, now. "I'm bad? That's ridiculous. What's wrong with a world where things run smoothly? Where there is no grief, or anger, or fighting? How can you question this now, when we're almost done?"

She shook her head. "You're wrong, and that's why I betrayed you. That's why I helped Altus. But now I can't help him anymore, either. I won't be able to help him stop you, or Mortis. I'm not strong enough."

"Betrayed me?" Niveus sat back. He had suspected Altus, but Aevi? "You have?"

"Maybe they will be enough," Aevi went on. She spoke as if she didn't know anyone was listening. "Maybe they will be strong enough without me to summon Niveus and Mortis, and lock them away forever."

Niveus jumped to his feet, backing away with revulsion pulsing through him. How many of his magi had betrayed him? Impossible! And why now? Why was she talking like this?

"I'm sorry, Niveus," she whispered. As he moved away from her, his unnatural influence over her lessening, she turned her face against the wall and began to sob once again, her words growing indistinct. "I'm sorry for what I did."

As he reached the door, he could no longer understand the words she spoke through the sobs, though he thought he caught one last phrase before he closed and locked the door once more.

"I hope she takes me soon."

And he had no doubt who Aevi meant.

Mortis.

Chapter 37

As Maenos hurried through the castle, an envelope clutched to her chest, key words from the memoranda she had read over the last few hours ran through her mind at odd moments. Phrases like *"moved to the castle for his protection"* and *"emotional outburst during surgery"* and *"precious cargo should touch down by mid-afternoon"*.

Everything was coming together in its own ponderous way, but like all important political operations, it was also on the edge of falling apart completely at any moment. Now, with Aevi in the dungeon, things were truly teetering on the brink.

She reached her destination and knocked. At the quiet "Come in", she opened the door and saw Altus at his desk, waving away a strange haze. The room was filled with the stench of scorched paper.

She closed the door. "Altus, I just came from seeing Aevi."

He rose to his feet to greet her, looking grave. "How is she?"

"Not good." Her lips pursed around the words. "A complete mental breakdown, I think."

"She's always been fragile," Altus said, grimacing. "Why she had to pick *now* to lose it—"

It was just too much. "A little compassion, Altus!" Maenos snapped, feeling her cheeks pale with a combination of horror and anger at his callousness. "Aevi is our friend."

"And we're relying on her to help us capture the nivevox," Altus said impatiently, "but she's allowed her emotions to get in the way – as usual."

"Some of us *have* emotions, Altus. For vox's sake—" Despite her anger, that smell of burning paper was distracting, and she wrinkled her nose. "Is something burning?"

Altus seemed glad for the distraction. He picked up an odd writing implement he'd been using, holding it up with pride. The metal nib was faintly glowing with heat, and a long, slender voxmar was embedded in the side of the wooden casing. "My invention. I call it a copen. Careful of the tip, it's very hot. It uses the heat of the covox to burn the paper, creating indelible text, like a laser printer that you can write with."

"It stinks," Maenos said, far too annoyed to appreciate its dubious value. "What's wrong with a ballpoint pen? We've used them for centuries."

Miffed, Altus capped the copen and pocketed it in his robes. "I prefer this. Pens are antiquated, and this is a magical age. In a few decades, everyone will have forgotten all about ballpoints."

Maenos rolled her eyes. Magic had enriched their lives in so many ways, but Altus had an obsession that frankly worried her. If something could be done with magic, he scorned any other type of technology. Instead of cars that belched smoke and ran along the ground, Laxam had brought the world airships. Every appliance now had a magical equivalent, and the world had gone mad for them.

But there were exceptions. Under Altus' leadership, guns had become all but unused by the Laxam army and police, since no one had been able to figure out a way to keep the recoil from shattering the voxmar that powered them. Yet once upon a time, people had manufactured gunpowder.

Even as a mage herself, Maenos sometimes wondered if magic was really making the world a better place. Altus wouldn't hear of any alternatives, though, and as Niveus' right hand and Maenos' direct boss, his preferences had all but controlled research and development for centuries.

It was a war she couldn't win, and she let it go, clenching her hands together tightly. "Anyway, I think we need to call this off."

"What?" Altus visibly stiffened. "Are you insane? The voxmar is landing in a few hours. We can't call it off."

Maenos lifted the envelope in her hand, waving it at him. Inside was the ritual Aevi had developed. "Aevi's done a great job cutting down the number of magi needed, but her ritual still calls for four powerful magi at the cardinal points. Without her, we have only three."

"I'm well aware of that, but everything is in place. We *must* do it now, or I'll have to begin planning again."

"Voxae ma, Altus!" Maenos exploded in frustration. "People are dying. Shouldn't we take care of Mortis first?"

"It's not as though *we* are going to die. Calm down. It'll all be taken care of in due course."

Maenos felt her cheeks pale. How could he be so uncaring? "I'm not afraid that you and I are going to die. I just don't understand why we're wasting time on Niveus right now. Doesn't it matter to you at all that people are dying out there?"

Altus drew in a breath. He looked as if he were barely holding himself together, and for the first time Maenos wondered why. "Of course it matters to me. But the simple fact is, I *cannot* call it off now."

"But—"

Altus pointed towards the window, his arm visibly trembling. "There is an assassin out there, right now, Maenos. She's already tried to put a knife in Garelon. I have no way to contact her, do you understand? If she doesn't have her chance at Niveus, whom do you think she'll come after next? Are you hearing me, Maenos?"

Maenos felt her breath catch in her throat. Altus had hidden yet another critical part of the plan from her. "An assassin?"

Altus nodded. "She's an integral part of the plan, but not one that was necessary for anyone to know about other than me." He leaned forward towards her, and Maenos had to resist the urge to recoil from him. "This is happening. We can either profit from it, or go down. Now, you will scour this place for someone to take Aevi's place. We can't contact the others – there isn't anyone we can trust for something like this who can get here without alerting Niveus."

He rubbed his lips thoughtfully. "It has to be someone local. Can you get placement records from the University? There has to be a third-tier mage with some talent and some discretion within six hours of here. There *has* to be."

There was nothing for it but to obey. She forced herself to nod, numbly, and then a thought occurred to her, and she felt relief spread through her body. "I think the governor is third-tier, and he's got some talent. We worked together on a paper once. He's a good man."

"Then get him. And make sure he doesn't screw things up even further." His voice turned soft, more sympathetic. "Once Niveus is dealt with, Mortis will come next. I promise. You have nothing to worry about."

With a shaky nod, Maenos left to carry out his order. She was just as glad to escape his presence, her stomach twisting with revulsion.

As she walked, for not the first time, she thought of going to Niveus and confessing it all. But just as quickly, as she had every other time, she discarded the thought. In the eyes of a vox who didn't understand human emotion, she would be just as culpable.

And if Altus weren't in charge, if he were imprisoned for treason against the prime minister, what then? There'd be no one left to oppose Niveus, to rein him in.

It was far too late. She had to see this through, distasteful as it was.

Chapter 38

It was like a dance, a ritual, a set of motions honed and practiced for centuries, all culminating in a single event that could change everything with the flash of a blade and a spurt of blood.

The ritual consisted of strapping blades to limbs; rubbing dust on skin to mute colours; dressing in loose, concealing clothing that blended with stone, brick and concrete. It consisted of moving through the city to a bolthole previously identified and concealing herself in that place, where she could watch the comings and goings and wait for the right moment.

Varil shifted faintly on the balls of her feet, an automatic gesture, barely visible from a distance of even a few feet, but enough movement to ensure she wouldn't get a cramp. She could stay still like this for hours – and had done so in the past – almost invisible against the colours of the urban jungle, and barely moving.

She had been waiting for several things – for darkness, for the change of the guard, for Turil to give her signal. When all the various factors came together in just the right way, then she would act.

A thick mist had been gathering all day, which would make getting to the building easier, but which made it harder to see what she was doing. It lay like a white blanket over everything, swirling and eddying in the cross-currents created by the wind swirling around buildings and stirred up by passing motor vehicles.

Turil was in the castle itself, posing as a maid cleaning bedrooms, sweeping floors, carrying dishes. Even Altus didn't know she was there.

But Varil was the one who would be let past the guards, the one expected by their treacherous friend, who would be given the clearest opportunity. So she would go, and if Altus betrayed them then, and only then, Turil would act.

Even as she ran this through her mind – that was part of the ritual as well, going over the steps of the dance to come so that when the time came she wouldn't mis-step – she saw it.

There was a flash of white at a window, a set of curtains being pulled back and a window being opened. Turil was in position in a small antechamber above the main audience chamber.

At that same moment, the guards at the door went inside. Now there were no guards at all on this side of the building. Varil knew she had only seconds, that the planned mistake in the change of the guard could only buy her a minute at most when she could get into the building without being seen.

Varil darted forward, a silent shadow on her slippered feet, invisible in the fog. She knew Altus would expect her to go through the door he had prepared for her, but she veered to one side towards a small window on the second floor, which Turil had unlocked earlier.

She leaped upwards as she reached the wall and scaled it as easily as a spider, her fingers digging into the worn stone and finding holds invisible to the eye. She reached the window and pushed it upwards, clinging to the sill with her other hand, the rubber soles of her shoes planted on the wall.

It rose up without a squeak, and Varil smiled. She slipped through the window into a bathroom, dropping down to the tiled floor with no more than a light plopping sound.

Before she moved to the door, she closed the window and latched it. She was inside, but Altus wouldn't know where she was.

Let him stew in fear as he waited and wondered if something had gone wrong with his precious plan. It was no more than he deserved.

Chapter 39

The Talgar War Room was massive. A huge table dominated the lavishly appointed room, surrounded by high-backed chairs. The walls were draped with tapestries depicting great battles of the past, some of them portraits of assassins with knives picked out in silver threads. Others were great battles set upon on green velvet fields outside the shining silver walled city.

Talgar had never been expansionist, but its people had jealously and fiercely defended their own lands over the centuries, since right back to the beginning of recorded history. As such, it wasn't surprising that the table bore a scale map of the city itself and surrounding lands. The map was touch-sensitive, and Garelon could make various areas light up and even zoom in to examine details.

It was the best possible place to plan and execute an offensive in the mountains to the north, short of actually being there. After Hason's death and now the assassination attempt, being on the battleground was not an option this time.

Right now, though, Garelon was just distractedly zooming in and examining the city itself and the area where the battle had taken place, pretty much at whim, without any real purpose. The day had gone well, so he'd heard, and they had broken through in several places, advancing the front right into the mountains.

Guerrillas had harried them all day, and there had been many deaths – something that Garelon's direct subordinates had struggled to keep quiet – but they had achieved the goals Certos had set them and that meant it was a victory.

The thick fog provided by the weather magi had given them a definite edge, but the tactic had been unwieldy and difficult to control. Now even the city was covered in a thick soup of fog. It seemed certain that the Monson Alliance was all but defeated. By spring, anyone left in holes in the mountains would have starved – assuming Mortis hadn't been recaptured by then – or been driven by hunger into the lowlands and arrested if she had.

Yet Garelon couldn't dispel his depression.

I'm just at loose ends because I'm used to being in the thick of things, he told himself, determined to set the feeling aside and ignore it. He had argued at length to be allowed to go back to the front, but Niveus and Altus had been immovable.

Glancing up, he studied Certos, who was sitting at the opposite end of the table. The boy was examining the map of the castle with curious eyes, expanding different parts and roving through the map apparently randomly. Perhaps he'd never seen a table like this before – certainly Garelon didn't think even Niveus had one this nice.

"Do you want to play a bit of chess?" Garelon asked. Getting a sound thrashing at chess didn't really sound like much fun, but at least it might distract him from his malaise.

"Hmm?" Certos murmured, eyes still focussed on the table. Garelon's eyebrows rose. He'd never seen Certos this distracted and unresponsive except when he *was* playing chess.

He raised his voice a little. "What are you doing, Certos?"

Certos jumped and glanced up at Garelon with a strangely furtive look. "I'm just... watching."

"Watching what?" Garelon got to his feet and walked around the table. He looked down at the map Certos had been playing with, but didn't see much of interest. And why should he? It was a planning device, not a true reflection of what was happening in the real world. There would be nothing there except what he or Certos put there, and the battle had been taking place miles away.

Certos shifted. "Something's happening," he said. "I can feel it. Someone's planning something. They're coming, now, with death on their mind."

Garelon felt himself go cold as suddenly as if a bucket of water had been upended over his head. Certos had felt the assassin coming for him the first time.

"Another assassin?" he asked, and as Certos nodded, he cursed roundly.

"Where?"

Certos frowned and pointed, his finger wavering around a wing of the second floor as if he knew the general area but not exactly.

"I think there. I'm not good with single people, but the plan has many people involved, so I feel *that*. But they're not coming for you,

Garelon." Garelon felt the boy's deceptively fragile hand grasp his own. "It's all right. You're safe."

Garelon couldn't say he wasn't relieved at that, but it didn't really end the matter, though it was obvious that Certos felt it did.

"Whom are they coming for, then?" he asked, his heart beating a rapid tattoo in his ears.

"Niveus," Certos said, then frowned again. "And...Altus, I think."

Garelon tugged his hand free. "Why didn't you tell me sooner?" he demanded, and knew that he had gotten too heated as Certos cringed in his chair.

The way the boy didn't respond, biting his lip and dropping his eyes, was sufficient to communicate the reason to Garelon. He probably couldn't care less if either of them died.

"Come on," Garelon said, modulating his tone with an effort. "I have to go warn them."

"But..."

Garelon wasn't interested in his protests. "I'm going to warn them, and that's final." He hesitated, then reached out and lifted Certos into his arms. He had to suppress a gasp, marvelling at how light he was. He scarcely felt the weight. Certos caught hold of the swinging end of the chain attached to his collar and wound the chain about his wrist to keep it from getting in the way.

"Yes, sir." At least he didn't sound afraid anymore.

Garelon left the room at a dead run, his arms full of vox and his heart pounding. He was pretty sure Niveus was in the main audience chamber, probably with Altus and possibly others from his inner circle. A talented assassin could probably take out several important people in one fell swoop if they attacked without warning. But it wasn't far from where he was right now. In the time it would take to send a messenger, he could be there himself.

He only hoped he could get there in time.

Chapter 40

"I've seen this report already, Altus," Niveus said, flipping through the pages and then setting it aside on the small, spindly legged table at his right hand. He had appropriated the throne room for the day's work – it was only right. Garelon and Certos had been in the War Room, and Niveus was here with his grand minister, runners bringing the news throughout the day in the form of thick reports that didn't really mean much in the grand scheme of things.

The room was huge, with many columns and rich tapestries. The vaulted ceiling was three stories high, and a long gallery ran around the upper level, draped in rich fabrics that just obscured the velvet seats where – he presumed – interested observers could have watched the queen make her pronouncements when she held Court.

Such an antiquated, *human* sort of place. All pomp and circumstance, and no real substance.

Niveus rather liked it, despite that. The rich colours were cheerful, and evoked a sense of power. As did the way he could watch each beleaguered runner trot all the way up the hall before finally reaching him. Not to mention the way the high-backed and richly carved chair was raised up on a dais, putting him slightly above everyone else. When Altus had suggested he use it, he had seen the value in it.

It was rather tempting to change his capital to Talgarora, after all this, though he would miss Laxamora, the city he built practically by his own hands.

"Oh, yes. Sorry, sir," Altus said, whisking that report away and then putting another one into Niveus' outstretched hand. "I think this one has some additional figures on the last few pages. You might want to read the beginning again to refresh your memory?"

Niveus gave him an irritated look, but pretended to read. Altus was acting *nervous*, and it was very distracting. More importantly, he was being very illogical, urging him to re-examine reports he had read already, as if the nivevox were capable of forgetting something so quickly.

As if he were trying to keep him here as long as possible, instead of retiring to his tower room or taking a relaxing flight, now that the sun had set.

The game was afoot, it seemed. And Niveus could only wonder what he was waiting for.

Well, he'd play along. He could easily insist on heading up to his tower room, but the game was so *obvious* right now that it seemed more hazardous to change the rules. He didn't know what Altus would do in that event, so better to play it safe, walk the clear path, and see what lay at the end.

He didn't have to wait much longer.

As he reached the end of the report he had *indeed* already read from cover to cover, a sound made him look up.

It was no more than a whisper, just a patter of slippers, and the sensation of something not quite right entering his sphere of influence. His head jerked upwards and he saw a woman leap off the balcony railing from the gallery above.

She'd somehow gotten to a balcony within twenty feet of the throne before showing herself. In the second between when he noticed her and when she landed on the tiled floor just five feet in front of him – having ricocheted somehow off of one of the smooth pillars to slow her descent – he wondered how many guards she'd killed to get that far.

She landed catlike on both feet and braced with one hand, her hood falling back to reveal a red sweep of hair caught up in a high ponytail. In her other hand she held a knife, the blade flashing in the havox light, wickedly curved.

Niveus rose to his feet as she launched it at him. The blade whistled past him, slicing through his right sleeve, and burying itself in the back of the throne with a ringing clang.

"Prime Minister! This way!" Altus seized him by the arm, pulling him backwards to put the throne between himself and the savage assassin.

Niveus' first instinct was to scoff. "It's not necessary—"

But Altus was insistent. "Let the guards deal with her. If she gets away, and knows what you are..."

Indeed there were soldiers converging on her from every direction. The woman whirled, kicking out with one foot and tripping one of the men, then plunged another wicked knife into his throat. Niveus felt the man's life flee as he gurgled on blood, but she hadn't stopped moving, using her own momentum to carry herself past the guard and out of range of the other men's swords.

Altus had suggested that Niveus' personal guards equip themselves for close combat only, so as not to damage the furniture or accidentally out his secret with badly aimed bolts. The suggestion had been made weeks ago, long before Niveus had suspected any hint of treachery.

Now he had an idea of just how well this had been planned.

But he was walking Altus' path, and there was nothing more he could do but see how far down it went.

"Let's go," Niveus said, moving to follow Altus before the woman could kill all his guards and turn her attention on him. There was a small door, he knew, concealed behind the throne. It was to this door that Altus pulled him, and he willingly let himself be led.

But just before they reached it, a side door about ten feet to their left flew open and Garelon burst through, holding Certos in his arms. "Sir!" the general exclaimed, setting the small vox down. "Certos felt something."

"You're too late," Niveus said. Altus shouldered the door open and went through, still holding tight to Niveus' arm. "She's already here. I'll be fine."

There was renewed shouting behind him and he looked back in time to see the woman launch herself at him from the top of the throne, red-stained blade flashing.

There was a queer moment when Niveus just stared at her, more interested than frightened – of course, he had no need to be frightened. Then he felt a solid impact as Garelon pushed him out of the way and stepped in front of the woman's blade.

Certos yelled, and Niveus caught himself on the wall. He lunged to protect Garelon, and felt the knife tear through his suit jacket and into his arm. But Altus still had a grip on him, and pulled him off course. "This way!" Altus shouted, and Niveus stumbled to one side, and through the door, which slammed closed behind him.

He could have slipped out of the human's grip easily, but he didn't. Garelon would have to take care of himself.

Then he was running down cool, spiralling stone steps, Altus just in front of him in the dimness, the mage's hand clamped hard around his forearm, with no idea where he was being led.

Chapter 41

Altus' breaths whistled in and out of his lungs harder than he thought was normal for the exertion as he raced down the cold stone steps. Pure adrenaline pounded through his veins and he felt his free hand curl into a tight, angry fist.

That bitch, Varil.

First she had kept him waiting until he despaired of her ever showing up. If Niveus had gotten impatient and headed up to his tower, the whole plan would have failed. There was no way he could have gotten Niveus into this corridor from the tower room – he had scarcely managed to get the recalcitrant vox to listen as it was.

And of course Niveus had had to be arrogant and decide he didn't need to worry about taking a knife to the chest, since he wouldn't die of the injury. Thankfully, Altus had managed to disabuse him of that idea, but only just in time. She had nearly reached them, and he was just grateful for the fortuitous timing of Garelon's arrival with the certovox.

He realized with regret that the man was probably dead, now. After sending one of her psychotic women after Garelon the other day, Varil would scarcely balk at killing him now, even if it cost her a few seconds before chasing her true prey.

He hadn't quite expected her to dispatch *all* the guards, either, even if he had reduced their complement to give her a better chance. The idea had been for her to be arrested after he and Niveus had taken their leave, not for her to kill them all and still come after them.

Even as their footsteps echoed against the stone, Altus listened hard for any sign that the assassin was chasing them. Of course, he likely wouldn't hear a sound until she buried the knife into one of their backs. Thankfully, that back would likely be Niveus', and then Altus had little doubt that the vox would turn on her and rip her head from her shoulders for ruining his fine white suit jacket.

Still, even knowing that, he couldn't relax. There was every chance she would kill Altus first, or somehow screw things up in a different way. He had to get to his destination before she caught up.

Even as he had the thought, Altus felt the steps even out, and they were running along a low-ceilinged tunnel, stooping slightly when the ceiling sloped down even further. The floor was largely earthen, though the walls and ceiling were shored up with stone.

"Where are we going?" Niveus asked. Despite the fact that they were theoretically running for their lives from an assassin, he sounded calm and collected.

"It's a panic tunnel, sir," Altus said. There was scarcely any light at all, few torches on the wall as it was, and at least every third one cracked and lightless. "I believe it opens out into the city."

"Hmm," Niveus mused. "Well, I do hope Garelon's all right."

"I'm sure that the certovox will preserve his life again," Altus said, though he wasn't sure of that in the least.

"Yes, quite."

The last of the lights were left behind as they turned a corner and ran into a more open space, utterly pitch black. Niveus hesitated, but Altus plunged forward without slowing, trusting to momentum to carry Niveus to the correct spot before he could realize what was happening. Voxae could see in near-total blackness, but this was dark even for him.

Five long strides, and they were dead centre in the room.

"Goteru sadakeba voxmaria!" Altus called commandingly, and the room blazed with light.

The magical circle that had been inscribed on the floor, each rune gouged out of the dirt and stone with painstaking care, flared with a white brilliance. Niveus cried out and threw up a hand to shield his eyes, and Altus let go of his wrist, stepping quickly out of the confines of the circle before the vox could recover. His own eyes were streaming, but he wasn't as badly off as Niveus.

Calam, Maenos and – yes, as he had hoped, the Talgaroran governor, looking nervous and confused – stood at the cardinal points of the circle. Their faces seemed pale and gaunt in the harsh white light, except for Calam's of course, whose chiselled features were cast into sharp relief and were, as usual, impossible to read.

Altus moved quickly to take up the fourth position. "Careful, everyone," he said, focussing his attention towards the vox in the centre of the circle as his eyes adjusted. "With only four of us it'll be more difficult than the last time. We have to get him into the voxmar before he manages to break out." The gleaming glass bulb in question sat on the floor beside the vox, waiting.

"A-Altus," Maenos said in a strangled voice, but Altus didn't have time to deal with her insecurities right now. Niveus lowered the arm he had used to shield his face from the bright – and apparently painful – light, and he glanced around the room at the faces of his Ministers.

"Calam," Niveus said, "I think we have what we need."

"Yes, sir," Calam replied, "we do."

"What—" Altus had barely opened his mouth to protest when he felt rough hands seize his arms and pin them behind his back. A plastic strip was cinched around his wrists and pulled tight before he could even begin to struggle.

*   *   *

Three hours earlier...

Niveus observed Calam exiting the airport, and waited as the man lit up one of the thick, blunt cigarettes he favoured. His clothes were loose and ruffled in the breeze that came down from the Talgar mountains. His bald head caught the sunlight, the black lines of his tattoos crawling over the dark skin and breaking up the yellow gleam.

While he puffed on the cigarette, two police officers stepped outside, escorting a handcuffed and hooded prisoner between them. After them came four people in mage robes, pushing a huge crate on a hover sledge with obvious care. A police van pulled up and both prisoner and crate were loaded onto it.

After overseeing the operation, Calam dropped his cigarette and crushed it under his shoe, then stepped forward – not to join his staff in the van, but with his eyes on an approaching taxi. Niveus put his own car into gear quickly and pulled forward to block Calam's way. The man stopped short and Niveus rolled down the window.

As the tinted window descended, Calam caught sight of the prime minister and his eyes widened with obvious surprise and dismay.

"Get in," Niveus invited him, and smiled with satisfaction as Calam obediently pushed his suitcase into the back seat, then slid into the car.

Niveus pulled smoothly away from the curb and merged onto the road, distinctly aware of Calam's gaze, watching him. After Aevi's chaotic emotional displays, Calam's quiet observation was like a breath of fresh air.

He knew that even though Calam was obviously burning with questions, he would wait for Niveus to speak before addressing them. Niveus took his time.

"How was your flight?" Niveus asked.

"Good," Calam replied.

"Your cargo arrived just fine, I see." He had no idea why they were transporting Mortis' new voxmar – for that's what it must have been. But he took satisfaction in pretending not to be ruffled by it.

Calam shot him an uncertain look. "Yes."

Niveus couldn't help but smile. He knew the man hated wasted words.

"Ask your questions, Calam."

Calam didn't hesitate once permission was given. "Why did you come to pick me up, sir? And alone. You have no security detail."

This question didn't come as a surprise. "I wanted to talk to you," Niveus said, "with no observers or interruptions. I've had a bit of trouble getting away from Altus lately."

Calam had excellent control over his face, and the tattoos only made him more difficult to read. But his eyes flickered before he turned away to watch the scenery passing by.

"What did you want to talk to me about, sir?"

Niveus hesitated, wanting to frame this question carefully. The biggest trouble with betrayal was questioning where one stood with everyone.

"I had an interesting conversation with Aevi... She's having a difficult time coping with recent developments. But in any case, I got the impression that you know something about me that I never told you."

"I know quite a few things about you that you didn't personally tell me, sir," Calam said.

Cagey, as usual, Niveus thought, more amused than annoyed. "Do you know that I'm not human, Calam?"

Calam was silent for a beat. "Yes, sir."

"And who told you that?"

216

"Grand Minister Altus."

"When?" Niveus murmured.

"A couple of days ago."

"So, shortly after Mortis escaped her confinement."

Another beat. "Yes, sir, I suppose that's true."

The two men drove on in silence for a short while. They had passed out of farmland now and slowed to a relative crawl as Niveus threaded the white sedan through the narrow city streets of Talgarora.

"I have always treasured our friendship, Calam," he said finally.

"Have you, sir?" Calam replied in a carefully neutral tone.

Ah, as I suspected. "I also know you treasure honesty and trustworthiness."

"I do."

Niveus sighed. "I realize now that I should have told you myself. To be honest, it's only Altus and Aevi who ever knew of my true nature. I discussed the question of who else might be appropriate to tell, and Altus advised that we keep the information to only the three of us."

Calam darted a look at him. "When did you have that discussion?"

Surprised by his tone, Niveus glanced at him. "Long ago, before I had even been elected prime minister."

Calam's lips thinned. "Altus claimed to have only learned you were a vox a few weeks ago."

Niveus didn't smile, though he felt a rush of triumph. Calam wasn't happy with Altus, that much was obvious. "He lied," he said simply. "Altus was in on it from the beginning. I met Aevi first, as she was doing her research on us, the more advanced voxae, and met Altus soon after. The three of us developed the plan, and I began impersonating a human. By the time I met you, after I was elected and we were preparing to capture Mortis and Certos, it had long been decided that none of the other Circle members would be told."

The silence that fell over the car this time was heavy, but Niveus wasn't concerned. He waited a few minutes, giving Calam some time to mull it over, and hopefully get very angry at Altus, then spoke again, quietly, his voice barely more than a breath.

"Calam, what is Altus planning?"

Calam's response came without hesitation. "He intends to gain control over you, like he did with the others. He wants to be prime minister."

The answer didn't come as a complete surprise. Niveus did, after all, know Altus. He did feel a burn of anger, however.

But that was the way with humans. They were unpredictable, petty and treacherous. He had been using those traits for his own ends for centuries, and it wasn't surprising that they were now turning around to bite him in turn.

"Calam, we've been associates – if not friends – for a very long time," he said. "Can I trust you?"

Dark eyes turned towards him from the passenger seat. The walls of Talgar were passing overhead, casting a shadow over the car as he rolled through the gate. The plates on his car told the guards all they needed to know to wave them through without stopping. There was little chance of the assassin who had attacked Garelon hiding out in the prime minister's vehicle.

"I gave you my loyalty first," Calam said.

Niveus smiled, but it was a grim expression. At least he still had one trustworthy ally in this whole mad world. "Excellent."

*   *   *

As Altus stood frozen, his world was crumbling around him, he watched as both the governor and Maenos were pushed forward a step, stumbling a little. He could now see that they, too, had their hands cuffed behind their backs, and secret police officers were holding them.

Calam stepped forward as well, and scuffed at the floor with one boot. A rune damaged, the magical light began to fade, and Niveus stepped out of the circle with a slight curl of disgust and irritation coming to his lips. The prime minister straightened his tie, and made a gesture to his police dog, Calam, who nodded once.

"Grand Minister Altus, Minister Maenos, Governor Moraiil," he said formally, "you are hereby arrested and charged with high treason and conspiracy against the prime minister himself. You are immediately removed from your positions and will be placed under armed guard until the disposition of your case."

Altus couldn't believe this was happening. All this had taken place in mere moments, and he could still feel himself gaping like a schoolboy, staring at the shining white man in front of him who had somehow ruined all his plans when he had *had* him in his grasp.

"How... how did you...?" he gasped in a strangled voice. And then it hit him. "Aevi. Or... or was it you?" He shot a glare at Calam, who merely stared at him unblinkingly.

"It was Aevi," Niveus confirmed. Damn him, there was even a hint of a smile on his lips. "But we can discuss it in more detail later, Altus." He gestured to the guards. "Take them to the dungeons. But be careful going out into the throne room, since there is a bit of a scuffle going on there."

"But he was in on it!" Altus cried, jerking his head desperately towards Calam.

"Yes," Niveus said, unruffled, "he knew. And you did a decent job of manipulating and lying to him. Fortunately, I do a better job." And now Niveus smirked, outright.

There was no point in protesting innocence. His head swam and he felt nauseous as three hundred years of life and work evaporated in an instant. Maenos only looked miserable, her dark eyes cast towards the floor and guilty expression creasing her delicate features.

The guard behind Altus pushed, and he had to turn away from Niveus and Calam just to keep his feet and see where he was going. They headed back into the tunnels, and they seemed to close suffocatingly around him.

Chapter 42

As Niveus and Altus fled, Garelon somehow managed to pull his sword out of its scabbard just far enough to block the assassin's next lunge with her wildly flashing knife.

She made a soft, urgent sound of frustration, and lunged at him again, but this time he freed his sword and her knife skittered down the blade until it hit the hand guard. Tiny springs in the guard let go at the impact and traps snapped out, pinning the knife blade.

The two fighters clasped both hands around the hilts of their weapons and struggled to rip their enemy's from their grasp by brute force. Garelon would have expected to win such a contest easily against the shorter, slight woman, but she was in excellent shape, evidently, while he was no longer in top fighting trim.

He was aware of several things as they struggled. The door behind him had closed, and he could only hope that Niveus and Altus were getting further away by the moment. Certos stood nearby, watching with obvious distress, jerking this way and that with each of their movements as if looking for an opening to intervene. There were faint groans coming from behind the woman, so not all the guards were dead, but none of them were rising, either.

"Garelon, be careful," Certos exclaimed suddenly, a split second before the woman's foot came shooting upwards. Garelon jerked backwards reflexively, then heard his pants rip and felt a bright line of pain drawn up his thigh. A tiny blade stuck out of the end of her boot.

The woman cursed softly and Garelon shoved forward, trying to keep the pressure on her so she wouldn't have a chance to try the blade again.

"Certos," Garelon said, pushing forward step by step and watching the woman's face contort with irritation as she was forced to take a step back, and then another. If he could just get her back to the throne and pin her, he might be able to take her prisoner. Maybe.

Voxae ma, how in Mortisor was he going to get out of this one?

"Yes, sir?" Certos replied eagerly.

"Go... go get help." The woman's eyes narrowed and she kicked out again. He grunted as the knife buried itself in the meat of his thigh, but the moment she regained her footing he stamped on her foot with all his force. She opened her mouth in a silent scream and he hoped he'd broken her foot, if not the blade.

"But sir—"

"*Go!*" Garelon roared, certain that Certos would do anything to save his life, but there was little the vox could do in this situation. There was no mob to kill this woman, and Garelon would be caught in the crossfire anyway. His heart squeezed at the necessity, but he was a general. He knew how to give orders. "I order you to go. Now! Get help!"

There was no acknowledgement but the patter of bare feet as Certos fled.

"That the way you talk to your son?" the woman said, her voice almost a grunt as she struggled against his greater weight.

Garelon nearly miss-stepped, but realized quickly what she intended by the remark, and he pressed forward again, glowering at her. "He's not my son."

Her mouth twisted wryly, and she tried another tack. "What happened to my blade sister, Garelon? We know she wasn't taken prisoner."

"My 'son' killed her," he said. Then, hoping to catch her off guard, he heaved at her, trying to barrel her back the last few steps to the throne and trap her. But she grinned and he found himself stumbling. She had let go of the knife, and he tottered forward, trying to catch his balance, his sword off-balance with the knife still trapped by the hilt.

The assassin danced out of the way of his blade, out of his immediate line of vision, and he felt the hairs on the back of his neck rise. He caught himself on the cool wooden back of the throne and whirled around, but she was nowhere to be seen.

He looked around wildly for a moment. She hadn't gone through the door after Niveus and Altus, or he would have heard it. With a flick of his finger, he released the knife from the catches, and it clattered to the floor at his feet. He panted for breath, and his neck prickled. But he still had no idea where she was.

"Up here." He heard her voice and looked up, seeing her perched on the top of the throne, right above his head, with two knives in her hand. She flashed him a smile, and the knives whistled through the air.

Garelon dived away, feeling the knives miss him by a hair.

Certos, hurry, he thought as he turned and raised his sword up to meet more flashing blades as she dived towards him. He backpedalled wildly, just trying to stay ahead of the knives. *Please hurry.*

Chapter 43

As Liiran came awake, a cool hand smoothed back his hair in a gentle rhythm. The room was well lit, the lamps shining through his eyelids as he regained consciousness.

"I finally woke him." It was Mortis' voice. He opened his eyes and found her looking down at him from only inches away.

His eyes didn't seem to be working right, but after a few blinks he managed to bring her face into focus. "Mortis," he murmured, but it came out indistinctly. He felt like he was swimming upwards from very deep water, and he wondered how long he'd been asleep.

"How do you feel?" she asked. In the white havox light, she looked oddly drawn and shadowed.

Experimentally, Liiran sat up and swung his legs over onto the floor. His head swam, but stilled almost immediately. He yawned and his jaw cracked explosively, then he stretched and heard his back crackle. He felt as if he had barely moved in hours. But he was feeling more alert and awake by the minute.

"A lot better," he decided. "How long have I been out?"

"Almost twelve hours," Phames said with deep resentment. "Are you able to move?"

Liiran looked up at him. "Yeah, I think so. Where are we going? Did you find Certos?"

The two voxae exchanged uncomfortable glances. At that moment, Liiran noticed that they were alone, that Varil and Turil weren't in the room. He wondered uncomfortably if they were off trying to kill Niveus.

"We found him. But there's something wrong with him. We think they've put some kind of magical compulsion on him," Mortis said.

"Compulsion?"

"We figure that's why he's willing to obey them," Phames said.

"What are we going to do about it?" Liiran asked. This was way out of his area of expertise.

"We're not sure," Mortis admitted, "but we hope that even if Phames and I can't do anything about it, you will be able to break it somehow."

Phames muttered something indistinct.

"Me?" Liiran echoed, startled. "Why would I be able to?"

"Well, you're human, aren't you? Magic only affects voxae," Phames said.

"But I'm not a mage. I don't know anything about magic."

Phames sneered at him. "Look, you wanted to come, and now we may have a use for you. You're going to pussy out now?"

Liiran opened and closed his mouth for a moment. "No, I'll do my best," he said. What else could he say? Phames was right that he had wanted to come, and up to now, he really had felt like nothing but a drag upon them.

"It's a good thing Liiran's here, isn't it?" Mortis said pointedly, looking at Phames.

The phamevox grunted, but gave a curt nod, and Liiran figured that was probably the most acknowledgement that he could expect.

"But after all this we are staging a prison breakout and all three of you voxae are going to help. We need to get my friend, too," Liiran said.

Phames looked for a moment as if he was going to object, but at Mortis' look, he glanced away. "Fine."

Liiran let out a breath. "So when is this happening?"

"Now," Phames said, and Liiran nearly choked. "Turil and Varil have already gone to prepare. You're lucky to have woken up in time. Are you sure you're able to come?"

You mean that you're lucky – if you really need me to break the spell on Certos, Liiran thought, but there was no point in baiting Phames. Instead, he hesitated, doing a thorough internal check. Now that he felt fully awake, he realized that he did feel miraculously recovered.

"Yeah. I really think it's going to be fine. I feel totally healthy." His face twisted wryly. "Though I could eat a horse. Is there any food?"

"We brought you some food," Mortis said.

"And it can be eaten on the way," Phames added. "But if the injuries are healed then you should break the connection now."

Liiran opened his mouth to ask what Phames was talking about, then felt Mortis' arms tighten around his neck and realized that Phames was talking to her, not to him.

"What connection?"

"I can't do it right now, Phames," Mortis said stiffly. "That would be foolish."

"What are you talking about? Look at you! It's sapping your strength. Why wait another moment?" Phames said.

"What connection?" Liiran asked, a little more loudly.

"Because I don't know what will happen when I do. I don't know if it'll hurt Liiran – I don't know if it'll hurt *me*. I can't take that risk right before we need to go rescue Certos. It's a critical time."

"*What* connection?" Liiran exclaimed. The two voxae looked at him.

"I'm sorry, Liiran, I should explain," Mortis said. "When I saved your life, it connected your life force to my essence."

"And that's why you're healing so fast. Feeding on Mortis somehow," Phames growled.

Liiran's jaw dropped. "What?" He jerked to one side, shifting enough to look at Mortis' face. It hadn't been his imagination – she was definitely looking drawn and tired.

She smiled softly. "I'm fine," she said. Then she turned to Phames again, her expression hardening. "Honestly. After this is all over, we'll figure out what to do about it. But now isn't the right time to be experimenting with dangerous magic."

Phames looked mutinous, and Liiran gave Mortis a hard, searching look, but she seemed determined.

"Fine," Phames said again, with his usual poor grace. "Then let's get this over with before you get even weaker." With that, he stomped towards the door.

Liiran made a face at his back, then turned to Mortis. "*Are* you all right?"

Mortis smiled and laid a hand on his arm, then rose to her feet. "I have to be. Come, Liiran. Let's go."

Once he was up and dressed in fresh clothing that hadn't been slept in, Liiran followed the two voxae through the fog-covered city, over the rooftops and the wall into the inner city via a route Varil had shown them. Then Mortis hugged him around the waist and they flew up to the castle, to a high tower with wide windows. Phames opened one of the windows and they all scrambled through.

Liiran glanced around curiously. "So, where now?"

"This is where I saw them," Mortis said, folding her wings against her back tightly before they disappeared.

Phames prowled the room in a restless manner, like a cat, and then opened the door, revealing a stone staircase heading down in a tight spiral. "Can you feel him, Mortis?"

Mortis closed her eyes for a moment, her brow furrowing in concentration, then she nodded. "I have him."

"Let's go," Phames said, starting down.

"Feel him?" Liiran's question echoed oddly off of the stone walls as they jogged downwards. Phames was in the lead, his own wings invisible as well, and Liiran right behind him, while Mortis brought up the rear.

"He's a vox, and a powerful one, and he's very nearby," Phames said. "For some reason, he feels different from the way he used to – probably the magic they're using. But Mortis knows what he feels like, now, so she can lead us to him."

"If vox can sense other vox, doesn't that mean Niveus can find us?" Liiran asked, and was met with a grim silence for a moment before Phames replied.

"Probably he won't be looking."

Somehow that didn't really reassure him. Though Liiran reflected that at least Niveus would likely be distracted by the women trying to kill him – for about ten seconds, anyway, before he blasted them to dust. Or whatever he could do. He wondered what nivevoxae *could* do, then realized he was only distracting himself from his task when he nearly ran into Phames, who had stopped at the bottom of the stairs.

"Shut up," Phames whispered. "Lead the way, Mortis."

Liiran followed the two voxae down the stairs and into a hallway, feeling horribly exposed. If anyone just happened to come around the corner – a guard, or even a maid – surely they would know they were intruders the instant they saw them.

But the castle did seem very quiet. Maybe they would be lucky.

Yeah right. After everything we've been through already? Our luck isn't that good.

"Shouldn't we steal some uniforms or something?" Liiran suggested as they skulked down another stairwell and down a hall.

Phames glanced at him with a mixture of disgust and confusion. "Why?"

"Uh..." It sounded stupid even in his head. "Never mind," Liiran said, abashed.

They had to dart into rooms four times to avoid people. Mortis gave warning each time and they ducked into an empty room – once into a broom closet, which was thankfully empty but still extremely cramped with the three of them pressed tight into the tiny space.

They rambled all over, it seemed to Liiran, but generally going down each time they reached a stairway. He began to wonder if Mortis really did know where she was going. Then she gave another of her low warning noises, a soft murmur in a language Liiran couldn't understand, and Liiran heard the rattle of blades against armour a moment later.

They were standing in a hallway lined with doors. Liiran quickly reached for the doorknob of the nearest room. As the door opened, Phames instantly slipped in through the crack, and Liiran put a hand on Mortis' shoulder to draw her in after, but she shrugged him off and raised a finger to her lips.

"You have to hurry! Garelon is in danger!" The words were pitched a little high, like a young teenager whose voice hadn't yet broken.

"We're going as fast as we can," a deeper voice said. "Who did you say you were?"

"I... I'm his son." The lie in this was obvious even to Liiran, at a distance, and he wondered why the boy would lie about something like that. Then again, it sounded to him as if the kid was terrified, and now he wondered what a young boy was doing in this half-deserted castle in the middle of a war zone.

Then Phames emerged from the room again and darted past him. Liiran lunged for him automatically. *Is he crazy?* he thought, but clamped his mouth shut on a cry to call him back. He watched as Phames slipped out of the hall right after the last of the guards had gone past, and grabbed the boy's arm, covering his mouth with his other hand.

The boy struggled, but Phames dragged him back towards Liiran and Mortis. "In," Phames said, and they all dove through the door, the whole operation all but silent and taking only seconds.

Liiran privately wondered whether the obviously irritated guards had simply ignored the little scuffle, or if it had been covered by the sound of their passage.

Phames let go of the boy once they were in the room, a small parlour with a couple of chairs set around a small coffee table. The room had no windows, being deep in the interior of the castle. The boy whirled around and backed up a few paces, putting a clear distance between himself and his abductors.

Then he paused and stared at the three of them. "Phames! Mortis!"

And only then did Liiran realize that *this* was Certos.

He also realized that Mortis had drawn close to him, almost shielding him from the small, fragile-looking vox.

"We're here to free you," Phames said in a low, rapid voice.

Certos' eyes darted from Phames to Mortis, and then landed on Liiran. He looked terrified.

"Who are you?" the boy asked, his eyes narrowing.

Liiran hesitated, then came forward when Phames waved at him impatiently. "This is Liiran Uwis. He's just a... well, he's a friend of Mortis' and he's not a part of the government or anything like that. They're trying to imprison him, too."

Certos' eyes narrowed with distinct distrust. "Well, what's he doing here? It seems very stupid to bring a human in here right now."

Liiran ignored the triumphant smirk Phames shot at Mortis, who rolled her eyes.

"I'm here because we weren't sure what kind of magic was going to be used to keep you prisoner, and I might be able to break it," Liiran explained, trying to pitch his voice soothingly. He didn't know if Certos really was a child in some way – though now that he was speaking, he didn't sound childlike at all – but he did at least seem scared and there was no need for that.

"Are you a mage?" Certos asked.

That brought Liiran up short. Obviously the only answer to give was the honest one. "Well, no. I'm a journalist, actually."

"Then I think you're all sort of stupid," Certos said, and strode straight towards Liiran, glaring. Liiran had to almost jump out of the way, not sure what the vox intended, but he just went straight by him, headed for the door. "I don't have time for this now."

"Certos," Mortis caught him by the shoulder. "What do you mean you don't have time? Time to be rescued?"

He shrugged her off and yanked the door open. Liiran noticed as he lifted his arm to turn the doorknob that he had a chain wrapped a dozen times around his wrist. "I have to rescue Garelon. You can come if you want, but I'm not staying here right now," he said.

228

And, while the rest of them stared at him in shock, he vanished out into the hallway.

"What the—" Phames said, and darted after him, Liiran and Mortis following after in close pursuit.

Certos raced down the hall ahead of them, seemingly determined to catch up with the guards, his feet silent on the stone floor. He didn't try to hide or avoid his three would-be rescuers, but he did cast annoyed glances back at them as they caught up.

"Isn't Garelon the new grand general? What are we rescuing him from?" Mortis asked, with a calm air that seemed incredible to Liiran under the circumstances.

"An assassin is trying to kill him right now. Only she's only after Niveus, so after she kills Garelon she'll probably get herself killed, because it's not as if *he* can die, and Altus is planning something. I just don't really know what, but I'm sure the assassin is just a distraction." Certos said all this in a matter-of-fact rush that seemed incongruous given the seriousness of his words.

"But, aren't we rescuing you from Garelon?" Liiran blurted out. None of this made any sense.

Certos eyed him sidelong and didn't answer.

"Certos!" Phames exclaimed hotly. "What has gotten into you? Let's *go.*"

Huge double doors opened ahead of the column of guards and they marched through without pausing, the three voxae and Liiran following doggedly behind.

"Garelon ordered me to get the guards and come back," Certos said.

And that was when Liiran understood what was going on, and his blood ran cold. "Voxae as nema uto," he swore. "He's brainwashed, or being controlled by that collar or something. We've got to stop him and take that damn thing off, or he'll just wind up leading us right to Niveus."

It seemed that Phames had thought of the same thing, because he lunged for Certos before the words were all out of his mouth.

Certos opened his wings, forcing Liiran to dive to the side, feeling the feathers brush his clothes as the wings spread wide. The feathers looked like knives, and sounded like them as they clattered together as well. Then Certos was aloft and out of reach.

Both Phames and Mortis exploded into the air, arrowing after Certos, who winged his way across the room towards the far end. It was a huge gallery, the vaulted ceiling three stories up at its highest point, so there was more than enough room for the three voxae to fly.

Liiran watched the three voxae dip and dive around the room, Certos evading the other two by inches, and moving faster and faster, until all Liiran could see were blurs that hurt his eyes to try to follow. He looked around and saw a furious melee breaking up at the far end of the room, a tall man with no uniform coat on and carrying a sword limping towards Liiran. There was blood staining the front of his leg and his shirt was torn, but he walked quite erect.

Behind him, a woman with red hair was being restrained by three guards at once. Liiran realized with a shock of recognition, but not surprise, that it was Varil. She was fighting like a wildcat, but the guards had forced a pair of handcuffs on her and were trying to take off her boots without getting kicked. Liiran saw a flash of light glint off of the boot and realized she had a knife attached to it somehow.

He took a confused step towards her, then stopped. What could he do to help? He wasn't even armed.

"You there." The bleeding man had addressed him, and was walking towards him as quickly as his injuries allowed, eyes narrowed. He had a rather intimidating face, with a square jaw set in harsh lines, and light-coloured, flinty eyes. He raised his sword, pointing it at Liiran. "Who are you?"

Liiran began to back away. He opened his mouth to answer, but little came out. "Ah..." He didn't have a ready lie. The man continued to advance.

Then suddenly there was a rush of air and Certos landed next to the man, falling straight to his knees. "They're trying to take me away from you, sir!" Certos said, cowering and all but clinging to the man's leg.

Liiran stared up at Grand General Garelon as Phames and Mortis landed, the three of them facing Garelon and Certos.

Now they stood in a standoff. Liiran was glad to have Mortis and Phames at his back, but he didn't know how they could possibly rescue Certos at this rate. Was this whole trip a waste?

"You're under arrest," Garelon said, his eyes still focused on Liiran. "Will you come quietly?"

Liiran's stomach roiled. This was one of the ones who had trapped that poor kid, who had brainwashed him, who was after Liiran and all the people he loved, and who had locked Mortis in a bottle for three centuries. He certainly looked like that much of an asshole from where Liiran was standing.

"What about them?" Liiran asked, jerking his head to indicate Mortis. "You can't arrest them."

Suddenly a new voice rang out through the room.

"I don't think they'll be a problem much longer."

Liiran hadn't even noticed that a large group of people had entered the room at the far end. More guards had entered, along with several other people, some of whom he recognized as members of the cabinet. And at their head was Niveus himself. It was he who had spoken, a wide, arrogant smile twisting his face.

"Well Phames, I had a feeling you'd show up," Niveus said, but he had eyes only for Mortis. "And Mortis, of course. Are you quite all right, my dear? You've got magic clinging."

He snapped his fingers.

Mortis started visibly, and Liiran panicked. But whatever Niveus had done, it didn't seem to have hurt her. She only shook herself for a moment, then glared at the prime minister with a queer look on her face. "Niveus..."

Niveus stopped beside Garelon. "I figured the two of you had met up by now and would be here sooner or later. I would have prepared a better reception for you, but I was a bit distracted."

Now he looked Liiran over in a way that made him feel about six inches tall. "So you're the one that's got Calam in such a tizzy."

The huge man was a pace behind Niveus. Liiran recognized the name and went cold. This was the man he's spoken to briefly at the police station – and his appearance fit the voice he remembered. He wasn't quite glaring at Liiran, but only because his face was so stony that Liiran couldn't detect any kind of expression. There was definitely a tightness around his eyes and mouth that was distinctly unfriendly.

"I was only..." Liiran started, but his voice came out a little weak, his throat too dry to form the words. The scuffling had now ceased and Liiran sensed rather than saw the prisoners – including Varil – being marched past him by the guards. He swallowed hard, to clear his throat.

"I was just trying to get my damn life back, Prime Minister," he said, as coldly as he could manage.

"And how did you expect to do that," Niveus replied, his lips curving in a smile, "while travelling in the company of death?"

Liiran gaped at him, stunned by the nerve of his words. But he rallied quickly. "You haven't caught me, yet!" Surely with Mortis and Phames with him, he could still get out of here. There were windows... somewhere. They could flee on the wing.

Niveus eyed him. "Haven't I? Calam, you brought someone with you, to prepare for this eventuality, didn't you?"

Calam nodded. "Mr. Uwis, at an undisclosed location in the castle, we are holding your friend, Tanen Siitar. If you don't surrender yourself to me immediately, my next order will be to execute him." His eyes flicked to Mortis, and he gave a nod. "And I expect you know that an execution now would mean true death for him."

Mortis grabbed Liiran's arm, but he shook her off, staring at Calam. Was he lying? Even if he was lying about where Tanen was located, he definitely could carry out his threat.

Liiran's mouth was completely dry. "I... I want to see him."

Calam's dark eyes bored into Liiran's. Whatever Liiran could see there, he saw no hint of a lie. "I make no guarantees. You *will* surrender. Now."

Triumphant, Niveus was already turning away, addressing a spare guard. "Take him with the others," he said, gesturing towards Liiran, and the uniformed man approached with handcuffs at the ready.

"Liiran," Mortis exclaimed. He looked at her. Was her skin always so papery-white? She looked ill, or terrified.

"It's okay," he said through numb lips. This had been coming for so long, hadn't it? How many times had he already been arrested, and now Mortis was paying for it by keeping him alive with her own essence. They *had* to break that connection, and rescue Certos and Tanen, and deal with all of this shit, but he couldn't do anything. He needed to buy time for Tanen, for Mortis and Phames to figure this out.

Rough hands grabbed him, and he didn't resist as he felt the cold metal circlets lock around his wrists.

Niveus glanced at Mortis and Phames. "He'll be surety," he said, indicating Liiran with a flick of his hand. "So long as I don't see either of you two again, he'll be safe."

Garelon bent and drew Certos to his feet, holding the gold chain connected to the collar around the fragile vox's neck. Liiran couldn't look away from him. Those cold grey eyes were locked onto his, and there was no remorse or doubt that Liiran could see.

That poor kid.

"Go on, I'll be okay. Find a way," Liiran said to Mortis and Phames.

Phames turned without a word and marched towards the doors, shouldering past the guards holding the other four prisoners. "Come on, Mortis." He sounded angry, and Liiran wondered if he blamed his presence for the failure.

Mortis hesitated. "Niveus, if you hurt him, I will destroy you in every way I can."

The prime minister waved a hand at her in farewell. "Hush, my dear. I have no reason in the world to harm him."

She gave him a hard look, then turned to follow Phames, her feet scarcely touching the ground as she darted past and through the guards like a wisp of smoke. And then she was gone, and Liiran was alone.

Chapter 44

Garelon hurried to follow the contingent of guards marching the prisoners away. They were a motley group – the grand minister, the two others Garelon didn't know, a Talgaran assassin with no shoes on and sporting a distinct limp, and a scared-looking man who apparently had vox friends. Garelon hadn't quite yet figured out how he fit into this mess, but when he saw the man, Garelon had figured the easiest thing to do was to arrest everyone he could and sort it out later.

Given how much planning Calam Veliir had obviously put into arresting the newcomer, Garelon felt he'd made the right choice.

He sheathed his sword, grateful that he'd taken the precaution to wear it. He was still bleeding, but he was only now beginning to become aware of the pain, and he pressed the heel of his hand to his thigh where the woman had kicked him with her boot knife, trying to staunch the flow of blood while continuing to walk.

He had been very, very lucky. She was good, but he had obviously hurt her badly when he stomped on her foot, and it had hampered her just enough. Otherwise, he was sure he wouldn't have survived long enough for the guards to arrive.

Certos was still sticking to his side like a limpet. "You're hurt. You should go to the hospital."

Garelon shook his head. "It's fine. I need to..." But what did he need to do? Did he really need to traipse about the castle, leaving a trail of blood? Adrenaline still coursed through him, but he knew he really should get the wound looked at.

Before he could finish the sentence, a hand landed on his shoulder and he turned to see the prime minister.

In stark contrast to Garelon himself, Niveus stood tall and calm, not a hair out of place. He certainly didn't look as if he'd been running. What had happened to him after he left the throne room?

Altus had taken Niveus away to protect his life, but now the grand minister was in handcuffs. It was completely baffling.

"Are you all right, Garelon?" Niveus asked. "You're limping."

Garelon felt Certos shrink away and grabbed the boy's shoulder with his bloody hand, keeping him close. "I'm fine, sir. It's shallow, and I'll attend to it once the prisoners have been secured." He eyed the man with a pointed expression, willing him to explain. But he wouldn't ask – it wasn't his place.

Niveus nodded, accepting his words without question. Garelon found his eyes drawn to Niveus' sleeve – the only place on him that wasn't completely put together. In fact, the white fabric was blood-stained and hanging loose from a nasty slice.

"What about you, sir? Are you all right?"

Niveus looked blank for a moment. "Of course. Why?"

"Your arm?" Garelon felt his eyebrows go up.

Niveus glanced down, looking at his arm as if he hadn't realized the cut was there. "Oh, yes, I'm fine. Er, I suppose one of the guards must have bled on my sleeve. See?" He spread the torn place and Garelon saw no sign of a cut, nothing but flawless skin.

But, your sleeve. Garelon almost spoke the words aloud, but then the realization hit him like a siege cannon bolt.

Niveus was a vox.

"Very good, sir. I'm relieved," he said, outwardly calm. Inwardly, he was shaken.

He found himself searching Niveus' face closely. He had seen the wings of the other voxae, seen them fly, but he also knew Certos could look completely human. He couldn't see any sign that Niveus was anything but human. But there was that almost eerie self-possession about him, that unruffled perfection that seemed too much to be real. He knew what it meant, now, and it unnerved him.

There was no sign of a collar, either.

"I wanted to thank you, Garelon," Niveus said, moving along with him down the hall. The tight knot of guards had gotten a bit ahead of them, and the two men lengthened their strides to catch up, though each step sent a bolt of fire shooting up Garelon's leg.

Garelon felt himself settle into parade-ground stride, though he was thrown off not only by the pain in his leg, but by the fact that Certos walked at his side, their hands clasped tightly. He didn't particularly want to talk to Niveus at all. It was too much to process, too quickly. The longer he remained in his presence, the more uncomfortable he became.

Somehow a vox was in charge, and the human most likely to have been managing what was going on was now just ahead, in handcuffs. Was Altus Niveus' handler, the way Garelon was for Certos?

"Thank me, sir? What for?"

"For coming to my rescue. That was a very brave thing you did."

Brave and pointless, apparently. "It was my duty to protect you, sir."

"Not exactly *your* duty, was it? I was surrounded by guards, who are far more easily sacrificed than a general." Niveus' voice was slightly bemused.

Garelon was silent for a moment, wondering if Niveus was fishing for something. "Nevertheless," he said finally, "I knew something was about to happen, and the guards were taken by surprise."

"Yes," Niveus said thoughtfully. "I was wondering about that. How did you know?"

With the question asked so blatantly, there was little Garelon could do but answer. "Certos sensed something was wrong, just minutes before it happened," he said. He felt Certos squeeze his hand. "He alerted me, and I came to stop it."

Niveus nodded, eyes widening fractionally. "I see. Well, I thank you. Things had gotten quite out of hand, and if it weren't for your intervention, they may have gone rather differently."

"I imagine so, sir," Garelon said. He hesitated. "At the very least, Grand Minister Altus might have been killed. She didn't seem very discriminatory."

Niveus glanced at him sharply. "Altus? Altus was paying her. I'm certain of that."

Garelon frowned. "But sir—" He stopped, confused. So that was why Altus was in chains, now? How could Niveus believe that Altus had paid an assassin to come after him? It wouldn't make any sense at all, if Altus knew Niveus was a vox. And surely he knew – he was a mage, and had been Niveus' right-hand man for the last three centuries. If Garelon figured it out, Altus had to know. "Why would he hire an assassin to come after you?" he asked weakly.

"Are you concerned that I've falsely accused him?"

A beat. He simply had to know. There was so much about this he was having trouble understanding. Why would Altus work for a vox? He obviously had such contempt for them, if he could be judged by his attitude towards Certos.

He drew in a breath, and took the plunge. "Altus is aware of your status, isn't he?"

There was a long silence. "My status?" Niveus' tone was light, but there was steel underneath.

Garelon dropped his voice so quietly that no one could have overheard. "The fact that you're a vox, Prime Minister. He knew that, didn't he? He had to have."

Niveus stopped dead, and turned to stare at him. The guards were getting away again. "You know," He sounded more bemused than angry, though consternation was thick in his voice. "Certos told you?"

There was no sense in denying it. "No, sir. I just figured it out a moment ago." Garelon drew himself up and stared coldly into Niveus' eyes, wondering if he were about to be arrested, too.

"Yet you didn't say anything immediately. It makes no difference to you?"

Even here, with so many thoughts swirling through his head, Garelon knew his answer. "Ultimately, it doesn't change anything. It's my duty to protect my superiors, no matter their race."

Niveus searched his face, and Garelon felt as if the prime minister were looking straight into his soul. "What about the human superior officers? Your duty to them doesn't supersede your duty to me?"

"You're the prime minister, not Altus Itolan." Garelon certainly hoped that was true, otherwise Niveus had just executed a coup, and both Garelon and likely also Calam were complicit in it.

"Altus plotted against me," Niveus said abruptly. "He was going to collar me like Certos."

"Then it's good that the plot was discovered and foiled," Garelon said. He only wished he could completely believe his own words.

Niveus was prime minister. He'd been elected, and he had been running the country all this time. Did it matter that he was a vox? The question plagued him despite his words.

"You're a loyal man, Garelon," Niveus said, and they moved on together again.

"I'm loyal to the Empire, sir," Garelon replied. *Not to you.*

Niveus seemed to understand the unspoken words, and he didn't look at him. "As it should be."

They moved on in silence, watching the guards up ahead move the prisoners through a wide junction between two corridors. Suddenly a door flew open with a bang and someone darted into their midst. Garelon caught only the momentary impression of a black figure before it disappeared from view. Screams and yells erupted from the tightly packed knot of people as pandemonium ensued.

Garelon, Certos and Niveus broke into a run, fire jolting up Garelon's leg with every step as he drew his sword. But he could do little in the tight corridor, filled with so many people.

"The prisoner! The prisoner is escaping!" someone shouted, and Garelon looked up to see two dark shapes running down the corridor, one of them limping badly, and the other helping them along.

"The Minister is hurt!" another person yelled, and then another voice, strangled and high, "Altus!"

Niveus was suddenly gone from beside Garelon, slipping through the crowd. Garelon followed in his wake. He was slower, as Niveus seemed able to slide between people too close together for anyone to get through. Garelon had to all but shove people out of the way.

"Hang onto the prisoners," Garelon ordered. "Don't let them escape. Someone go after the ones who ran off." He grabbed hard onto one of the other prisoners himself and pushed him into the arms of one of the guards, trying to count heads even as he moved. Several of the guards at the front of the group had already detached themselves from the melee and were racing down the hall, boots and armour clashing loudly. Calam himself was at the head of this group.

But Garelon knew that they'd never catch them. It was clearly the assassin who had escaped, and the other shadow must have been her accomplice.

Suddenly Garelon found himself beside Niveus again, in a circle of stunned men and women. The grand minister lay on the floor, half propped up in Niveus' arms, as the nivevox knelt on the stone. Blood bubbled from Altus' lips as they moved soundlessly.

A knife hilt jutted from his breastbone.

"Relax, old friend," Niveus whispered. "Accept her kiss." Garelon felt Certos press close against his side and he slipped his arm around the

238

boy, frowning. Niveus had spoken so quietly, that in the general confusion of regaining control over the prisoners and trying to recover the escaped one, Garelon was sure none of the guards had heard him.

Altus seemed to expend a great effort and opened blood-reddened lips to speak. "I was... never... your friend," he gasped.

"I know," Niveus said. Garelon felt a chill, though whether it was because of the words, or because of the possibility that Mortis had returned to take the life of the dying man and he had somehow sensed it, he didn't know.

Moments later, Altus was still and silent, and Niveus lowered his head to the stone and rose to his feet. There was more blood on his white suit. "Clean that traitor's body up," he said, "and secure the remaining prisoners."

Niveus turned away. He slipped past the circle of watching men like smoke, and headed down the hall. He didn't hurry, or move in any way that Garelon could see as unnatural, and yet he vanished from sight so quickly it seemed to be by magic. In bare moments, he was gone.

Garelon stayed with the guards and personally ensured that no more of them escaped, and didn't leave to attend to his own wounds until he had seen them locked into the dungeon. Calam returned, but said nothing, a silent presence as Garelon ordered his guards around. Garelon didn't care if there was any kind of conflict of authority between them, but Calam didn't seem to mind, either, as he raised no overt objection.

Nevertheless, they never found the assassins.

When Garelon finally left the doctor, with new bandages on his legs and arms, he felt like falling straight over and sleeping for a week. It seemed outrageous that he would have to run another battle tomorrow.

It seemed outrageous that anything should happen tomorrow. Today had been so strange, so many things had been turned upside down, that it seemed as if he was in another world.

The grand minister was a traitor, and he was dead. Actually dead. Niveus was a vox, and there was no one in the world who knew and cared but him and a couple of other traitors locked in the dungeon. At least, so far as Garelon knew.

Assassins were hiding in every shadow, it seemed, and Garelon didn't even know who the last prisoner was. The man who travelled in the company of voxae.

He entered his bedroom and began to undress mechanically, his fingers moving so tiredly that it seemed he could scarcely undo the buttons. Certos just watched him change, pale and silent as always.

Despite his exhaustion, as he sat down on the edge of the bed, preparatory for a long sleep, he couldn't help but broach the subject.

"They were trying to take you," he said. "That man, and the two voxae."

Certos sat down beside him on the bed and stared down at his feet. "Yes."

"Who were they?"

"Mortis, the vox of death, and Phames, the vox of decay, and a man named Liiran Uwis that I've never seen before," Certos said.

Mortis, the vox of death. Her release was why his son had...

No, he couldn't even think the words. But the strange developments over the last week were coming into focus. "And Phames? Why was he here?"

Certos shrugged. "We are friends. All three of us. Always."

Garelon sighed. Sometimes the things Certos said made no sense at all. But more disturbing were the things he wasn't saying. "I don't understand you. Don't you want to be free? You hate Altus and Prime Minister Niveus for trapping you."

Certos squirmed. His hand, enclosed by Garelon's fingers, closed into a fist. "Of... of course I do."

Garelon studied him. "Then why didn't you just go with them?"

"Because... because you needed me," Certos said unconvincingly. "You ordered me to go get help, and I was bringing the help back."

Garelon snorted. "You did that, and yes, I did order you. I'm sure you couldn't have disobeyed. But you could have gone with them after that. You had the opportunity, while the guards were subduing the assassin."

Certos was silent for a long time. "I... I don't know," he said finally, in a very small voice. "I'm scared. I used to be scared to stay, but I'm scared to go, too."

This was only verbal confirmation of something Garelon had begun to suspect long ago. He closed his eyes and leaned his head back against the wall with a sigh. "Is that why you didn't run away when Hason was injured? Is that why you didn't take the opportunity to run when the assassin came after me? It is, isn't it?"

"Yes," Certos said, with obvious reluctance. "I guess it is."

"If you don't leave, then Niveus will get everything he wanted. You'll win this war for him, even though you hate him. Altus is gone now, but Niveus is still in charge."

Certos looked up. "But you helped Niveus today. If you hadn't helped him, then he might have been put in a voxmar, and then we could have killed Altus, and all of it would have been over."

With a quick shake of his head, Garelon dismissed that idea completely. "No, Certos. My sense of duty wouldn't have allowed me to do anything of the sort, and you know that about me."

"...Yes, I do."

Silence fell over them for a few long minutes. "Are you content, then?" Garelon asked. "For this to be your life? Is this what you want?"

"What... I want?" Certos said, as if he hadn't considered that question before.

"Certos. Are you content with this, as it stands?"

Certos was silent for a long, long time now. Garelon was so exhausted, all he wanted was sleep, but he didn't move or speak. He sensed that the vox was thinking, really *thinking* about the answer to his question, and he told himself a hundred times as he waited that whatever Certos decided, Garelon would try to fulfil.

He – no, the entire Laxam Empire – owed him that much, at least.

Finally the boy spoke once more. "I don't think it's very nice that the man who tried to rescue me is in the dungeon. And I don't want Mortis to be captured again, or for Phames to be captured. I want Niveus to pay."

Garelon could think of a half-dozen things to say to this, some suggestions, some condemnation. All he said was, "So what are you going to do?"

"I... I want to help them," Certos said in a very small voice. "I don't want to help Niveus anymore."

Garelon nodded. "I will help you, if I can."

Certos looked up, his eyes wide. He didn't say it, but the question was obvious in his eyes.

Garelon was far from sanguine about any of it. *Do I even know what my duty is? What do I want to do?* He shook his head. "I may not be able to come with you, but I'll help you as far as I am able to."

"But I want you to—"

"Certos," Garelon said sharply, "sometimes we don't get everything we want."

Chapter 45

"Wait, stop," Varil panted as they ran down a cobbled alley some blocks from the palace, Turil's hand still tight around her upper arm. She had a stitch in her side, caused by trying to run with her arms cinched tightly behind her back. Not to mention that her foot was killing her. In the battle of slippers vs. military boots, boots had had a decisive victory.

There was also no way she was going to get over the wall – or past the gate – with handcuffs on.

Turil stopped obediently, and Varil bent over slightly, trying to catch her breath.

"Are you injured?" Turil asked tersely, catching Varil's wrist. Varil heard the clink of metal and a scraping, and one of the handcuffs sprang open.

Varil took a quick internal inventory. "Just my foot. Other than that, General Unitar managed a scratch or two, but that's all." The other cuff opened and she straightened, rubbing one chafed wrist with her palm. "What the hell happened?"

"Niveus Exalan obviously figured out that Itolan had betrayed him," Turil said. "Arrested him and his co-conspirators."

"We pretty much knew I was just a distraction for his plan, whatever it was, from the beginning," Varil spat. She stretched her arms out wide to work out the kinks in her shoulders. "Please tell me you killed him."

"Knife to the heart," Turil confirmed.

"I'm sorry I couldn't deal with Unitar, or Exalan," Varil said. "What a damned waste."

"At least Itolan is out of the picture."

Varil shook her head. "You should have gone for Unitar or Exalan. Or Calam Veliir. Itolan was going to prison, anyway."

"He knew too much about us," Turil said coldly. She was probably miffed that Varil had second-guessed her, but Varil was too frustrated to care much. She was right, though, much as Varil hated to admit it.

She sighed. "Yeah, I guess you did the right thing, at that." She turned to Turil. "Head north now. We have to report to the queen, and if you hurry, you may be able to get into the mountains before Itolan's men find out that we're not on their side anymore. Assuming that they were ever supposed to let us get back through the lines, anyway."

"They probably won't just let me go," Turil pointed out, but raised a hand to forestall Varil's next words. "I'll go right now, and kill anyone who tries to stop me. But what are you going to do?"

Varil hesitated. There were theoretically two options. She could stay, and try to complete her mission – with almost no chance of success – or she could go home in defeat and await another opportunity.

But that wasn't really the choice she was trying to make. She had seen something that Turil hadn't, and it weighed on her mind – how had Mortis and Phamile sprouted wings? What did it mean?

She quickly told Turil what she'd seen. As the other woman gaped in surprise, Varil made her decision. "I'll stay here. Try to see what I can do."

Turil nodded. "It'll only take one of us to ensure our Queen knows what happened here. You can stay here and learn more. Perhaps you'll have some kind of opportunity."

An opportunity like blackmail, perhaps. Either way Varil knew she *had* to know what was going on with the trio they had been helping for the last day.

"Right," she agreed. "Safe journey, Sister."

"May no one hear your steps," Turil replied. She put a hand on Varil's arm for a moment as she spoke the ritual parting, and then she darted out of the alley, vanishing quickly into the darkness. The unnatural mist had finally lifted without weather magi maintaining it, but the night swallowed her almost immediately, and Varil was alone.

And alone she felt – very alone – as she made her way over the rooftops and down to the outer city, and then to the door to their hideout. For a moment as she stood outside the door, she hesitated and wondered if the two would even be there. Perhaps they had gone somewhere else – flown away, or tried to hide in the castle to rescue Liiran. For a moment she hoped it was so.

Then she twisted the knob and opened the door, striding into the room to see the two sitting together on the edge of the cot, their heads bent together closely.

Varil shut the door, and the pair turned their heads to look at her. Try as she might, she couldn't see any sign of wings, but that didn't surprise her.

"Varil! You escaped." Mortis started to get up, but Phamile grabbed her by the arm and forced her back down. She struggled for a moment before relenting. "Where is Liiran? Is he all right?" she asked, tugging her arm out of Phamile's matchstick-thin fingers.

"In the dungeons, I expect. Last I saw, he was unharmed, and I doubt that they'll hurt him without reason." The assassin pulled her gloves off, one finger at a time. "So," she said, "what in Mortisor are you two?" She fixed Phamile with a severe look.

Phamile merely looked at her expressionlessly. "We're voxae. My real name is Phames, and my sphere of influence is decay."

Varil felt a bit of the wind go out of her sails. She'd run this confrontation through her mind a few times as she made her way back, and she had expected to meet resistance. She rallied quickly, though. "And Liiran?"

"Human," Phamile – no, Phames – informed her. He rose from the cot, giving Mortis a look as she made to rise, and the woman once again sank back down to the mattress. Varil held her ground as Phames moved towards her. "You understand why we didn't tell you?" Despite the up tilt of Phames' tone, it didn't sound much like a question to Varil.

"Why would you tell me?" Varil replied curtly, her eyes narrowing. "But since I know... I didn't know that voxae could be so big." She looked at Mortis. "What are you?"

"I am the mortivox – the highest of the voxae of death. I am the reason why death has returned to the world. And because of Phames' presence, the supply lines have been difficult for the Empire to manage. Their food is withering as it passes through the city," Mortis said quietly.

Varil's eyes widened. The words were like a physical blow, and she moved quickly towards the dark-haired woman sitting on the cot. "You... you're *Death*?" she breathed, feeling a glow, almost like rapture, run through her. Before either vox could react, she sank to her knees in front of Mortis. "Where have you been?" Varil whispered.

There was a short, stunned silence. "What... are you doing?" Phames demanded.

"Phames, it's all right," Mortis said softly. "Varil, please get up."

For a moment, Varil hesitated. By everything she'd been taught, it seemed right that she should show the mortivox the kind of respect she would show the queen. But at the same time, it had never been contemplated – at least, not by *her* – that she would ever meet one, nor that she would be of a nature such that one *could* kneel before her.

Reluctantly, she rose to her feet.

Mortis had changed in the past few hours, Varil was sure of it. She had seemed frightened before, worried about Liiran, who had obviously been so badly injured, though he didn't have a mark on him. She had been kind. Now her black eyes were even more bottomless than Varil remembered, and her voice was cold. Not cruel – the kindness was still, somehow, there.

But it was the kindness of a sharp knife, which could kill before its victim knew they were dead. Soundlessly and painlessly.

Was it just Varil's perception that was different, or had something really changed in Mortis since this morning? Varil had no idea, and her mind was swirling with too much emotion to work it out for herself. Thankfully, Mortis was speaking, and that gave her something to focus on other than her confusion.

"I'm sorry if your people have been inconvenienced by my absence," Mortis said. "I was sealed in a voxmar by Niveus and his magi."

Varil's head came up and she stared at Mortis for a moment before she mastered herself. "Then you'll be pleased to know that one of those magi is dead," she said. "Altus Itolan. Please forgive me for not reaching my mark tonight. I will give my own life in exchange, if you ask it of me."

Mortis' black eyes widened fractionally, and she shook her head. "I... did know that Altus was dead," she said, in a distracted tone. "Though I hadn't realized it until you mentioned it. And of course you must not blame yourself, Varil. Niveus couldn't have died no matter what you did."

"Mortis," Phames snapped.

The mortivox waved a delicate hand in dismissal of Phames. "She already knows this much, Phames. What difference does it make? You trust this woman, don't you?"

Phames hesitated. "I trust her," he said. "For what it's worth."

"It's worth a great deal," Mortis said. And then, with more energy, "Varil, Niveus is a vox as well. His realm is that of order."

If Varil had thought she was surprised before, that was nothing to how she felt now. "Oh, voxae as nema uto," she whispered, fervently. But then the rest of what that implied caught up with her, and she rounded on Phames as anger surged through her. "You *knew*, and you said nothing."

Phames looked as if he was trying to remain unruffled, but it was spoiled by the fact that he couldn't look her in the eye. "Yes, we knew."

"I could have been killed, on a useless mission." Varil couldn't keep her voice down. "Not telling me about your nature is one thing, but why didn't you tell me about him?"

"Varil." Mortis' voice cut through her anger. "Please, forgive us. We felt that the secrecy of our own mission would be jeopardized if we told anyone about Niveus' true nature. We knew that you would be on your guard as it was, and we chose to trust your skills to carry you through."

It was difficult to forgive so easily. Varil turned away from Phames with a huff and threw herself into a chair, glaring into space, her back to both voxae.

"Sulk if you want," Phames said. "But tell us, what are you going to do now?"

Varil closed her eyes for a moment, leaning her head back against the chair. There was really only one answer she could give, but she didn't want to say it. Instead she said the next thing to come to her mind. "My mark cannot die," she said, "so I have failed. I could turn my knife upon myself, or upon Grand General Garelon, the secondary target, or I could go back to the queen and receive new orders. I don't really know which would be best right now."

"Don't throw your life away, Varil. I will take it if you ask me, but I would rather you live for a while longer," said Mortis.

The assassin was silent for a moment. Then she said, "I will of course do as you command."

The ensuing silence was brittle, like a thin sheet of ice over deep water.

"What is this?" Phames asked, testily.

Varil opened her eyes and rose, turning to face them. "It means that I know what I have to do," she said, glaring at Phames. "I have to help you, if you have any need of me, or go back to the queen in her exile if that's all that is left for me to do."

Mortis rose to her feet. Phames made a gesture towards her, but she waved him off with an edge of impatience. "I'm fine, Phames. I was just a little tired."

The mortivox moved towards Varil, who had to resist an urge to run. Even for her, the approach of death was terrifying. But Mortis' fingers were soft as they folded around Varil's hand. They were cool, too cool to be human, but gentle.

Mortis folded both hands around Varil's fingers and looked into the assassin's eyes. Varil forced herself to meet those bottomless pits without flinching.

"Can you rescue Liiran?"

Varil started, her fingers tightening reflexively around Mortis'. It seemed impossible that such an inhuman being would still care for one human. Or was he simply important to her plan, whatever it was?

"I will do it, or die in the trying, mistress," Varil said.

Phames made a noise of disgust. "Just do it, and don't die," he said.

Chapter 46

Liiran sat on the cot in a prison cell, his head in his hands. When he was first shoved into the room and the door had locked, he'd decided that he wasn't going to waste his time brooding. But the only light in the room filtered through a tiny window in the door, and he was sure he could hear the sound of rats chittering in the walls. After only a few minutes of exploring his tiny prison by feel he had moved to the bed and drew his legs up tight towards his chin, sure he'd feel a rat climb over his feet any moment.

He wasn't sure how long he'd been here, in this exact position, but he supposed it would definitely have to qualify as brooding by now.

He had never wanted a cigarette so much in his entire life. Why had he thrown them away? Even if by some chance Mortis stayed free, so he would die in a mere five or six decades, those years would be spent in prison. At least he could have had the pleasure of one last smoke, instead of making a futile gesture simply to prolong his pointless life.

He could hear the faint sounds of crying from somewhere nearby, a woman's voice, and he wondered if it was Minister Maenos. After Altus Itolan's death, she had pleaded with the guards at length to let her speak to Prime Minister Niveus, but the pleas had fallen on deaf ears.

At least he knew Varil and Turil had gotten away. No other prisoners had been brought in since he arrived, and he was sure if they had been captured they would have been tossed into the dungeons with the rest.

Unless they'd been killed. But no, he wouldn't think about that. The two assassins, Mortis, and Phames were even now trying to hatch a plan to rescue him. He was *sure* of that.

He had to be sure of that, or he was going to go crazy.

Why didn't Mortis do something when she came to take that man's life? he wondered, burying his face against his knees. He hadn't been able to see her, but he was sure he could *feel* her. And anyway, if it was so easy for her to get in and out, why couldn't she rescue him and Tanen in a moment? Why had they gone through so much grief trying to get at Certos?

Certos, who had just wound up betraying them to his own captors.

It was all just a big fucking mess.

He wondered when they would transfer him to the main prison. Or would he just be left here to rot? Did they think that he had something to do with Varil's attempt on Niveus' life? Would they torture him to find out more?

His thoughts were spiralling out of control, and the one thing he couldn't think of was any way out of this.

The sound of a key turning in the lock and the heavy tumblers moving brought his head up and set his heart to pounding in his chest. He just had time to shift into a less pathetic position when the door opened and he had to raise his arm to shield his eyes from the light streaming in from the torches in the hallway. Tears sprang to his squinting eyes and it took him a moment to recognize the figures that had entered his cell.

Garelon and Certos.

Liiran lowered his arm, glaring at the intruders – in particular, up at the cold-eyed general. "What do you want?"

"Quiet," Garelon said in a low tone. He carried a lamp, and he shut the door firmly, then hung the lamp up on a bracket on the wall.

Mutinous, Liiran jumped to his feet. "I said what do you want?" he said, just as loudly as before. "I want to talk to my lawyer, damn it."

Garelon snorted. "You don't get to talk to your lawyer when you're arrested by secret police for committing treason. Now sit down and shut up for a minute, and we'll tell you why we're here."

Despite Liiran's anger and determination not to let the man intimidate him, he felt himself deflate a little at Garelon's words. He hesitated, then sat down on the edge of the bed, glaring up at him with his jaw set.

When Certos stepped out from behind Garelon and spoke, he was startled for a moment. He'd almost forgotten the vox was there.

"I want to help you," Certos said.

The words made no sense. Liiran stared at the boy for a moment. "Help me?"

Certos nodded. "You want to bring down Niveus, right? You want to free me, and punish them, and put things back the way they were." There was an odd glint in Certos' eyes, which sent a shiver down Liiran's spine, a glee in his voice that sounded bloodthirsty.

Liiran had to swallow twice before he could speak. "Yes," he managed. "Ah, that's the general idea, yes." He snuck a look up at Garelon again, but the general was standing with his back to them, his hands clasped behind his back. As far as Liiran could tell, he was looking out the barred window in the door.

"General?" Liiran said. "Are you—"

"Whatever you two might have to say, I know nothing about it," Garelon interrupted in a clipped tone. "I'm just here in my capacity as Certos' handler, as it is my duty to stay with him at all times."

Liiran hesitated, then looked back at Certos. "If you wanted to get out of here, why did you lead us into a trap? We could be out of here already, if it weren't for you."

Certos shifted from foot to foot. "I needed to bring help to Garelon," he said lamely. "He was in danger."

Liiran glanced at Garelon again involuntarily, but he hadn't moved. He jumped to his feet. "Well, now that the danger has passed, let's get the hell out of here. Hey, how do I take this collar off Certos?" he asked, addressing Garelon's back.

"No!" Certos backpedalled as if Liiran had taken a swing at him. "I... I mean, that's not going to work."

"What do you mean?" Liiran took another step towards Certos, who leaped backwards and pressed himself against the wall with a cry.

A heavy hand landed on Liiran's shoulder and jerked him backwards. Liiran looked up to see Garelon's face inches from his, and he looked livid. "Don't scare him." The general shoved Liiran back hard enough that he stumbled back a step and sat down hard on the edge of the cot again.

To Liiran's amazement, Garelon turned to Certos and dropped to one knee, catching his hands and speaking soothingly in a low voice. Liiran stared as the boy vox slowly relaxed and wrapped his arms around Garelon's neck, who rose with him cradled in his arms as if he weighed nothing.

Garelon turned and glared at Liiran. "I've got you, Certos. Explain it to him."

Certos looked far more confident held in Garelon's arms. "If we leave now, then Garelon will be implicated. We're not supposed to be here at all, and no one is to know we had contact with you. Niveus believes I want to leave, and he already suspects that Garelon is too attached to me. He will be looking for treachery, and I won't allow Garelon to be hurt."

That last was said in such a fierce voice, that Liiran couldn't help but believe him.

Liiran took a deep breath, and let it out again, calming himself. "All right, then what do we do?"

"We wait," Certos said. "One of two things will occur. Either your people will attempt a rescue, or you will be moved out of the city. Either way, there will be an opportunity. Where you are, right now, you're in the best position to get what you need to escape."

This was his plan? "How long do I have to wait—"

"Listen to him," Garelon said. "Certos is a vox of tactics, after all."

"And what about you, General?" Liiran demanded. He wanted to know what role Garelon had in this, but Garelon just shook his head, retrieved his torch, and started for the door.

Certos looked at Liiran over the man's shoulder, solemn. "Be vigilant. You'll need to take an opportunity. I can't make you act – you have to do it yourself. All I can do is try to arrange the circumstances for you to succeed, but the rest is up to you. When we're outside of the castle, you can break my collar. But not before. I don't know what will happen when you do, and it might be very dangerous."

That gave Liiran a chill. He remembered the museum, where Mortis had killed a roomful of people upon being freed from her voxmar. Would Certos destroy everything around him when the collar was broken?

What would happen to Liiran if he did?

"Okay," he said, his voice sounding hollow and nervous to his own ears. Maybe prison was safer. "I'll be ready."

The heavy door banged shut and the key turned with a hollow clunk.

* * *

"Hello? Hello, are you there?"

The voice was muffled, and at first Liiran wasn't sure he actually *had* heard anything. Since Certos and Garelon left, he had waited in agony for *something* to happen, but all he had been able to hear was more sobbing from not far away. The sound finally faded away only a few minutes ago, replaced by this calling voice. But he couldn't tell where it was coming from. Muffled as it was, it didn't sound as though it could be coming through half a foot of solid stone.

"Yes, I'm here. Who are you?"

"Come down. They'll see you. I can't hear you very well. Please, come down."

Liiran was pretty sure the owner of the voice was the one who'd been crying earlier. There was something tremulous in her tone, as if the tears weren't buried deeply.

"Uh, what do you mean?" Liiran slipped off of his bed, searching the dark corners of his room for some sign of the source of the voice.

"The hole is near the floor. *Please*, someone will see you."

A hole? With the torch left by Garelon, he was sure he would have seen a hole in the wall. He got up and explored, but couldn't see any sign of a hole in the wall.

Then his eyes widened with realization and he dropped to his hands and knees. He peered under the cot with trepidation. He couldn't see any light at all, no chink in the wall. It was nothing but impenetrable darkness under there and his mind supplied images of cockroaches and rats that would surely be hiding in that blackness.

But the mysterious voice had to be coming from under there. It was the only place where a hole had to be, where it wouldn't be noticed, and where he could hear the voice come through so clearly while sitting on top of the bed. He swallowed hard, and then bent down and wriggled under the bed, feeling his way forward with his fingers.

He nearly screamed as something large scuttled over one of his outstretched hands. He bit down on his lip, holding the sound in until it stopped bubbling in his throat. Gasping softly, he squirmed forward a little bit further until he touched the wall, then felt around nervously. It was musty and dank under here, and smelled of what he imagined was mouse droppings.

He felt around for a few moments before his fingers touched a small hole just wide enough to fit perhaps three fingers inside.

Shifting forward to place his mouth almost to the hole, he tasted a bit of fresh air coming from the other side of the wall. "Hello?"

The voice came back through the hole, clear to his ears now. "Yes, I'm here."

It was close and claustrophobic under here. He hadn't thought anything could feel claustrophobic compared to the prison cell itself, but he'd been wrong.

"Who are you?" Liiran whispered. Was it Maenos? But he knew Maenos' voice, and this didn't sound like her. That meant that this woman had been here before Liiran had been brought down. How long had she been here?

"I'm Aevi," she murmured. "Aevi Nexalum. Not Eve, not Eve Nellexe. Not that, I'm *Aevi*." There was something off-putting about the way she spoke, too fast, *too* urgently, as if her thoughts were scattering and she had to speak quickly before she lost hold of them.

And the things she said made no sense. "Aevi Nexalum?" he echoed. "But..."

"I know, I know," she said. "I'm supposed to be dead. I *should* be dead. They gave me a new name, a new face, but I'm *me*, and I'm alive."

Eve Nellexe was a name he knew vaguely. It was the name of the administrator of the largest long-term care and research hospital in Laxamora. And Aevi Nexalum was supposed to have been a doctor.

This was all starting to come together. "There was no serum that cheated death, I already knew that. Did you take part in trapping Mortis in that voxmar? And they just said it was an injection, and pretended you were killed to cover it all up?"

"Yes, yes," Aevi said, and her voice had turned brittle. "I was the one who came up with the runes they needed for the spell. I designed the voxmar. I killed *everyone*."

"What do you mean, killed everyone?" Liiran demanded, the words hitting him like a bucketful of cold water. "Is everyone going to die?" He shook his head quickly, clenching a fist. "No, I won't believe Mortis will kill everyone now that she's free. She's just not like that."

"Everyone dies," Aevi said, a sob in her voice. "Everyone is supposed to die."

Liiran closed his eyes. He was clearly talking to a madwoman.

That doesn't mean she's not right. What is going to happen if Mortis remembers who she really is, a voice whispered in his head. *Do you really think she won't change?* But he ignored it as best he could.

"Look," he said forcing his tone to calmness. "Why did you call out to me? What do you want?"

254

There was a short pause, broken by soft, ragged breaths, before Aevi spoke again. "I heard you talking to the certovox."

He winced. "Does that mean you're going to tell someone about our plans, or do you want to escape with me?"

"No, no, not escape. I'll die right here. Near my only friends... Alone. But... But I can help you."

Liiran pressed two fingers to the bridge of his nose. "I could try to bring you with me. You don't have to die, Aevi. Let's get out of here together."

"*No!*" The word was shouted so forcefully that Liiran nearly cracked his head on the underside of his cot in surprise. "I won't go," she went on in a calmer tone. "Why won't you listen to me?"

"I'm trying to listen to you," Liiran said ruefully, rubbing his scalp. "I just want to help."

"I don't need help," Aevi said, so softly he now had to strain to hear her. "But I heard that you walk hand in hand with death. You can fix my mistakes."

Liiran flushed with anger. "You're the one who should fix your *own* mistakes. Why should I do it for you?"

"Please, please," Aevi whispered. "I can't do it. It's too late for me. I need you to do it."

He drew in a breath and swallowed his rage, knowing it was pointless. The woman was nuts, and she was offering him help. He should take it. Why force her to take help she didn't want?

"All right," he said. "You said you could help me. How?"

She drew a breath and let it out in a rush loud enough that he could hear it through the tiny hole in the wall. "Take this. It's all I have," she said, and there was a soft rattling sound inside the hole as she shoved something into it.

Liiran hesitated, then wormed his fingers into the hole, touching something warm and smooth. It took a moment, but he managed to extract the object. He couldn't see it, but a bit of investigation and a nicked finger told him that it was a broken piece of glass. It was slightly curved and had a symbol etched into it – part of a large voxmar.

"How in Mortisor did you get this?"

"No... no time," she said. Her voice was getting softer, and she gasped as if winded. "You can use it, right?"

Liiran swallowed. "Yeah, I'm sure it'll come in handy. Thank you, Aevi."

She didn't respond, and there was silence for a few moments. "Aevi?" he asked. "Why did you do it? Why did you put Mortis in that voxmar?"

No response was forthcoming to this question either, and Liiran waited, straining his ears, but to no avail. Finally he shook his head and crawled out from under the bed, deciding it was probably best not to tempt fate. Someone could look in the cell at any moment, see him missing and raise the alarm.

As he straightened up, the light coming in through the doorway fell on the piece of glass in his hand and flashed wetly. He stared for a moment, unable to believe what he was seeing.

Almost the whole shard was shining with fresh blood.

"Aevi?"

He turned and dove under the bed again, calling out. "Aevi? Aevi? What did you do?"

There was no answer.

Chapter 47

For the second time in as many days, Niveus walked down the narrow steps to the dungeon level. It was a great deal more crowded down here than the last time he had come, the hallway well-lit by torches, which cast the shadows of the four guards, stationed at intervals along the hallway, into flickering relief on the freshly swept floor.

He glanced curiously through the windows in each door as he walked, slowing only just enough to catch a glimpse of each prisoner.

The stranger who had been with Mortis and Phames – Liiran Uwis according to Calam's reports – was sitting on his cot with his knees drawn up tight against his chest and his face hidden. Niveus couldn't tell if he was sleeping or just afraid.

He continued past, making a mental note to meet with him later. Right now he had a different goal.

Aevi's cell was dark, the lamp extinguished. But he could see she lay on her cot, calm and reposed for once. He was relieved to see that, at least.

The next cell held Governor Moraiil. He would likely be released in the end – the man hadn't had a full understanding of what he was participating in, and was merely a minor player in this drama. Across from him was the prisoner Calam had brought from Laxam, also a minor player, but one who likely could not be released, given his association with Uwis. A pitiable waste.

And with that, there was only one prisoner left to check on. He nodded to the nearest guard, making a gesture, and the man approached quickly to unlock the door and pull it open.

Maenos was awake and sitting up as he entered. She looked fragile, but composed, and Niveus wondered if she had been crying earlier. If there was anyone who mourned Altus, it was she.

Niveus had only needed a moment to compose himself after Altus' death, of course. He had experienced some strong sensations, but it had been only the surprise, not sentiment that produced the odd reaction. He only hoped Maenos didn't become distraught again – he really didn't want to deal with more raw, chaotic human emotion than he absolutely had to.

Maenos looked up as Niveus entered. Her eyes widened, the whites cream in the coffee of her face, made large by fear.

"Niveus, what are you doing here?" she asked, hope rising in her voice.

"I came to find out who else was in on it," he said gently, and watched her face fall.

"I don't know," she said. "Please, Niveus, you have to believe me. I didn't want to do this to you."

"Then why did you?"

"Because... I thought he'd succeed, no matter what I did." Maenos' reply had the ring of truth to it.

Niveus' eyes narrowed. Did all the humans really think he was such a fool? But of course, why wouldn't they? They had already trapped two voxae, with no difficulty. Why should Niveus – decadent, arrogant, lulled into a false sense of security – be any harder to subdue?

"He didn't. And now he's dead."

Maenos looked at him, and he almost recoiled from the look in her eyes. Was that sympathy? Pity?

He straightened quickly, smoothing a hand down his lapels. "Tell me everything he told you, Maenos, and maybe there'll be a pardon in it for you. You're not a treacherous person. You're not usually the type to get yourself entangled in politics and back-stabbing."

She laughed hollowly, a short bark of a sound that didn't fit her delicate features at all. "You really think Altus would have told me anything?" she asked, shaking her head. "Trust me, Niveus, if I knew anything I would tell you."

"So who did he tell?"

There was a long pause. "I'd have said Calam, but... maybe Aevi?" In that moment Niveus knew she really didn't know.

He shook his head. "Aevi was the one who alerted me. If she had known more, I'm sure she would have told me."

Maenos spread her hands. "Then you have the answer, Niveus. He played us all, told us only what he thought we needed to know. If the others of the Circle of Magi are involved, then I don't know how. So far as I know, they're not, and even if they are they probably won't admit it now that Altus is dead."

He hated not knowing things. Shaking his head, he turned towards the door, trying to cling to the calm that had once been literally second nature to him. It seemed to slip through his fingers. *Voxae ma, have I really spent so much time around humans that I'm starting to lose myself?*

It was a possibility that was beginning to weigh on him. The fear in Mortis' eyes when she looked at that human haunted him. He had tried to restore her to order, but he had no idea if it worked. He himself was so disordered, and he had had only moments before she left. Plus it was difficult for voxae to affect each other with their powers. For all he knew, there was nothing he could do to return her to herself.

Even more frightening to him was the fact that he hadn't sensed their presence in the city, at all. How could he have overlooked something so significant?

"Niveus?"

The soft voice recalled him to his surroundings and he looked back at Maenos. "Yes?"

"Are you really going to leave me down here?" she asked, her brows drawing together and her hands curling into small fists.

He opened his mouth to flatly confirm that he would, but then hesitated. Maenos' feelings for Altus had made her weak, but he was out of the picture now, and Niveus believed that – at her core – Maenos was an honest person. Assuming he could even trust his own beliefs any longer.

Could he trust them? He didn't know.

But he had to make a decision. She stared at him as the silence drew out, and he knew that he was acting... inhuman.

"I'll let you out if you submit to being under guard," he said. "And you won't try to talk to anyone for now, will you?"

"Yes, of course. Thank you, Niveus." He tried to tell himself that her relief didn't strike some chord inside him.

"Try to do something for Aevi, if you can," he said, turning away. He wished he knew what was wrong with him.

Calam met him at the top of the stairs. "Did she know anything, sir?"

Niveus shook his head silently, and made his way to his tower room. Up there he felt powerful – not as safe as he would feel in his own office back in Laxamora, but better than he felt right now. He felt a strange sensation in his middle that he couldn't identify. He didn't know what it meant, or perhaps didn't want to think about what it might mean.

Though he hadn't been invited, Calam was a constant shadow at his shoulder as they walked. It irritated Niveus.

It *irritated* him. That wasn't right at all.

When he reached the top he strode to a window and threw it open wide, inhaling the scent of wind and sunlight and the moisture in the clouds. The wrenching sensation in his middle softened and dissipated, though not completely. He wondered if it would ever go away.

"Trust," he said suddenly, turning around and regarding the man standing by the door with his hands clasped behind his back.

Calam looked as impassive as Niveus wished he felt. "Trust?"

"How do you do it?" Niveus demanded. "I trusted the nine of you for centuries, yet Altus betrayed me. All of you betrayed me. Some others may have betrayed me and I may never know it. So what am I to do now?"

The other man stared at him. "Why are you asking me? If you don't trust me after what's happened, then any advice I give you is suspect."

It was the most infuriating answer possible. Niveus whirled around and stared out the window, at the dance of light and wind and water. It was infuriating, but somehow it calmed him.

"Altus only told me what I wanted to hear," he said, realizing for the first time that it was true. He had suspected it sometimes, but he had caught Altus at it enough times that he thought he'd trained the human to tell him the truth. It turned out instead he'd taught him to be craftier in his lies.

"Is that what you want me to do?" Calam asked.

Niveus glanced at him over his shoulder, his eyes narrowing with irritation. "Would you?"

"No, Prime Minister." Calam shook his head. "I'm afraid I'd have to ask to be excused. Besides, I'm a policeman, not a politician."

The nivevox felt something break inside him at the words and he strode towards the human. Calam tensed, but Niveus only grabbed his hand and held it tightly in both of his. "Yes, *yes*." It was a revelation.

"Yes, I understand. I can trust you, Calam. And perhaps I'm wrong again, but I think it mustn't matter, since I trust you anyway. Is that... about right?"

Calam smiled, a flash of white teeth. "Yes, sir," he said, gripping Niveus' arm with his other hand in return. "I think that's about right. Trust is like that."

"So human," Niveus muttered, releasing Calam and moving back towards the window. "So damned human."

"What else would it be, sir?" Calam intoned.

Niveus just shook his head, staring out the window for a few moments as his thoughts settled into their familiar grooves once again. Yes, he knew where he was, and what he wanted. He knew who he was.

Time to move on. That was the best way to deal with issues, he'd found. When life went strange, he focused on the problem, dealt with it, and then moved on.

"That man who arrived with Phames and Mortis," Niveus said after several minutes, "who is he, exactly? I feel as if I've seen him before." He turned, expecting Calam to still be there, and he wasn't disappointed. The man stood where he had been, his hands clasped behind his back, as if waiting to be dismissed.

So dependable, Calam was. Why had Niveus never fully appreciated that about him?

"Liiran Uwis," Calam said. "Newspaper photographer and journalist for the Laxam Daily News. Last assignment resulted in the accidental discovery of our facility in the south of the Sincovati Desert. He was not present when Mortis' voxmar ruptured, and he dropped out of sight within hours of that. He's popped up again a few times in the company of the rebel voxae. All attempts to apprehend him have resulted in deaths at the hands of the mortivox. Shall I go on?"

It sounded as if he was reciting from an official report or biography. It was also the longest speech Niveus had ever heard him make.

The prime minister shook his head. So, since he was a journalist, Niveus had probably seen him during press conferences, or done an interview or two. One mystery was solved, but it didn't really help. "No, that doesn't tell me anything. It doesn't tell me why he became involved with Mortis, or how he gained her trust. It doesn't tell me why he left his comfortable job, his comfortable life, and travelled halfway across the world to take Certos from us."

"I don't have the answers to those questions, sir," Calam said, his lips twisting wryly. "I think if you want to know those things, you'll have to ask him."

Niveus smiled and started for the door. "Exactly."

Chapter 48

Liiran tensed once more as the lock disengaged with a clang and he saw the shadow of someone's head beyond the door to his cell. Was it Garelon and Certos, maybe back with a more concrete plan? Yeah, right.

The door opened to admit Calam and two guards, and for a wild instant he was sure they knew. There was a shard of glass tucked into his sleeve, and there was blood on the blanket where he'd wiped it off as best he could before hiding it. For a moment it was all he could do to keep guilt off of his face, sure that they were going to accuse him of killing Aevi Nexalum. He had the murder weapon, after all, though so far as he knew her body had yet to be discovered.

Calam's expression was mild, though. Not the sort of face one presented to murderers. Especially murderers who had somehow committed their crime from inside a locked cell.

Calam produced a set of manacles. "Stand up, please. The prime minister requires an audience."

Liiran stood obediently and held his hands out. It would probably be best not to try to mess around with the manacles, even if he had any idea how to go about it in the first place. The less time the minister of laws spent around his wrists and the hidden piece of glass, the better.

Nevertheless, the click of the manacles closing felt like the loss of a chance. Maybe he should have rushed the guards.

Another look at the hulking guards standing behind the even larger Calam dashed that thought to pieces. This couldn't have been the opportunity Certos mentioned. He hoped.

"Come," Calam ordered the moment the second manacle clicked into place, and turned away. Liiran had to pass between the two guards to follow, and they seemed to loom over him as he squeezed past them into the corridor.

Voxae ma, why wasn't I born big and muscular like these guys? I'd never have had to worry about finding a job, he thought resentfully as they fell in behind him. It was like being herded by three mountains.

He had to fight panic as they ascended the spiralling staircase. His heart was pounding so hard he was certain it was going to burst right through his chest. Sure, he'd been in situations of danger before, but there was a huge difference between standing at a safe distance from a battleground, on a high ridge that gave a good vantage point, and being arrested for treason.

Liiran tried to look around himself. How could he take an opportunity if he was chained up and covered by three armed guards who were twice his weight, all muscle? The glass shard seemed tiny and useless.

As they approached the throne room, a group of guards passed them, and the sight of red hair caught his attention. A female guard tucked the errant lock of red hair under her cap again. She wasn't looking in his direction, but he saw she was limping slightly, and his heart leaped into his throat. Could that be Varil?

Could she have infiltrated so quickly? He'd only been stuck in here for a matter of hours. Surely they'd increased the guard.

On the other hand, maybe she had never left. It could be her.

It was difficult to keep his head down and hide the rising tide of his hope. He could feel the glass cold against his forearm, but perhaps he wouldn't have to find a way to use it at all.

Double doors opened ahead and he was being marched down the long hall towards Prime Minister Niveus, who sat on the throne at the far end like a reigning king. He rested his elbow against one arm of the chair, his fingers steepled against his temple and his thumb resting on his chin.

But it wasn't Niveus' presence that made Liiran's heart nearly stop. Standing beside him, flanked by two guards, was Tanen, looking pale and confused. But at the sight of Liiran, Tanen lit up and tried to step forward, only to be instantly restrained by the guards.

Niveus ignored the scuffle. "Well, well, Liiran Uwis. Good of you to join us. I was hoping we could have a little chat."

Liiran was brought to a halt a few paces away from the man by a touch to his upper arm. Calam continued on and took up a place next to Tanen, a third guard for his innocent friend.

Garelon stood nearby, hands clasped behind his back. Liiran glanced around automatically and spotted Certos, far to his left, sitting on the floor and apparently playing chess with himself.

264

He struggled to ignore the vox's presence and focused on Niveus. "Why is Tanen here? You've got me now. Why won't you just release him?"

His friend shook his head and smiled crookedly. "Pretend I'm not here, Lii. I've just been sitting around eating bon-bons, entertained by our friends, here. I'm totally fine."

Liar. But Liiran appreciated the attempt.

Niveus waved a hand. "Quiet, please. Mr. Uwis, I brought him here as a gesture, so you could see that we continue to look quite seriously upon what you've done. But he has not been harmed, as you can see. Depending on how our conversation goes, I might be inclined to release him – he was merely an innocent victim of your treason, after all."

"Stick it up your ass, Prime Minister. There's nothing innocent about me," Tanen snapped.

"Tanen, shut up," Liiran said desperately. His own escape seemed nearly impossible, even with the help of his allies. How was he going to rescue Tanen, too?

Liiran turned to Niveus again, struggling to fake a calm he didn't feel. "What exactly is my crime?"

Niveus leaned back against the chair. "How does treason sound?"

"It's treason to shelter a lost girl?" Liiran fired back, hoping Tanen would keep his mouth shut, for once.

But Niveus just snorted. "It's treason to steal a priceless weapon of war. Two of them. You might have gotten the hint when we tried to arrest you back in Laxamora. Three times."

"Mortis came to me. I tried to turn her in, and the police tried to arrest me. What else was I supposed to do?" Liiran asked, but he was losing energy. He could protest until he was blue in the face, but he really had no leverage at all.

"Yes, I know. All of that is in your file," Niveus said, his lips twisted ironically. "But it didn't tell me what I wanted to know."

Liiran drew a breath. He had nothing to hide, right? He let it out. "What do you want to know?"

Niveus leaned forward, elbows on knees. Liiran was amazed at how *human* he was. Phames and Mortis had always seemed a little off, somehow, but even knowing that there were vox that could masquerade as humans, he didn't think he'd ever have figured out that Niveus was one of them.

"I want to know why you left everything you love, everything you worked for, to help Mortis. Why are you here, Liiran Uwis?"

Liiran stared into those cold blue eyes. It was a question he had a lot of answers for, and none.

He opened his mouth. "I... love her."

And that was when it happened.

Surprise flickered in Niveus' eyes and he straightened up, but before he could respond the wooden throne he was sitting on let out a groan and cracked right up the middle. Niveus yelped as it collapsed in on itself and on him, and he spilled onto the stone dais below.

The room filled with dust, obscuring Liiran's vision, as every tapestry and curtain hung on the walls simply collapsed and dissolved explosively. The guards at his shoulders and ranged around the room yelled as their uniforms fell right off their bodies.

This is it, Liiran's mind yelled as he stood there, gaping. *The opportunity. What are you waiting for, idiot?*

The thought propelled him into action.

With the manacles on, he could just barely reach the shard of glass hidden up his sleeve. He turned suddenly and thrust his hands forward, shard sinking deep into the stomach of one of the two guards.

The man screamed and stumbled backwards, clutching at the bleeding wound, and Liiran lost his grip on the slick glass. Liiran mourned the loss of his only weapon even as he bolted through the space that was left.

He felt fingers clutch at his arm and yanked hard, pulling free of the other guard.

Then he sprinted through the choking dust, coughing and awkwardly trying to cover his mouth with his bound hands.

A shape loomed out of the dust and he skidded to a stop, but recognized Varil as she blurred past him. "Go," she said, and Liiran dove forward again, hearing the thumps and cries as she dispatched the guard on his heels. He could only hope she was getting Tanen.

Certos was right where he'd last seen him, standing solemnly by the wall with his chess board packed into its box and tucked under his arm.

"You're coming... with me," Liiran said, gasping and struggling to get air. "Right?"

The boy turned away, looking towards where Garelon had last been. Liiran couldn't see anything at the moment, but he could hear the sounds of struggles and shouting coming from that direction.

"I'm scared," Certos said.

"No time to be scared." He meant every word. "I didn't risk my life to find you just for you to stand there. Come *on*."

He curled his fingers around Certos' wrist and felt the cold links of the metal chain under his palm, wrapped around Certos' wrist. Together he and Certos raced towards the door.

Varil joined them halfway. She held a blood-soaked knife in her hand, and her eyes flashed with glee. "Can't you guys hurry?"

"I'm running as fast as I can," Liiran said. "Where's Tanen?"

"Alive, but his guards got him away before I could catch up." Liiran nearly stopped, but she gave him a hard shove. "*Go*. We'll have to get him later. They won't execute him if they can still use him as bait."

Swearing, and giving a mental, heartfelt apology to his friend, Liiran put his head down and concentrated on not tripping over his own feet as she hauled him along, Certos bringing up the rear like a lop-sided conga line. He could only hope they'd have another chance, and that Tanen would ever forgive him for leaving him behind *again*.

The speed took them through the double doors at the end of the room. At the next junction there was a phalanx of guards coming towards them, and the guards drew their weapons when the threesome burst into the hallway.

"There they are," someone shouted, and Liiran, Varil and Certos turned in the opposite direction.

A winged shape arrowed past them overhead, and Liiran caught a glimpse of Phames, his face set in a grim mask. Liiran couldn't help but turn to look even as he ran on. He saw Phames, his black, bat-like wings spread to slow him as he gestured towards the guards.

Again, dust exploded to choke the corridor as the guard's uniforms burst apart, and the whole group dissolved into confusion. Phames flew back and kept pace with them, dodging overhead lamps with a whisper of wings like the flap of a cloak in a high wind.

"How the hell are we going to get out of here?" Liiran gasped. The dust was still clearing his lungs, and he wasn't used to such sustained running at top speed. And with his arms bound, even in front, it was even more awkward.

"Go left," Certos said. "A little faster."

The voice was so unexpected, that Liiran nearly stumbled. He glanced back at the boy, and saw only a set expression on his face. Could he trust him, really? Wasn't it possible that he would only lead them into another trap? This could all be some kind of elaborate trick to capture Varil and Phames, beginning back when Garelon and Certos came to his cell.

The fact that he was the vox of war meant that he might know a way to win. But was he really on their side? Liiran didn't know, but he had to make some kind of decision, if no one else would, and neither Varil nor Phames was speaking up.

"Do what he says," Liiran said firmly, and he saw Varil nod fractionally, before putting on another burst of speed.

His lungs burned, and his feet ached, but as they flew down the corridors they heard shouts receding behind them. They managed to squeak past another phalanx of guards just before they could have reached a cross-corridor and cut them off.

Then Certos spoke up again. "Third door on the left, go in." He didn't sound winded at all. Even Varil sounded strained as she spoke up.

"But that's the way we came in. How did you know—"

"I know."

It was a small bathroom, the window slightly ajar. Liiran closed the door behind them and locked it, then leaned against it and bent over, gasping.

Certos tugged at his hand. "No time." Liiran looked up and found Certos' face was very close to his, his eyes huge in his thin face. "We have to go."

"Why are you really helping us?" Liiran asked. "What's changed?"

"I have to. I want to hurt Niveus for what he's done to us." The boy's eyes flickered away. "I have to stay with you, now."

Liiran felt strangely as if there was more to what he was saying than he understood. But there was no time to question him further. Phames had slipped out the window as nimbly as if he were no more than a shadow.

He turned and gestured. "Liiran, come on. I'll help you." Varil was standing back, waiting for Liiran to go next.

Something heavy slammed against the door, and Liiran darted forward. He could hear talking and someone giving orders on the other side. How long before Niveus caught up to them himself? Large numbers of human guards were one thing, but a vox was something else, even if Liiran did have two with him.

He wondered why Mortis hadn't come.

But there was no time for such thoughts. He climbed up onto the toilet and put his arms and head out the narrow window. Phames grabbed onto his arms and hauled him bodily outside. In seconds, Liiran was standing on the ground outside, looking up at the tall, dark buildings.

He could hear the sounds of many running footsteps coming up the street. Guards were on their way.

Certos slipped outside and dropped down to stand next to him, and then Varil joined them.

"We're flying," Phames said, touching down next to them. "Certos, take Varil."

"But I can't," Certos protested. "The magic makes me weak."

Phames' face grew stony. "You're a vox and you can't carry a human?"

"I need..." Certos' eyes darted from side to side, and then to Liiran. "I can carry you. We've got to hurry."

"Then carry me," Liiran said. There was no time, no *time* to worry that this was some kind of weird trick, no time to try to understand what the hell was going on.

"Yes, sir," Certos said, the fear and concern apparently melting away. The boy spread his wings and wrapped his arms around Liiran's waist. Phames made a derisive sound, and grabbed Varil. In a moment, they were all aloft, leaving the castle behind and disappearing high into the night.

Chapter 49

Garelon couldn't stop coughing, though the room was slowly beginning to clear. Whatever the rebels had done, it had filled the room with dust, destroyed every bit of fabric in the room – though thankfully, those at this end of the room had been spared their clothing.

"What...in hell was that?" he gasped, wiping his streaming eyes. Dimly he could see Niveus had gotten to his feet, but the vox merely stood stock still, staring towards the other end of the hall.

"That was Phames," Niveus said, turning towards Garelon. Not a speck of dust had landed on him. "He is quite adept at destroying vegetable matter. I'd never have thought to use that power so... creatively, though."

Garelon didn't need to look to see that Certos was gone. He'd felt something a few moments ago, a sharp wrenching inside him.

The bond between them, which had allowed him to give Certos orders and forced the boy to obey him, was gone. He wasn't sure if he was relieved, after all. It felt like a loss, an aching hole inside him, but he schooled his expression, just in case. Niveus was looking at him, and Garelon wondered if he suspected him of complicity in the escape.

Then Niveus' eyes turned away and fixed on Calam. "They'll be out of the castle soon, and I doubt the guards are going to be able to stop them. Mobilize our forces to search the city." Niveus hummed softly, pressing a forefinger to his lips as if in thought. "The gang is back together again," he added. "They'll free Certos as soon as they have the chance." Despite his words, Niveus seemed strangely calm.

"What are you going to do?" Garelon asked. "What'll happen when Certos' collar is broken?"

Niveus smiled. "Who knows what'll happen. Calam... don't hurry with those guards. They could be caught in the backlash."

Calam bowed his head, then started for the door. "Sir," he said, his back already receding from view into the fog hanging in the air.

"Besides," Niveus said, so softly Garelon could barely hear him, "I doubt it'll take long before they come knocking on our door again."

Garelon's eyes widened. What did Niveus know? "Sir..." he began, then abruptly changed his mind. "Permission to get started planning today's battle. With Certos working against us, I'll need to start from scratch and come up with something he may not expect."

Niveus gestured offhandedly. "Of course, Garelon. Do you think it'll make a difference?"

Garelon sighed. Did it matter what he did? "I don't want to assume one way or another." He paused. "Surely even Certos can't turn the tide now. Even if he makes things hard for us, even he can't turn a few guerrillas with sticks into an army with enough might to stop our people." He wasn't sure whom he was trying to convince.

Niveus glanced at him out of the corner of his eye. "Still," he said, and he was definitely smiling wryly now. "Make a *good* plan. And execute it as soon as you can, while Certos is focused on other things."

"I'll do my best, sir," Garelon said, then bowed and started off through the falling dust, his boot heels muffled by the fine grains on the floor. It seemed he wasn't going to be thrown into Liiran's recently vacated cell, just yet.

Winning the war would hopefully keep any lingering suspicion from falling on him. He could only hope that, even with the magic broken, Certos would grant him that one last kindness.

Chapter 50

The flight was uneventful, without any sign of pursuit. Certos' breathing was laboured and Liiran wondered if his weight was too much for him after all, until a cold droplet fell on the back of his neck and he realized that Certos was crying.

"What's wrong?" he called out over the wind and the clashing sound of Certos' beating wings, but Certos didn't answer.

They landed heavily outside the door to their hideout, Liiran's feet hitting the ground so hard a shock ran up his feet, exploded in his ankles and radiated up to his knees. He gasped and staggered as Certos released him, but slender, strong hands caught him before he could fall.

He looked up, expecting to see Varil, and looked straight into Phames' sunken eyes.

Phames looked at him only briefly, then past him. "Was he too heavy for you?"

Certos shook his head. "I was... distracted."

"It's fine," Liiran said, hoping to forestall a fight. Besides, he was all right. It had been more shocking than painful.

But it didn't work. "The last thing I need you to do is hurt him right now," Phames said, stepping past Liiran to confront Certos directly.

"I didn't mean to," Certos said, hunching his shoulders and looking away. Liiran couldn't help but think he looked guilty.

"If he meant to hurt me, he would have dropped me from higher up," Liiran found himself saying, hoping it was true.

"Right, because it would have looked like an accident if you dropped him from a hundred feet in the air."

Certos looked as if he was trying to sink into the cobbles. "I *didn't* mean to hurt him. I didn't *mean* to."

Liiran's heart rate was beginning to rise and he clenched his teeth. Why couldn't Phames just give it a *rest* already? "That's enough," he said, stepping forward and grabbing Phames by the shoulder. "He didn't mean it. What is *wrong* with you, Phames?"

He had meant it in a more global sense, but Phames looked up and for the first time Liiran felt he could read those strange sandy-coloured eyes of his.

In them, he saw fear. Immediate fear.

"Nothing that's not *your* fault, human," Phames snarled. Then he was gone, pulling out of Liiran's grasp so deftly it was as if Liiran had tried to grasp smoke, and vanishing through the doorway into their hidey-hole.

Varil was nowhere in sight, and Liiran found himself suddenly alone with Certos.

The vox was still staring at the ground, and Liiran thought he saw a small tremor in his hands. Exhaustion? Guilt?

Fear?

"Come on," he said, holding out the chess set towards the boy. It rattled slightly as the pieces inside shifted, and Certos looked up with the startled, wide-eyed expression of a rabbit caught outside of its hole. "Let's get inside before someone sees us," Liiran said, trying to pitch his tone soothingly.

Certos reached out and took the box, then wrapped it in both arms and held it in front of him like a shield. "Yes, sir."

Liiran wondered at that, but not too much. Certos had been around the military for three centuries, and might not have even met a civilian before. He gave the kid an encouraging smile and then turned and headed for the door, Certos trotting obediently along at his heels.

Inside, he forgot all about Certos' oddness. Inside, he found Mortis and Varil, and another argument.

Mortis sat in one of the chairs, a blanket wrapped around her shoulders. Phames was in mid-pace, his long-fingered hands gesticulating wildly. Varil stood before Mortis like a shield, or a supplicant.

"My lady, maybe he's right," Varil said in a pleading tone that shocked him. He couldn't have imagined the assassin begging for anything. Let alone calling anyone 'my lady' – that was new.

"I *am* right," Phames said. "I've been saying it all along. Well now he's back, safe and sound, and out of danger. It's *time*, Mortis."

"Time for what?" Liiran asked, walking toward the trio. Mortis rose from her chair, and he stopped dead in his tracks.

She looked like a pale ghost of herself. Her cheeks were sunken almost as much as Phames', and if he had thought her skin was pale before – now it was the bluish white of a corpse.

But it wasn't just that. It was the way she moved. Just getting up from the chair looked like an effort, and Varil leaped to take her elbow as if she might fall.

Before Liiran meant to move, he was in front of her, taking her into his arms as she caught his shoulders in her bone-thin hands.

"Liiran," she whispered, her voice a rasp. "It's good they got you out of there." She didn't smile; in fact, her expression was almost solemn, as if being happy at his return was an effort that was beyond her.

"Voxae ma, what's wrong with you?" Liiran asked.

"Nothing, Liiran," she said, but Phames cut in, as sharp as a blade.

"It's that connection between you. You're sucking her dry."

A surge of guilt met the surge of relief coming and overwhelmed it. She hadn't come to rescue him because she *couldn't*, not because she hadn't wanted to. But how could he be relieved that he was killing her?

"Then we have to break this connection," Liiran said, looking up and meeting Phames' accusing gaze. "Right now."

"That's exactly what *I* said."

"Then how?" Liiran asked. "How do we do it? There's no reason to leave it now. I'm fine."

Mortis shook her head. "We don't know. We've never seen anything like this before, and we don't know how to fix it. So let's leave it for now. I won't fade away so quickly."

Fade away? "Is that what's going to happen if we don't fix this? You'll fade away?" Liiran asked.

She shrugged. "Who knows? But it won't come to that. Come, Liiran, let's focus on something else. Perhaps a solution will present itself."

She drew back, and he let her go reluctantly. Something felt off, and he searched her expression. "There's something else. Something else has changed."

Varil made a soft sound, almost a chuckle, but too muted to really qualify. "Journalists. They can't stop prying."

Liiran looked around at Varil as Mortis sank back down in her chair. "What do you all know that I don't?"

"It's all right. I was about to tell you, Liiran," Mortis said. It was a cool, repressive tone that he'd never heard from her before, and it ripped his attention from Varil and right onto Mortis again. Her eyes were as bottomless as they had ever been. No, more. He had to focus elsewhere before he fell into her eyes. "Niveus gave me back my memory. I'm myself again."

It was as if the colour drained out of the world. Of course, that's what was missing – her humanity. She seemed distant, removed from him, and that was because she was. It had been ridiculous to call him a man who walked hand in hand with death – Niveus should have known better. He had never touched death, until just now. And she had never been so cold until now, now that she'd lost the humanity she'd learned from him.

"That's great," he said through numb lips that he forced into a parody of a smile. "I'm really happy for you."

"You'd better be," Phames said, and Liiran wondered why. Why bother to snipe at him at all? Liiran was no threat to him now – Phames had won, and gotten the cold mortivox back, just as he had wanted from the beginning.

Varil's face was a mask of bemused concern. He couldn't look at her, but the alternative was to look at Mortis – to look into those bottomless eyes and be swallowed up.

Liiran looked away from both of them, away from Phames as well, unable to bear any of their gazes. And his eyes landed on Certos, crouched in a corner, laying out chess pieces.

"If we don't know how to break the bond right now, then we should do something we *can* figure out," he said, watching the boy place a last pawn into its designated square and then study the board with focused attention. "We should focus on something else right now. We should free Certos."

Certos' head came up in a jerk and focused on him. The boy's mouth opened, then closed with a snap.

"You're right," Mortis said. He imagined that there was relief in her voice, but it was a lie. She didn't feel anything. How could death feel? If death could feel, it would be the most torturous existence possible.

"Right," Liiran said, and headed for Certos. The boy jumped to his feet and backed away until he hit a wall.

Suddenly Varil was at Liiran's shoulder. "What are you going to do? He looks scared."

"I'm not scared," Certos said in a rush, and shrank against the wall as if trying to press himself through it.

"I thought I'd try to break that collar," Liiran said, but Certos' body language made him stop a few feet away. "Voxmarae break pretty easily. Shouldn't the collar be similar?"

"The collar is pretty sophisticated," Phames said, gliding up towards them obliquely and looking from Liiran to Certos and back. "It might not be the same."

Liiran shrugged. He wanted to do this now, so he could stop thinking about the way Mortis looked at him, the way her slender figure had felt in his arms, the cool smoothness of her skin. Besides, it needed to be done, and there was no time like the present. "Then we'll try something else. Certos, don't you want me to do this?"

Certos' eyes darted back and forth, then focused on him for perhaps the first time. "I want to be free," he said, "but what if something horrible happens when you take the collar off?"

Liiran took another couple of steps forward and sank down to one knee, moving slowly as if to tame a cornered animal. The slower pace seemed to calm Certos somewhat. "Horrible like what?"

"I could kill you all." Certos' eyes were the colour of dried blood, and bored into Liiran's. "I hate them so much. And my power's been sealed up for so long. Maybe it'll explode."

Again the memory of yellow police tape outside the museum flashed before Liiran's eyes.

"I'm death," she said. "You're war, Certos. It's not the same."

"But it's not very different. People could die, not directly, but because they hurt each other," Certos said, his voice high and tight.

Phames reached out, his arm darting forward like a striking snake. "I say we risk—" he said, but sparks jumped between the collar and his reaching fingers, and he jerked them back, hissing with surprise and pain.

"Everyone cool it a second," Liiran said, then he reached out and grasped the boy's shoulders in both hands. "Listen to me, Certos," he said. "We're all going to trust you to *control* your powers when I break this seal. You're forewarned. You know what's coming. Now you have to ask yourself whether you can do this."

Certos made a small sound in the back of his throat, like a soft whimper. "Why are you trusting me?"

Liiran could only be honest. "Because I don't have any other choice. Either we do this, or what was the point of getting you away from Niveus? You'll just fall under someone else's control – mine, maybe, or the Talgaran queen, or who knows who? No one should have that kind of power."

There was a long, long pause, then Certos nodded. "I'll try."

"Don't try," Liiran said. "Do it. Ready?"

The boy's Adam's apple bobbed. "Yes," he breathed, and squeezed his eyes shut tightly, his brow furrowing deeply in concentration.

As Liiran reached for the collar and worked his fingers in between its cool surface and the boy's warm throat, he hoped he really could break it by hand. Otherwise that whole exchange would have been a lot of drama for nothing.

With only the slightest pressure, the collar snapped.

Chapter 51

Liiran's first impression when he awakened was not pain. Oh, he felt pain, but it didn't matter. He bounced up from the floor with the hot metallic taste of adrenaline in the back of his throat and his heart thundering in his ears.

There was a figure in front of him, hazy behind the film of rage, but he didn't care. He barely noticed it as he wheeled around and saw the one he *really* wanted.

"What's wrong with y—" That was as far as Phames got before Liiran launched himself bodily at him, fists swinging. He wanted Mortis back, and *this* was the bastard who had stolen her from him. It was his fault that she knew what she was, his fault that she'd lost what humanity she'd gained with Liiran. In his blinding rage, he blamed Phames for the near-arrests, for the fact that they were far from home and in danger, for every bad thing that had happened to him in the last week.

It was *all* his fault.

Liiran felt himself connect. He *felt* the cool, yielding skin of the other man under his fingers. He wrapped his hands around that slender, chicken-like neck and began to squeeze.

Then two things happened.

Phames slipped from his grasp like smoke, and hands grabbed him. Slender hands. Strong hands, but somehow insubstantial at the same time.

"What's wrong with you, Liiran?" Mortis said. In his wildness, he thought he detected concern in her tone.

He could hear someone screaming with inchoate rage, and he fought the grasp, struggled to get to his enemy. His throat hurt from the shrieks, but they sounded as if they came from far away.

Now someone else was shouting. Varil. "What did you do to him?" Even in his distraction he saw her run at the figure he'd seen before, blades flashing. The creature spread massive wings and sidestepped her, did something with one and Varil went sprawling. The knives clattered across the stone floor and she didn't move.

Liiran's ire changed direction. He reversed and leaped forward at Varil's attacker, but again those gentle hands held him back.

"No, Liiran, you've got to calm down. Certos, please stop what you're doing to him," Mortis said.

"Why?" The voice might have sounded petulant, if it hadn't rumbled like the sound of distant cannon fire. "Besides, I didn't mean to do it. He shouldn't have connected himself to me with the magic, or it wouldn't have backlashed onto him."

"Because I'm asking you to."

"And I'm *telling*." Phames' voice was hard as stone. "We don't have time for this." Liiran stopped fighting Mortis and looked around for him, searching for the source of the voice so he could rip his throat out.

Certos huffed. "It isn't as easy as that," he said, but Liiran abruptly felt heavy. The adrenaline began to ebb, and he sagged in Mortis' arms as if lead weights had been attached to his limbs.

"Thank you," Mortis said coolly. "I'm taking him out of here for a bit to calm down. See to Varil."

"But you can't," Phames said. His voice no longer aroused more than a stirring of jealous ire, and he sounded as if he were speaking from the other end of a long tunnel.

Distantly, Liiran wondered if he were passing out. If so, it was sure taking a long time.

"I can," Mortis snapped. "I'll be fine taking a short flight, Phames." Then the world swung crazily as she lifted him bridal-style into her arms.

"No, this is backwards," he murmured nonsensically, wrapping his arms around her neck and burying his face in her fragrant hair. Dust and ash and lilies.

She didn't hush him, or acknowledge his words in any way as she strode towards the door. In a moment she landed on top of one of the nearby buildings and then laid him out on the roof.

He rolled onto his back and forced his eyes open. All he saw was sky for an instant, and then his vision filled with Mortis' face.

This time he was sure. She was worried. For some reason, that was a relief.

"What happened?" His voice sounded slurred to his own ears. His emotions felt disconnected and distant, and his mind reeled from the experience. He'd never felt such complete and uncontrolled rage against anyone before.

Did he really hate Phames that much, or had it just been Certos' influence? He knew he had no reason to like the man, but he hadn't thought his feelings went so deep. Liiran shuddered – he had tried to kill Phames. He'd never even considered doing something like that to anyone before in his whole life.

But now he was beginning to calm down, his mind clearing of the unnatural emotions.

Mortis took his hand, holding it in both of his. Her skin was so thin that it felt like paper, but her bones were still strong underneath. "The magic Certos had pent up inside him seems to have run into you when you broke the collar."

Liiran closed his eyes for a moment and realized that he knew that already. That was what Certos had meant when he talked about backlash. He opened them again, frowning. "I didn't make a connection with him like I did with you, so why?"

"I don't know. Maybe because you touched the collar."

That made him remember something – the cool shift of chain links under his palm, and a strange warmth at that touch. Collars and leashes were used to control, right? Certos' demeanor had completely changed after that. "No, I touched the chain," he said, his voice darkening. "I bet that's what it was. I was Certo's owner or something, at that moment, so it fell on me."

Cool fingers touched his forehead, smoothed hair back out of his eyes. He still didn't much feel like moving, but his thoughts were becoming clearer. If there had been any lingering doubt about what he was doing, it was gone now. They had enslaved that man, had even given him a collar and leash like an animal, and then used him to take over the world.

The world needed to know the truth, and he was pretty sure he knew how he was going to make sure they did.

But first he had to deal with this, figure out where he stood with Mortis and convince the others that they had to go straight back to Laxamora now – before Niveus got on his fancy jet and beat them back there, or somehow figured out what they were going to do next and alerted the police to expect them.

"You're probably right," Mortis said, her gentle tones breaking into his determined thoughts.

He looked up, searched her expression. He needed to understand. "You really remember everything now?"

"Everything."

He pushed himself up onto his elbows, then reached for her, cupping her cheek. It wasn't the lingering effects of Certos' magic, he was sure, that gave him the energy to do it.

It was desperation.

"Then you haven't forgotten me, right?"

Confusion flickered in her dark eyes. He could meet them now, without falling in, but he didn't know why. Perhaps it was the presence of emotion within them that gave a bottom to the well, gave it dimensions and depth, rather than going on forever.

"Of course I haven't forgotten you, Liiran. I'm talking to you, aren't I?" He got the definite impression that she was humouring him.

"Mortis, please don't dismiss me. I have something very important to tell you." Her eyes widened faintly – more confusion, and surprise.

He drew a breath, girded himself. "I told Niveus that the reason I was with you, helping you all this time, was because I loved you."

This was it. This was the moment that was supposed to come in a real relationship. He had never met a woman like this, let alone loved one. This was his moment.

The silence drew out for a long while.

"I'm sorry, Liiran," Mortis said. "I don't know what you want me to say."

The words were a physical blow.

Liiran let out a breath and lowered his hands away from her face, his eyes dropping to examine the gritty surface of the roof.

"Nothing," he said. "I just... wanted you to know how I felt. I suppose."

"I've upset you."

Liiran's lips twisted. "It's all right." His chest felt as if a hot knife had slipped right between his ribs. "You're a vox. You're just different from me. I knew that pretty much from the beginning."

Her brow furrowed faintly. "Liiran," she said. "If I weren't a vox, and you told me something like that, how would you have expected me to react?"

He laughed, a soft mirthless sound. But at the way she drew back at the reaction, her eyes flickering with confusion again, he forced himself to answer her honestly. "I suppose I would have *hoped* you'd have said you loved me, too."

Her hand slipped into his, much to his surprise. "And given I'm a vox, you don't want me to say that?"

Hope flared, then died almost at once. He shook his head. "I'd want you to tell me the truth, that's all."

"I see." Her hand slipped out of his, and he nearly tried to recapture it, but she lifted her hands to cup his cheeks the way he had done with her just a moment ago. "Liiran, the truth is that I don't know what I feel for you."

His face, which had been turned up towards her with that swell of hope and wonder once more, fell.

He saw her smile ruefully. "The truth is that I don't know much about human emotions, or love. But I do know that you've changed me. I know that I feel *something*. I know that when you're in danger, it makes me feel as if I am in danger. I know that when you're hurting, it makes me hurt. And I don't think that's just because of the connection between us."

She smiled. "I remember who I was, who I am, but I also remember that I never felt this sort of thing before I met you." And now she leaned close, so close he felt her lips brush against his as she spoke. "And I think I know this is what I'm supposed to do."

And she kissed him.

Liiran felt as if the ground had fallen out from under him. He was flying and falling at once. Could he really believe what she was saying? Yet he was certain she would never intentionally lie to him – at least, the Mortis who had come to him one night, lost and confused and alone, would never lie.

Would this Mortis? No, he couldn't make himself believe she would try to manipulate his emotions like this.

Their lips parted once more and Mortis drew back from him, but not far. Her lips were curved in what looked like a nervous smile, and her hands were still cupping his cheeks.

He looked into her eyes, his jaw slack, but a smile beginning to grow on his lips. "I don't know that much about love. No one really does. But that... sounded pretty good to me."

She nodded, and he leaned forward for another kiss, only to be stymied as she looked up abruptly. He turned to follow the direction of her gaze and saw Phames and Certos come in for a landing just a few feet away. Varil was cradled in Certos' arms, her eyes open and alert. Apparently Certos' attack hadn't hurt her significantly, and she dropped down lithely to stand as soon as they touched down.

Certos had grown three feet in height and at least one in width. His clothing, formerly loose and overlarge, strained against his muscled chest and thighs. But there was still something boyish and uncertain in his reddish, darting eyes, something subservient in the way he landed just behind Phames and let him take the lead. As with Mortis, his time with humans had left its stamp upon him.

Liiran turned back to Mortis and studied her. Would that mark, that change remain forever? Would she always be capable of loving him, or would that humanity evaporate quickly now that her true memories had returned to her?

"We need to break the bond," Phames said briskly, almost before his feet touched the ground. "If Liiran's recovered enough."

Despite his irritation at the interruption, Liiran knew Phames was right. Mortis' fragility was obvious, and he didn't even know if she could manage the flight that he was going to ask of her in her current condition. He got to his feet and faced Phames.

Phames lifted his chin and narrowed his eyes. It was obvious that he was spoiling for a fight. But this time, for once, Liiran wasn't going to give him one.

"I'm sorry about what just happened," Liiran said, looking Phames right in the eye. "I know we don't like each other, but it doesn't matter. We're on the same side, and what really matters right now is taking care of Mortis, and taking down Niveus. Are you with me on that?"

For a moment, Liiran wasn't sure if Phames was even going to respond. The vox stared at him as if he couldn't believe his ears, then nodded, slowly. "I'm with you. And there's nothing for you to apologize for. It was Certos that made you do it."

"Maybe," Liiran agreed, his lips twisting in a wry smile. "But the emotion came from somewhere."

Now he turned his attention to Certos, who stood in an awkward stance that looked completely unnatural on his new, huge frame. Certos' wings flared a little, unsettled, as Liiran looked at him.

"Did I take control of you somehow when I touched that chain?" Liiran asked.

Certos nodded. "But you can't control me now," he said, an edge in his tone. "I'm free, now. No human can tell me what to do."

It wasn't a reassuring response, but Liiran forced himself to smile. "That's the way it should be. Will you help us deal with Niveus?"

The red eyes narrowed. "Definitely."

Now he looked at Varil. She was rubbing a spot on the back of her neck, wincing, but otherwise looked fine. "What about you? Are you sticking around?"

She lowered her hand, darting a look at Mortis before answering. "Quite frankly I don't completely understand everything that's going on here. But what I do know is that stopping Niveus is not only my assignment, it's the first step in freeing my country. And it's my duty to go where Mortis needs me. So if I can do something to help, then yes, I'll stick around."

Liiran opened his mouth to ask what Mortis had to do with anything, then closed it again. Right now, that was an irrelevant question. Maybe he'd find time to ask it later, but for now he just nodded. "I'm sure we could find a use for you," he said wryly.

"Great," she said, folding her arms and returning his smile.

"Liiran," Phames said. "This is all very heartwarming..."

Liiran nodded and turned back to Phames. He'd said what he had to say, and asked the questions he needed to ask. Back to business. "Right. Any ideas?"

He looked from face to face and saw expressions ranging from bemusement to discomfort, but not a single answer was forthcoming.

Finally, it was Mortis who spoke. "From what I understand of magic, it is mostly about willpower. Maybe if you just *try* to break the

284

connection, it'll break. I've tried myself, but it may need both of us working together."

Liiran wanted to protest that he had no idea how to *do* that, but he sighed and nodded. Nothing ventured, nothing gained. "All right, I'll try."

Some impulse made him grasp her hands in his and he closed his eyes. He didn't know what he was looking for, but he was certain that if he wanted to break this connection, he needed to know what it felt like first.

Struggling to ignore the eyes of his spectators, not to mention all the little distracting noises and sensations that came with the city, he reached deep onside himself. There had to be something there, something foreign.

And yes, there it was. It felt like a fleeting sensation of warmth, in the place where his wound had been. It was so faint, he thought at first that it was nothing, but as he concentrated on that spot, he felt the current of it, the way the heat entered him and flowed through him on the pathways of his veins and arteries.

That was what it felt like to suck the life out of the woman he loved, apparently.

But what to do about it? He mentally prodded at the spot, tried to will it to stop, to grow cold and stop flowing. He tried visualizing a door closing, visualizing a dam blocking the way. He could sense Mortis trying as well. Somehow through the connection, he could feel her fear, feel her trying to choke off that stream, or cut it with a knife.

But still it kept flowing, bit by bit, drawing the life out of Mortis and into him.

He opened his eyes and saw Mortis do the same, saw helplessness and frustration in those black depths to match his own.

"I don't think I can do it."

"Damnit, Liiran!" Phames exploded, clenching his hands into fists. "Don't you know that if we don't do this Mortis could die? You have to try harder!"

Liiran released Mortis' hands and rounded on Phames. "I know that." Anger rose up inside him again, this time tinged with despair. And this time it was all him. "I've tried everything I know how to do, and everything I can think of, but it's not *working*. We have to try something else."

"What, then?" Phames snarled. "What should we try?"

The rage died, crushed by a wave of fear and hopelessness that was almost overwhelming. "I don't know," Liiran said, turning to glance at Mortis who stood still and white, her hands clasped together tightly. "I have no idea what to do."

Chapter 52

Liiran had been walking restlessly for an hour when a rustling above him made him look up with a rush of fear. Mortis was going to die because of *his* stupidity. It would just be the icing on the cake if she died all the more quickly because he got himself hurt again.

Thankfully, it was only Varil, who dropped down from a nearby rooftop and stood before him, hands on her hips. Despite her injured foot, she landed so silently he wondered if the rustling sound had been deliberate, to warn him that she was coming.

"How long are you going to mope? I'm tired of following you around."

The words prompted a flare of anger. He didn't want company right now – shouldn't that be obvious? "Then don't follow me around." He stalked off down the street in a random direction, but she kept pace with him with an easy stride that he knew there was no way he could outpace.

But though she stayed with him, she didn't speak. Slowly, his shoulders began to unknot themselves and he found her company oddly soothing. He had been alone with voxae so long it was hard to remember what human company was like. The little sounds and movements of a human being, which a vox could only imitate.

His irritation and restlessness weren't her fault. It was that he knew what he needed to do about Niveus, but he just couldn't bring himself to do it, when the exertion it required would probably kill Mortis. Anyway, if she were gone, what difference did it really make if Niveus were still in power? At least he was used to ruling over a world that had no death. At least he didn't have Certos, now.

"Why are you still here, anyway?" he asked finally, ready to be distracted from his morbid thoughts. "You said something before about staying with Mortis. But you never seemed to care that much about what we were doing before."

Varil's lips twisted wryly. "That was before I found out what they were," she said, her expression strangely uncertain. "My people have always worshipped Mortis, the goddess of death. When I found out who she was, I knew I had to help her with whatever she needed."

Liiran spoke without thinking. "But she's not a goddess. She's a vox. She's not really any different from the sparks in that lamp there," he said, pointing to a nearby lamppost, the havox dancing merrily in the bulb.

"Do you really believe that, Liiran?" Varil asked, catching his arm and bringing them to a halt. "You seem to think Mortis is pretty special yourself."

He jerked his arm out of her grip, averting his gaze. "That's different. I don't *worship* her. I don't worship *death*."

"No," Varil said coldly. "You wish she was human, rather than what she is. And you want to hold onto her, to change her. Isn't that pretty selfish?"

Liiran opened his mouth to deny that, but closed it. He had no answer.

And her words brought another ugly possibility to the surface. Was it his fault that they couldn't break the connection, because he wanted to keep her with him, not lose the last bit of her that he had left?

Varil's eyes seemed to penetrate him, and after a moment, she shook her head. "Don't give me that puppy-dog look," she sighed. "I could say the same about every man or woman who's ever fallen in love."

Liiran couldn't look at her. She was right, he knew. He made his way to a nearby bench and sat down, dropping his head into his hands. "I don't know what to do. If we don't break this bond between us, she'll die, and it'll be my fault."

She sat beside him, arms akimbo and body loose and comfortable. "This isn't all about you, Liiran. And if you just get over yourself, you'll figure out what you've got to do next. Think you can do that?"

Liiran glared at her. "It's about *Mortis*. Something needs to be done, damn it, and you don't even care."

"Oh, I care," Varil returned, her eyes narrowing. "I care enough to give you the smack you so richly deserve."

"How can I fix something if I don't even know how?" Liiran exploded. "I don't know anything about magic, or voxae or anything. I can't put anything right—"

He stopped, staring at her, open-mouthed. Her eyebrows rose. "You thought of something?"

Liiran jumped up and grimly started back the way he had come. "Yeah, there's just one person who can fix anything."

He stepped into their room a few minutes later, Varil a shadow on his heels.

"I think we need to ask Niveus for help with Mortis," he said.

"*What?*"

This exclamation came, predictably, from Phames, who strode towards Liiran with such vigour that for a moment Liiran thought he was going to strike him.

Liiran made a gesture of dismissal, hoping without much faith that he could cut Phames off before he really got going. "Look, I know what you're going to say. I'm crazy. It'll just land us all right back where we were before, with Mortis in danger or even in a voxmar again. But don't you see that we have no choice?"

"We have a choice," Phames hissed. "We can try something *else*."

"What?" Liiran asked, spreading his hands wide. "What should we try? I'm no mage, Phames. I don't know how to break magical connections with voxae, if anyone in the world even does. I don't know what else to do. But I do know one thing – Niveus is the vox of order. He brought Mortis' memories back with a snap of his fingers. Isn't there a good chance he can fix this, too?"

Phames began to pace, gesturing wildly with his spider-thin hands. "He won't just help her and leave us in peace, damn it. He'll make us promise something we don't want to give. That's what he's like. We'd have to make some kind of deal with him, and we *won't* like it. And when he's got Mortis in his hands, we'll realize we made a big mistake."

Liiran shook his head. "We have to risk it."

Certos stepped forward slowly. "Is this what he's waiting for?" the vox asked in his booming voice.

Liiran looked from Phames over to Certos so fast his neck creaked. "What do you mean?"

"We've detected little sign of pursuit since we escaped," Certos said. "Niveus wants me back, and he wants Mortis to surrender herself. He's searching for us, but if he really wanted to find us, he would commit more resources."

Liiran felt his jaw fall towards his chin. "Are you trying to tell me he's already realized we'll come to this conclusion?"

Certos' massive shoulders rose and then fell again. "It's what I would tell him to do."

"Well what do you tell *us* to do, then?" Liiran asked, grasping at straws. There had to be another way.

"Be unpredictable," Certos said. "Go elsewhere, away from Niveus, and do something else. Bring him down, like you were going to do. Then maybe he'll deal with us on even footing."

"Yes," Phames said, turning to face them. "Yeah, that's exactly what we need to do. If Niveus isn't on top of the world, with all his armies and magi and everything, then he'll have to do what *we* tell him to do."

"He's got a point, Liiran," Varil said.

Liiran bit his lip, and looked to Mortis. She was the only one who hadn't spoken up, and this was *her* problem. She should be the one to decide.

When their eyes met, Mortis came forward to join the group, but still she said nothing.

He couldn't tear his eyes away from her, but Liiran couldn't stand the silence. "By the time we do all that, Mortis could be dead. Then it'll be pointless."

"We must risk it," Certos said. "Mortis won't die easily, sir. She is weak, but not dead yet. And if we focus our attention on the task at hand, it'll go quicker."

So long as Mortis was in danger, so long as he was sucking the life out of her, could he really focus on political machinations?

Wasn't her life more important than anything else right now?

Mortis came forward a few more steps until her face filled his vision. "Liiran," she said, her cool hands cupping his cheeks. "It's all right. I can wait."

"Do you even know how much longer you have?" he asked, jerking back out of her grasp, though all he wanted to do was throw his arms around her. If he let himself sink into her touch now, he'd do anything she asked.

Even risk killing her.

"I don't know," Mortis said, shaking her head gently as she let her hands fall. "But it's not over yet, Liiran. I will live a bit longer."

Phames spoke up snidely. "And if you can keep yourself from getting hurt again, it'll be that much longer."

Certos drew himself up. "We'll all protect Liiran's body. Maximize Mortis' life until we have a good opportunity."

Liiran sagged, defeated. "All right. We'll do it your way."

He closed his eyes. There had been a plan forming before, before he'd gotten side tracked on the roof with the failure to break the bond. Now all they could do was put it into action, and hope that it was enough.

"In that case," he said, straightening and opening his eyes, "we have to go back to Laxamora, now. It's time to show the world who Niveus really is."

They all exchanged glances, and Mortis nodded. "We'll follow your lead, Liiran."

*   *   *

It didn't take long for them to get ready to go, moving with purpose and determination. They worked efficiently as they packed up their few belongings and, under Varil's direction, eradicated any sign that they had been there at all.

But there was a moment of hesitation when it came time to take off. The group of five clustered together in the street outside, and Mortis reached automatically for Liiran, but Phames shook his head and put up a hand to stop her.

"I'll take him. Are you even up to flying that distance?"

Liiran had been ignoring that exact worry. Now he looked at Mortis and saw her hand falter.

"I... I'm sure it'll be fine," she said.

"No," Liiran said, forcing her hand down with gentle pressure. "You should concentrate on getting well and conserving your strength. There are three voxae and two humans."

To his chagrin, Mortis backed down without a fight, offering him a wan smile and withdrawing her hand. "Yes, you're right, Liiran. Very well. You go with Phames, and Varil with Certos, and I'll fly along beside you."

"No." This time the objection came from Certos. Everyone looked at him in surprise, but he was looking fixedly at Mortis, ignoring the sudden attention. "You should stay here and wait for us to return."

"We shouldn't leave her alone," Phames objected. "What if Niveus finds her?"

Certos shrugged. "Niveus is down at least two magi since the last time he summoned and entrapped us. I doubt he has the manpower to do it again right now."

"Mortis is weaker than the last time. Maybe seven is enough," said Phames.

"Then ultimately it doesn't matter where we go. If he traps Mortis we can get her out again as soon as we finish our mission."

"*If* we can find her. If they haven't buried her at the bottom of the Pharosian Gorge in the meantime."

"Transporting her safely will leave tracks we can follow if we act quickly."

Liiran had watched his argument as long as he could stand. Phames and Certos weren't showing any signs of backing down, and they were starting to attract attention from passersby.

"We can't just leave her alone here, Certos," Liiran said, scarcely able to believe that he and Phames had agreed on something. "We can't go that fast, anyway, since Varil and I can't handle it, so we'll just have to take rest breaks."

But then Mortis spoke up. "No, Liiran, Phames. Certos is right. I'll slow you all down, and we must deal with Niveus."

"But—"

She smiled, and it cut off Liiran's protest as abruptly as a slap. "But I can't stay here, by myself, and cause more problems for all of you, either." She straightened slightly. "So I'll scatter. I'll meet you all there."

"Scatter?" That was Varil, echoing the question that Liiran had only begun to ask.

"She'll split apart into smaller mortivoxae and travel that way." The wind seemed to have gone out of Phames' sails. He spoke quietly and evenly, keeping his eyes fixed on Mortis. "She does it all the time in small ways. Any time someone dies, a part of her travels there to do it. It'll take less energy than coming with us."

Liiran couldn't quite relax without some clarification. "Oh, so this is safe, right?" he asked, looking from Phames to Mortis and back. He was getting an odd vibe, yet Phames wasn't objecting to this idea. If it were dangerous, he definitely would.

"It's safe," Mortis said. "Like Phames said, it's a natural process for us."

It was the only suggestion that hadn't prompted vociferous objection by anyone, and Liiran could feel the minutes ticking by. How long before Niveus realized that they weren't going to take the bait? How long before he gave up and put all his considerable resources into arresting Liiran and Varil again, and got the University magi together to put Certos, Phames and Mortis in bottles and bury them somewhere they'd never be found?

He had to trust Mortis, trust that she knew what was best.

"All right," he said before he could change his mind. "We'll see you when we get to Laxamora. Meet us in my apartment. They should have stopped watching it by now, and there are some things I have to get there anyway."

Mortis smiled and nodded. "Of course."

In an instant, Liiran realized he'd made some kind of mistake. He leaped forward. "Wait!"

But it was too late. Mortis was dissolving in a shower of gold sparks, small winged creatures detaching from her body, only to break into even smaller version of themselves, until all that Liiran could see were billions of stars, flying in all directions.

Mortis slipped through his fingers, literally, and Liiran was left holding the Talgaran clothes Varil had lent her.

In that moment he was sure he would never see her again.

"Come on," Phames said, grabbing Liiran by the arm. "We've got to go."

Liiran nodded and complied, holding still and bundling the clothes into his duffle bag just before Phames wrapped his arms tightly around his waist and lifted off. He barely paid attention to the scenery as it rushed past, unable to dispel his last sight of Mortis' face.

The last thing he'd seen before she closed her eyes was naked and terrible fear.

Chapter 53

The trip back to Laxamora was hellish.

They pushed the limits of human endurance, not knowing how long they had, so the buildings and fields whizzed by nauseatingly. Liiran shivered in the wind, Phames' arms no shield at all against the elements. They even ran into a rainstorm at one point, leaving Liiran shuddering with cold as the rainwater dried on his skin.

They had to fly quick and low. Low enough that the humans could breathe at their speed was low enough that people would notice. They would attract attention any time they came close to a town, so their course had to describe wide arcs around any settlement. In broad daylight, they would surely be noticed, and it was possible – even likely – that word would get back to Niveus.

Taking a circuitous route meant that they had to travel all the faster, to make up the time, with all its attendant discomforts.

But he didn't call for any breaks or stops. He hoped at times, prayed that Varil would call a halt, but she hung stoically in Certos' massive arms, her eyes closed to slits against the wind and her arms hugging herself. He didn't imagine that she was any more comfortable in her tight jumpsuit than he was, but she never complained.

And neither did Liiran. The quicker they got to Laxamora, the more likely it was that they would outrun pursuit.

Not only that, but the sooner they got there, the sooner he could satisfy himself that Mortis was all right, and that the fear he thought he had seen had nothing to do with the fact that she had scattered herself – literally – to the four winds.

The ocean winds were even colder, but it didn't take long to traverse the channel between the two main continents. Soon they were dodging buildings. Phames arrowed straight for Liiran's apartment building, and before he realized it, they were slowing down.

They landed jarringly on his patio, as Liiran's knees buckled the instant Phames let go of him. The vox had to grab him again to keep him from hitting the patio door hard enough to possibly shatter the thick glass.

Varil fared scarcely better. Certos landed a moment after Phames and waited for Varil to nod before letting go. However, the instant she lost his support she crumpled like a ragdoll, her chest heaving and her limbs trembling.

It took some time before Liiran felt able to stand, but he managed finally to shake off the numbness and weakness, and to catch his breath. Then he shrugged off Phames' supporting hand and hobbled to the door.

Living on the twentieth floor had its advantages, and the door was still unlocked as he'd left it. It slid open with nary a whisper.

"I'll check for security," Certos murmured and spread his wings again, taking off and circling the building, quickly moving out of sight.

"So will I," Varil said, drawing a knife from a boot and moving stealthily towards Liiran's front door.

"Don't kill anyone," Liiran called after her in a desperate, carrying hiss.

She raised her hand and waggled the knife blade in a distinctly uncaring manner. "No promises."

Whatever she was going to do, Liiran didn't want to know. He moved straight for his bedroom, trying not to listen for the sounds of falling bodies. Phames shadowed him, close behind.

In his bedroom, Liiran hurried to the closet and pulled the door open, pushing clothing aside. He was sure they had searched the apartment, but they hadn't tossed it like burglars. Everything seemed to be in its place, undisturbed. Surely they hadn't found his box.

But it was gone.

He sat for several moments, numb, scarcely able to believe his senses. Centuries of carefully gathering evidence, risking his job – his *freedom* – each time he added to the little stash, and it was all wasted.

"What's wrong?" Phames asked, and Liiran nearly jumped out of his skin. He'd forgotten he was there.

He turned, still kneeling on the floor. "We're fucked. My plan isn't going to work."

Phames dropped to the floor beside him, forehead wrinkling. "Why?"

Liiran could scarcely talk. "My evidence. Everything I've gathered that could be used to show what Niveus has really done. The police took it."

"You gathered evidence?" Phames asked, eyebrows rising as an expression of newfound respect spread across his face.

"Yes. I've been gathering it nearly my whole life." Phames was smiling, and that pissed him off. "Don't you get it? This was my plan!"

"Liiran," Phames said, reaching out and squeezing his shoulder. "Remember who I am?"

"Phames... vox of decay," Liiran said, confused.

"And Phamile, editor of *The Truth*."

Liiran's eyes widened, and he gripped Phames' arm. "You have footage we can use? In Laxamora?"

Phames nodded.

Varil darted into the bedroom. "Got rid of some officers outside. I stashed them in your hall closet. Hope you don't mind," she said. Then she arched an eyebrow at the sight of them holding each other, grinning. "Did I interrupt something?"

Liiran was pulled out of his relief by the announcement of murder done on his property. "I told you not to kill anyone!"

The assassin shrugged, but there was a smirk playing about her lips. "They're unconscious. So I suggest we hurry, if you've got everything you need?"

Liiran got to his feet. "What I came for has been stolen. Phames is going to go get a replacement, but..." He hesitated, but Phames finished the sentence for him.

"Where's Mortis?"

Liiran had been trying not to think too hard about it. Mortis had said she'd beat them here, and she *should* have – she hadn't had to go slower to accommodate himself and Varil. She should have been here waiting. He turned to Phames, studying him, and watched the other man's eyes turn away and study a photograph on the wall.

It was such blatant guilt that Liiran felt his anger flare. "Tell me what really happened. What did she really do to herself?"

"I already told you," Phames said, his tone oddly listless. "She scattered herself into smaller parts."

"And?"

Phames was silent for so long that Liiran had to resist the urge to grab him by his spindly neck and shake the answers out of him. Finally he shrugged. "And she was probably so weak that she's having trouble pulling herself back together again."

Liiran's temper broke like a wave. He took a step towards Phames, raising his fists. It was so intense he might have thought that Certos had used his magic again, if it weren't so justified by what Phames had just said. The moment of camaraderie they had just shared was completely gone. "And you don't even care. You did it on purpose. You said it was natural, that it was just something normal for her to do, but it's not! You've killed her!"

"I... what did you say?" Phames face, already pale, had gone completely white. His eye sockets were stark black, staring like the holes in a skull. "How dare you.... accuse me... dirty human." Phames was so angry that he could scarcely get the words out, as if they got jumbled up before they could come out of his mouth, jostling together like a crowd fleeing a smoke-filled theatre.

Liiran couldn't care less what Phames had to say. "You couldn't stand that she wanted to be with me. Now you've gotten exactly what you wanted. She's just dust now, like the damned covox in my toaster!"

"No!" Phames took two rapid steps back. "No, I didn't know this would happen. It's because of the bond, weakening her."

"She hasn't been the same since she came out of that voxmar. And you're a vox just like her. You must know if it's some kind of effort to scatter and then reform." Liiran could see the truth of that in Phames' wide, staring eyes, and pressed onwards. "She knew it was dangerous. She *knew* it. Why'd she do it if there was a chance she wasn't going to be able to come out of it? Because she trusted *you*."

Phames fell very still and silent. Liiran couldn't hear anything for a few moments but the rushing of blood in his ears and his own laboured breathing.

Finally Phames' face fell. "I didn't know," he said, wretchedly. "I thought it would be okay. I thought... maybe it would even break the bond, and she'd be the way she used to be."

"Yeah," Liiran said, "but where is she now?"

Phames closed his eyes. "Everywhere, and nowhere."

It was over. Mortis was gone, and it was their fault. Both of them.

Chapter 54

Garelon sat at the table in the War Room, poking and prodding virtual infantry from place to place without much attention. It was difficult to focus and his mind wandered continually back to Certos. Had he done the right thing by not lifting a finger to stop him from escaping? In fact, actively assisting him?

His conscience said yes, so what was the part of him that insisted on feeling guilty?

Probably the same part of him that insisted that no matter what he came up with, if Certos wanted them to lose, they would. It was futile, since Certos certainly wanted nothing more than for his captors to suffer.

Only the hope that Certos might still hold some affection towards him kept an embarrassing fear at bay.

He was brought out of his reverie by a soft tap on the door. "Come in," he called, straightening up in his chair and hoping it looked as if he'd been working rather than moping.

The door opened to admit Calam, and Garelon rose to his feet immediately. "Is something wrong, Minister?"

Calam's face creased into a frown. "Perhaps. I wanted to discuss what happened today with you."

Garelon nodded curtly, smoothing his face into a frown that he hoped was free of guilt. He had expected something of this nature, even if no actual suspicion had fallen upon him. "Of course. Would you like to sit?" he invited, gesturing towards one of the other chairs around the large table, and taking a seat himself.

Calam hesitated visibly, but then took the offered chair, sitting ramrod straight. "You visited the prisoner before he escaped."

Direct. Garelon forced his eyebrows to rise and allowed himself to look guilty. "Yes, I did. Certos wanted to speak to him, to ask him about the other voxae, and I saw no harm in allowing it."

Calam' eyes actually widened. "You saw no harm?"

Garelon had spent a substantial part of the last few hours thinking about what he was going to say when Calam or someone asked him these very questions. It had been one of the only things he could focus on, since the war was definitely not able to hold his attention.

"Yes," he said rubbing the bridge of his nose with the tips of his fingers. "I know it was naive of me now. I remained with them, of course, and heard the entire conversation, but somehow Certos must have communicated some kind of signal to Mr. Uwis that I didn't recognize. I've been thinking about it all day, and I can only surmise that Certos had some ability I wasn't aware of."

Calam leaned forward towards him across the table. "An ability?"

Garelon nodded. Was it working? Was he going to make it?

Calam leaned back, apparently accepting this, though his eyes were narrowed with suspicion. "And did you visit Eve Nellexe as well?"

This was a tack that Garelon hadn't anticipated, and for a moment he was nonplussed, his mind whirling as he struggled to figure out what Calam intended to trap him into admitting by asking him this question.

"No, why?"

"She's dead."

Garelon knew that Calam was looking for a reaction, but he didn't try to censor his own. He couldn't have, in any case. The news took him completely by surprise. "Dead? How?"

Calam seemed to relax minutely, but only minutely. "Yes, her lamp was broken and it seems her wrists were slashed by a piece of the voxmar. I wouldn't be suspicious of her suicide – she was had grown unstable – but the piece that slashed her was missing, until we found a piece much like it in the stomach of an injured guard after the escape. Uwis had stabbed him with it in order to break free."

"How the hell did he get a piece of her lamp?" Was that what Certos had meant when he talked about an opportunity? Garelon had been pretty sure he was talking about the distraction Phames had provided. Maybe he meant both.

"I believe that they had assistance," Calam said coolly.

Garelon glared at him. "You think I killed Dr. Nellexe – an act for which I have no motive – then gave a the murder weapon to Mr. Uwis so he could use it to escape – a second act for which I have no motive."

"I have accused you of nothing, Grand General."

Garelon was starting to lose his cool, and he knew it. "But you implied it."

"Maybe it didn't happen that way," Calam began, but Garelon interrupted him, inspired.

"It seems to me you would better be looking to your own people. After all, you brought Liiran Uwis within a few feet of the prime minister with that weapon on him."

He hadn't won any points by that salvo, and he regretted it the moment Calam' eyes narrowed with faint irritation.

"Indeed. But I know I didn't do it. There's no reason to believe the glass magicked itself through a solid wall into Uwis' cell, so he had help."

"Well, it wasn't my doing," Garelon snapped with real anger.

Calam rose to his feet with a kind of finality. "Grand General Garelon, I hereby accuse you of treason. Will you come quietly?"

"Going to fill the vacancy in the cells left by the escape?"

Calam didn't rise to the bait. "Will you come quietly?" he repeated, withdrawing a set of handcuffs from a pocket.

Garelon got to his feet and held out his hands. "Of course," he said coldly, but inwardly his heart was sinking. He had committed treason, and it was only right that he be arrested. They would have likely figured it out sooner or later, but he had hoped.

Certos' plan hadn't included his master's safety, though. That was clear, now. What was going to become of him?

Chapter 55

Despite his own grief and anger, Liiran couldn't help but feel sorry for Phames.

When he'd accepted that Mortis was gone and might never be coming back, the vox literally folded. He sat down abruptly on the floor, as if his legs were cut out from under him, then folded his wings around his head and legs.

So he did have a bit of human emotion in him, after all, Liiran's mind observed callously. But even as he thought it, he felt ashamed.

He knew how Phames was feeling. He could feel the cold, crushing misery squeezing his own heart. But he had to deal with it later, after their mission was over. For now, he had to set it aside and confront what was in front of him, step by step, until they were safe.

And right now, the first thing he had to confront was Phames.

He crouched down beside the vox and touched his shoulder. "Maybe we can find a way to get her back." The words felt like a lie on his lips.

Phames lifted his head. Liiran was almost surprised to see no tears in his eyes, just a hollow, cold look of resignation.

Liiran wondered for the first time just how lonely and bereft of hope Phames had felt for the last three centuries, with his two closest friends taken prisoner. What must that have been like for him?

"We *will* get her back," Liiran repeated, more urgently. "But first, we need to deal with Niveus."

It worked. Phames' eyes hardened and he nodded once. "You're right."

Liiran straightened and, to his own surprise, offered Phames his hand. To his further surprise, Phames took it, and Liiran drew him up to his feet.

For a moment, the two men stood where they were, a shared understanding passing between them for the first time.

It was at that moment that Certos stepped through the door. "It's time to go."

Liiran and Phames broke apart like guilty lovers, though Varil had been standing there silently watching the whole thing.

301

"Did someone report that we're here?" Varil asked. The words doubled Liiran's heart rate.

"Yes," Certos said, which only made it worse. "We were spotted entering the city. However, they now believe that we are headed for the Parliament Building by air. All units are converging on that location." Certos looked at Liiran. "We aren't going there, right?"

Liiran shook his head. "No, we aren't. Why do they think we're going there?"

The corners of Certos' lips curved upwards slightly. "Because they saw me headed in that direction, carrying a passenger, and there was some confusion about how many of us there are. Some may believe that our group split up, but I am definitely headed there with a passenger fitting your description."

"How the hell did you pull that off?" Varil asked, voicing Liiran's next question before he could formulate it. "Where did you get a passenger?"

Certos shrugged. "I used the materials I found on the street."

"You mean *a person*?"

"What else?"

Liiran was incredulous, but they were getting wildly off track. "Fine, fine, good job, Certos. Let's get out of here before they figure out they were led on a wild goose chase."

He headed for the living room, but another thought struck him. "They're going to figure out it was a ruse when we fly out of here, right?"

Certos nodded. "Most likely they're still watching the skies for the rest of our party."

"Then we go on foot," Phames said. His tone was still subdued, but at least he was engaging again.

For once, Liiran agreed with him. "Right, on foot. We don't have far to go, anyway, and we won't attract as much attention. Are there media alerts out for us?" he asked, turning back to Certos. "On the television?"

Certos shook his head. "I suspect either they have not yet had time to feed our descriptions to local media, or they are attempting to keep things under wraps."

"Probably the latter," Varil put in. "They don't want people knowing that voxae like Certos, Phames, and Niveus exist."

Or Mortis, Liiran's mind supplied, though he was grateful that Varil hadn't mentioned her as well. The very thought of her was painful, and he tried to thrust it away.

It was difficult, though, as he wondered why Certos was leading them out the door without once asking where Mortis was, or suggesting that they wait. As Liiran stepped into the elevator and it began to descend, it occurred to him why.

Of course, Certos must have always known what would happen.

But did that mean that it wasn't the disaster that it seemed? Or had he simply known there was no other option, that the alternative was death?

When they stepped outside, a third option occurred to him.

Maybe Certos didn't really consider her to be gone, just because she had been scattered into pieces, each one too small to be self-aware. After all, the evidence of her presence was everywhere in the street.

A man lay stretched out in a doorway across the street, unmoving. Several crows stood on his chest, their beaks darting in and out busily. Pedestrians gave him a wide berth and even from here Liiran could smell the sickly sweet scent of putrefaction. There was no official organization set up to take the body, and no one who was willing to do it themselves.

The buildings were faring almost as badly from people's fear. Graffiti sprawled over almost every clear surface, much of it declaiming dire warnings of doom. Some writings seemed sarcastic, but the freshest paint was more ominous. Warnings that death would come to all were most common, followed by anger at the government and the hospitals.

Liiran automatically glanced at a newspaper box as he passed, noting the headline. When he saw mention of the Nexalum serum, he stopped and bought one.

Apparently the official story was that the injection was wearing off, an unanticipated, but minor problem. People could go to their local hospital to get a booster, and there was no reason to panic. Judging from the graffiti, people weren't buying it.

A flyer heavily covered in black ink with white lettering blew past them on an errant breeze and Phames bent to pick it up. It was a copy of *The Truth*, his own newsletter.

Liiran glanced at him questioningly as Phames read it over, and the vox handed it to him wordlessly. Liiran read the sarcastic article, debunking much of what the government was saying, though there was no mention of Mortis.

"Your work?" Liiran asked in surprise. When had he had time to write it?

"No," Phames said with a slow shake of his head. "I have a few copycats. I deal with them if they start to get out of line, but most of them do a decent – if naïve – job."

"They're missing a few details," Liiran said, letting the page fall from his fingers.

"Not their fault," Phames replied, his lips pulling wryly to one side.

Even a smile as tiny as that was good to see, though Liiran wasn't sure right now if he would ever smile again.

But Phames sobered quickly. "I still need to get that material."

Liiran nodded. "Go now. We need anything you have that proves that Niveus is a vox. Video footage would have the most punch, but photographs are all right."

Phames nodded, eyebrows rising. "I have some things like that. I never quite dared to show anything that overt before – it would have destroyed my reputation."

Liiran chuckled softly. Would his reputation ever recover? Probably not. "I know what you mean. Get as much as you can and meet us at Laxam Daily News Headquarters." They had reached a bus stop now, and a bus trundled towards them, swaying drunkenly. It looked as if a mob had taken baseball bats to it, but it was still operating.

"I will," Phames said, and immediately turned away, trotting down the street and quickly lost to view.

They climbed onto a bus at the stop. It seemed amazing to Liiran that any infrastructure was running, given that half the Ministry was jailed, and the city was enveloped in riots. As they passed through the downtown core, Liiran saw gangs of people breaking windows, and others spraying more signs of warning. He even saw a wild-looking man standing on a concrete block gesticulating to a crowd.

Doomsday religion had been out of fashion for so long that it took Liiran a few minutes to realize what he must have been saying to the rapt mob.

"This is going to take so long to deal with," Varil murmured into his ear, startling him out of his thoughts. They stood side-by-side, holding onto overhead loops and gazing out the window. Certos and Phames might not fully appreciate the gravity of what they were seeing, but Varil definitely did.

"I thought you were happy that Mortis was back," Liiran asked, then immediately wished he could take back the petty words. Wasn't he happy, too? He hadn't exactly been jonesing to get her back into her voxmar or he wouldn't be on this smelly bus right now.

Varil shrugged. "I am. This is what's supposed to happen. People *should* be scared of death – death is scary, and it happens to everyone. At least, that's the way it should be." She sobered and lifted her shoulders in a shrug. "But that doesn't mean I like to see all this social disorder. None of this needed to happen."

"We've been free of it for so long, we forgot what it was like to be afraid of death," Liiran said.

"No, we've been free of it so long, we only got more afraid. It's like when you've done something so many times you don't think about it anymore, but if you don't do it for a long time, it stops being second nature, even if you haven't forgotten how."

Liiran looked at her. "Did you just say that dying is a bit like riding a bike?"

The assassin just shrugged and gave a wry smile, and that was answer enough.

Before Liiran could think of a better analogy, he had to pull the signal, and soon they stood on the sidewalk in front of the Laxam Daily.

Walking into the building had once made Liiran feel excited, as if he were about to do something important, but he hadn't felt that way in decades. Yet today he certainly had butterflies again.

He found himself quickening his steps, so that the others had to hurry to follow him, and even the sight of the tape holding together a cracked pane in one of the plate glass front doors didn't dampen his excitement.

For now, he wasn't thinking about the death all around him. He was focused on what he had to do.

The security guard at the front desk stood up as Liiran powered past him. "M-Mr. Uwis?" he called. "They were saying you were d... d..."

"Just on a scoop, Alon," Liiran tossed over his shoulder, moving to the bank of elevators and jabbing his thumb into the call button. The

305

elevator opened instantly, thankfully, and the foursome crowded inside before the guard could question who they were.

He drilled his thumb into '12' and the elevator began to rise.

"So," Varil said conversationally, "going to let us in on the plan?"

"We're going to take down Niveus. Just follow my lead and do what I tell you. I'll need all the hands I can get once we're inside." He was in his element, and once they got there, his plan would hopefully become obvious. Trying to explain it would take more time than they had.

The doors opened and Liiran took the lead again. Down a hall and take a right, then he pulled out his card and swiped it through a reader.

The red light failed to turn green.

Liiran stared at it for a moment in consternation, though he wondered immediately why he hadn't considered the possibility of them being stymied by this. Of course they would have cancelled his security access once he was convicted of treason. The card had probably been cancelled before he'd even met Salmo in that park.

Varil poked him. "Let me try, Secret Agent Man." Liiran gladly gave way, and Varil took a couple of steps back.

A few seconds later and with the judicious application of a boot heel, the door opened.

"Thank you, Varil," Liiran said and then headed down the hall. Heads turned as they passed offices, the queer threesome likely attracting attention even if Liiran hadn't been reported deceased and/or fired a week before.

He reached his office before anyone thought to try to stop him, and found someone he'd never seen before sitting at his desk.

The sight was so shocking that for a moment he simply stared. Then he gestured, striding forward and grabbing the woman's chair, pulling it backwards on its wheels. "You're sitting in my chair."

"Who the hell are you?" she exclaimed, jumping to her feet.

"Certos," Liiran said, spinning the chair around so he could sit down and get to work.

In seconds the stranger had been firmly ejected by the huge war vox and Liiran was sitting at his computer, pulling up a fresh document. "Bar the door, please, and don't let anyone in. I need to put some things together."

Certos turned to look out the small window in the door. Varil slunk around the room, opening drawers and looking through files, turning electronic equipment over.

"Do you know that you have a bug in your phone?" she asked conversationally as she set it back down on the desk.

"I figured as much," Liiran said, his fingers flying over the keyboard.

It wasn't going to be his best work, but it would have impact, he hoped.

After ten minutes, Liiran slowly became aware that the noise outside the door was growing. Certos was physically holding the door shut, and Liiran silently thanked him for being ridiculously strong, but eventually the handle itself would break off.

Then a rapid knock at the window startled him out of his work. Varil crossed the room to peek carefully through the blinds in such a way that Liiran wondered if she feared snipers. Probably she did.

"It's Phames," she said with relief. "He's got a box or something."

"Let him in," Liiran said. Varil opened the catch on the window and turned the lever to open it its entire six inches. Phames shoved the box through the gap and then eeled through himself.

"I've got some stuff I think will help," Phames said, grabbing the box back from Varil and leaning over Liiran to put it on his desk. "Look at this one."

Extracting a memory stick from the jumble, he pushed it into the slot on Liiran's computer and opened a file.

It wasn't the greatest picture quality, a bit wobbly from being filmed on a hand-held camcorder, and whoever was taking the film had been standing quite some distance away. But for all of that, the roof of the Parliament Building was identifiable.

As the video rolled on a speck appeared in the sky. The hidden cameraman zoomed in to the maximum the camera could manage, and Liiran saw a fuzzy impression of beating wings. The figure grew quickly, and descended, and as it grew closer the picture sharpened.

As it landed, it turned its head, and Liiran caught a clear shot of Niveus' face. It was unmistakeable, and lasted more than long enough for recognition as Niveus glanced about and straightened his jacket, his great white feathered wings vanishing.

Altus Itolan suddenly came into the picture, and the two men walked off together, chatting amiably as they entered the building from the rooftop door. Then the picture wobbled and went black.

"Voxae ma," Varil breathed at Liiran's shoulder. "Why didn't you ever release that?"

Phames shook his head. "People would have said it was just camera tricks and special effects. People will *still* say that."

Liiran shrugged. "Now people are looking for an explanation, or someone to blame. All we can do is try. Hopefully if we put together enough footage, it'll overcome skepticism, and this will be the video we start with." With a few clicks of his mouse, he began incorporating clips into a montage. He worked for several minutes, faster than he had ever done anything, but he didn't have time to do more than make a dent in the volumes of material Phames had brought him. The vox stood at his shoulder, making suggestions about which files to use.

Finally he felt he had enough, and sat back. "I think that's all we've got time for. Let me finish encoding it and then we're on to stage two."

"What's stage two?" Varil asked.

"Getting this on every news station we can," Liiran said, "and while the world is busy watching that, I'll be writing down everything I know, so it can appear on the front page of tomorrow's newspaper. People will listen. They're too scared not to want an explanation, and the official ones aren't cutting it anymore."

"Sounds like a plan if we can pull this off. And if people aren't dumber than you think. People don't really want the truth, Liiran. They want comfortable lies."

Liiran punched the button to encode the video and twisted around to glare at her. "Then why aren't people believing their lies anymore?" he asked, gesturing towards the window. "If they want comfortable lies, why aren't they heading to the hospital to get their next bogus injection?"

Varil hesitated, but before she could answer, Phames gestured at her dismissively. "Leave him alone. We'll make it happen, and it'll work if I have to spread my wings and tap-dance on the roof of the Parliament Building myself to prove that there are voxae like us around."

Varil's lips thinned skeptically. "I don't doubt we can make it happen. But what do we expect it to accomplish? Niveus isn't going to disappear just because we out him as a vox."

"I know," Liiran said.

Phames stiffened and looked at him. "What?"

Liiran looked up and saw betrayal in Phames' eyes. "Nothing we do right now will probably make a difference today. But maybe, someday, if the information gets into the right hands, it will."

Phames seemed to droop, and he looked away. There was nothing more to be said, and Liiran turned back to his work.

"Liiran, there is someone here to see you," Certos said.

Everyone turned to look at him as he stood at the door, still fighting to hold it closed. "Sounds like there are a lot of people here to see him," Varil said, nonplussed.

"Yes, but this one says he's your sup— boss," Certos said, frowning. "I think you should talk to him."

Liiran looked up, then back down at what he was doing. "Let Salmo in. But no one else." Varil drifted to the door, drawing a blade so she could help Certos keep the rest of the people out.

Liiran wasn't surprised that the instant Salmo entered the room he started blustering.

"Lii! Damn it, what are you doing here?" Salmo pushed into the room, then gave the various people – particularly Certos – nervous glances.

Liiran didn't look up again. He was way too busy copying files. "My job, Sal."

"Your job? Your *job*?" Salmo sounded as if he'd never heard of something so crazy as someone doing their job at their place of employment. "Didn't the fact that your card didn't work and there was someone else at your desk give you a clue that you don't have a job anymore?" He didn't sound angry so much as distressed. Liiran could see his former boss wringing his sausage-like hands out of the corner of his eye.

"Just because you fired me doesn't mean I don't have a job to do."

"But Lii... I mean, you know we've been friends forever and I think the world of you..." Liiran wasn't paying close attention, but he got the gist. The gloves were coming off now. "But you *can't* be here. I've already called the police. They're on their way."

"I know, Sal," Liiran said. "And I understand you had to do that." He pulled three memory sticks out of his computer and jumped to his feet.

Salmo's face smoothed with relief. "So you and your friends are going to leave now? You know I didn't want to see you arrested again."

That prompted a flare of anger. "Yeah. I bet that was really traumatic when I bled on you after I trusted you to meet me alone."

"That's not what I meant and you know it—"

But Liiran wasn't listening. He handed out the memory sticks to Certos, Phames and Varil. "Take these to LBC, NRC and TCC. They're the three top broadcasting companies in the city other than ours."

Pages shot out of the printer, and he handed them out as well, keeping a copy for himself. "Get yourself on camera, on a live feed, and read these. Add personal touches if you want, and I want to see wings. And *make* them broadcast the videos on the memory sticks I gave you. Don't let them tell you no."

Everyone nodded, except Salmo, who gaped then took a determined step towards him. "You... you can't be serious. I don't know what's on that video, but what are you trying to prove, Lii? What do you think they're going to do when they show up and demand broadcast time?"

Liiran ignored him. "Oh," he added as the voxae and assassin turned to go. "And don't *kill* anyone."

"You're such a worrywart," Varil said, and tipped him a wink before she slipped out the door. From the exclamations that Liiran heard, she was pushing through the crowd of would-be observers, and they were shouting questions at her, but Liiran had no doubt she could handle it.

Meanwhile, Certos and Phames spread wings and slipped out the window, causing Salmo to make a strangled sort of noise and stop trying to convince him that this was a bad idea.

That was exactly what Liiran was hoping would happen. He had one more thing to do before he almost certainly went to jail for the rest of his – hopefully not endless – life, and since he'd just sent everyone off on their own missions, he had no one to help him do it.

No one but Salmo Lina. If he could persuade him to.

He pulled the last memory stick from its drive and put a hand companionably on Salmo's shoulder. "Walk with me, boss."

"Where are we going?" Salmo stammered, still obviously in shock.

"Just down a floor or two," Liiran said, steering him to the door. He pulled it open and the staring crowd of his former coworkers pulled back as if he had an infectious disease.

"Salmo? Liiran? What the hell's going on?" one of them called out, but Liiran flapped the paper at the group and they pulled back a few more feet, allowing Liiran to draw Salmo out of the room.

The crowd followed them as far as the elevator, but Liiran barred the door until it closed. No one seemed willing to force the issue, possibly because they'd seen the company he was keeping now.

The elevator began to descend, and Salmo seemed to come alive again.

"Where the hell are you taking me?" Back to blustering again.

"I'm not kidnapping you, Sal. I need your help with a little something, and then I'll go and never bother you again, if that's what you want. Though really after everything I've been through, I deserve a promotion."

"A promotion?" Salmo exclaimed. "For committing treason?"

"I haven't committed treason," Liiran said. "It's treason to report on the truth now? If that's treason, then there's something wrong with this world we've built."

Salmo laughed, and it wasn't a pretty sound. "You've known for decades that that's the world we live in, Lii. We've all accepted it long ago. Eating is more important. Having a job and not being on the street or in prison is more important."

"No. Nothing's more important."

The doors opened on the pregnant silence that ensued after that pronouncement, and Liiran led the way once again. Salmo shuffled after him as if he didn't dare fail to follow, but was afraid to see what lay at the end of their journey.

It made Liiran sad to see him like this. He had always admired the way Salmo seemed to dance through life, but he wasn't dancing now.

They came to another locked door, and this time Liiran unceremoniously took the card key clipped to Salmo's suit jacket and swiped it. The doors unlocked and they stepped into the broadcasting studio.

A news broadcast was going on, and Liiran didn't linger and watch the anchors reading their copy and smiling into the camera, but went straight to the booth. He didn't listen to what they were saying. It would all be lies anyway.

"You can't seriously expect me to play that video, to let you read whatever is on that paper," Salmo said. He'd turned to pleading now. "Damn it, Lii, I'll lose everything. This whole company could be shut down if it looks as if we're supporting traitors. It was hard enough staying in business the last few weeks as it is, with the police crawling all over, questioning all the employees, searching for any 'i' we didn't dot, any 't' we didn't cross. Do you really want to have the jobs of hundreds of employees on your conscience?"

Liiran pushed a technician on a wheeled chair out of the way, eliciting a cry of protest. The man jumped to his feet, but Salmo gestured frantically at him and he backed off. Liiran was grateful for that, but didn't know what it really meant. Probably he was just waiting for the police to arrive and didn't want to cause a scene before then.

He bent over the console, puzzling out the controls. "Sal, do you remember when I first interviewed with you?"

"Sure... sure I do, Lii." Salmo's tone had grown more careful, as if he was dealing with a wild animal who might turn on him.

"Remember you asked me why I wanted to become a journalist? Remember how naïve I was?" Liiran looked up, looking his friend full in the face almost for the first time since he walked into the building. "Remember that?"

Salmo smiled reminiscently, though there was still that nervous, careful look in his eyes. "Sure, I remember. You didn't have a clue how the world works, Lii. You told me that you wanted to find out the truth and broadcast it to other people."

"I remember, too," Liiran said. "I remember you said that you had had a time when you felt the same way, that that was the reason why you became a journalist, too. Of course, you were wiser, even by then, but we had that in common. Of course, I got wiser eventually, too, and I started to keep my head down, and do what I was told."

"Right, we got wiser. I know that that kind of idealistic thing doesn't—"

"It *can* exist," Liiran said. "If we have the strength to do it. If we aren't afraid."

"We have every reason to be afraid," Salmo protested. "Haven't you been listening to me?"

"Sure. But you don't really believe what you're saying, Sal." Liiran took a step towards his friend, pleading now himself. "Sal, *listen*, you know that there's something wrong here. You've seen all the things that they repressed. I've probably only seen a fraction of the things you've seen, and *I* knew there was something wrong with the world long before I went to the desert and found out for real."

Salmo's eyes darted quickly from side to side, as if looking for a rescue. "Lii, it doesn't matter. I mean, the world works fine the way it is. If you push the wrong button it could all explode."

Liiran felt a flash of anger, and he gestured wildly towards the nearest wall. "Voxae ma, Sal. What do you think has already *happened*? The world is exploding right now, and it's going to keep on exploding. Don't we have an obligation to do something about it?"

"There's nothing we can do, Lii. All we have are words and pictures. We can't change anything with them."

"We don't just have words and pictures. We have the *truth* on our side."

Finally, Salmo seemed to have nothing to say.

Liiran's voice dropped and he put his hands on Salmo's shoulders. "Come on. Wouldn't you like to do one thing that matters, after all these years? Something that just might really make a difference?"

Salmo's face was pale, with two bright red spots high on his cheeks. "Lii..."

Liiran nodded and pressed the sheet of paper into Salmo's hand. "Go on camera and read this. Please. I can't do it. There's been too much publicity showing me as a traitor."

Salmo bit his lip and looked down at the sheet of paper in his hand. He read it, and the man who looked up afterwards was a different person. "All right. All right, Lii. I'll do it. Damn you, but I'll do it."

He squared his shoulders and gestured to one of the techs. "Do a special report transition," he said authoritatively, striding towards the door. "And if the police come to the door, don't let them in. Stall them if you have to. Just don't unlock the door."

Liiran smiled and handed the memory stick to one of the techs. "Play this at the first cue."

Salmo was dancing again, as if all the weight had been taken from his shoulders. He believed in something again.

313

Salmo headed out to the booth and shooed the surprised news anchors out of their seats, then took a position in front of the centre camera. When the director gave him his cue, he held up the sheet of paper and started to read aloud. At the same moment, Liiran heard the police start banging on the door.

"Good evening. My name is Salmo Lina, chief editor of Laxam Daily Newspaper, and Laxam Business Chronicle. What you're about to see is completely real. Some of the images you will see were shot by amateur citizens of our great Empire, while others were taken by our very own photographers and cameramen. These images have been repressed by the Laxam government, by Niveus Exalan himself, and by the secret police. But now it's time for our citizens to see them, at long last."

He looked up from the sheet of paper, and straight into the camera. "It's time for these repressed and censored images to be shown. Now, in this dark time of death and uncertainty, it's time to know why this has come to pass."

He gestured, and Liiran saw his hand was trembling. "Roll the video."

The tech, wide-eyed, hit a few switches, and on the monitors Liiran saw the video Phames had captured begin to play as Salmo continued to read, commentating. That small dot grew larger and larger, until Niveus was revealed winging his way to the top of the Parliament building. As one, everyone in the room drew a gasp.

Liiran sat back and closed his eyes as the video played through, and began to repeat. At some point, the police broke down the door and cuffed him.

He didn't resist. He told them he had forced Salmo to do it, but they arrested his boss, anyway.

As they were marched past their coworkers, Liiran felt nothing but a deep numbness settle over him. Now he'd done all he could do. Even if he went to jail now, even if only one person truly believed what he had shown them today, he'd die knowing his life had made a difference. With Mortis gone, and his career ruined, that was enough.

When he reached the lobby, Niveus Exalan was waiting for him, a wide smile on his face. "Hello, Mr. Uwis. You've been busy."

Chapter 56

Garelon expected to be taken straight to the prisons to await more questioning. They had the room, after all. But instead Calam brought him up into the tower, to Niveus' office.

He wasn't sure if it was a good sign or a bad one, so he kept his face completely impassive and calm.

The one he needed to convince, if it were possible to convince anyone he wasn't a traitor, was Niveus. Calam was a smart man, a suspicious man, but he seemed loyal to Niveus, and Garelon felt he would follow the prime minister's orders even if he disagreed with them.

Niveus was waiting at his desk, leaning back in the chair and reading a document.

"Sir," Garelon said immediately, before Calam had a chance to speak. "I assure you that these accusations—"

"Are entirely founded, and completely true," Niveus said in a bored tone, his eyes still moving over the page in front of him. "You might or might not have actively helped Certos escape, but you certainly knew about it, and you did nothing. You didn't alert anyone, nor did you make any move to try to stop him when he was abducted."

Niveus looked up and smiled. "I'm just swimming in traitors today."

Garelon felt a flush rising up his neck. "If you believe that, why didn't you arrest me hours ago, sir?" he asked, feeling his voice begin to lose its composure despite his best efforts.

"Because it didn't really matter," Niveus said. Garelon heard Calam made a soft sound, and only their proximity let him hear the quiet exclamation. Well, at least it wasn't just him who was confused.

"But it matters now?"

"It might," Niveus said. He set the sheet down. "Garelon, why did you do it? No lies now, there's no escape from the fact of your treason, so be candid with me. Please."

Something about Niveus' tone made Garelon answer honestly. It wasn't magic. Niveus was listening, and wanted to know. And Garelon was pretty sure he wouldn't have lied anyway – it was too late for that. He was caught, and he might as well tell the truth.

"I don't believe Laxam is served by using slaves to dominate the world," he said. "This... this entire thing was wrong from the beginning, sir. I believe our country has much to offer everyone in the world – and by now, it *is* the world. All of the world's people are our citizens, even the voxae."

He shook his head. "But if it's built on lies and deceit, built on unnatural warping of the natural order of things, then what have we built? Instead of bringing the best of Laxam to the world, like you always said we were doing, all we've done is build a castle with slave labour, on a rotten foundation."

He drew himself up, knowing how this sounded, but unable to disguise his feelings now that he'd begun. "If the only way we can accomplish our goals is by cheating this way, we don't deserve to win."

Finally he fell silent, almost stunned at his own words. He *sounded* like a traitor, even to his own ears. Calam stared at him with a fierce expression in his eyes, and Garelon couldn't blame him. But wasn't he loyal to Laxam even now?

That part of Laxam that wasn't built on lies, anyway. If there was anything left of that.

Niveus listened to this with an impassive expression, his elbows resting on his desk as he leaned forward towards Garelon, his fingers steepled in front of his face.

After a long pause, he spoke. "I see," he said simply, then sat back. "Garelon, Calam, I'd like you both to watch something."

He turned his computer monitor around so they could see it, and tapped the keyboard. Garelon frowned as he saw an unfamiliar man reading from a sheet of paper, reading slowly and haltingly, as if he weren't used to public speaking.

No, not a man, a vox. When Garelon saw the wings rising up from behind the massive shoulders, saw the glint of the blades as the studio lights reflected off them, he gaped.

"That's Certos," he breathed.

"So it is," Niveus said. "Listen, and watch."

He turned up the volume, so they could hear what was said, just as Certos abandoned the page and looked up at the camera, his body language growing more confident.

"...I am Certos, the vox of war. Niveus is not who he pretends to be. He is the vox of order, and he's been lying to everyone to control all the humans. Grand General Garelon helped me to escape, and sent me out into the world to bring you this message. You are all safe, so long as you don't fear death. But so long as Niveus is your leader, you are living a lie, and you will always have much to fear."

He hesitated, then made a gesture, the chiming of his wings audible even over the tinny computer speakers. "Roll the tape. This will prove my words."

Garelon gasped and heard Calam draw in a sharp breath at the first image, of Niveus flying and Altus meeting him on the top of the building.

Niveus turned the computer back around and cut off the sound. Garelon's emotions swirled.

"Variations of this began playing on all of the major networks for the first time ten minutes ago, and they're replaying it now," Niveus said gravely. "It's several minutes of video, and there are a few different introductions. I don't know how they gathered this footage, but it's obviously been accumulating somewhere for a long time despite our efforts."

Calam cleared his throat. "I'm very sorry, sir. It was my failure."

"No. It was inevitable." Niveus' lips curved upwards. "As you said, Garelon. It's a castle built on a rotten foundation. I didn't mean it to turn out that way, but you were right about that. Everything that's happened in the last week has proven that to me."

He rose to his feet. "Take off those cuffs," he said, and after only a moment's hesitation, Calam complied.

Garelon was still rubbing his chafed wrists when Niveus stuck out a hand for him to shake. "It's over for me now. It's time for me to move on, and pass on the mantle to someone else."

Surprised, Garelon hesitated a beat before reaching out and taking Niveus hand. "If you don't mind me asking, sir, why did *you* do this?"

"I'm a creature of order, and humans are creatures of chaos, striving for some semblance of order in their lives. I thought that if I helped them along more directly, it would be better for everyone. At least," Niveus' lips twisted wryly once more, "better for the humans, and for me. Not so good for those voxae who thrive on chaos and violence."

Garelon was stunned, and didn't know what to say, but Niveus didn't wait for him to come up with something.

"But I was wrong. Humans need both order and chaos in their lives to thrive. To be honest, it's a relief. I've been feeling trapped inside this structure I built for some time." Niveus arched an eyebrow. "Garelon, would you like to be my successor?"

Garelon started, and spoke without thinking. "No, sir, I... don't think I'd make a particularly good politician."

"Exactly," Niveus said. "Besides, all those things you said before, I think they were very wise. And I'd be willing to bet that you have Certos' support." He paused, sobering. "Smooth the way for another politician, if you feel you must, but take this offer. Please."

Garelon's eyes darted from side to side, landing on Calam. "I... I can't just say that I'm the leader of the Empire with no backing. You'll be gone."

"I will be here," Calam said quietly. He seemed shocked, but resolute. "And I believe those of us who remain will back you once I explain it to them. You have the support of the vox, and perhaps even his friends."

"It has to be you," Niveus said. "You lack the taint of my regime. You made this government fall. But you have the knowledge, the strength, and the leadership abilities you need to do this."

Garelon stared at Niveus, into those crystal blue eyes. It made sense – but of course it did, since it came from this man.

But it *did* make sense.

"Temporarily," he said weakly. "If the people will have me."

Niveus clapped him on the shoulder and stepped back. "Good," he said. "Thank you. I know I'm leaving my world in good hands, this way."

He turned towards one of the windows, and his wings spread from his back, a waterfall of white feathers. Garelon took a quick step towards him, sudden panic in his chest.

"Will you be around? If I need any... anything?" Niveus wasn't the first person he would have wanted to go to for advice, but he was suddenly feeling very much alone and adrift.

Niveus glanced at him over his shoulder, a soft smirk on his lips. "I'll be everywhere."

318

He spread his wings, and then he was out the window and flying away.

For a few moments, Garelon and Calam stood together, staring after their former leader. He dwindled to a dot far faster than seemed possible.

Garelon couldn't process what had happened in the last few moments. He had gone from traitor to prime minister in less than five minutes, and he scarcely even believed that it had happened.

But he couldn't just stand here gaping like an idiot. He was prime minister now, even if it were only temporary. The world was in chaos. There was a war on.

There was a hell of a lot to do.

He turned to Calam. "Send an envoy to the queen of Talgar. Tell her the war is over and we're pulling out of her country. Over the next few weeks, I'll meet with any surviving government of any other countries we've conquered, but right now the priority is to bring order to the cities. Get your men on it now."

Calam nodded and bowed. "Yes, Prime Minister."

Chapter 57

Mortis was everywhere.

Somewhere... a woman leaped from a great height and gladly accepted her kiss when she hit the ground.

Somewhere... a heart choked with fatty deposits beat in a stuttered rhythm, and at her touch, it stopped.

Somewhere... a child born too soon never took her first breath, and slipped away into her arms.

Somewhere... a mob surged against policemen. Swords flashed, bottles were thrown. Some broke and ran, and some were crushed in the melee. And she was there.

She was everywhere but where she wanted to be. She could find everyone, but the one she wanted eluded her touch.

Liiran...

Chapter 58

Liiran was led outside to a white car, idling in the tow zone out front. To everyone's surprise, Niveus got into the driver's seat and ordered Liiran to be placed in the passenger seat, without a guard. Liiran didn't see what happened to Salmo, the press of people and the chaos separating them like toys carried down a river.

To be honest, Liiran didn't know what game Niveus was playing now, and he didn't care. For the most part, he just felt tired. Too tired to worry about what would happen to him now.

He didn't lack a tiny sense of accomplishment, though. As Niveus drove, Liiran saw a huge crowd of people gathered around the front of an electronics store, watching the video he'd cobbled together. It had to be on its second, maybe its third run.

Other than that, Liiran still felt numb. He knew there was no reason to lose all hope – Varil was still out there, and Phames and Certos. There was every chance they would break him out again.

But that didn't really comfort him at all. His life was over, and it was just a matter of time before his body caught up. He'd done the one thing he had left to do, the one thing he had been preparing his whole life to do. He had no employment, he was a criminal, his love was effectively dead.

So what was left?

"Are you all right, Liiran?" Niveus asked. He dropped something into Liiran's lap.

A key.

He was smiling. That irritated Liiran the most.

Liiran unlocked his cuffs on autopilot, but set his jaw and raised his chin. "Fine, Mr. Exalan. Decided to supervise my transfer to your deep dark hole personally?" He had to have flown, or he'd have his chief of secret police at one shoulder, and the asshole who had kept Certos on a leash at the other. There hadn't been enough time for him to get here by a human-safe method, even on the Cloudtoucher, his government jet.

"No," Niveus said. Why did he sound kind? Why was he still *smiling* like that? Why had he given him the key? "I had the opportunity to see your video—"

"Did you like it?" He wasn't in the mood to chat with the prime minister, and was really just hoping he would get to the point.

"It was very interesting." The smile flickered a little. The sight of him losing his composure helped Liiran's mood a bit. "I came to congratulate you for a game well played."

Anger flared and Liiran stared at the hand Niveus had extended towards him as if it were a dead rat. He was so stunned, he couldn't even think of a good reply. After a moment or two Niveus returned his hand to the steering wheel and went on.

"Anyway, I've arranged for all charges against you and your associates to be dropped, and everything will be cleaned up before word reaches Laxamora that I'm no longer prime minister." Then Niveus fell silent, and waited for Liiran to find his tongue.

It took a few seconds. "No... longer prime minister?"

The car came to a stop and Liiran realized they were in front of his own building. "No, Liiran. As I said, I came to congratulate you. You won."

Freedom was staring him in the face, but Liiran was still pissed. "This... this wasn't a *game* to me, you gigantic asshole. This was my *life*! Thanks to you, everything is fucked up, *everything*, and Mortis is dead."

"Yes, I know, and I'm very sorry about tha— dead?" Niveus stared. "What do you mean she's dead?"

He leaned over, getting right in Niveus' face. "She connected herself to me somehow, by using her powers to save my life. It weakened her, so she scattered herself to make the trip here. But she was too weak, or something. She's just gone, now."

He didn't want Niveus to bow out like an actor on a stage whose role is finished. He wanted him to taste at least some of the destruction he'd wrought.

But Niveus, far from looking horror-struck, merely looked thoughtful. "I sensed the connection when I saw you together. I could see it was going to give you problems, but she's not gone." He glanced around as if expecting to see her. "If she were gone, no one would have died in almost a day, and I'm sure that's not the case."

He looked down at Liiran. "I think I can remove the connection."

"Fat lot it'll do now."

Niveus shook his head. "It'll make all the difference, if what you're saying is true."

Niveus put a hand on Liiran's chest, and Liiran felt a concussion, as if he'd punched him. Liiran wobbled for a moment, gasping, wondering why he hadn't fallen back into the seat, but Niveus simply lowered his hand.

"There, that should do it. Are you feeling all right, Liiran?"

Liiran rubbed his own chest. He felt weak and exhausted, but he wasn't dying; he was still whole and alive. "Yes, yes, I'm fine."

"It may take her some time to regain her strength, but— wait, that's her now."

Liiran looked around, following the direction of Niveus' startled gaze, and saw a shower of sparks swirling together just in front of the car. In seconds, it resolved into Mortis, nude and her skin still glittering a little.

Mortis glanced around, her eyes landing first on Niveus, and then Liiran. The moment she saw him, she started forward quickly, eyes wide with concern. "Liiran, are you all right?"

Liiran opened the door and lunged towards her. He felt his arms go around her, felt the cool smoothness of her skin, felt her hair tickle his neck as she laid her head on his shoulder. "Yes... yes."

Niveus was already gone, but he barely noticed. He was flying.

*   *   *

Later, Liiran lay in bed with Mortis in his arms, his fingers caressing her soft skin.

After Mortis had flown him up to the apartment, they were quickly lost in the thrill of discovery and pleasure. He found himself utterly charmed once again by her innocence as he touched her intimately for the first time. The voxae duplicated human anatomy right down to the nerve endings, but they didn't use their bodies the way humans did. The sensations were entirely new to her.

They kissed and he pulled her close against him, her hair soft under his fingers and smelling of lilies and roses. He slid fingers over skin so flawless and perfect, it couldn't be human, and as she touched him she laughed with delight at the gasps and moans she pulled from his lips.

As he entered her, they fit together seamlessly. She rode him, wings spread for balance, and his fingers on her bare hips, steadying her. She threw her head back and cried out her pleasure as she came, and he followed soon after, pleasure crashing over him in a wave that left him stunned and gasping.

Still joined with her body as feathers fell around them onto the blankets, he held her close against his chest and panted, his world filled with her scent and his overwhelming love of her.

When they grew calm again, she shifted and slid her arms around him, laying her head on his shoulder.

"I'll have to go," she whispered.

He closed his eyes. Somewhere along the line from the point at which he had been freed and reunited with Mortis, the crushing hopelessness of earlier had left him. Now even though he felt disappointment settle over him at her words, it was nothing in comparison. Maybe it was just the post-coital lassitude, but he didn't think so.

He had been expecting this, that was all. "When will you be back?"

"I don't know. Liiran, I'm sorry. I don't want to hurt you."

Too late, he thought, but it was devoid of bitterness. Somehow, he found a smile. "It's all right, my dear."

"I'm not like you. This— all this is wonderful." She drew a breath and let it out, the gesture so painfully human. Her fingers tightened, nails scraping against his bare chest. "But this isn't me. I don't think I can do this for you, in the way you really need it."

He opened his eyes and looked at her, into her bottomless eyes. Not bottomless now; they were filled to the brim with worry.

The longer she stayed with him, the more human she'd be, he knew. It had happened to Niveus, had happened to Certos, had happened to her when she didn't remember who she really was.

A selfish part of him wanted it anyway. He suspected that despite her words, that if he asked her to, she would stay. And then he would grow old, and one day she would take his life, and it would be but a blip, an anomaly in her endless life. But even so, it would have an impact on her, perhaps forever.

324

It *was* selfish, and he knew it wouldn't be the perfect life he envisioned. He would resent her flawlessness, would miss his own endless youth. She would be confused and uncomfortable, spending her life in human skin, living a human life. It could even affect her ability to *be* death, and that was something he, reluctantly, believed his world needed.

He sighed, held her tightly, then let go. "I'll be all right." They were weak words, but at least he knew they were true. "You should be yourself."

She shifted up, kissed him. She tasted of ash, but to him it was like the finest thing he'd ever savoured. He felt tears sting his eyes, but didn't let them fall. They'd only confuse her, and he didn't think he could bear it if she didn't understand and made him explain.

"I love you, Liiran. As best I can."

"I love you, too," he said. "As best I can." She smiled and slipped from his arms, padded barefoot and perfect across the room.

"I'll be around. I'll visit."

"Goodbye, my dear."

She was gone in a whisper of wings.

Chapter 59

Liiran leaned back in his chair, staring fixedly at the computer screen, the phone pressed between ear and shoulder to free both hands for typing.

"How late are you going to be working? I'm cooking tonight." Tanen's voice wheedled. It was a tactic that sometimes worked, only because Liiran didn't really want to say no.

But he wouldn't make it that easy. "You mean you unearthed the kitchen?"

"I've been cleaning since you moved in a month ago," Tanen said, affronted. "Haven't you noticed?"

"I've noticed the efforts, I just haven't noticed any progress," Liiran said, bringing up a couple of photographs and considering which one he wanted to include. He was tempted to include the one of Prime Minister Unitar with his special – and unnamed – aide visible in the background, but he figured he owed it to Certos not to let him show up on camera too often. Instead, he cropped it differently, including Maenos and Calam, who stood on Garelon's other side.

After word had come from the new prime minister himself that Liiran was not only exonerated, but to be decorated for unspecified service to the state (there had been a ceremony and everything; the medal was sitting in his desk drawer), Liiran had gotten his job back, with a promotion.

He was now the only full-time press secretary to the prime minister. No more ridiculous assignments to the ass-end of nowhere, and he got to keep a close eye on Garelon. He had made no secret of his suspicions, but somehow he sensed that Garelon appreciated having someone like him around.

Though secretly, Liiran really felt that if Certos supported Garelon enough to show up from time to time and skulk in the wings while Garelon was being questioned by the press, Garelon had to be worth something.

Tanen was still sputtering about Liiran's lack of appreciation. He'd been released from prison the same time Liiran had, or nearly so, and within a couple of weeks Liiran had sold his apartment and moved in with him. It was... not the perfect solution, and the commute was hell from that side of the city, but Liiran felt better not being completely alone in his apartment.

"Anyway, I won't be home late," Liiran said, taking pity on his friend. "I'll be stopping at the store to pick up cigarettes on my way home. Do you need anything?"

"I thought you gave up smoking."

Liiran shrugged and almost upset the phone. "Eh, I figure everyone's got to have one nasty habit that'll probably kill them."

"And here I thought yours was investigative journalism," Tanen laughed.

"Very funny." He was grinning. Tanen had a point.

He missed whatever Tanen said next as he heard a tapping sound at the window, which startled him badly enough to drop the phone. Considering he was on the 14th floor of a 15-story building, he wouldn't expect anyone but window washers to be up here, and window washers didn't tend to knock.

No one human, anyway.

He retrieved the phone. "Sorry, Tan, someone's at the door. I gotta go."

"Okay— don't work too hard, Lii," Tanen said, just before Liiran hung up the phone.

He parted the blinds and looked outside, turning the lever to open the window with his other hand before he'd even seen his visitor. He stopped immediately when he recognized him, but Niveus slipped through the gap anyway, landing lightly in the middle of the floor.

"Well, well," the former prime minister said agreeably, glancing around. "Looks as though things are falling back into place for you again, Liiran. That's good to see."

Liiran dropped back down into his chair. "I have no complaints," he said, cautious. He didn't know why Niveus had come to see him, and he didn't think he'd ever count the man as a friend after what he'd done, though he no longer feared him, nor did he think he had plans to trap his friends and take over the world again.

Somehow, Niveus looked a lot happier than he had the last time Liiran had seen him. That, more than anything else, reassured him.

"To what do I owe the honour?" Liiran prompted, hoping to get the interview over with quickly.

Niveus leaned against the desk, and his attention was attracted by a short stack of papers on Liiran's desk, clipped together. He picked it up and flipped through it. "Phames is still publishing?" He sounded bemused.

"Don't think so." The first edition of *The Truth* that had come out after Niveus' 'disappearance' had been very thick, and contained a lot more information than Liiran had managed to fit into his slapdash video – everything Phames knew, it seemed. Reading through it, Liiran had even sensed a touch here and there of Certos, and possibly Varil, though so far as he knew, Varil had returned to Talgarora almost immediately.

Liiran had gone out of his way to get a copy of each issue since then, but he was quite certain Phames hadn't had a hand in any of them. Maybe he didn't know Phames that well, even at the end, but he was pretty sure he knew him well enough to tell his writing style and choice of subject matter.

No, after having the last word, Phames had gone back out into the world, the way the others had, to focus on doing what was in his nature to do. He had no reason to concern himself with human affairs now.

Niveus nodded and set it down again, precisely where it had been. "I'm sorry if my presence here startled you," he said, the corners of his mouth pulling down slightly. "I really did just come to make sure that there wasn't anything that I missed."

He glanced around with obvious satisfaction. "But it seems things are going well for you now. You're keeping watch on my successor, you've been forgiven the crimes I accused you of, and you have your life back."

Liiran leaned back until the chair creaked. "I even have someone new in my life. Though he's not Mortis." He wasn't entirely certain *what* it was with Tanen, either, but he knew he wasn't planning on dating any women any time soon. He suspected strongly that no one would measure up.

Besides, he had time. And if he didn't find anyone, he and Tanen were compatible enough that he was happy for now. Maybe more than just compatible. Their experiences had created a bond that he didn't want to ignore.

Niveus nodded. "That's good. I have to admit, I wondered what she would do. You haven't seen her since?"

Liiran felt a chill settle over him, just a little. He knew Niveus didn't mean anything by the question, and he felt he'd done the right thing, but it was still painful. "I've sensed her, I guess. But I haven't seen her, no."

"She won't forget you, Liiran," Niveus said, and the kindness in his tone only hurt all the more. "I'm sure of that."

Liiran could only shrug and look away, uncomfortable. "Why does it matter to you how I'm doing?" he asked. "Really? You nearly had me killed, but you caused a lot of other misery, too. So why me?"

Niveus was silent for a moment, and when Liiran glanced up he looked thoughtful. "It's really simple, actually. You saved me, just as much as you saved Mortis and Certos. I'm... grateful for that."

"You could have left any time. If you'd changed your mind about what you were doing, you didn't have to keep doing it."

"It's not that easy." Niveus shook his head. "Leaving just like that would only have brought chaos, and that's not something I could do. The right conditions needed to be in place, so I could leave with a clear conscience – as clear as possible, considering." He smiled. "You granted me that, Liiran. You brought all the cards together into the winning hand."

"Funny you using card metaphors," Liiran muttered, "considering a game is all about luck."

"Even I rely on luck, a little," Niveus said, chuckling.

Liiran glanced up at him. "Can I ask you a question?"

"Anything."

"Did you really think the world would be better without death?"

Niveus glanced at him curiously. "Isn't the difficult question whether the world would be better *with* death?"

Liiran shrugged again. "There was a time I asked that. But having lived it, I think not having death means you don't really have life, either. It's just existence, even if you don't really realize it at the time." He smiled wryly. "I certainly didn't notice until I had that fear of death back that I hadn't really been living life all that time, either. I was just moving from day to day, doing the same things. Existing. What a waste that was."

Niveus grinned superiorly. "Then I've given you something as well, haven't I?"

Liiran scowled. Arrogant to the end, wasn't he?

"And the look in your eye tells me that it's time to leave," Niveus said, straightening up. "Truly, Liiran... I do thank you, and I wish you the best."

Despite himself, Liiran smiled and nodded. He got to his feet and offered Niveus his hand. "Maybe we'll see each other again."

"Oh yes," Niveus said, shaking it warmly. "You'll see me everywhere, if you just look. And I'll see you from time to time, too."

Liiran nodded. "Goodbye, Prime Minister."

"Goodbye, Liiran." Niveus took a step and spread wings, then vanished out the window.

Liiran rose and parted the blinds, looking out over the city. The world was the world, with all its pain, joy and confusion – anyone could see that, just looking around. But yet somehow, he felt it. Things weren't easy, but they were also the way they were supposed to be.

As he stared out at the sky, for a moment he thought he saw four shapes, dipping and spiralling around one another, wing beats in counterpoint, and their dance in perfect harmony.

The End

Coming Soon From the Author...

Grim Disguise

Marseilles was a beautiful city, though like many European cities, it subscribed to the 'densely packed' school of architecture. The stone buildings practically climbed on top of each other as they marched up the sides of the hill that the city was built into, and the roads were so narrow and parking at such a premium, that most people drove their little cars up onto the sidewalks to park.

Those few who had cars in working condition, that was. Petrol was hard to find these days - as James well knew - and working car parts even more so. There were many vehicles that looked to have been abandoned in place for years, if not centuries. Rusting hulks barely recognizable anymore as vehicles hunched in place on the sidewalks, slowly flaking apart.

At this time of night, the roads were virtually empty, but the cobblestones and cracks in the road made it impossible for him to open up his motorcycle and go quickly. As a result, James was forced to take in a lot of the sights, whether he wanted to or not.

Closer to the water, things widened out a bit and he was able to speed up, the purr of the engine practically swallowed by the susurration of the sea. The famous Old Port was a wide harbour filled with little boats and bordered with a quaint boulevard. Presiding over the mouth of the port, on a spit of land that extended out into the Mediterranean Sea, was a smallish castle-like building, though James happened to know it was actually a fort.

Someone had taken up residence there. As James passed by the area on his way to the local police headquarters where his contact was supposed to be, he saw that several of the windows were lit with what looked like the warm glow of lamplight.

Perhaps that was the reason why there were hardly any people on the streets. Those who were out now, after sunset, moved with a rapid pace and furtive, frightened expressions. But James Grim scarcely noticed the oppressive weight of fear that had settled on the ancient city - he was too used to it.

No one ever invited a vampire hunter to a town that didn't have a vampire, after all.

There was a single lamp hung outside the door to the police station, the flame dancing merrily inside its glass cage. It could have been seen as a beacon of welcome to the city's saviour, but James saw its more practical purpose as he knocked on the heavy steel door and a small metal trapdoor slid aside to reveal one frightened brown eye.

It was there so they'd be able to see his face.

"Sorry!" the voice said, muffled by the intervening door. "We're not open right now."

James tilted his hat back slightly so the man on the other side could see his face, too pale, angular, framed with black hair and set with startling blue eyes. "The names James Grim," he said. "I was sent." His French was articulate, but accented from his British heritage.

Clearly he was understood, though, because the eye widened fractionally and the window was shut with a clang. James folded his arms and waited, listening as the heavy bolts were slid aside before the door swung open. A painfully young-looking police constable regarded him for a moment. "Um, you're the hunter?" he asked nervously.

"I don't carry the stakes and silver knife for nothing," Grim replied. "Aren't you going to invite me in?"

The young man ducked his head and stepped back. "O-of course, please come in."

James smiled and stepped into the lobby area, removing his wide-brimmed hat and shaking out his long black hair, before looking up and glancing around. There were only two other people in the room besides him - the constable who'd let him in, and a middle-aged heavy-set man with the uniform of a highly-placed officer.

"Police Chief Doucette, I presume?" Grim asked, stepping forward with a faint smile to shake the officer's hand.

It was then that they saw his fangs.

The police chief recoiled, crossing himself and exclaiming a plea to God in French that made Grim's ears smart. The young constable had his gun out and was pointing it at Grim, the hand shaking badly enough the vampire was quite certain he wouldn't hit anything important even if he was foolhardy enough to fire.

Unfortunately, James wasn't surprised by the reaction. The vampire held the chief's gaze for a moment, and then glanced at the constable out of the corner of his eye. "Put that away, boy," he said. "I'm here to help your stupid ass, and all you'll do if you fire that thing is put a hole in my coat. And I *will* make you buy me a new one." The long leather duster was custom made, and it hadn't come cheap.

There was silence for a moment before Doucette nodded fractionally. "Put it away, Jacques," he said, his voice rasping.

Grim watched as the young man clicked the safety back on and, trembling, put the gun back in the holster at his hip. Then he turned his head and met Doucette's gaze again. "Glad that's out of the way. Tell me about the vampire problem."

Doucette swallowed. "The Vatican really sent you?" he asked suspiciously. "This is...not...acceptable."

Grim rolled his eyes and stuck a hand in his inside pocket - one of many - and he pulled out a square plastic card. "You want proof?" he asked, holding the card out to the man. "My visa, issued by our Mother the Holy Church."

Doucette hesitated, then took the card and picked up a reader on the desk behind him. In a moment he'd swiped it and was looking over the data on the screen. "James Alexander Grim," he read aloud. "The passport is in order."

"But it can't be you!" Jacques burst out. "We need someone else!"

"Look," James snapped, turning his glare on the young man. "Yes, I'm a vampire - all the better to kill the monsters with, my dear. What do you care how they die, so long as they're dead? I'll be out of town before you know it."

"That's not the issue, Monsieur Grim," Doucette said quietly. He seemed to have regained his calm and as he held out James' card to return it, his hand didn't tremble.

"What's the issue, then?" James asked. "We're burning darkness, sir, and I doubt you people have time to wait for the Vatican to send a replacement."

"There is no issue," Doucette said, shooting a glare at the younger man. "I think the young man is merely hoping you can take care of things quickly and that you do not linger in our city too long."

"Like I said, that's the plan," Grim growled. He sensed there was something here that he was missing, but he was getting impatient with these people. "Look, just tell me what I need to know so I can put my back to this city. It'll make you happy, and it'll make *me* happy, and everyone can be happy. Okay?"

There was a moment of silence, and then the police chief nodded fractionally. "Okay." He straightened slightly, clasping his hands behind his back. "The vampire, who calls herself Lady Gwenhwyfar the Beautiful, has taken over Fort St. Jean, which you will see at the mouth of the Old Port. She's been...infecting many people. We don't know how many vampires are in there now, but perhaps a dozen?"

"A dozen vampires, inside a fortified castle," James said wryly. "Sounds like fun. No wonder everyone's hunkering in their houses like the plague has come. What about the zombies? How are your cemeteries?"

Vampirism was a disease - a sexually transmitted one. But it didn't just make people photosensitive and crave blood. That was if you were lucky.

If you were *really* lucky, you just got bitten and survived the experience. You might have a few days of fever and mild sensitivity to light. A good priest could drive it off in a couple of hours. If not, you could wait it out and hope you didn't get hit by a bus before it worked its way out of your system.

If you were mildly fortunate, you got a taste of the vampire's blood and fully contracted the disease. You'd live out the rest of your - exceptionally long - life as a monster, but at least you would *have* a life, and a will of your own. That's what had happened to James Grim some time ago.

Many people, especially those who encountered the real monsters - the vampires so heinous in their crimes that Grim was sent to kill them - were not so fortunate. They died with the disease-laced saliva or blood still in their system.

Usually such people were burned when their bodies were found, but sometimes the symptoms weren't recognized in time, or the body was left somewhere remote and not discovered. Those people became monsters of a different type. Mindless and vicious, the creatures still craved blood, but unlike vampires, were immune to pain. They'd attack until literally dismembered, and even then might manage to regenerate given enough time. The only way to stop a zombie permanently was to burn them to ashes.

At Grim's question, the chief went a little pale and swallowed. "There have been a few, but most have been caught and burned before they rose again," he said hollowly. "Gwenhwyfar has been kidnapping most of her victims and keeping them at the fort. Some of her progeny have been less careful."

James started, his eyes widening. "So there might be people still kept captive at the fort?" he asked. In that case, there wasn't any time to lose. Between a quickly growing army of vampires and the captives who could be added to their ranks at any moment, no wonder the city had called for help. What was actually surprising was that the city wasn't devastated already, given the math.

One thing was sure, though: sooner or later, this Gwenhwyfar would unleash her vampires on the city and it would be a right bloody mess.

Literally.

The chief nodded, though without much certainty. "There's no way to know, but I pray to God that some of them are still alive," he said, crossing himself again.

James winced and looked away at the gesture. Most people couldn't produce that kind of reaction with a simple movement of their hands, but when it was backed with real faith, even something so small packed a punch. Clearly he had a believer on his hands. Good thing they were on the same side.

"God doesn't have much to do with it," he growled. It was time to go. "I'll go take care of it." He turned away, placing his hat on his head again as he started for the door.

"Monsieur Grim," Doucette called after him, a hesitant note in his tone. "How are you going to get in?"

James paused, his hand on the door handle, and glanced over his shoulder. "What difference does it make to you?" he asked frankly.

Doucette blinked, taken aback. "I...I just mean, it may be difficult," he said awkwardly. "It's a fort, and you're a man -- by which I mean to say, just one man. The rumours of your prowess are impressive, but how can you storm a castle by yourself? The Lady doesn't take just any visitor."

James shook his head faintly, opening the door. "I don't expect you care much, chief," he said. "But vampires have a...camaraderie. She won't turn away a fellow monster at the door. Now are you going to let me go take care of your problem, or keep asking questions all night?" he added in an annoyed hiss.

There was a pause. "I'm sure you know better than I, Monsieur Grim."

"Yes," James said, striding through the door into the night. "I do."

*   *   *

Grim Disguise is the first story in the Hunter Grim Anthology, a short story collection by Jessica Steiner, slated to be released in spring 2013!

www.ingramcontent.com/pod-product-compliance
Lightning Source LLC
Chambersburg PA
CBHW061324170626
46817CB00001B/306